A BLAZING WORLD:
THE UNOFFICIAL COMPANION TO
THE LEAGUE OF EXTRAORDINARY GENTLEMEN,
VOLUME TWO

Other MonkeyBrain Books titles
by Jess Nevins

*Heroes & Monsters: The Unofficial Companion to the
League of Extraordinary Gentlemen* (2003)

The Encyclopedia of Fantastic Victoriana
(Forthcoming, 2005)

The Enyclopedia of Pulp Fiction
(Forthcoming, 2006)

monkeybrain, inc.

A BLAZING WORLD

THE UNOFFICIAL COMPANION TO

THE LEAGUE OF EXTRAORDINARY GENTLEMEN

VOLUME TWO

BY JESS NEVINS

INTRODUCTION BY
ALAN MOORE

COMMENTARY BY
KEVIN O'NEILL

A Note on the Type

The cover typography was set in Treacherous Corners and Curves, a typeface produced and licensed by Comicraft. For this font and other fabulous font designs, please contact:

Comicraft
Richard Starkings, President
8910 Rayford Drive
Los Angeles, CA 90045
www.comicbookfonts.com

Additional cover typography was set in Adobe Woodtype Ornaments, a typeface licensed by the Adobe Corporation.
For this font and more, please see: www.adobe.com

TABLE OF CONTENTS

Acknowledgments

As in *Heroes & Monsters*, much of the text here was the result of a large number of people contributing their comments, suggestions, and corrections. Quite literally, this book would not have been written without their help.

My thanks to "Kurt A.," Jason Adams, Philip Adams, Scott Adsit, "Adventurer," Neil Alderton, Youssef Alaoui, Boyer Alseth, Ted Anderson, Paul Andinach, Leandro Antolini, Pierce Askegren, Matt Austern, Timothy Avery, Peter Ayres, José Luis Bárcenas, Edward Bart, "JoeyBags," Stephanie Bagstaff, Simeon Bankoff, Neale Barnholden, Matthew Baugh, Rob Beattie, HC Beck, Aaron Bibb, Ryan Bibb, Keith Bieberly, Sean Blair, Rene Blais, Fabio Blanco, Henry Blanco, Matt Board, Kate Bolin, Rob Boyte, Rupert Brackenbury, Kevin Brettauer, Ben Brighoff, Andrew J. Brook, Will Brooker, Adrian Brown, Peter Brüell, Ray Brunt, James Burt, Ronald Byrd, "Simon C.," "Steve C.," David Cairns, Jim Cannon, Stephen Cappiello, Loki Carbis, Rob Carr, Jonathan Carter, "Carycomic," "Cefo," John Chadwick, Tim Chapman, Joseph Charneskie, Mike Chary, Simon Cheeseman, Christian Chelman, Alberto Chimal, Dave Choat, Tim Christopher, Terence Chua, Adam Eli Clem, "CleV," Mark Coale, Philip Cohen, Loren Collins, Spencer Cook, Steven Costa, Dave Cotter, John Coulthart (artist extraordinaire), Andres Couturier, Kieran Cowan, Josh Cramer, Chris Cratsley, Liam Creighton, Ian Crichton, Adam Cuerden, Mark Cummins, "Cyberperson," Ian Dall, Chris Davies, "John_Dee," Timi del Toro, Michael Denton, Zoltán Déry, Rick Diehl, Carla DiFonza, Ron Dingman, Marc Dolan, Kelly Doran, Dr. Sharon Dornhoff, Neil Dorset, Carolyn Dougherty, Ian Driscoll, Tim Driscoll, Paul Duggan, Scott Dunbier, Martin Dunne, Peter Dyde, Win Eckert (editor of the forthcoming *Creative Mythography: An Expansion of Philip José Farmer's Wold Newton Universe*), Dickon Edwards, Mark Elstob, "EmarZero," James Enelow,

Joseph Eros, Mike Everett-Lane, Taina Evans, Julian Fattorini, Zak Fejeran, Richard Flanagan, Jack Fletcher, Dave Fogel, Craig Fox, Dominic Fox, "Francis," Michael Frank, Harry Gaffing, Joe Gallagher, Shawn Garrett, Greg Gick, Jeff Giddens, Steven Gilham, Jim Gillogly, Mitchell Glavas, David Goldfarb, Adam Goldman, Marcus Good, Philip Graves, "Great Bear," Kelvin Green, Steve Green, John Gregory, Tom Grzeskowiak, Robert Gurskey, John Hall, Mags Halliday, Scott D. Hamilton, Isak Hammar, Martin Hancock, Billy Haney, J. Keith Haney, Ryan Harlick, Sean Harnett, Rob Harris, Timothy Hatton, Lukas Haule, Ola Hellsten, Terry Higgins, Ben Hilton, the sui generis Ken Hite, Rick Hodge, Steve Holland, Steve Holroyd, Michael Holzer, "Hoopster," Seth Hunter, Kathy Igo, Mark Irons, Rafael Jasso, Harold Jenkins, Ken Jennings, Adam Jimenez, Leo Johansen, E.S. Johnson, Dave Joll, Rosemary Jones, Doug Jourgensen, Elliott "Mr. Television" Kalan, Heather Kamp, Robert Karol, Alexx Kay, John Kelly, H Jameel al Khafiz, David Kindler, Mike Kirk, John Klima, John Klump, Keith Kole, "General Kong," Ori Kowarsky, Tim Kreider, Sophie Lagacé, Rick Lai, Brett Lashuay, Kevin Lauderdale, Ryan Laws, Dennis Lien, Martin Linck, Håkan Lindh, Paul Lloyd, Shaun Logan, Ed Love, "Lukeskawalker," Krzystztof Lipka-Chudzik, Simon, McAndrews, Gabriel McCann, Patrick McCaw, Robert McCord, John McDonagh, Brendan McGuire, Ian McDowell, Andrew McLean, Bob McMahon, Joe McNally, Marc Madouraud, Will Mahoney, "Mistress Malevolent," David Marantz, Rafael Marín, Brad Marshall, Charles Martin, James Martin, Keith Martin, Frank Mascari, Masoud, Parke Matru, Jeff Meyer, Michael Meyer, Dean Milburn, Andrew Miller, Maurice Mitchell, James Moar, Robert Mohl, Ben Moldover, "Mole King," "Moony Girl," Chris Morris, Matt Morrison, Kevin Mowery, "mslbdll," Doug Muir, Chris Murphy, "Murrutala," Chris Myers, Robert Myers Stuart Nathan, Alex Naylor, Gabriel Neeb, "Duc de Nevers," Joseph Nevin, Kiat Han Ng, Joseph Nixon, Shaun Noel, Mike Norris, Michael Norwitz, "Vampyre Nute," Bill Nutt, Kate O'Brien, Toby O'Brien, Dapo Olasiyan, Nick Orwin, Pete Overstreet, Anthony Padilla, Steven Padnick, David Palmer, Clara Pandy, Jeff Patterson, William Paton, David Patton, Dan Pearce, Leigh Penman, Nick Perks, "Pete," Neal Peters, Christopher K. Philippo, Craig Pilling, Eli Pipik, Jim Pipik, Greg Plantamura, Allyn Polk, Paul Polton, "PoohBah42," Nowie Potenciano, Richard Powell, Dennis Power, Spencer Prokop, Igor Prudkin, Sean Quigley, Ed Quinby, Brendan Quinn, Hisa Rania, Colin Rankine, Michael Rawdon, Eric

Reehl, Sean Reynolds, Alasdair Richmond, "Rob," John Robie, Al Roderick, Juan Venancio Rodríguez, Edward Rogers, Jean Rogers, Bede Rogerson, Charles Roig, Peter Royston, John Rudolph Jr., Paul Rush, Timothy Rutt, "Ray S.," Beppe Sabatini, Matthew Sabonis, George Sandeman, Tristan Sargent, "Saturn2012," Adam Savage, Cliff Schexnayder, Darren Sellars, Tim Serpas, Emmanuel Seyman, Masoud Shadravan, Colin Sheaff, John Sherman, Stu Shiffman, David Silberstein, Jason Silvey, Darren Slack, Peter Slack, Daniel Smith, Nick Smith, Paddy Smith, Phil Smith, S.P. Smith, Steve Smith, Ralph Snart, John Snead, Uwe Sommerlad, Henry Spencer, "Stimps," Bill Stiteler, Allen Strange, Jim Strickland, Greg Sullivan, Michael Patrick Sullivan, Bill Svitavsky, Jeff Sweeney, Joseph Tan, Brian Taves, Sheridan Taylor, Andrew Teheran, Traven Terzich, Arnaud Thévenet, David Thiel, Lang Thompson, R. Thomsen, Kelly Tindall, Roger Todd, Geoffrey Tolle, John Toon, Ed Toshach, "tphile," Doug Tribbe, John Trumbull, Django Upton, Mike Valdivielso, Sean van der Meulen, Rick Veitch, Arturo Villarubia, "Visitor," Peter von Sholly, "Mike W.," Brian Wallace, Jamie Ward, Tara Wells, Travis Wells, Geoffrey Wessel, Chris Whiley, Dean White, Jérôme Wicky, Kurt Wilcken, Ian Wildman, Chris Whiley, Jackie Williams, Tony Williams, Gareth Wilson, Simon Wilson, Giles Woodrow, Rev. Kevin Wright, Tom Wright, "Xanadude," Ray Yamka, and Andrew Yeo.

For services above and beyond the call of ordinary fandom and friendship, my very special thanks to Steve Higgins, Martin Linck, Win Eckert, Damian Gordon, and Jean-Marc Lofficier.

Thanks for emotional and moral support and lasting and valued friendship to Judith, Cindy, Susanna, Elena, Maggie, and Abe.

Special thanks to Don Murphy for various things, to John Picacio for the wonderful covers, to Chris Roberson & Allison Baker for giving me the chance to publish this, and Kevin O'Neill and Alan Moore for their generosity with their time.

And, again, thanks to Alicia, my treasure beyond rubies.

INTRODUCTION

You know, I felt sure that *The New Travellers' Almanac* would finish him off. God knows, it finished off my copy of Manuel and Gaudalupi's *Dictionary of Imaginary Places*, and near enough finished me, so why should Jess Nevins be exempt? Maybe the proximity of Pepperland with Argentina, or the oblique nod to Mark Danielewski's *House of Leaves* would do it: he'd fail to catch the reference and his head would explode in a shower of green sparks and seafood. But no. Here he is again, every element of *The League of Extraordinary Gentlemen's* second volume neatly catalogued and cross referenced, and here I am again, as promised, writing the introduction.

If anything, my appreciation for the service that Jess provides in these companion volumes has only grown over the intervening period since the issue of *Heroes & Monsters*. As *League* itself has grown more complex and ambitious since its first conception, so too have I become obsessed with expanding the book's remit to include even the most remote and obscure corners of the fictional landscape. At the same time, I've grown concerned that this might eventually serve to alienate the readership, if they came to feel that we were showering them with unreconisably arcane literary winks and nudges for no greater purpose than to demonstrate how much research Kevin and I have done.

With Jess at hand to field even the wildest lobs over the ballpark gates of audience comprehension, these anxieties melt away. Thanks to his tireless work and enthusiasm at the academic margins of our project, unpacking the increasingly densely referenced thesis that our comic book and its collected volumes have become, then there is no reader, of whatever age or background, who need feel excluded. Now, with the turn of a page or the click of a mouse, the most tenuous allusion can be instantly decoded. This allows everybody, including the book's authors, readers and commentators, to relax their clenched and anxious intellects and simply luxuriate in how much fun this whole glorious car-crash of different fictions actually is. Without these two companion volumes, I doubt that the experience of the original work would be as complete, and I also doubt that Kevin and I would have felt sufficiently liberated or encouraged to push the concept quite as far as we currently are doing. As with *Heroes & Monsters*, *A Blazing World* is not a mere appendix to the books themselves, since an appendix is an organ that serves no vital function and which explodes on inconvenient occasions. Rather, I think of these companion volumes as having a necessary organic place in the body of the work itself, a kind of useful and symbiotic gut flora (and I wince at the bacterial analogy for something so inherently grand), essential to the organism's survival, an irreplaceable aid to its digestion.

Also, of course, never having met myself or Kevin, he does make us look brilliantly clever, when in actuality we are more often low-minded gutter scum. That bit about me referring in the *Almanac* to Captain Pugwash as "not cut out for life on the high seas" because of the cut-paper animation style that the character was rendered in would be absolute cast-iron proof of my wit and genius as a wordsmith if I'd noticed the pun before Jess pointed it out to me. On the other hand, the suggestion that I might have labeled the amphibious humanoids of South America's Black Lagoon "Silurian throwbacks" as a link to *Dr. Who* is nothing short of slanderous. The Silurian period is a stage of Earth's development typified by a proliferation of mostly aquatic life-forms, and for the record can I just make clear that I don't even particularly like *Dr. Who*, and that personally I've always felt that the Doctors following the marvelous and sinister William Hartnell dressed and behaved like unusually flamboyant child-molesters?

Even the choice of title for this current volume, *A Blazing World*, seems to sum up the essential nature of what our originally simple idea of a Victorian hero-team has evolved into, with the Duchess of Newcastle's visionary allegorical terrain become a symbol for the entire blazing landscape of the human imagination that *The League of Extraordinary Gentlemen* is now dedicated to excavating and exploring. This incandescent planet of our species' fictions, with all its hilarious, noble, tragic or terrible inhabitants, all of its towers and islands and countries and shimmering cities, has been with us since we first grunted tall tales to each other, squatting in the firelight of the cave; has been with us as long as its material, terrestrial twin. For many of us, especially here in the leisure-intensive western world, it may be that we will spend significantly lengthy stretches of our actual mortal lives at play in this imaginary territory, will come to know some of its population better than we know our real acquaintances, will have a clearer memory of Arkham, Gormenghast or Barsoom than we have of the real places that we've passed through on our way through life.

If this is true, that to all intents and purposes the world of fiction may be seen as a real place, a place we regularly visit and spend our real time immersed in and that has been a necessary, constant solace and companion to humanity since our inception, then perhaps this explains the occasional feeling that comes over Kevin and myself, the sense that somewhere amidst all this endlessly enjoyable cross-continuity mucking about, we might genuinely be handling something that is, unexpectedly, rather important. And of course, the conscientious and intensely serious effort which Jess lavishes on these companion volumes, along with the continuing gratification of what is probably one of the most well-read and intelligent readerships enjoyed by any comic book in recent history, only serve to reinforce these dangerous delusions concerning the work's worth and relevance, goading us on to even more ambitious extremes. My sincere thanks to everyone concerned.

Of course, this gush of appreciation for Jess doesn't mean that we're going to be letting up on him in any way. Quite the reverse: by encouraging us towards a deeper and richer level of creative complexity, he is in fact conspiring in his own inevitable ruinous breakdown and demise. What I'm saying is that even if by some fluke he somehow managed to survive *The New Travellers' Almanac* unscathed, our next salvo will utterly destroy him. Or us. Or you.

Failing that, I'll see you all here next time, and we can nurse our head-wounds and reminisce about a magnificent campaign. Until then I remain, your friend,

Alan Moore
Northampton,
April 29, 2004

FOREWORD

Welcome to *A Blazing World*, the companion to the second *League of Extraordinary Gentlemen* series. Like its predecessor, *Heroes & Monsters* (2003), *A Blazing World* is intended to explain the many references *League* makes to Victorian literature and popular culture.

I'm extremely pleased to be writing this introduction. I wasn't surprised that *Heroes & Monsters'* reception was positive, but I was surprised at how positive it was: interviews, store signings, a positive review in *Locus*, and even some award nominations. It's all been quite flattering, and I hope that *A Blazing World* is equally well received.

Like *Heroes & Monsters*, *A Blazing World* began life as posts on Internet newsgroups and then migrated to my Comic Book Annotations site. Most people, when they write acknowledgements for their books, say something like, "This book could not have been written without the following people." In my case, however, it's literally true. *A Blazing World* would not exist if the people noted on my acknowledgements page had not contributed to it, and I am thankful for their help, as I am for the great patience and trust that Chris Roberson and Allison Baker of MonkeyBrain Books have in me and in these books.

I am even more thankful for the generosity of Alan Moore and Kevin O'Neill. I was lucky enough to meet Mr. O'Neill at the San Diego Comic Con in July 2003, and he was kind enough to tell me that I was surprisingly normal looking, and even kinder to agree to be interviewed. He was as genial and forthcoming over the phone as he was in person. Likewise, Mr. Moore put up with a three-and-a-half hour interview, which many people wouldn't, and provided me with thousands of words of interesting material. It is in many ways a shame that most fans won't have the chance to speak with him, because he is a fascinating man to listen to, and quite giving with his time and energy.

A few notes about the format of the annotations in *A Blazing World:*

When I refer to a page and panel number, as in "Page 9. Panel 5," I am referring to the page and panel number of the collected edition of *League of Extraordinary Gentlemen, Volume 2.*

When possible, I describe panels from left to right and top to bottom.

In general I try not to spoil any of Moore and O'Neill's surprises in my annotations, so occasionally I will defer revealing information until the appropriate time. This is not always possible, however, and I apologize in advance if I ruin any surprises for any readers.

Jess Nevins
March, 2004

Annotations

Front Cover: This scene, which does not appear in the series itself, takes place in the British Museum, which is the League's headquarters. In the series the Museum is shown to be full of objects from various works of literature.

Starting with Mr. Hyde and moving clockwise around the room:

The portrait in the upper right, beneath the America's Best Comics logo, is of Orlando, who is referred to in the *New Traveller's Almanac* beginning on Page 181 and is discussed in the notes to that page. Orlando appears in Virginia Woolf's *Orlando* (1928).

The figure on the right is a large version of Punch, originally Punchinello, a popular comic character in Italian theater in the Seventeenth century. He made his appearance on continental Europe in puppet shows in 1662 and first appeared in England in 1703 at the Bartholomew Fair in a puppet play of the creation of the world. Punch is a quarrelsome, disagreeable character who fights with the other characters, beats his child, argues with his wife Judy and then kills her. He is put on trial and sentenced to death but escapes being executed through his own cleverness. Here, however, he did not ultimately escape, as can be seen by the rope around his neck.

The skull beneath Punch is a unicorn's.

The one-eyed skull beneath the unicorn's is likely a cyclops'.

The papers beneath the unicorn's skull are newspapers published during the events of H.G. Wells' *War of the Worlds*. For more information, see the notes to Page 31, Panel 4 below.

The "C. Cave, Naturalist and Dealer, Seven Dials" paper is a reference to H.G. Wells' "The Crystal Egg" (*New Review*, May 1897). See the notes to Page 25, Panel 3 for more information.

The book Mina is holding is *La Planète Mars* (*The Planet Mars, Rêves Étoilés*, 1888), written by French astronomer and writer Camille Flammarion. *La Planète Mars* is a detailed description of Mars accompanied by Flammarion's suggestions about possible Martians.

The bust in shadow is of Britannia, the personification of the British Empire, just as Uncle Sam is the personification of the United States. Britannia's head, topped by the arc of a question mark, is the icon of the second *League* series in the same way that the Question Mark Man was the icon of the first *League* series.

The scrap of paper in the lower right hand corner reads "Nacumera. Nemo Exp." This is a reference to Nacumera, an island written about by Sir John Mandeville in his *Voiage and Travayle of Sir John Maundevile* (1357). The "Nemo Exp." refers to Captain Nemo's expedition around Africa in 1890, which is explained on Page 185.

The arms of the shield are *Vert, a Hound Passant Or*. It is a Nacumeran shield, as can be seen in the illustration on Page 185.

The enormous beetle in the glass tube is the Beetle, from Richard Marsh's *The Beetle* (1897), in which novel a malign shape changing Egyptian princess, who can take the form of a giant scarab beetle, a beautiful androgyne, and an old woman or man, pursues a vendetta against a British Member of Parliament. The initials "K.O." at the base of the tube stand for Kevin O'Neill, the artist of *League*.

The portrait in the upper left, beneath "Volume II," is likely of Dr. Moreau, from H.G. Wells' *The Island of Dr. Moreau* (1896). Dr. Moreau appears on Page 120.

Kevin O'Neill notes:
> Yes, portrait in upper left is Dr. Moreau in his straw hat, and Noble's Island in the background.

Inside Front Cover: This is the Martian Red Weed, from *War of the Worlds*. The Red Weed appears on Pages 104-105.

Page 2. This is a painting of the planet Mars. The object in the upper left is Gullivar Jones in his carpet. See the notes to Page 7 for more on Jones.

The writing beneath the painting is in the Martian script, which is only understandable when viewed in a mirror.

The first line reads, "(incomprehensible), Jones, Gullivar, And, John."
The second line is incomprehensible to me.
The third line is incomprehensible to me.
The fourth line contains the word "Lofficier."
The fifth line contains the phrase "This is for Jess Nevins."
The sixth line contains the words "Jean-Marc Lofficier." Jean Marc Lofficier is an expert on French popular literature and is the author of *French Science Fiction, Fantasy, Horror and Pulp Fiction* (2000) and *Shadowmen* (2003). Lofficier suggested several of the figures who appear in the "Les Hommes Mysterieux" section on Page 171.

Page 3. This is a silhouette of a Martian Tripod. A full view can be seen on Pages 66-67.

Pages 4-5. This is the cover illustration for *League* vol. 2 no. 1 Gullivar Jones is in white and the Hither People, the Martians Jones encountered in *Lieutenant Gullivar Jones*, are in red. See the notes to Page 7 for more information.

Page 7. The man on the carpet is Gullivar Jones. Gullivar Jones was created by Edwin L. Arnold and appears in *Lieutenant Gullivar Jones: His Vacation* (1905). (Jones is referred to as "Gullivar" in *League*; varying editions of the book have his name as "Gulliver" or "Gullivar"). *Lieutenant Gullivar Jones* is about an American naval officer who is transported to Mars via a flying carpet. Once on Mars he has adventures with a group of friendly Martians and finds love with a Martian woman, Heru, before returning to Earth.

There are obvious similarities between Arnold's work and Edgar Rice Burroughs' John Carter of Mars stories, in which John Carter travels to Mars via astral projection and falls in love with Dejah Thoris, a Martian princess. But *Lieutenant Gullivar Jones* predates "Under the Moons of Mars," the first John Carter story, by seven years. It is not known whether Burroughs read Arnold, but the similarities between Arnold's work and Burroughs' work are intriguing.

Arnold wasn't the first author to write about an American military officer traveling to Mars. In 1894 Gustavus Pope wrote *Romances of the Planets No. 1: Journey to Mars*, in which Lieutenant Frederick Hamilton is shipwrecked in the Antarctic. His life is saved by a group of Martians, whose skins vary in color, and he is eventually taken to Mars by them. There he meets and falls in love with the beautiful Princess Suhlamia Angelion. As with *Lieutenant Gullivar Jones*, the similarities between Burroughs' work and Pope's are pronounced.

Nor was Burroughs the first to use the idea of travel to Mars via astral projection. In 1875 the Argentinian writer Eduardo Ladislao Holmberg wrote *Viaje Maravilloso Del Senor Nic-Nac* (*The Marvelous Travels of Mr. Nic-Nac*), in which the titular Argentinian starves himself until his soul separates from his body and travels to Mars. Holmberg's Martians are intelligent and complex, and Holmberg uses their culture to satirize Argentinian society.

In *Lieutenant Gullivar Jones* the carpet is described this way:

> ...the strangest thing about that carpet was its pattern. It was threadbare enough to all conscience in places, yet the design still lived in solemn, age-wasted hues, and, as I dragged it to my stove-front and spread it out, it seemed to me that it was as much like a star map done by a scribe who had lately recovered from delirium tremens as anything else. In the centre appeared a round such as might be taken for the sun, while here and there, "in the field," as heralds say, were lesser orbs which from their size and position could represent smaller worlds circling about it. Between these orbs were dotted lines and arrow-heads of the oldest form pointing in all directions,

while all the intervening spaces were filled up with woven characters half-way in appearance between Runes and Cryptic-Sanskrit. Round the borders these characters ran into a wild maze, a perfect jungle of an alphabet through which none but a wizard could have forced a way in search of meaning.

In *Lieutenant Gullivar Jones* the carpet does not work like an *Arabian Nights* carpet, which is sat or stood upon while in flight, but rather wraps up its passenger and then carries him to Mars:

Even as I spoke the magic carpet quivered responsively under my feet, and an undulation went all round the fringe as though a sudden wind were shaking it. It humped up in the middle so abruptly that I came down sitting with a shock that numbed me for the moment. It threw me on my back and billowed up round me as though I were in the trough of a stormy sea. Quicker than I can write it lapped a corner over and rolled me in its folds like a chrysalis in a cocoon. I gave a wild yell and made one frantic struggle, but it was too late. With the leathery strength of a giant and the swiftness of an accomplished cigar- roller covering a "core" with leaf, it swamped my efforts, straightened my limbs, rolled me over, lapped me in fold after fold till head and feet and everything were gone—crushed life and breath back into my innermost being, and then, with the last particle of consciousness, I felt myself lifted from the floor, pass once round the room, and finally shoot out, point foremost, into space through the open window....

The format of this page, beginning with a close shot of part of Gullivar's carpet and then either pulling back into the sky or remaining static while Gullivar descends, is similar to the first page of Alan Moore and Dave Gibbons' *Watchmen*.

A complete image of the carpet can be seen on Page 226.

Page 8. "Phases of Deimos" is both an astrological and a mythological reference. Deimos is one of the moons of Mars and was named after one of the attendants of the Roman war god Mars. *Deimos* means "panic" in Latin, and so the story's title refers to the events of the story and the mood of the main characters as well as to the phases of the moon.

Mars is covered with canyons much like the one seen here. The largest of the canyons, the Valles Marineris, is around twenty-five hundred miles long and up to four miles deep. By comparison, the Grand Canyon on Earth is less than five hundred miles long and only one mile deep.

Page 9. **Panel 5**. Gullivar's buckle may be a stylized question mark, which might mean that Gullivar is associated with the League. The question mark was a recurring motif in the first *League* collection, and as mentioned above in the notes to the cover, the Question Mark Man was the icon of the League in the first collection.

Kevin O'Neill notes:
> The buckle is an accident of design.

Panel 7. As mentioned in the notes to Page 2, the language the Martians speak is understandable if viewed in a mirror. The second word of the dialogue is "Hither," which is a reference to the Hither People.

Page 10. **Panel 1**. In *Lieutenant Gullivar Jones* Gullivar Jones learns to speak Martian by telepathic transferral when one of the Hither People touches him.

The giant four-armed creature who speaks to Jones on the previous page and whom Jones speaks to here is one of Edgar Rice Burroughs' Martians. Burroughs wrote eleven novels about the adventures of John Carter, a Civil War veteran, on Mars, beginning with "Under the Moons of Mars" (*All-Story Magazine*, Feb-July 1912). As adults Burroughs' Martians are fifteen feet tall, carry huge spears (some as long as forty feet), and are ferocious looking. Burroughs describes them as follows.

> There was no hair on their bodies, which were of a very light yellowish-green color. In the adults, as I was to learn quite soon, this color deepens to an olive green and is darker in the male than in the female. Further, the heads of the adults are not so out of proportion to their bodies as in the case of the young.

The iris of the eyes is blood red, as in Albinos, while the pupil is dark. The eyeball itself is very white, as are the teeth. These latter add a most ferocious appearance to an otherwise fearsome and terrible countenance, as the lower tusks curve upward to sharp points which end about where the eyes of earthly human beings are located. The whiteness of the teeth is not that of ivory, but of the snowiest and most gleaming of china. Against the dark background of their olive skins their tusks stand out in a most striking manner, making these weapons present a singularly formidable appearance.

Moore's stated goal with this series is to bring together various fictional version of Mars and portray them as co-existing. Arnold's Mars and Burroughs' Mars are the first two.

Jones' dialogue is incomprehensible to me.

Panel 3. The Martian's dialogue is incomprehensible to me.

Page 11. **Panel 1.** The Martian's dialogue is incomprehensible to me.

Panel 2. This scene may be an homage to the Wadi Rum scene in *Lawrence of Arabia* (1962), when T.E. Lawrence, played by Peter O'Toole, approaches the encampment of the Lord Feisal's Hasami Bedouin in the Wadi Rum section of Jordan.

Kevin O'Neill notes:
> Not an intentional reference to David Lean's *Lawrence of Arabia*. However, after reading the Edwin L. Arnold book I was struck by how lame a character Gullivar Jones is— for the most part a spectator in his own story whose naval uniform slowly falls to bits and sword rusts. Thinking about the Martian deserts brought T.E. Lawrence to mind, a flawed but fascinating figure. The image of a troubled man in flowing robes seemed to invest Gullivar with a mystery and gravitas lacking in Arnold's book, but does not contradict it.

Panel 4. The dialogue in Martian is incomprehensible to me.

The seated, cross-legged Martian is smoking from a hookah or water pipe.

Page 12. Panel 2. The dialogue in Martian is incomprehensible to me.

Panel 3. Gullivar Jones is greeting Edgar Rice Burroughs' John Carter. Carter is a Virginian—note his Southern manner of speaking here—and a Civil War veteran who is astrally transported to Mars in 1866 after falling asleep in an Arizona cave. Once on Mars Carter has a series of adventures, eventually becoming the Jeddak of Jeddaks, or Warlord of Barsoom (Mars), and marrying Dejah Thoris, a Martian Princess.

Carter has traditionally been portrayed in book and comic illustrations as clean shaven. The mustache, beard, and metal decorations in his hair are Moore and O'Neill's invention.

In the background is a military map illustrating the progress of the war against the invaders. The three-legged symbols in red are Tripods, which can be seen in full on Page 20. The double-barred cross symbols in yellow represent the Hither People. The ornate cylinder presumably represents the Hither People's cannon.

Kevin O'Neill notes:
> For the record, the yellow symbols represent the green Martians. The two dashes on the vertical line are a graphic for four arms.

> The three-leged symbol represents the Tripods.

Page 13. Panel 1. The "Hither People" are the friendly Martians whom Gullivar Jones joins in *Lieutenant Gullivar Jones.* They are human-looking, as can be seen on Page 17, Panel 2.

"Varnal, the Green City" comes from Michael Moorcock's Martian trilogy. See the notes to Panel 2 below.

Panel 2. Michael Moorcock, under the pseudonym of Edward P. Bradbury, wrote *Warriors of Mars* (1965), *Blades of Mars* (1965), and *Barbarians of Mars* (1965), a trilogy of stories about Michael Kane, a physics professor at the Chicago Special Research Institute who transports himself to Mars, or "Vashu," during the Cretaceous Period on Earth. The trilogy is Moorcock's homage to Edgar Rice Burroughs, and the similarities between Kane and John Carter and Shizala and Dejah Thoris are deliberate.

"Varnal, the Green City," mentioned in Panel 1 above, is the capital of Vashu, and the home of Shizala, Kane's love.

In the Moorcock series Kane is from "Negalu, the third planet of the solar system."

Panel 3. One reason that Jones and Carter have not heard of Kane is because he traveled from Carter's and Jones' future to their past.

Jones' eyes are a striking blue. This may be a dual reference to both *Lawrence of Arabia*, which showcased Peter O'Toole's eyes to good effect, and to Frank Herbert's *Dune*, in which the Fremen of the desert planet Arrakis have eyes turned blue-on-blue from use of the spice melange, a look that is similar to Jones' blue-on-blue eyes here.

Panel 4. The "Sorns" are from C.S. Lewis' Space Trilogy. See the notes to Page 22, Panel 1.

By using the word "molluscs" Carter is describing the Martians of H.G. Wells' *The War of the Worlds* (1898). For more on this, see the notes to Page 20.

Panel 5. The use of the term "alien leeches" implies that Wells' Martians are not really native to Mars. See the notes to Page 27, Panel 3.

When Jones calls the Martians "leeches" he is being accurate. In *The War of the Worlds* the Martians subsist on blood:

Strange as it may seem to a human being, all the complex apparatus of digestion, which makes up the bulk of our bodies, did not exist in the Martians. They were heads— merely heads. Entrails they had none. They did not eat, much less digest. Instead, they took the fresh, living blood of other creatures, and INJECTED it into their own veins. I have myself seen this being done, as I shall mention in its place. But, squeamish as I may seem, I cannot bring myself to describe what I could not endure even to continue watching. Let it suffice to say, blood obtained from a still living animal, in most cases from a human being, was run directly by means of a little pipette into the recipient canal....

Jones' comment about "the Princess" is curious. In the original Burroughs novels bad things rarely happened to Dejah Thoris, John Carter's wife, and the "Princess" referred to here, but Gullivar Jones' words imply that something did. The internal chronology of the Burroughs novels was never completely resolved, but as best can be figured, the first John Carter novel, *A Princess of Mars*, takes place from 1866 to 1886; the second John Carter novel, *The Gods of Mars* (serially published in *All-Story Magazine* in 1913 and then as a novel in 1918) takes place in 1886; the third John Carter novel, *The Warlord of Mars* (serially published in *All-Story Magazine* in 1913-1914 and then as a novel in 1919) takes place from 1887 to 1888; the fourth Mars novel, *Thuvia, Maid of Mars* (serially published in *All-Story Weekly* in 1916 and then as a novel in 1920), takes place sometime between 1888 and 1898; and the fifth Mars novel, *The Chessmen of Mars* (1922), takes place sometime between 1898 and 1917.

League v2 takes place in 1898. Dejah Thoris does not appear in *Thuvia*, a novel about Thuvia, a Martian princess, and Carthoris, the son of Dejah Thoris and John Carter. Dejah Thoris does appear in *Chessmen*, but seems in perfect health. This may be a case where Moore and O'Neill are deviating from the original texts. If we disregard the interior chronology of the Burroughs stories, as Moore and O'Neill have occasionally done with other source texts used, it is possible to fit the events of this issue in between two of the Burroughs novels. *Gods of Mars* ends on a cliffhanger, with Dejah Thoris trapped in a room which will not be accessible for another two years, and the last thing John Carter sees is one of the women in the room attempting to murder Dejah Thoris while Thuvia tries to save her. John Carter is forced to wait for two years while believing his wife is dead. It could be that *League* v2 takes place during that two-year interval.

In *War of the Worlds: Global Dispatches* (1997), an anthology of stories about what happened around the world during the *War of the Worlds* Martian invasion, George Alec Effinger's "Mars: The Home Front" tells the story of what took place on Mars during *War of the Worlds* (hereafter *WotW*). In this story Dejah Thoris is abducted. If Moore is incorporating "Mars: The Home Front" into the continuity of *League* v2, Gullivar Jones may be referring to this abduction.

Panel 6. Carter is a self-proclaimed worshiper of Mars/Ares, the Roman/Greek war god, which is why he bids farewell to Gullivar with the Roman salute of the raised arm.

Page 14. Panel 3. In the Burroughs novels the atmosphere of Barsoom (the Martian word for Mars) is kept breathable by an "atmosphere factory." At the end of *A Princess of Mars* the atmosphere factory is inoperable, but in the rest of the Burroughs novels the factory is working. It may be that Wells' Martians have damaged the atmosphere factory, which is why Jones and Carter need the breathing apparatuses which they wear. (See the note to Page 24, Panel 2 below). Or possibly the masks are simply filters to keep out the sand and dust of the atmosphere.

Kevin O'Neill notes:
> The masks and breathing apparatuses are to filter out the sometimes violent sand and dust disturbances on Mars.

Page 15. Panel 1. The dialogue in Martian is incomprehensible to me.

Panels 2-4. The creatures which Carter and the other Martians are riding are thoats, from Burroughs' John Carter books. Burroughs describes one this way:

It towered ten feet at the shoulder; had four legs on either side; a broad flat tail, larger at the tip than at the root, and which it held straight out behind while running; a gaping mouth which split its head from its snout to its long, massive neck.

Like its master, it was entirely devoid of hair, but was of a dark slate color and exceeding smooth and glossy. Its belly was white, and its legs shaded from the slate of its shoulders and hips to a vivid yellow at the feet. The feet themselves were heavily padded and nailless, which fact had also contributed to the noiselessness of their approach, and, in common with a multiplicity of legs, is a characteristic feature of the fauna of Mars. The highest type of man and one other animal, the only mammal existing on Mars, alone have well-formed nails, and there are absolutely no hoofed animals in existence there.

Panel 3. The dialogue in Martian is incomprehensible to me.

Panel 5. The dialogue in Martian is incomprehensible to me.

Pages 16-17. The canyons on Mars can be miles deep, which is why the Martians and the thoats are climbing up them, rather than through and around them. The lower gravity of Mars is what makes climbing the canyon wall in this way possible.

Most of the thoats in the Barsoom novels have flat, nailless feet. These thoats may have been bred for use in the canyons.

The Martians have Roman- and Greek-style helmets and spears. The iconography of Ares/Mars, John Carter's god of choice, is the spear and the helmet.

Page 17. Panel 4. The dialogue in Martian is incomprehensible to me.

Page 18. Panel 1-4. The dialogue in Martian is incomprehensible to me.

Page 19. Panel 1. The clothes of the Hither People have some resemblance to later Islamic cultures such as the Ottomans, while the Barsoomians' are similar to those of pre-Islamic Arab nomads.

Panel 2. The Martian's dialogue is incomprehensible to me.

Panel 4. From left to right, "Shit!" "Look out!" "Oh, fuck!"

Page 20. This is one of the Martian Tripods from H.G. Wells' *The War of the Worlds*. On page 13, Panel 4 John Carter describes Wells' Martians as "molluscs." This is how Wells describes the Martians in *WotW*:

> But, looking, I presently saw something stirring within the shadow: greyish billowy movements, one above another, and then two luminous disks—like eyes. Then something resembling a little grey snake, about the thickness of a walking stick, coiled up out of the writhing middle, and wriggled in the air towards me—and then another.
>
> A sudden chill came over me. There was a loud shriek from a woman behind. I half turned, keeping my eyes fixed upon the cylinder still, from which other tentacles were now projecting, and began pushing my way back from the edge of the pit. I saw astonishment giving place to horror on the faces of the people about me. I heard inarticulate exclamations on all sides. There was a general movement backwards. I saw the shopman struggling still on the edge of the pit. I found myself alone, and saw the people on the other side of the pit running off, Stent among them. I looked again at the cylinder, and ungovernable terror gripped me. I stood petrified and staring.
>
> A big greyish rounded bulk, the size, perhaps, of a bear, was rising slowly and painfully out of the cylinder. As it bulged up and caught the light, it glistened like wet leather.
>
> Two large dark-coloured eyes were regarding me steadfastly. The mass that framed them, the head of the

thing, was rounded, and had, one might say, a face. There was a mouth under the eyes, the lipless brim of which quivered and panted, and dropped saliva. The whole creature heaved and pulsated convulsively. A lank tentacular appendage gripped the edge of the cylinder, another swayed in the air.

Those who have never seen a living Martian can scarcely imagine the strange horror of its appearance. The peculiar V-shaped mouth with its pointed upper lip, the absence of brow ridges, the absence of a chin beneath the wedgelike lower lip, the incessant quivering of this mouth, the Gorgon groups of tentacles, the tumultuous breathing of the lungs in a strange atmosphere, the evident heaviness and painfulness of movement due to the greater gravitational energy of the earth—above all, the extraordinary intensity of the immense eyes—were at once vital, intense, inhuman, crippled and monstrous. There was something fungoid in the oily brown skin, something in the clumsy deliberation of the tedious movements unspeakably nasty.

Carter's use of the term mollusc seems apposite.

The Martian Tripod is described by Wells in this way:

And this Thing I saw! How can I describe it? A monstrous tripod, higher than many houses, striding over the young pine trees, and smashing them aside in its career; a walking engine of glittering metal, striding now across the heather; articulate ropes of steel dangling from it, and the clattering tumult of its passage mingling with the riot of the thunder. A flash, and it came out vividly, heeling over one way with two feet in the air, to vanish and reappear almost instantly as it seemed, with the next flash, a hundred yards nearer. Can you imagine a milking stool tilted and bowled violently along the ground? That was the impression those instant flashes gave. But instead of a milking stool imagine it a great body of machinery on a tripod stand....

Seen nearer, the Thing was incredibly strange, for it was no mere insensate machine driving on its way. Machine it was, with a ringing metallic pace, and long, flexible, glittering tentacles (one of which gripped a young pine tree) swinging and rattling about its strange body. It picked its road as it went striding along, and the brazen hood that surmounted it moved to and fro with the inevitable suggestion of a head looking about. Behind the main body was a huge mass of white metal like a gigantic fisherman's basket, and puffs of green smoke squirted out from the joints of the limbs as the monster swept by me.

Page 21. Panels 1-4. In *WotW* the Martians use the "black smoke" Carter refers to in Panel 4 to wipe out great numbers of humans.

Panel 3. John's dialogue is incomprehensible to me.

Panel 5. The Martian on the left says, "By the gods, we're" with the last word being incomprehensible to me. Perhaps "saved"?

The Martian on the right says, "(incomprehensible) hurts look at (incomprehensible)."

Page 22. Panel 1. The tall, spindly creatures are the Sorns. The Sorns were created by C.S. Lewis and appear in *Out of the Silent Planet* (1939), the first book in Lewis' Space Trilogy; the other two are *Perelandra* (1943) and *That Hideous Strength* (1945). The Space Trilogy is about Dr. Elwin Ransom, a human who is kidnaped by an evil scientist and taken to Malacandra, a.k.a. Mars. On Mars Ransom befriends the Malacandrans and helps capture the evil scientist. In *Perelandra* Ransom goes to Perelandra, or Venus, and helps prevent a second Fall of Eve. In the third book evil is fought on Earth.

The Sorns are one of three species of Malacandrans. There are the Hrossa, poet-farmers; the Pfiltriggi, the artisans; and the Sorns, the scholar-philosophers. Lewis describes the Sorns as

> spindly and flimsy things, twice or three times the height of a man...so crazily thin and elongated in the leg, so top-heavily pouted in the chest, such stalky, flexible-looking distortions of earthly bipeds.

Page 23. Panel 5. John Carter previously described the Martians as "molluscs." The shells around the compound in this panel might be their shells.

Page 24. Panel 2. Gullivar Jones removes his breathing mask here and is able to speak and breathe. It may be that the Martian atmosphere is only partially damaged and so can be breathed by humans for short periods of time. Alternatively, the breathing apparatuses may be used to protect Jones and Carter from the Martians' Black Smoke.

Panel 3. The idea of "flesh-mechanics" is not one which appears in the Martian works of H.G. Wells, Edgar Rice Burroughs, Edwin Arnold, or C.S. Lewis. It may be a reference to the tactics of the sadistic Martians in the "Mars Attacks" bubble-gum card set, created by Len Brown, Woody Gelman, Wally Wood and Bob Powell for Topps, Inc. in 1962.

However, in *WotW* Wells does describe another Martian race, which the Martians brought with them to Earth during the invasion:

> Their undeniable preference for men as their source of nourishment is partly explained by the nature of the remains of the victims they had brought with them as provisions from Mars. These creatures, to judge from the shrivelled remains that have fallen into human hands, were bipeds, with flimsy siliceous skeletons (almost like those of the siliceous sponges) and feeble musculature, standing about six feet high, and having round erect heads, and large eyes in flinty sockets. Two or three of these seem to have been brought in each cylinder, and all were killed before earth was reached. It was just as well for them, for the mere attempt to stand upright upon our planet would have broken every bone in their body.

This creature has some resemblance to the Sorns seen here. Perhaps Moore and O'Neill are implying that the Wells' Martians use "flesh-mechanics" on Sorns and use the resulting creatures as food? Alternatively, Moore and O'Neill may be referring to another Martian, the winged telepathic Martian which appears in Ritson and Stanley Stewart's *The Professor's Last Experiment* (1888).

Page 25. **Panel 1.** In *Lieutenant Gullivar Jones* the Hither People are a thin, slight, fair race, quite different from the darker types seen in this panel on the right.

Kevin O'Neill notes:
> I wanted to have a touch of Arabian fantasy about the Hither People, who are clearly here a more warrior-like people than in Arnold's book.

Panel 2. The image of Gullivar Jones is, I think, from that moment in *Lieutenant Gullivar Jones* when he first wishes to go to Mars. The image of John Carter and Dejah Thoris is not from any specific moment in any of the Burroughs books.

Kevin O'Neill notes:
> Gullivar Jones is shown in his naval uniform.

Panel 3. The "glass egg with moving pictures" which Gullivar is examining is actually the Crystal Egg from H.G. Wells' "The Crystal Egg" (*New Review*, May 1897). In that story C. Cave, a dealer in antiquities, looks through the Egg and sees Mars. Cave sees other crystals and wonders if the Martians sent the crystal to Earth as a viewing device. In *Sherlock Holmes's War of the Worlds* (1975) Manly Wade Wellman speculated that the Egg was a reconnaissance device for the invading Martians.

In "The Crystal Egg" Cave sees various flying creatures. It may be that the winged Sorn subjected to flesh-mechanics is a reference to the winged Martians in "The Crystal Egg." Cave also sees tentacled Martians as well as what might be a Tripod:

> On another occasion a vast thing, that Mr. Cave thought at first was some gigantic insect, appeared advancing along the causeway beside the canal with extraordinary rapidity. As this drew nearer Mr. Cave perceived that it was a mechanism of shining metals and of extraordinary complexity.

And the tentacled Martians in "The Crystal Egg" seem to feed on "certain clumsy bipeds, dimly suggestive of apes, white and partially translucent," which may be the same race of bipeds mentioned in the notes to Page 24, Panel 3 above.

The bust seen in the Crystal Egg is of Queen Victoria.

The Martian may be saying, "Outside, quick."

Panel 4. The Martian says, "Look!"

Page 26. In Chapter One of *WotW* it is hinted that the Martians are using huge cannon to fire their ships at Earth, in much the same way that the Baltimore Gun Club sends a manned capsule to the moon in Jules Verne's *De La Terre a la Lune* (*From the Earth to the Moon*, 1865). Given the illustration here, it may be that the Martians are using a combination of cannon and rocketry, or perhaps a laser to propel the shells.

Page 27. Panel 3. In *League* Wells' Martians are not native to Mars. In an interview Moore said that "H.G. Wells' Martians, they are not from Mars. They are from some other galaxy. And they tried to take over Mars but have been driven out by the combined Martian resistance...and that's when they come to Earth." This idea is not wholly new to Moore, having been used before in Christopher Priest's *The Space Machine* (1976), which combines Wells' *The Time Machine* and *WotW*, in Manly Wellman's *Sherlock Holmes's War of the Worlds*, and in George Alec Effinger's "Mars: The Home Front."

Page 28. Panels 1-3. This panel may be a reference to the Oscar Wilde comment, "We are all of us in the gutter, but some of us are looking at the stars."

Panel 5. The "V.R." on the side of the carriage stands for Victoria Regina or Queen Victoria. The "V.R." is a kind of official emblem for the British government and is sometimes seen as "V.R.I.," or "Victoria Regina Imperatrix" (Victoria Queen and Empress).

Page 29. Panel 4. Generally in *League* characters who appear in the background of panels, as the dog with the black ring around its eye does in this panel, are not described in the scripts by Moore and are put in by Kevin O'Neill. This dog may not be a reference at all, and might have been included simply as local color. Or it could be a reference. The dog might be Tige, the talking dog friend of Richard F. Outcault's comic strip character Buster Brown. A similar-looking dog appears in the "Bellman Expedition" illustration on Page 164.

Kevin O'Neill notes:
> No reference intended. Dog is just a dog.

Page 30. This is the moment in *WotW* when the Martians have first landed but not emerged from their impact crater.

The "smug Frenchman, licentious Spaniard, and the blustering Hun" text in the next issue panel is typical nineteenth- and early twentieth-century boys' story text, describing the French, Spanish, and Germans in stereotypical fashion.

Page 31. Panel 1. Campion Bond makes his first appearance in *League* v2 in much the same way that he was first seen on Page 1 of *League* v1 #1, down to his Aubrey Beardsley cigarette case.

Kevin O'Neill notes:
> On the chapter in particular I was careful to mark up and pass onto colorist Ben Dimagmaliw very clear notes on weather—sky color, time of day, etc.—to match same details in Wells' book.

Panel 2. The symbol on the rear of Bond's carriage is the Masonic compass and right triangle. The ties between Bond and MI5 and the Masons were made explicit on Page 101 of the first *League* collection.

League v2 generally adheres quite closely to the timeline of events in *WotW*. Chapter 3 of *WotW* has the following passage, from the time after the first Martian shell has landed but before the Martians have emerged: "There were half a dozen flies or more from the Woking station standing in the road by the sand pits, a basketchaise from Chobham, and a rather lordly carriage." The "lordly carriage" might be Bond's.

Panel 4. The newspaper Griffin is holding comes from *WotW*, Chapter 3:

> In the afternoon the appearance of the common had altered very much. The early editions of the evening papers had startled London with enormous headlines:
>
> "A MESSAGE RECEIVED FROM MARS"
>
> "REMARKABLE STORY FROM WOKING"

The other legible headline of the paper contains the words "Doctor Nikola." This is a reference to Guy Boothby's supervillain Dr. Nikola, who was introduced in an eight-part story in *Windsor Magazine* which was later published as *A Bid For Fortune* (1895). Nikola appears in four sequels to *A Bid For Fortune*, and is one of the great mad scientists and archvillains of nineteenth-century popular literature. Nikola's name appears on Page 110 of the first *League* collection on a paper on Professor Moriarty's desk as a possible alternate identity for Sherlock Holmes. In the world of *League* Dr. Nikola is obviously at large.

"The new M" Campion refers to is Mycroft Holmes, the older brother of Sherlock Holmes. In the first *League* collection Mycroft appears on Page 149, taking over MI5 as the new "M" after Professor Moriarty's disappearance.

It is a part of Sherlockian canon that Mycroft does not like to travel. In "The Adventure of the Greek Interpreter," Sherlock describes his brother this way:

> Mycroft lodges in Pall Mall, and he walks round the corner into Whitehall every morning and back every evening. From year's end to year's end he takes no other exercise, and is seen nowhere else, except only in the Diogenes Club, which is just opposite his rooms.

Panel 5. The girl in the left-hand side of the panel resembles the John Tenniel drawings of Alice, from Lewis Carroll's *Alice's Adventures in Wonderland* (1865). The girl in this panel is not Alice, however; Alice's fate is described on Page 164 below.

"The Prussians" were the Germans, one of the rivals to the British Empire at the turn of the Twentieth century. Prussia was an eastern German state, along the Polish border. Prussia and many of the lesser Germanic states were united and became the German Empire in 1871.

Page 32. The title of this issue, "People of Other Lands," is a reference to the *Bible*, 2 Chronicles 32:13:

> Know ye not what I and my fathers have done unto all the people of other lands? Were the gods of the nations of those lands any ways able to deliver their lands out of mine hand?

The enormous capsule is one of the Martians' space ships. In *WotW* Chapter 2 the craft is described as "a huge cylinder, caked over and its outline softened by a thick scaly dun-coloured incrustation. It had a diameter of about thirty yards."

Page 33. Panel 1. To answer Campion's question, in *WotW* Stent, the "Astronomer Royal" Hyde mentions, directed the workmen excavating the cylinder.

Panel 2. The head of Campion Bond's cane has the Morse Code for "007."

Panel 5. The dialogue here is reproduced verbatim from Chapter 4 of *WotW*.

Panels 6-7. In *WotW* the cylinder lid is described in this way:

> The end of the cylinder was being screwed out from within. Nearly two feet of shining screw projected. Somebody blundered against me, and I narrowly missed

being pitched onto the top of the screw. I turned, and as I did so the screw must have come out, for the lid of the cylinder fell upon the gravel with a ringing concussion.

Page 34. Panel 1. For a description of the Martians' first appearance in *WotW*, see the notes for Page 20.

Page 35. Panel 1. The Martian falling from the cylinder into the pit occurs in Chapter 4 of *WotW*.

Panels 3-5. The man trying to crawl from the pit is from *WotW*, Chapter 4:

> And then, with a renewed horror, I saw a round, black object bobbing up and down on the edge of the pit. It was the head of the shopman who had fallen in, but showing as a little black object against the hot western sun. Now he got his shoulder and knee up, and again he seemed to slip back until only his head was visible. Suddenly he vanished, and I could have fancied a faint shriek had reached me.

Page 36. Panel 3. The pair between Quatermain and Hyde are from *WotW*; they are the novel's narrator (on the left, with his back to us) and one of his neighbors. The relevant passage, from Chapter 5, follows:

> One man I approached—he was, I perceived, a neighbour of mine, though I did not know his name—and accosted. But it was scarcely a time for articulate conversation.
>
> "What ugly brutes!" he said. "Good God! What ugly brutes!" He repeated this over and over again.

Panel 4. The man on the right who says, "D-Did you see a man in the pit? That chap that fell....," is the narrator from *WotW*. From Chapter 5:

> "Did you see a man in the pit?" I said; but he made no answer to that.

The narrator is drawn to resemble H.G. Wells.

Page 37. Panel 1. The expedition, with the lead man waving the flag, is from Chapter 5 of *WotW*.

"That Reverend Harding who writes to the newspapers so often" was mentioned in the first *League* collection, on Page 39. He is the Reverend Septimus Harding, from Anthony Trollope's *The Warden* (1855) and the succeeding Barsetshire novels.

Panel 5. From Chapter Five of *WotW*:

> Suddenly there was a flash of light, and a quantity of luminous greenish smoke came out of the pit in three distinct puffs, which drove up, one after the other, straight into the still air.

Page 39. Panel 1. The group here is described in *WotW*:

> ...The group of bystanders...among these were a couple of cyclists, a jobbing gardener I employed sometimes, a girl carrying a baby, Gregg the butcher and his little boy, and two or three loafers and golf caddies who were accustomed to hang about the railway station.

Panels 2-3. From Chapter 5 of *WotW*:

> Forthwith flashes of actual flame, a bright glare leaping from one to another, sprang from the scattered group of men. It was as if some invisible jet impinged upon them and flashed into white flame. It was as if each man were suddenly and momentarily turned to fire.
>
> Then, by the light of their own destruction, I saw them staggering and falling, and their supporters turning to run.
>
> I stood staring, not as yet realising that this was death leaping from man to man in that little distant crowd. All I felt was that it was something very strange. An almost noiseless and blinding flash of light, and a man fell headlong

and lay still; and as the unseen shaft of heat passed over them, pine trees burst into fire, and every dry furze bush became with one dull thud a mass of flames. And far away towards Knaphill I saw the flashes of trees and hedges and wooden buildings suddenly set alight.

Page 40. Panels 1-2. From Chapter 5 of *WotW*:

It was sweeping round swiftly and steadily, this flaming death, this invisible, inevitable sword of heat. I perceived it coming towards me by the flashing bushes it touched, and was too astounded and stupefied to stir. I heard the crackle of fire in the sand pits and the sudden squeal of a horse that was as suddenly stilled. Then it was as if an invisible yet intensely heated finger were drawn through the heather between me and the Martians, and all along a curving line beyond the sand pits the dark ground smoked and crackled. Something fell with a crash far away to the left where the road from Woking station opens out on the common. Forthwith the hissing and humming ceased, and the black, dome-like object sank slowly out of sight into the pit.

Page 42. Panel 1. Kevin O'Neill notes:
The barrow with (exploding) bottles of ginger pop is a detail from *War of the Worlds*.

Page 43. Panel 4. The inn, "the Bleak House," is a reference to Charles Dickens' *Bleak House* (1852), Dickens' savaging of the British legal system. In the novel Bleak House is the home of John Jarndyce, a part of "this scarecrow of a suit," the interminable Jarndyce v. Jarndyce.

The Bleak House Pub is an actual coaching inn and public house. It is on the Chertsey Road (the A320) in Woking, Surrey, south of London, and has been there for several centuries. The pub may have been the inspiration for the fictional pub in *Bleak House*.

Kevin O'Neill notes:
I made a trip to Woking station and asked a local taxi driver to take me to the sand pits at Horsell Common. He couldn't find them, but did drop me off at the Bleak House for

directions—they told me to dismiss the taxi and stay and have a drink—which I did. A very friendly afternoon all in all. And in fact the sand pits are across the road, a little ways into the woods. Our Bleak House interior and exterior is pure invention. The present inn on the site is rather more recent than was called for.

Page 45. Panel 4. "I always thought of it as something that sheltered humanity, but now it frightens me, Mr. Quatermain."

Mina's words may be Moore's way of illustrating the change in fictional presentations of aliens which H.G. Wells, through *War of the Worlds*, caused. Before the publication of *WotW* the great majority of fictional aliens were benign and were essentially humans and Earthly animals, even if sometimes in strange shapes. Aliens and alien societies were primarily used for satirical or utopian purposes by writers. Even those writers who created truly alien beings, like Camille Flammarion in his *Real and Imaginary Worlds* (1864), portrayed them as well-meaning. Wells changed this.

There were predecessors to Wells who created hostile aliens. J.H. Rosny aîné, in his "Les Xipéhuz" ("The Shapes," 1887), described mineral aliens fighting with human cavemen. And the German writer Kurd Lasswitz, in his *Auf Zwei Planeten* (*Between Two Worlds*, 1897), described a Martian landing on Earth and subsequent conflict with humans. But *War of the Worlds* had a far greater impact on writers than the work of Rosny or Lasswitz. Its depiction of a war between aliens—specifically Martians—and humans spawned many imitators and sequels, such as Garrett Serviss' *Edison's Conquest of Mars* (1898). In *Edison's Conquest of Mars* the attack of the Martians is more widespread and damaging than in *WotW*, and so Tom Edison creates weapons to counter the Martians' weapons and then leads the human counterattack on Mars. It was H.G. Wells, through *War of the Worlds*, who popularized the idea of a human war with invading aliens, and it may be this is what Moore is referring to with Mina's statement.

Panel 5. Quatermain's comment that "This whole affair reminds me of a dream I once had" is a reference to his dream in the text piece "Allan and the Sundered Veil" in the first *League* series.

Page 46. Panel 1. These troops appear in Chapter 8 of *WotW*:

> About eleven a company of soldiers came through
> Horsell, and deployed along the edge of the common to
> form a cordon. Later a second company marched through
> Chobham to deploy on the north side of the common.
> Several officers from the Inkerman barracks had been
> on the common earlier in the day, and one, Major Eden,
> was reported to be missing. The colonel of the regiment
> came to the Chobham bridge and was busy questioning
> the crowd at midnight. The military authorities were
> certainly alive to the seriousness of the business. About
> eleven, the next morning's papers were able to say, a
> squadron of hussars, two Maxims, and about four hundred
> men of the Cardigan regiment started from Aldershot.

"Major Henry Blimp" is a reference to Colonel Blimp, a cartoon character who was created by Sir David Alexander Cecil Low and appeared in various newspapers around the world in the 1930s, beginning with the *London Evening Standard*. Low described Colonel Blimp in this way:

> Blimp was no enthusiast for democracy. He was impatient
> with the common people and their complaints. His remedy
> to social unrest was less education, so that people could
> not read about slumps. An extreme isolationist, disliking
> foreigners (which included Jews, Irish, Scots, Welsh, and
> people from the Colonies and Dominions); a man of
> violence, approving war. He had no use for the League
> of Nations nor for international efforts to prevent wars.
> In particular he objected to any economic reorganization
> of world resources involving changes in the status quo.

The Blimp seen here is obviously a younger version who has yet to be promoted.

The Inkerman Barracks were located in Woking; formerly a prison for invalid convicts, it was converted into infantry barracks in 1892.

The British infantry troops shown here are wearing the standard-issue British Home Service uniforms, circa 1898. British troops in the Boer War wore almost exactly the same uniform, although in foreign service, a white pith helmet was worn instead of the black home service helmet depicted here. The metal spike protruding from the helmets was no longer in use in in 1898.

The rifles the troops carry are Lee-Metfords or Lee-Enfields, bolt-action "magazine rifles" that replaced the venerable Martini-Henry single-shot rifle in the early 1890s. The Lee-Metford had Metford rifling, which was adequate for black-powder cartridges. The Lee-Enfield had Enfield rifling, which was necessary to deal with the smokeless-powders cartridges introduced at around the same time. Externally, both rifles are identical. By World War I, all British soldiers carried Lee-Enfields.

Panel 2. The Maxim Gun Major Blimp mentions was the first modern machine gun, adopted for use by the British Army in 1889. It was the most significant technological difference between the British Army and its native opponents and was largely responsible for the British military triumphs of the late Nineteenth century. Blimp's invocation of it indicates the level of confidence the British military had in the Maxim gun in 1898.

Panel 3. "It'll all be over come Monday morning" is a reference to the expression, "It will all be over by Christmas," which was often said in Britain in the opening days of World War I. A young Field Marshal Bernard Law Montgomery was actually quoted in August 1914 as saying, "Fortunately the whole thing will be over by Christmas." In *WotW* those people who had not seen the Martians were similarly optimistic about how easily the Martians would be defeated. In Chapter 9 of *WotW* the narrator's neighbor "was of the opinion that the troops would be able to capture or to destroy the Martians during the day" (the Sunday following the first use of the Heat Ray).

Page 47. Panel 2. The "buggering noise and clanging from the Common" are from Chapter 8 of *WotW*:

> A curious crowd lingered restlessly, people coming and going but the crowd remaining, both on the Chobham and Horsell bridges. One or two adventurous souls, it was afterwards found, went into the darkness and crawled quite near the Martians; but they never returned, for now and again a light-ray, like the beam of a warship's

searchlight swept the common, and the Heat-Ray was
ready to follow. Save for such, that big area of common
was silent and desolate, and the charred bodies lay about
on it all night under the stars, and all the next day. A noise
of hammering from the pit was heard by many people.

Panel 3. The word "nine" spelled out in matchsticks is the answer to a
riddling game. The riddler takes six matchsticks and lines them up
vertically, like so:

The riddler then hands his opponent five matchsticks and says, "Add
these five to these six and get nine." The solution to the riddle is to place
them so that they spell the word nine, like so:

```
!\ ! ! !\ ! !—-
! \ ! ! ! !\ ! !—-
! \! !! \! !—-
```

Page 48. Panel 1. The descent of the second cylinder appears in
Chapter 8 of *WotW*:

> A few seconds after midnight the crowd in the Chertsey
> road, Woking, saw a star fall from heaven into the pine
> woods to the northwest. It had a greenish colour, and
> caused a silent brightness like summer lightning. This was
> the second cylinder.

Pages 50-51. The exchange here between Hyde and Mina is
reminiscent in spirit of Sydney Carton's farewell to Lucie Darnay in
Charles Dickens' *A Tale of Two Cities* (1859), in which Carton declares
himself a bounder and wretch, a "poor creature of misuse," and asks
Lucie to keep a soft spot in her heart for him.

Page 55. Panel 1. This is the first instance of a discrepancy between
the chronologies of *League* and *WotW*. In *WotW* the shelling of the first
Martian craft begins, in Chapter 9, on Saturday night, "about six in the
evening."

The "Jonathan" Mina refers to here is Jonathan Harker, Mina's husband in *Dracula*. In *League* they are divorced. For more on this see the notes to Page 109, Panel 1.

In the bottom left corner of the panel is what appears to be a Hussar, a type of light cavalry introduced during the Napoleonic War. Although obsolete, there were still active British Hussar units in 1898.

The British artillery team in the center of the panel is aiming what appears to be an Armstrong Twelve Pounder. The Twelve Pounder was a breech-loading field artillery piece used during the the Boer War.

Major Blimp, on the right side of the panel, is leading the troops while also making himself into a target. During the Boer War officers who led from the front had a very short life expectancy. Boer commandos and snipers targeted leaders and worked their way down the ranks until the British troops were a demoralized and leaderless rabble.

Panel 3. In Chapter 9 of *WotW* the second Martian craft lands at the Byfleet Golf Links.

The muzzle of a Maxim gun is visible on the left edge of the panel.

Page 56. "And the Dawn Comes Up Like Thunder" is a quote from Rudyard Kipling's "Mandalay," from his *Barrack-Room Ballads* (1892). The line is from the poem's refrain; the first stanza is this:

> By the old Moulmein Pagoda lookin' eastward to the sea,
> There's a Burma girl a-settin' and I know she thinks of me.
> For the wind is in the palm-trees, and the temple bells they say,
> "Come you back, you British soldier, come you back to Mandalay."
> Come you back to Mandalay,
> Where the old Flotilla lay.
> Can't you 'ear their paddles chunkin' from Rangoon to Mandalay?
> On the road to Mandalay,

Where the flyin' fishes play,
And the dawn comes up like thunder out of China 'crost
the bay.

The men on horseback are Hussars. The Hussar holding the telescope is wearing the Home Service uniform and has the carbine version of the Lee-Metford rifle in his saddle holster. The gunner is holding a shell for the Armstrong Twelve Pounder. The equipment of the British troops here and their tactics are consistent with those of the real British Army in 1898.

The gore of this panel and of the other British engagements with the Martians is no more violent or bloody than most other battles during World War I, when British tactics had not caught up to the horrifying capacity of high-explosive shells and machine guns.

Page 57. Panel 3. In Chapter 32 of *Bleak House* Mr. Krook dies of spontaneous combustion, a possible foreshadowing of the scene here.

Page 58. Panel 4. The identity of the coachman is revealed in the notes to Page 61, Panel 5.

Page 59. Panel 4. The red-coated gentleman and the young lady in pink to whom he is about to present a bouquet of flowers are references to the illustrations on the boxes of tins of Quality Street sweets. The pair originally appear in the J.M. Barrie play *Quality Street* (1901), a love story about Valentine Brown, a doctor home from the Napoleonic Wars, and Phoebe Throssel, the woman he loves. In 1936 the two characters were chosen for the logo of Mackintosh's Quality Street chocolates and toffees. Quality Street sweets are currently made by Nestlé Rowntree.

Kevin O'Neill notes:
No Quality Street reference intended.

Page 60. Panel 1. Moving clockwise, beginning at the top of the panel with the large human skeleton:

The giant humanoid skeleton is a reference to the Edward Lear limerick, "An Old Man of Coblenz," which runs

> There was an Old Man of Coblenz
> The length of whose legs was immense
> He went with one prance
> From Turkey to France
> That surprising Old Man of Coblenz.

"An Old Man of Coblenz" first appears in Lear's *A Book of Nonsense* in 1846, hence the "1846" date on the plaque at his feet.

To the right of the skeleton of the Old Man of Coblenz is pictured part of a stature of the Reverend Dr. Syn, seen from the back in the crossed-guns pose shown in his picture on Page 53 of the first *League* collection. The Reverend Dr. Syn is from Russell Thorndike's *Doctor Syn* (1915) and its six prequels. In *League* v1 Dr. Syn was shown to have been a member of the eighteenth-century League.

The painting on the right is the final version of the portrait of Dorian Gray, from Oscar Wilde's *The Picture of Dorian Gray* (1891), in which the painting of Dorian Gray reflected Gray's sins. The joke here is that the painting is being restored, as can be seen by the "Danger" sign and the pots on the scaffolding. The painting here is similar to the one seen in the 1945 film version of *Dorian Gray*. In that film the final appearance of the painting is the sole use of technicolor in the film.

In the lower left, the straight razor on the plaque reading "Kettlewell, Yorkshire, Mr. W. C. Cording" is a reference to C. J. Cutcliffe Hyne's "The Lizard" (*The Strand Magazine*, February 1898), in which an explorer discovers a dinosaur in a cave in Kettlewell.

José da Silvestra is the Portuguese explorer who in 1590 discovers the mines of King Solomon in H. Rider Haggard's *King Solomon's Mines* (1885), the novel which introduced Allan Quatermain.

The bust to the right of da Silvestra is that of Karl Friedrich Hieronymus, Baron von Münchhausen (1720-1797). Baron Münchhausen is best known for his extraordinarily tall tales. A collection of his tales first appeared from 1781-3, under the title *Vademecum fur Lustige Leute* (*Manual for Merry People*), but Münchhausen was made into the epitome of the European tall tale teller with the 1785 *Baron Münchhausen's Narrative of His Marvellous Travels and Campaigns in Russia.*

The enormous skeleton in the upper left may be that of the whale which swallowed Baron Münchhausen during one of his adventures, or it may be one of the dinosaurs brought back from Maple White Land by Professor Challenger in Arthur Conan Doyle's *The Lost World* (1912).

Kevin O'Neill notes:
> The enormous fish is associated with Baron von Münchausen.

Panel 2. The corpulent gentleman speaking with the League is Mycroft Holmes.

Panel 3. Holmes' injunction against using the word "invasion," as "the panic alone could kill hundreds," may be a reference to the 1938 Orson Welles radio adaptation of *WotW*, whose broadcast caused panic among some listeners.

Page 61. Panel 4. Hanging from Mycroft Holmes' watch chain are various Masonic symbols, including the eye in the pyramid and the compass and square. The eye in the pyramid, which also appears on the United States dollar bill, represents the all-seeing eye of God and of the Freemasons. The compass and right angle are the tools of the Masonic trade as well as being the instruments that God used to measure and circumscribe the boundaries of the universe. The square also reminds Masons to square their actions, to keep them socially acceptable, while the compass tells Masons to circumscribe their desires and to keep their passions restricted.

In "The Red-Headed League" (*Strand Magazine*, August 1891) Sherlock Holmes explains to Jabez Wilson how he deduced that Wilson was a Freemason:

"I won't insult your intelligence by telling you how I read that, especially as, rather against the strict rules of your order, you use an arc-and-compass' breastpin."

It seems that Mycroft similarly flaunts his membership.

Panel 5. "Mr. William Samson Senior" is not a pre-existing character, but is rather an example of what Moore calls "back-engineering," the addition of a new character as a relation, ancestor, or descendant of an existing character. Starting in 1922 the character "the Wolf of Kabul" appears in the British comics *Wizard* and *Hotspur*. The Wolf of Kabul, whose real name was Bill Sampson (often shown as "Samson"), is an agent for the British Intelligence Corps operating on the Northwest frontier of India. William Samson, Sr. is the father of the Wolf of Kabul.

Moore said that the timing was right for the Wolf's father to have fought against the forces of the Mad Mahdi. The "Mad Mahdi" was Mahdi Muhammad Ahmad (1844-1885), the Muslim religious leader of a movement against the Egyptians ruling the Mahdi's native Sudan. This goal brought the Mahdi into conflict with British forces, which led to the Battle of El Obeid, on November 5, 1883, in which the Mahdi's forces completely wiped out an Egyptian force led by General William Hicks. This defeat was shocking to the British public, as was the defeat six weeks later of another Egyptian force led by the British rogue Valentine Baker, but neither horrified Britain so badly as the Mahdi's taking of Khartoum on January 26, 1885, in which General "Chinese" Gordon and the entire British garrison of Khartoum were massacred. The British quickly retaliated, sending Major General Sir Horatio Kitchener and 26,000 men to hunt down the Mahdi's successor and eliminate the Mahdist dervishes at the Battle of Omdurman.

Page 62. Panel 3. The bust on the right is of Sir Percy Blakeney, the Scarlet Pimpernel, from Baroness Emmuska Orczy's *The Scarlet Pimpernel* (1905) and its ten sequels. Sir Percy was shown in *League* v1 #2 to have been a member of the eighteenth-century League. He appears in *The New Traveller's Almanac* beginning on Page 161.

Page 63. Panel 3. William Samson Senior, as a British veteran, undoubtedly fought the Pathans and Kurds in the British campaigns in the North-West Frontier of India from 1855-1863.

Page 64. Panel 1. "Anti-Stiff" was a real product sold in the Nineteeth century; athletes used it to strengthen the body. A period advertisement for it can be seen on Page 158.

Chips, used as a rain cover in the lower middle of the panel, was a real comic. An Alfred Harmsworth publication, the *Illustrated Chips* was published from 1890 to 1952.

The child in the upper left may be Little Lord Fauntleroy, from Frances Hodgson Burnett's *Little Lord Fauntleroy* (1886).

Page 65. Panel 1. The newspaper headline is a reference to the newspaper headlines mentioned in Chapter 9 of *WotW*:

> The Martians did not show an inch of themselves. They seemed busy in their pit, and there was a sound of hammering and an almost continuous streamer of smoke. Apparently they were busy getting ready for a struggle. "Fresh attempts have been made to signal, but without success," was the stereotyped formula of the papers. A sapper told me it was done by a man in a ditch with a flag on a long pole. The Martians took as much notice of such advances as we should of the lowing of a cow.

Panel 2. The hamlet of Maybury is the narrator's home in *WotW*. In Chapter 10 of *WotW* the narrator encounters a Martian Tripod in Maybury.

Pages 66-67. Panel 1. For Wells' description of the Martian Tripods, see the notes to Page 20.

The Tripod seen in this panel is likely the Tripod which the narrator encountered in *WotW*.

Page 68. Panel 1. The bust may be of Sherlock Holmes.

The giant beetle in the vacuum tube, also seen on the cover of this collection, is the Beetle, from Richard Marsh's *The Beetle*.

The top picture on the right could be of a number of characters named "Thomas" from Victorian literature. Possibly it is a picture of a grown up Tom Sawyer, from Mark Twain's *Tom Sawyer, Detective* (1896).

The bottom picture is of Dr. Nikola, from Guy Boothby's novels.

Panel 2. The books are a reference to Arnould Galopin's *Le Docteur Oméga - Aventures Fantastiques de Trois Français dans la Planète Mars* (*Dr. Omega - Fantastic Adventures of Three Frenchmen on the Planet Mars*, 1905). *Le Docteur Oméga* was about Doctor Omega, an inventor-adventurer, who goes to Mars and encounters various Martian races.

Panel 7. Mina is looking at the death mask of Napoleon Bonaparte. The hat in the glass case is similar to the one Napoleon is traditionally shown wearing, and it has a "6" in its middle, a reference to the Arthur Conan Doyle Sherlock Holmes story, "The Adventure of the Six Napoleons" (*Collier's Weekly*, 30 April 1904).

The "Eyes Only - Docteur Omega" sheet, with "J.M. Lofficier" on the bottom, is another reference to *Le Docteur Oméga*. "J.M. Lofficier" is a reference to Jean-Marc Lofficier, one of the world's leading experts on French science fiction, fantasy, and pulp fiction and the author of an outstanding book on the subject, *French Science Fiction, Fantasy, Horror and Pulp Fiction* (2000). Lofficier is a friend of Kevin O'Neill and suggested several characters for inclusion or mention in *League* v2.

Un Habitant de la Planète Mars is a reference to the 1865 novel of the same name by the Frenchman François-Henri Peudefer de Parville. In that novel the calcified body of an ancient Martian is discovered in America.

Page 69. Panels 1-3. The map on the wall which reads "Sea of Drea" is a reference to the Rudyard Kipling story "The Brushwood Boy" (*Century Magazine*, December 1895). In that story a boy named Georgie goes on a series of dream adventures in a land on the shore of the Sea of Dreams.

Panel 5. The skeleton of the centaur is likely a reference to the centaurs of the Marvellous Islands, which are mentioned on Page 178.

Page 70. **Panel 6**. Kevin O'Neill notes:

> Mina is knocked into a side table. The vase sent flying on the extreme left is the Portland Vase—this rare and beautiful example of Roman glassware was damaged by a madman in 1845 while on display in the British Museum.

Page 73. **Panel 2**. The giant skull, seen at various points in *League* v1, is the skull of one of the Brobdingnag giants, from Jonathan Swift's *Gulliver's Travels* (1726).

Panel 4. Nemo's statement, "Growing up in Mombai, in Calcutta, one learns differently," cannot be taken literally. In the world of *League*, Nemo's origin is the one given in *L'Ile Mystérieuse* (*The Mysterious Island*, 1874), the sequel to *20,000 Leagues Under The Sea*: Nemo is "Prince Dakkar, the son of a rajah of the then independent territory of Bundelkund and a nephew of the Indian hero, Tippu-Sahib." Bundelkand (misspelled "Bundelkund" by Verne) is in the north central section of India, quite a distance from either Mombai or from Calcutta. Nemo, as the son of a rajah in pre-Mutiny India, would not have grown up in Mombai or Calcutta. As a metaphoric comment, however, Nemo is quite correct; hoping for the best was not wise for most Indians in pre-Mutiny India.

Page 75. **Panel 2**. Mina's inability to write Griffin's name is reminiscent of a similar moment in *Dracula*, in Chapter 27, after she has been bitten: "But then the boat service would, most likely, be the one which would destroy the...the...Vampire. (Why did I hesitate to write the word?)"

Page 76. **Panel 1**. The man with the arrow tattoo on his back, working on the side of the *Nautilus*, is Broad-Arrow Jack, previously seen in *League* v1. Jack is the hero of an eponymous 1866 penny dreadful written by E. Harcourt Burrage.

Page 77. **Panel 3**. The "Nutwood, Just So Good" ad above Mina's head is a reference to Nutwood, the idyllic village home of Rupert Bear. Rupert is one of the most popular of any of the British humanized animal cartoon characters. He was created by Mary Tourtel and first appears in the *Daily Express* on November 8, 1920. Since then he's appeared in over 500 books in 18 countries, and his adventures continue to appear today.

Page 78. The text panel here is a reference to British politics. The reference to "proof of loyal citizenship" and "God save the Home Secretary," is a reference to a controversial proposal by the British Home Secretary, David Blunkett. In 2002 Blunkett proposed that all immigrants to England should be forced to take a citizenship test and to speak English rather than their native tongue, even in their own homes. The reference to "cricket on the green and ladies bicycling to Evensong" is a reference to a 1992 Tory Party conference speech by John Major in which, while evoking a nakedly nostalgic and pastoral image of England, he mentioned "an old maid cycling to Evensong."

Page 79. Panel 1. The placard on the right reads "Barnes B," a reference to the Barnes Railway Bridge, one of the western bridges over the Thames. "Barnes Bridge" is also the name of the rail station on the Bridge. The Barnes Bridge was opened in 1849.

Page 80. In the real world the Barnes Bridge was served in the late Nineteenth century by the London and South Western Railway, whose locomotives were painted in an elaborate light green livery.

Page 82. The balloon just visible in the sky may be a reference to the opening of Chapter 17 of *WotW*: "If one could have hung that June morning in a balloon in the blazing blue above London...."

Page 83. Panel 4. In Chapter 12 of *WotW* a fallen Tripod boils the Thames to steam.

Page 84. Panel 4. As seen on Page 21, Panel 1 of the first *League* collection, the steering wheel of the *Nautilus* is a statue of the god Siva in his identity as Siva-Nataraja, the lord of the cosmic dance.

Page 85. Panel 2. Hyde's comment is a reference to the events in Cchapter 1 of *The Strange Case of Dr. Jekyll and Mr. Hyde*, in which Hyde "trampled calmly" over a child. This scene appears on Page 180 of the first *League* collection.

Panel 5. The Thames has a series of locks put in place to control its flow. The Shepperton lock is on the Windsor-to-Twickenham stretch of the Thames.

Nemo's comment is a reference to Chapter 12 of *WotW*, in which a hidden group of artillery bring down one of the Tripods:

> In another moment it was on the bank, and in a stride wading halfway across. The knees of its foremost legs bent at the farther bank, and in another moment it had raised itself to its full height again, close to the village of Shepperton. Forthwith the six guns which, unknown to anyone on the right bank, had been hidden behind the outskirts of that village, fired simultaneously. The sudden near concussion, the last close upon the first, made my heart jump. The monster was already raising the case generating the Heat-Ray as the first shell burst six yards above the hood.
>
> I gave a cry of astonishment. I saw and thought nothing of the other four Martian monsters; my attention was riveted upon the nearer incident.
>
> Simultaneously two other shells burst in the air near the body as the hood twisted round in time to receive, but not in time to dodge, the fourth shell.
>
> The shell burst clean in the face of the Thing. The hood bulged, flashed, was whirled off in a dozen tattered fragments of red flesh and glittering metal.

Panel 6. In Chapter 12 of *WotW* the Martians retrieve the wreckage of the Tripod destroyed by artillery: "Then I saw them dimly, colossal figures of grey, magnified by the mist. They had passed by me, and two were stooping over the frothing, tumultuous ruins of their comrade."

Nemo here refers to his courier. In *20,000 Leagues Under the Sea*, Part 2, Chapter 6, Nemo makes use of a courier named Nicholas Pesca to smuggle gold to the rebels on Crete.

Panel 9. The statue in the background might be that of Ganesh, the Hindu god of, and destroyer of, obstacles.

Page 87. **Panel 3**. Quatermain's comment about "how big these bloody woods are" may be a reference to the Hundred Acre Wood, from A.A. Milne's Winnie the Pooh novels. These woods are on the South Downs in Sussex, as mentioned on Page 86, Panel 2; the Ashdown Forest on the South Downs was Milne's inspiration for the Hundred Acre Wood.

Panels 4-5. Nature being "red in tooth and claw" is a reference to a passage in Alfred, Lord Tennyson's "In Memoriam" (1850):

> Who trusted God was love indeed
> And love Creation's final law—
> Tho' Nature, red in tooth and claw
> With ravine, shriek'd against his creed—

Page 88. Panel 1. Perhaps coincidentally, the steam from the *Nautilus* ends in a question mark.

Kevin O'Neill notes:
    Question mark was deliberate.

Panel 3. Jimmy Grey is a reference to "The Iron Fish," a comic strip which began appearing in the British comic *Beano* in 1949. "The Iron Fish" is about two twins, Danny and Penny Gray, who pilot two "Iron Fish" submarines, both of which are built by their father, Professor Gray. The Jimmy Grey here is a childhood version of Professor Gray.

One possible inference that might be drawn about Jimmy Grey/Professor Gray is that he is or is based on Sir James Gray (1891-1975), a prominent English zoologist. He's best known for applying mechanical principles to the analysis of animal movement and thereby coining "Gray's Paradox," which compares swimming efficiency in fish and in submarines. Energetics calculations suggest that fish are more efficient swimmers than submarines, while theoretical hydrodynamic calculations imply that they are not.

Page 90. Panel 1. This is Teddy Prendrick, who introduces himself in Panel 4 below. Prendrick appears in H.G. Wells' *The Island of Dr. Moreau* (1896). In the novel Edward Prendrick is shipwrecked on Moreau's island and discovers Moreau and his handiwork. His comment that "the stars...they told me I should meet people" is a reference to the end of *The Island of Dr. Moreau*, in which Prendrick, now a hermit withdrawn from human society, takes up astronomy, finding "a sense of infinite peace and protection in the glittering hosts of heaven."

Panel 6. At the end of *The Island of Dr. Moreau* Prendrick is more than a little unstable, finding that the humans he meets reminds him of Moreau's creations:

> My trouble took the strangest form. I could not persuade myself that the men and women I met were not also another Beast People, animals half wrought into the outward image of human souls, and that they would presently begin to revert,—to show first this bestial mark and then that. But I have confided my case to a strangely able man,—a man who had known Moreau, and seemed half to credit my story; a mental specialist,—and he has helped me mightily, though I do not expect that the terror of that island will ever altogether leave me. At most times it lies far in the back of my mind, a mere distant cloud, a memory, and a faint distrust; but there are times when the little cloud spreads until it obscures the whole sky. Then I look about me at my fellow-men; and I go in fear. I see faces, keen and bright; others dull or dangerous; others, unsteady, insincere,—none that have the calm authority of a reasonable soul. I feel as though the animal was surging up through them; that presently the degradation of the Islanders will be played over again on a larger scale. I know this is an illusion; that these seeming men and women about me are indeed men and women,— men and women for ever, perfectly reasonable creatures, full of human desires and tender solicitude, emancipated

from instinct and the slaves of no fantastic Law,—beings altogether different from the Beast Folk. Yet I shrink from them, from their curious glances, their inquiries and assistance, and long to be away from them and alone. For that reason I live near the broad free downland, and can escape thither when this shadow is over my soul; and very sweet is the empty downland then, under the wind-swept sky.

When I lived in London the horror was well-nigh insupportable. I could not get away from men: their voices came through windows; locked doors were flimsy safeguards. I would go out into the streets to fight with my delusion, and prowling women would mew after me; furtive, craving men glance jealously at me; weary, pale workers go coughing by me with tired eyes and eager paces, like wounded deer dripping blood; old people, bent and dull, pass murmuring to themselves; and, all unheeding, a ragged tail of gibing children. Then I would turn aside into some chapel,—and even there, such was my disturbance, it seemed that the preacher gibbered "Big Thinks," even as the Ape-man had done; or into some library, and there the intent faces over the books seemed but patient creatures waiting for prey. Particularly nauseous were the blank, expressionless faces of people in trains and omnibuses; they seemed no more my fellow-creatures than dead bodies would be, so that I did not dare to travel unless I was assured of being alone. And even it seemed that I too was not a reasonable creature, but only an animal tormented with some strange disorder in its brain which sent it to wander alone, like a sheep stricken with gid.

Page 94. Panel 1. The London General Omnibus Company was the largest of the London bus companies in the 1890s and the early decades of the twentieth century. It was formed in 1855 and closed in 1933.

Blackfriars Bridge is one of the bridges over the Thames. The bridge was completed in 1875 on the site of an earlier (1769) bridge and is the oldest bridge currently crossing the Thames.

Kevin O'Neill notes:

> Visible in Southbank background is a building marked "I.P.
> Seeds." This is roughly where IPC Magazine's offices in
> Kings Reach Tower stand today. I used to work there in
> the 1970s, and from the offices of *2000AD* we had a
> spectacular view of the Thames. I'd liked to have included
> another landmark here, the OXO Tower, but this was not
> built until some years later.

Page 95. Panel 4. Nemo's comment here may be Moore's way of reminding us that Nemo is, after all, a fanatic, a dedicated enemy of the English, and someone who would see the death of hundreds of English as only fitting, given what they did to his country.

Page 96. Panels 1-2. The Olde Stumpe, Miss Mopp, and Bell End are references to *It's That Man Again*, a.k.a. *I.T.M.A.*, a weekly radio comedy on the BBC which first aired in 1939 and aired through 1949. On *I.T.M.A.* "Mrs. Mopp" was an "office char." She later got her own radio series, "The Private Life of Mrs. Mopp," in 1946.

Kevin O'Neill: notes:

> "Bell End" is an amusing sexual reference—prefigures
> Allan and Mina's first sexual encounter.

> "The Olde Stumpe" is also of low humor.

Panel 3. In *I.T.M.A.* Mrs. Mopp's catchphrase, uttered every time she entered a scene, was "Can I do you now, Sir?" In *I.T.M.A.* Mrs. Mopp was in her sixties or seventies, so she would have been alive and working during the time period shown here.

Page 102. Panels 3-6. In interviews Moore has said that Dracula's teeth are not human teeth but rather the saw-toothed fangs of a vampire bat, which is why Mina's neck is so horribly scarred.

Pages 104-5. The thing choking the river is the Red Weed from *WotW*. The Red Weed is described in this way:

At any rate, the seeds which the Martians (intentionally or accidentally) brought with them gave rise in all cases to red-coloured growths. Only that known popularly as the Red Weed, however, gained any footing in competition with terrestrial forms. The Red Creeper was quite a transitory growth, and few people have seen it growing. For a time, however, the Red Weed grew with astonishing vigour and luxuriance...I found it broadcast throughout the country, and especially wherever there was a stream of water.

Page 105. Panel 2. The background to Nemo's comment that Hyde "can't walk through London, even if it's half-evacuated" is the state of London in *WotW*. After the Martians' display of technological superiority most of the south of England, including London, is evacuated, so that in the latter stages of the novel the narrator meets only one or two humans as he wanders across London and its outskirts.

Page 107. Panels 1-2. Allan's comments are a reference to his second wife, Stella Carson. Allan's first wife was Marie Marais, and in *Marie* (1912) Allan says of her, "She was my first wife, but I beg you not to speak of her to me or to anyone else, for I cannot bear to hear her name." Marie died saving Allan's life. Later, in the events of *Allan's Wife* (1889), Allan meets his childhood friend Stella Carson, falls in love with her and marries her. Stella dies giving birth to Allan's son Harry.

In *Allan's Wife* mention is made of the burns on Stella's neck. The burns are not Moore's invention, although the degree of severity described by Allan here differs from their description in *Allan's Wife*. When Stella receives the burn, this is how it is described:

As she did so her sleeve, which was covered with cotton wool, spangled over with something that shone, touched one of the tapers and caught fire—how I do not know— and the flame ran up her arm towards her throat. She stood quite still. I suppose that she was paralysed with fear; and the ladies who were near screamed very loud, but did nothing. Then some impulse seized me—perhaps instinct would be a better word to use, considering my age. I threw myself upon the child, and, beating at the fire with my hands, mercifully succeeded in extinguishing it before it really got hold. My wrists were so badly scorched that they had to be wrapped up in wool for a long time afterwards, but with the exception of a single burn upon her throat, little Stella Carson was not much hurt.

Then, later, when Stella and Allan meet again as adults:

"It is wonderful," she said, "but I have often heard that name. My father has told me how a little boy called Allan Quatermain once saved my life by putting out my dress when it was on fire—see!"—and she pointed to a faint red mark upon her neck—"here is the scar of the burn."

Page 109. Panel 1. Mina's husband Jonathan is Jonathan Harker, from *Dracula*. In *League* Mina never gives the reasons for her divorce from Jonathan; his withholding of physical affections from her would be one good reason psychologically, if not legally. In England in the 1890s divorce was not easy to obtain, and a lack of intercourse would not have been permissible as a reason for Mina divorcing Jonathan. A woman could not divorce her husband unless he had committed, in addition to adultery, bigamy, incest, cruelty, or bestial acts, while a husband could divorce his wife for simple adultery.

Panel 2. It's understandable that some modern readers find the asterisking of certain curse words (Allan's "Mina, I want to **** you") distracting. What must be remembered is that Moore intends *League* to be at least partly a pastiche of Victorian boys' literature, and the asterisking of obscenities, viz. "D*** your eyes, sir!" was a practice in those stories. Moore is simply being faithful to his source literature.

Panel 3. Mina's comment, "As if I were some...native girl," is a reference to a common stereotype among upper class British during the Nineteenth century. Native women, particularly Indian women, were seen as being sexually uninhibited, as opposed to proper upper class English women. This stereotype arose not because of the actions of Indian and African women so much as English men indulging themselves while abroad. One of the "benefits" for English men traveling abroad was the opportunity to indulge in sexual adventures that were not possible in England at the time. Rather than blame English men for this, however, English women (and men) shifted the blame to the foreign women.

Page 110. **Panel 1**. The unpleasant-looking ursine is a mutated Rupert Bear, one of the most popular of British cartoon characters.

Page 111. Panel 5. From left to right:

- The elephant might be either Edward Trunk, a friend of Rupert Bear, or Jumbo the Elephant, a friend of Tiger Tim (see below).
- The tiger is Tiger Tim. Tim first appears in the *Daily Mirror* in 1904 and is still appearing today in his own comics, making him the oldest regularly appearing character in British comics.
- The badger is Mr. Badger, from Kenneth Grahame's *The Wind in the Willows* (1908).

Kevin O'Neill: notes:
  The elephant is Tiger Tim's chum Jumbo.

Page 112. Panel 1. In *WotW* London is as deserted as it appears to be here.

The headline of the paper in the lower left alludes to the destruction of Richmond, one of the towns destroyed by the Martians' black smoke in *WotW*.

Panel 2. The character drinking from a flask is Ally Sloper. Ally, seen in *League* v1, is a British comic character who was created by Charles Ross and Marie Duval and first appears in *Judy* in 1867. Ally was one of the first rogues in British comics to be featured as a hero. The character on the right side of the panel with the cap and pipe is Weary Willy, also last seen in *League* v1. Weary Willy is an amiable tramp who was created by Tom Browne and first appears in the British comic *Illustrated Chips* in 1896.

Kevin O'Neill notes:
  In the centre of the panel is Captain Kettle, creatd by author
  C. J. Cutliffe. *The Paradise Coal Boat* (1897) was the

first Captain Kettle short story collection. Here Owen Kettle has clearly picked a bad time for shore leave. To his right Weary Willy is urinating on Tired Tim's hat! The drunkenness and debauchery are true to this point in *War of the Worlds*.

Panel 3. The dog watching the looters steal a gramophone is likely a reference to Nipper, the subject of Francis Barraud's 1898 painting *His Master's Voice* and later the trademark for HMV and then RCA.

Page 114. Panel 1. The giant skull is the same Brobdingnagian skull seen on Page 73, Panel 2.

Page 115. Panel 4. The *Daily Mail* is a real British newspaper. It was active during the Victorian era and is mentioned in *WotW* as the first newspaper to resume service after the Martians die. Currently the *Mail* has a reputation for jingoistic and ill-informed "journalism," so it's no surprise that the racist Hyde reads it.

Page 117. Panels 5-7. *Dr. Jekyll and Mr. Hyde* is notably lacking in the presence of women, and one prominent interpretation of the novel, most notably by Elaine Showalter, is that Hyde is Jekyll's gay side, with the novel being "a fable of fin-de-siècle homosexual panic, the discovery and resistance of the homosexual self." So there is a tradition of seeing Hyde as a gay man, although Hyde's sins are left undefined by Jekyll:

> The pleasures which I made haste to seek in my disguise were, as I have said, undignified; I would scarce use a harder term. But in the hands of Edward Hyde, they soon began to turn toward the monstrous. When I would come back from these excursions, I was often plunged into a kind of wonder at my vicarious depravity. This familiar that I called out of my own soul, and sent forth alone to do his good pleasure, was a being inherently malign and villainous; his every act and thought centered on self; drinking pleasure with bestial avidity from any degree of torture to another; relentless like a man of stone.
>
> Henry Jekyll stood at times aghast before the acts of Edward Hyde; but the situation was apart from ordinary laws, and insidiously relaxed the grasp of conscience.

But rape is a crime of violence rather than sexuality, and heterosexual men rape other men far more often than gay men do. What Hyde is doing here has nothing to do with his own sexuality. Rather, he has chosen the most degrading way possible to avenge Mina on Griffin.

Ironically Hyde's last words to Griffin in *League* v1 were, "Bugger you, Griffin."

Kevin O'Neill: notes:
> [on Panel 5] Amusingly, this panel may have cost us publication in Greece.

Page 119. Panel 1. The reason that Rupert is upset with Tim is that in *The Island of Dr. Moreau* Dr. Moreau imposes rules upon his Beast Folk:

> "Not to go on all-fours; that is the Law. Are we not Men?
> "Not to suck up Drink; that is the Law. Are we not Men?
> "Not to eat Fish or Flesh; that is the Law. Are we not Men?
> "Not to claw the Bark of Trees; that is the Law. Are we not Men?
> "Not to chase other Men; that is the Law. Are we not Men?"

In *Moreau* lapping up water on all fours is one of the crimes which results in the deaths of the various Beast Folk.

Panel 4. This is Mr. Toad, from *Wind in the Willows*, driving the newfangled motor car which he so loves. In *Wind in the Willows*, however, Mr. Toad is comical, rather than sinister as he is here. The car he is riding is the same car in the Disneyland ride, "Mr. Toad's Wild Ride."

Kevin O'Neill notes:
> The same as Toad's car on the Disneyland ride—I suspect not. Our car is steered by the rather old fashioned (even for 1898) steering handle. My guess is the ride sticks to a more Edwardian confection.

Panel 9. The Beast Folk in *The Island of Dr. Moreau* bow and scrape and cringe in the presence of Dr. Moreau, just as Mr. Toad does here.

Page 120. Panel 1. This is the Doctor Moreau of *The Island of Dr. Moreau*. In the novel his first name is not given. His name here, Alphonse, may be a reference to the television animated series *South Park*, which features a Dr. Moreau parody, "Dr. Alphonse Mephisto," who is based on Marlon Brando's portrayal of Moreau in the 1996 *The Island of Dr. Moreau* film. In the novel Moreau is a cruel eugenicist, although it is not commonly remembered that Wells intended Moreau to be the novel's hero.

Moreau has sustained some injuries. There is a dent on the left side of his head, and there is a chunk missing out of his right arm. In *The Island of Dr. Moreau* he is attacked by one of the Beast Folk and killed, or so Prendrick thinks:

> We came upon the gnawed and mutilated body of the puma, its shoulder-bone smashed by a bullet, and perhaps twenty yards farther found at last what we sought. Moreau lay face downward in a trampled space in a canebrake. One hand was almost severed at the wrist and his silvery hair was dabbled in blood. His head had been battered in by the fetters of the puma.

Moving clockwise from Moreau, the other characters in this panel are

- Algy Pug, Rupert Bear's best friend'
- Jemima Puddle-Duck, from Beatrix Potter's *The Tale of Jemima Puddle-Duck* (1908)'
- Puss-in-Boots, the character from the French fairy tale'
- Peter Rabbit, from Beatrix Potter's *The Tale of Peter Rabbit* (1904). (He may be skinless because he was eventually caught by Mr. McGregor);
- Joey the Parrot (being eaten by Peter Rabbit), one of Tiger Tim's friends from *The Rainbow Comic*;
- Mr. Mole and Ratty (at Jemima Puddle-Duck's feet), from *Wind in the Willows*;
- various rats and/or mice, possibly from Beatrix Potter's *The Tale of Two Bad Mice* (1904);
- Mr. Toad;

- The Third Little Pig, the one who built his house from bricks, from the children's story "The Three Little Pigs." His hands may be bandaged because he has built Moreau's house from sticks;
- Podgy Pig, one of Rupert Bear's friends;
- Georgie Giraffe, one of Tiger Tim's friends; and
- Jacko Monkey, one of Tiger Tim's friends. His dress, and the copy of *The Iliad* he holds, may be a reference to Thomas Landseer's etchings for his satirical *Monkeyana* (1827).

Kevin O'Neill notes:

> No, not the third little pig, but our own Toby Twirl. Toby Twirl had an annual series from 1946-1957, with stories by Sheila Hodgetts and art by E. Jeffrey. Toby was a sort of harmless Rupert competitor.

> The larger pig is a *relative* of Napoleon from Manor Farm/ George Orwell's *Animal Farm* (1945).

Panel 4. The dog to the left of Quatermain is Fido Dog, one of Tiger Tim's friends.

Page 121. **Panel 4**. The dead dog is Bonzo the Studdy Dog, a cartoon character created by George Studdy Bonzo and appearing in *Sketch* magazine in the 1920s and 1930s.

"It perished under the anaesthetic." Moreau's methods have improved. In *The Island of Dr. Moreau* he experimented on animals without benefit of anesthetic.

Panel 6. The food tray has rodents, insects, and birds on it, possibly a reference to the Victorian naturalist and divine William Buckland (1784-1856), a forerunner to Darwin who was known to delight in a snack of grilled mice on toast.

Page 122. **Panel 5**. The portrait seemingly staring at Hyde is of Robert Louis Stevenson, Hyde's creator. A similar image can be seen on the cover to the Bumper Edition of *League* v1 n1-2, which is included in the first *League* collection on Page 185.

Page 124. Panel 6. In *Dr. Jekyll and Mr. Hyde* Hyde is, originally, rather short, a "very small gentlemen." But as time goes by and Hyde emerges more often, he grows, so that in "Henry Jekyll's Full Statement of the Case" Jekyll says:

> That part of me which I had the power of projecting, had lately been much exercised and nourished; it had seemed to me of late as though the body of Edward Hyde had grown in stature, as though (when I wore that form) I were conscious of a more generous tide of blood; and I began to spy a danger that, if this were much prolonged, the balance of my nature might be permanently overthrown....

Panels 7-8. *Dr. Jekyll and Mr. Hyde* is fertile ground for analysis; the psychological issues involved are primal, which invites differing interpretations. The interpretation of Hyde as unchecked Id is one of the more common, and one supported by Jekyll's statement in Chapter 10 of *Dr. Jekyll and Mr. Hyde*:

> With every day, and from both sides of my intelligence, the moral and the intellectual, I thus drew steadily nearer to that truth, by whose partial discovery I have been doomed to such a dreadful shipwreck: that man is not truly one, but truly two. I say two, because the state of my own knowledge does not pass beyond that point. Others will follow, others will outstrip me on the same lines; and I hazard the guess that man will be ultimately known for a mere polity of multifarious, incongruous and independent denizens. I, for my part, from the nature of my life, advanced infallibly in one direction and in one direction only. It was on the moral side, and in my own person, that I learned to recognise the thorough and primitive duality of man; I saw that, of the two natures that contended in the field of my consciousness, even if I could rightly be said to be either, it was only because I was radically both; and from an early date, even before the course of my scientific discoveries had begun to suggest the most naked possibility of such a miracle, I had learned to dwell with pleasure, as a beloved daydream, on the thought of the separation of these elements. If

each, I told myself, could be housed in separate identities, life would be relieved of all that was unbearable; the unjust might go his way, delivered from the aspirations and remorse of his more upright twin; and the just could walk steadfastly and securely on his upward path, doing the good things in which he found his pleasure, and no longer exposed to disgrace and penitence by the hands of this extraneous evil. It was the curse of mankind that these incongruous faggots were thus bound together—that in the agonised womb of consciousness, these polar twins should be continuously struggling. How, then were they dissociated?

Panel 9. The portrait on the right might be of Charles Darwin. If so, Darwin is looking on while Hyde describes how he is essentially replacing Jekyll through a process of natural selection.

Page 125. Panels 1-2. In *The Invisible Man*, a similar development takes place when Griffin dies:

Suddenly an old woman, peering under the arm of the big navvy, screamed sharply. "Looky there!" she said, and thrust out a wrinkled finger.

And looking where she pointed, everyone saw, faint and transparent as though it was made of glass, so that veins and arteries and bones and nerves could be distinguished, the outline of a hand, a hand limp and prone. It grew clouded and opaque even as they stared.

"Hullo!" cried the constable. "Here's his feet a-showing!"

And so, slowly, beginning at his hands and feet and creeping along his limbs to the vital centres of his body, that strange change continued. It was like the slow spreading of a poison. First came the little white nerves, a hazy grey sketch of a limb, then the glassy bones and intricate arteries, then the flesh and skin, first a faint fogginess, and then growing rapidly dense and opaque. Presently they could see his crushed chest and his shoulders, and the dim outline of his drawn and battered features.

When at last the crowd made way for Kemp to stand erect, there lay, naked and pitiful on the ground, the bruised and broken body of a young man about thirty. His hair and brow were white—not grey with age, but white with the whiteness of albinism—and his eyes were like garnets. His hands were clenched, his eyes wide open, and his expression was one of anger and dismay.

Page 126. Panel 3. In Chapter 6 of *WotW* the narrator says this of the Red Weed:

Some way farther, in a grassy place, was a group of mushrooms which also I devoured, and then I came upon a brown sheet of flowing shallow water, where meadows used to be. These fragments of nourishment served only to whet my hunger. At first I was surprised at this flood in a hot, dry summer, but afterwards I discovered that it was caused by the tropical exuberance of the red weed. Directly this extraordinary growth encountered water it straightway became gigantic and of unparalleled fecundity. Its seeds were simply poured down into the water of the Wey and Thames, and its swiftly growing and titanic water fronds speedily choked both those rivers.

In the finale of *WotW* the narrator finds "nearly fifty" Tripods clustered together.

Pages 128-129. The name of the train stop, Wildwood, is a reference to the Wild Wood in *Wind in the Willows*.

The "Pears" is an advertisement for Pears Soap, an English soap produced by the Pears family from 1789 through 1914 and still sold today.

The Fry of "Fry's Cocoa" is a reference to J.S. Fry & Sons, a British chocolate and confectionary maker. In 1847 Fry & Sons sold a *Choclat Delicieux a manger*, thought to be the first chocolate candy bar. In 1919 Fry's merged with Cadbury's.

The rabbit being torn to pieces by foxes in the lower right hand corner of this panel is Beatrix Potter's Peter Rabbit. The foxes tearing him apart may be the Fantastic Mister Fox and two of his cubs, from Roald Dahl's *The Fantastic Mr. Fox* (1970).

Kevin O'Neill: notes:

> [On panel 1] The fox and cubs are generic, but nice idea. NOTE: Some people may have noticed our railroad operative on the superior (but more expensive) Brunel Broad Gauge (7 feet). I like it because it dwarfs the figures next to it—the proportions are unsettling to our eye more used to the 4&8½ in standard guage.

Page 130. Panels 3-5. "Luckily, a Gypsy woman lives nearby, who can placate him...I mean that for a substantial sum of money, she will have congress with him. She is a robust woman, I understand, though of mature years. In fact, if I recall correctly, I believe I heard she was a grandmother."
This is a reference to the *Oz* trial of 1970. *Oz* was an British underground magazine published from 1967 to 1973. In May 1970 the magazine ran a cartoon montage put together by fifteen-year-old Vivian Berger. The montage superimposed a Rupert Bear cartoon on an R. Crumb cartoon, so that one panel showed Rupert having sex with an unconscious "Gypsy Granny." As a result of this cartoon, the editors of *Oz* were put on trial in 1971 for conspiring to "corrupt the morals of young children and other young persons."

Panel 5. The head of Moreau's cane may be a reference to the flamingo croquet mallets in *Alice in Wonderland*.

Page 131. Panels 1-4. Presumably the black trains of MI5 would be the equivalent of modern black helicopters: the craft by which the agents of the conspiracy (in this case, the Freemasons—note the Masonic symbol on the front of the train and, as seen on Panel 4 below, on its side) travel the country.

Panel 4. The .007 on the side of the train is a reference to the Rudyard Kipling story, ".007" (*The Day's Work*, 1898). ".007" is about the life and times of train engine .007. Reportedly Ian Fleming took James Bond's number from the Kipling story.

Panel 6. The soldier's tunic overlaps his trousers, mimicking the wearing of the Masonic apron.

Page 132. Panels 2-3. "I've a nephew, who sometimes visits. An artist living abroad, sometimes he comes up here and paints my 'chimerae,' as he calls them. I tell him, 'Gustave, your work is excellent, if only you would finish it!'"
This is a reference to the French Symbolist painter Gustave Moreau (1826-1898). His 1884 painting *Chimeras* featured true chimerae, mixtures of beasts.

Page 133. Panel 7. The tunnel mouth is quite similar to the Clayton Tunnel, in Sussex on the London to Brighton line.

The windmill is the Jack windmill of Sussex, whose location in our world is some distance from the Clayton Tunnel.

Page 135. Panel 1. The "H. Smith" of the newsstand is a reference to British bookseller W.H. Smith.

The "Food Stores Crisis" on the placard is a reference to the starving state of Londoners before the complete evacuation of London during *War of the Worlds*.

Panel 5. The obscured placard on the right-hand side of the panel is for Wills Gold Flake, a popular brand of cigarettes.

The placard on the far right of this panel is a reference to the British tabloid *News of the World*, one of the most widely read of the Victorian "scandal sheets."

Page 137. Panel 1. This panel is very similar to a scene in the 1953 film *The War of the Worlds*, when the U.S. military is observing the results of an atomic bomb dropped on the Martians.

Kevin O'Neill notes:

> Hmmm—never occurred to me. I avoided watching the
> George Pal film again. I enjoyed it as a kid, but even then
> recall being a little disappointed it wasn't the real *War of
> the Worlds*. But terrific manta ray designs for the machines.

The uniforms worn by the British Army troops are khaki drab, much closer to World War I uniforms than the nineteenth-century uniforms seen on Page 46 above. The blue uniforms worn by the men in the center of this panel and in Panel 2 below are those of non-commissioned officers in the British Royal Artillery Corps.

Pages 138-139. Panel 1. The pillar on the left is the Monument, in Pudding Lane, designed by Sir Christopher Wren and erected from 1671-1677. In our world it is topped by a cippus and blazing urn. In the world of *League*, however, a figure stands atop it. The figure may be a member of the seventeenth-century League who was responsible for halting the fire, but Kevin O'Neill has said that he includes in *League* pieces of architecture which were theorized but never came to pass, such as the version of Wren's St. Paul's Cathedral seen on Page 126 of the first *League* collection.

Pages 140. Panel 1. "And inside that, there's just a useless, wheezing blancmange."
This may be a reference to the *Monty Python's Flying Circus* skit "Blancmanges Playing Tennis" (Season 1, Episode 7, November 30, 1969), in which Earth is invaded by alien blancmanges whose ultimate goal is to win Wimbledon. At the end of that skit, the aliens are defeated by being eaten, which mirrors events on Page 161, Panel 8.

Page 142. "You should see me dance the polka, you should see me cover the ground," is a reference to the 1941 film version of *Dr. Jekyll and Mr. Hyde*, in which Ingrid Bergman sings this song and Spencer Tracy hums it before he transforms into Mr. Hyde. The song itself was composed in 1887 by George Grossmith, a member of Gilbert and Sullivan's troupe.

The way Hyde walks in full view toward the Tripod is similar to the narrator's suicidal march to the Tripods in Chapter 8 of Book 2 of *WotW*.

Page 145. Panel 1. This panel is similar to the scenes of the Martian "spycam" in the 1953 *War of the Worlds* film.

Page 146. Panel 1. The men falling from the Tripod are humans that the Martians are using as feedbags; Wells' Martians do not eat but, as mentioned in the notes to Page 13, Panel 5, "took the fresh living blood of other creatures, and injected it into their veins."

Panel 4. The secret to the Martians' language is to read it reflected in the mirror. Hyde is saying to the Martian, "Can you hear me in there?" and it is being translated by the Martian's Tripod into Martian.

Page 149. Panel 5. In H.G. Wells' *The War of the Worlds* the Martians are brought low by their susceptibility to Earth bacteria and because their culture is free of bacteria and the like:

> The last salient point in which the systems of these creatures differed from ours was in what one might have thought a very trivial particular. Micro-organisms, which cause so much disease and pain on earth, have either never appeared upon Mars or Martian sanitary science eliminated them ages ago. A hundred diseases, all the fevers and contagions of human life, consumption, cancers, tumours and such morbidities, never enter the scheme of their life.

Page 150. Panel 3. The "wife and child on Lincoln Island" are Moore's invention. In *The Mysterious Island*, Nemo lives alone on Lincoln Island. As seen in the notes to Page 201, this is not the case in the world of *League*.

Page 151. Panel 4. "Why, I hear they're planning to rename Serpentine Park here after Hyde."
In real life Hyde Park was named after the manor of Hyde, the owner of the park before King Henry VIII acquired the park in 1536. There has never been a Serpentine Park in London, although the Serpentine, an artificial lake, still exists in Hyde Park.

Panel 7. The "ladies' commune in Scotland called Coradine" is from W.H. Hudson's *A Crystal Age* (1887) and is a utopia set in northern Scotland.

Page 152. Panel 1. The parting scene between Mina and Allan has a heavy emphasis on autumn leaves. Jeff Wayne's 1976 rock opera *War of the Worlds* had, on its soundtrack, a love song called "Forever Autumn" with the refrain, "Now you're not here."

Page 153. "I feel a wonderful peace and rest tonight. It is as if some haunting presence were removed from me. Perhaps..."
This line is from Bram Stoker's *Dracula*, at the point in the novel when Dracula has left England and is returning to Transylvania.

The date given, 5 October 1891, is interesting. In the first *League* collection Moore and O'Neill's rule of thumb for dating was that the year a book or story was published was the year that the events in the book or story took place. This led to the internal dates of some stories having to be ignored. *Dracula* was published in 1897, and while no year is specified in the novel for the events the epilogue says, "Seven years ago we all went through the flames." In *League* v1 the events of *Dracula* are described by Dupin, on Page 36, as having taken place "last year." In *League* v2 the events of Dracula, according to this portrait, took place in 1891. This contradiction is similar to the one in *The Mysterious Island*, where Jules Verne revised Captain Nemo's personal history and contradicted what he'd written in *20,000 Leagues Under The Sea*.

Kevin O'Neill notes:
> Date confusion is my fault—or Dupin is senile. I think it's
> my fault.

Page 154. "...Edward Hyde, alone, in the ranks of mankind, was pure evil."
This line is from *The Strange Case of Dr. Jekyll and Mr. Hyde*, when Jekyll describes his reaction when he sees, for the first time, Edward Hyde's face in the mirror:

> I have observed that when I wore the semblance of
> Edward Hyde, none could come near to me at first without
> a visible misgiving of the flesh. This, as I take it, was
> because all human beings, as we meet them, are
> commingled out of good and evil: and Edward Hyde, alone
> in the ranks of mankind, was pure evil.

The painting is dated 1886 because that is the year of *The Strange Case of Dr. Jekyll and Mr. Hyde*'s publication.

Page 155. "This is day one of year one of the new epoch—the epoch of the Invisible Man. I am Invisible Man the First."

In this line from *The Invisible Man*, Griffin announces himself to the hostile people of Burdock:

> You are against me. For a whole day you have chased
> me; you have tried to rob me of a night's rest. But I have
> had food in spite of you, I have slept in spite of you, and
> the game is only beginning. The game is only beginning.
> There is nothing for it, but to start the Terror. This
> announces the first day of the Terror. Port Burdock is no
> longer under the Queen, tell your Colonel of Police, and
> the rest of them; it is under me—the Terror! This is day
> one of year one of the new epoch—the Epoch of the
> Invisible Man. I am Invisible Man the First.

The painting is dated 1897 because that is the year of publication of *The Invisible Man*.

Page 156. "I am not what you call a civilized man! I have done with society entirely, for reasons which I alone have the right of appreciating. I do not therefore obey its laws."

In this line from *20,000 Leagues Under the Sea*, Nemo rejects appeals from his prisoners to be treated like civilized men:

> "Professor," replied the commander, quickly, "I am not
> what you call a civilised man! I have done with society
> entirely, for reasons which I alone have the right of

appreciating. I do not, therefore, obey its laws, and I desire you never to allude to them before me again!"

The painting is dated November 1867 because that is the month and year in which Nemo told the captured Arronax that he is not a civilised man.

Page 157. "I've killed many men in my time, but I have never slain wantonly or stained my hand in innocent blood, only in self defence."

This line is from *King Solomon's Mines*, when Quatermain is introducing himself to the reader and describing his personality and history:

> At any rate, I was born a gentleman, though I have been nothing but a poor travelling trader and hunter all my life. Whether I have remained so I know not, you must judge of that. Heaven knows I've tried. I have killed many men in my time, yet I have never slain wantonly or stained my hand in innocent blood, but only in self-defence. The Almighty gave us our lives, and I suppose He meant us to defend them, at least I have always acted on that, and I hope it will not be brought up against me when my clock strikes. There, there, it is a cruel and a wicked world, and for a timid man I have been mixed up in a great deal of fighting.

The painting is dated 1880 because that is the year, according to the internal chronology of *King Solomon's Mines*, when Quatermain made the preceding statement.

Page 158. In *League* v1 Moore and O'Neill included a number of advertisements from real Victorian magazines along with a few advertisements which they made up. The "Batchelor's Friend" ad is their own creation. The other advertisements on this page are real.

Page 159. *The New Traveller's Almanac* is Moore and O'Neill's attempt at creating a more widespread and encompassing shared world than has been created before, using the conceit of a traveler's almanac. The red material that the Almanac seems to be covered in was common for books published by the British government (note the "H.M. Stationery Office" stamp at the bottom of the page) in the 1930s, when *The New Traveller's Almanac* is supposed to have been published. The illustration on the cover does not have a specific reference that I'm aware of, although it is similar to Mayan and Aztec stone calendars. It can be seen as a watermark on Page 165.

Kevin O'Neill notes:

> The image used on the *Almanac* cover is a design I came up with for a watermark on the first *Almanac* chapter, a mix of alchemy and Mayan calendar images forming an unusual compass.
>
> Our good friend Todd Klein has helped give this series a real glow when it comes to all the extra pages and special features—working with him has been a great pleasure. Todd's attention to detail on the *Almanac* in particular is fantastic. I know what I want, but he always goes that extra mile for us. The *Almanac* was a lot of work for Alan, then Todd has this mass of material to track… I think I got off lightly just drawing the illustrations.
>
> The ex-libris book plate belongs to Campion Bond [with the top figure representing "007," the middle figure being a "C" for Campion, and the tail being a "B" for Bond.]

Page 160. These stamps are similar to those appearing on passports, albeit from fictional locations.

Moving clockwise, beginning with the British Library stamp:

The "British Library, Do Not Remove" stamp is similar to other stamps appearing in books in the British Library, but the real British Library stamps do not have the helmet-and-question-mark logo of the League.

"Fantippo" appears in Hugh Lofting's novels *Doctor Dolittle's Post Office* (1924) and *Doctor Dolittle and the Secret Lake* (1949). Fantippo is a kingdom in West Africa which adopted the English postal system after Fantippo's ruler, King Koko, heard about the system and was impressed by it.

"Kor" appears in H. Rider Haggard's *She: A History of Adventure* (1886), the novel which introduced Ayesha, She Who Must Be Obeyed. Kôr is a city in central East Africa ruled over by Ayesha. Kôr is close to the rejuvenating "Fire of Life," which granted Ayesha immortality.

"Skull Island," a.k.a. the Island of the Mists, appears in the 1933 film *King Kong*, which was based on Edgar Wallace's serial "King Kong" (*Boys'Magazine*, 1933). Skull Island is King Kong's home. Entry to it is forbidden for obvious reasons.

"Manghalour" appears in Louis Rustaing de Saint-Jory's novel *Les Femmes Militaires* (1735). Manghalour is an island, location undetermined, with several different cultures, including a Muslim community which supports equal rights for women and the Valley of Iram, or "Earthly Paradise."

The stamp in Greek is a reference to Xiros, which appears in Jorge Luis Borges' short story "El Zahir" (*El Aleph*, 1949). Xiros, an island in the Aegean Sea (hence the Greek of the stamp), is a haunting island which gives to its visitors a bliss so powerful that it is deadly.

"Ruritania" and "Zenda" appear in Anthony Hope Hawkins' novels *The Prisoner of Zenda* (1894), *Rupert of Hentzau* (1898), and *The Heart of Princess Osra* (1906). Zenda is a small town in the European country of Ruritania which is home to the Castle of Zenda, the traditional country residence of the kings of Ruritania.

"Wonderland" appears in Lewis Carroll's novel *Alice's Adventures in Wonderland* (1865). The reason that the word "Wonderland" is a mirror image is given below, on Page 164.

"Fragrant Island" appears in Alfred Jarry's novel *Gestes et Opinions du Docteur Faustroll, Pataphysicien* (1911). Fragrant Island is a monarchy where everything is sensitive, even the plants. "Be in Love, Be Mysterious" is the double formula for happiness which the gods of Fragrant Island pronounce.

"Klopstokia" appears in the 1932 film *Million Dollar Legs*, written by Joseph L. Mankiewicz. Klopstokia is a Ruritanian country whose government officials, impressed by the Klopstokians' athletic ability, enter the country into the Olympics.

"Freeland" appears in Dr. Theodor Hertzka's novel *Freiland* (1890). Freeland, in East Africa, is a communist utopia.

"Laputa" appears in Jonathan Swift's novel *Gulliver's Travels* (1726). Laputa is a flying island whose culture is preoccupied with music, mathematics, and astronomy.

"Noble's Island" appears in H.G. Wells' *The Island of Dr. Moreau*. Noble's Isle is the island on which the disgraced Dr. Moreau continues his experiments and where the action of the novel takes place. The "disinfected" on the stamp is necessary due to the danger of various diseases emerging from the island.

"Ex Libris," or "from the library of," is usually seen on labels or bookplates of books, identifying their true owner. *The New Traveller's Almanac* was assembled for British Intelligence—in the world of the League, the Freemasons—therefore this bookplate is full of Masonic iconography, including the triangle-and-compass, the all-seeing-eye-in-the-pyramid, and three masked women about to stab a fourth masked woman, just as, in Masonic legend, Jubelo, Jubela, and Jubelum, or the "Juwes," killed Hiram Abif, one of the two master temple builders of the Temple in Jerusalem. In *From Hell*, his fictional treatment of the Jack the Ripper murders, Moore and illustrator Eddie Campbell show the (real) appearance of the word "Juwes" on an alley wall next to one of the Ripper's victims as well as in a letter sent by the Ripper to the police, and explore the (possible) ties between the Ripper and the Freemasons.

Page 161. "About the earliest such gathering of unique individuals in service to the Crown, little is known save that they were reputedly convened during the seventeenth century and were referred to unofficially as 'Prospero's Men.'"
This refers to one of the earlier Leagues of Extraordinary Gentlemen hinted at in *League* v1. (A complete list of the Leagues is given in the

notes to Page 185). "Prospero" refers to Prospero, the Duke of Milan, from Shakespeare's play *The Tempest* (1611). In *The Tempest* Prospero is set adrift by his brother and washes ashore on an island of various exotic animals and spirits. At the end of the story Prospero promises to return to Milan and rule it as is his right. In the world of *League* Prospero later left Milan and entered the service of the British Crown.

"...A Duke of Milan with interests in the occult sciences..."
Prospero has various sorcerous powers, including the ability to conjure up storms.

"Two of the group were rumored to be conjurings of sorcery rather than mortal beings..."
This may be a reference to the sprite Ariel and the brute Caliban, both from *The Tempest*, although Caliban is "the natural-born child of the witch Sycorax" rather than a magically conjured being.

"...The wide-eyed traveller called only 'Christian,' claimed that he had wandered into our world from some neighbouring etheric territory..."
Christian is from John Bunyan's *The Pilgrim's Progress from This World to That Which Is to Come* (1678-1684). In *Progress* Christian, an Everyman, travels from the City of Destruction to the Celestial City, visiting the Slough of Despond, the House of the Interpreter, and various other locales on the way.

"...The marvellous archipelago known as The Blazing World..."
The Blazing World is from *Observations upon Experimental Philosophy. To Which Is Added the Description of a New Blazing World. Written by the Thrice Noble, Illustrious and Excellent Princess, The Duchess of Newcastle* (1666), by Margaret Cavendish, Duchess of Newcastle. The Blazing World is an archipelago of island which extends from the North Pole through the Greenland and Norwegian Seas almost to the British Islands. On the islands of The Blazing World are men of various colors and races, from blue to orange and from bear-men to parrot-men, with each type of person belonging to a different profession.

"...The fated and disastrous Bellman Expedition into the interior of a puzzling well or pit near Oxford in the 1870s."

The Bellman Expedition is from Lewis Carroll's poem *The Hunting of the Snark* (1876). In the poem the Bellman Expedition goes hunting for a snark, only to find that the gentle snark is in fact the dreaded boojum. The "puzzling well or pit near Oxford" is a reference to the hole down which Alice L. fell in Carroll's *Alice in Wonderland*. The Expedition is gone into more detail on Pages 163-164 below.

"Other members of this new fraternity would seem to have eventually included a mild-mannered clergyman from Kent, a Mr. Bumppo from America, a married English couple called the Blakeneys and a Mistress Hill..."

This is a reference to the eighteenth-century League of Extraordinary Gentlemen, seen in a portrait in Panel 2, Page 53 of the first *League* collection: The Reverend Dr. Syn, from Russell Thorndike's *Doctor Syn*; Natty Bumppo, from James Fenimore Cooper's "Leatherstocking" novels; Sir Percy and Marguerite Blakeney, from Baroness Emmuska Orczy's *The Scarlet Pimpernel*; and Fanny Hill from John Cleland's novel *Fanny Hill* (1749).

The "mild-mannered clergyman from Kent" is a possibly-coincidental bit of wordplay. Another word for "reverend" is "cleric" or "clerk." So Dr. Syn is the mild-mannered Clark of Kent.

"...Those notes accumulated by Miss Wilhelmina Murray in the period from 1899 to 1912..."

Bram Stoker, Mina's creator, died in 1912.

Page 162. "The Streaming Kingdom..."

The Streaming Kingdom is from Jules Supervielle's novel *L'Enfant de la Haute Mer* (1931). The Streaming Kingdom is an aquatic kingdom under the English Channel, near the mouth of the Seine. It is inhabited by water-breathing humans who must drown before they can enter the Kingdom.

"The notorious 18th century pirate, Captain Clegg..."

In *Doctor Syn* Captain Clegg is a ferocious smuggler and pirate. He is also the alter ego of the kindly Reverend Dr. Syn.

"...Something not unlike 'His Royal Wetness'..."
The Streaming Kingdom is ruled by a creature called His Royal Wetness.

"...The four-inch aquatic infants found within the submarine caves of St. Brendan's Isle..."
St. Brendan's Isle and the "aquatic infants" are a reference to Charles Kingsley's novel *The Water-Babies* (1863). *The Water-Babies* is about Tom, a chimney sweep, who is hounded across the English countryside until falls in a river. His body dies, but his soul is changed into a "water baby" by a group of fairies.

"...The concealed cave in the cliffs just east of Helston, where it is believed that Arthur's mentor Merlin was incarcerated by his rival thaumaturge, the sorceress Nyneve."
In Arthurian myth Nyneve is Merlin's lover and student, but she ultimately betrays him, and after he creates a cave refuge for the both of them she traps him in there.

"...The French authorities claim to possess the mummified remains of Merlin, found inside an oak somewhere in Brittany, believed to be the prior location of Broceliande Forest."
In the sequels to the Old French prose romances about Merlin he is trapped in the forest of Brocéliande by the sorceress Niniane. This passage may also be a reference to Robert Holdstock's novel *Merlin's Wood* (1994), in which Merlin is trapped in an oak in Broceliande Forest by the sorceress Vivian.

"...The cave is, rather than the tomb of Merlin, the retreat used by the famous lovers Tristan and Isolde when they were banished from the court of Cornwall by the jealous rage of Isolde's husband, Mark."
In Arthurian myth the knight Tristan, second only to Lancelot in valor, falls in love with Isolde, the wife of King Mark of Cornwall, and the two are banished by Mark after being trapped by courtiers who envy Tristan. The pair have an idyll in the forests of Cornwall, but Isolde eventually returns to Mark and Tristan goes into exile.

"Most well-known is Victoria..."
Victoria is from James Buckingham's *National Evils and Practical Remedies, with a Plan of a Model Town* (1849). Victoria is a model

town, built to be a kind of urban utopia under the rules Moore describes here.

"...It may be useful to compare Victoria with the model town established further north as recently as 1899, in Avondale..."
Avondale is from Grant Allen's story "The Child of the Phalanstery" (*Belgravia*, April 1884). A "phalanstery" is a self-sustaining commune. In "The Child of the Phalanstery" the Avondale Phalanstery is a well-managed commune with the unfortunate habit of killing all crippled or deformed children.

"...The delightful village known as Commutaria..."
Commutaria is from Elspeth Ann Macey's short story "Awayday" (*Absent Friends and Other Stories*, 1955). Commutaria is an Avalon of sorts for the weary commuter; whatever she or he wishes for can be found in the village. It was founded by a descendant of Merlin as a way to reward tired commuters, especially on Monday mornings.

"An enthralling tome by Donford-Yates..."
Dornford Yates was the pseudonym of Cecil William Mercer (1885-1960), an English author of mystery/adventure books with series characters Berry Pleydell, Jonah Mansel, and Richard Chandos. In the 1920s and 1930s Dornford Yates novels were very popular.

"...More sinister evasive sites, like Abaton in Scotland...."
Abaton is from Sir Thomas Bulfinch's My Heart's novel *In the Highlands* (1892). Abaton is a Scottish town of varying location, somewhere between Glasgow and Troon. It's never where it is sought for, and only a few rare men and women manage to catch a glimpse of it, always at sunset and sunrise; those who see Abaton are always affected strongly by it, either with great joy or great sorrow. No one ever makes it to Abaton, however; it is only ever seen from a distance.

"...The mind-warping horrors of 'Snark Island'...."
Snark Island is from Lewis Carroll's *The Hunting of the Snark*. Snark Island is the home of various deadly animals—the jub-jub, the bandersnatch, and the boojum, as well as the snark. The Island is filled with "dismal and desolate" valleys and jaggy crags, and is generally unpleasant.

"Yalding Towers Garden, Hampshire."
Yalding Towers Garden is from E. Nesbit's novel *The Enchanted Castle* (1907). See the notes to Page 163.

Page 163. "...Bleak, magnificent Baskerville Hall..."
Baskerville Hall is a reference to Arthur Conan Doyle's novel *The Hound of the Baskervilles* (1902). In the novel Sherlock Holmes and Dr. Watson visit Baskerville Hall to solve the mystery of a giant, ghostly hound.

"...To Crotchet Castle there in the Thames Valley..."
Crotchet Castle is from Thomas Love Peacock's novel *Crotchet Castle* (1881). In the novel Ebenezer MacCrotchet, Esq., one of the rare Scottish Jews, reads that London magistrates have ordered that all statues of Venus must appear in the streets wearing petticoats. MacCrotchet's response is to bring all of the offending statues of Venus to his home.

"At Yalding Towers..."
Yalding Towers appears in E. Nesbit's *The Enchanted Castle*. Yalding Towers was built decades ago by a man who owned a magic ring. When worn, the ring makes the ring-bearer invisible. It also grants the ring-bearer the power to make the dinosaur statues come to life.

"...At Ravenal's Tower outside Ivybridge in Kent..."
Ravenal's Tower is from E. Nesbit's *The Wouldbegoods* (1901). In the novel Richard Ravenal suffers from the curse as Moore describes it.

"...An isolated cottage called 'The White House,' bordering a gravel pit where there have been reported sightings of a stalk-eyed monster known to the locals as a Psammead..."
The "White House" and the Psammead are from E. Nesbit's novels *Five Children and It* (1902) and *The Story of the Amulet* (1906). The White House is a holiday cottage in Kent where five children discover the Psammead, an extremely cranky fairy.

"...Wilhelmina Murray, in 1904, visited (for reasons best known to herself) an elderly bee-keeper who resided near the seaside cove of Fulworth..."
This is a reference to Arthur Conan Doyle's short story "The Adventure of the Lion's Mane" (*Liberty*, 27 November 1927), in which Sherlock

Holmes is described as having retired to Fulworth to pursue his interest in bee-keeping. In the internal chronology of the Sherlock Holmes stories Holmes is only fifty years old in 1904, although in films the younger Holmes is usually played by older actors.

"...Folklore surrounding the 'Wish House' at 14 Wadloes Road in Smalldene..."
The "Wish House" and Smalldene are from Rudyard Kipling's short story "The Wish House" (*Maclean's*, 15 October 1924). The Wish House is a small basement-kitchen house in which visitors, by wishing aloud into the house's letter-box slot, can take upon themselves the ills of their loved ones.

"...Murray was referred to the Starkadder family farm..."
The Starkadder family farm, and Miss Ada Doom, are from Stella Gibbons' novel *Cold Comfort Farm* (1932). Miss Ada Doom of the Starkadder family saw "something nasty in the woodshed" when she was a child, and rarely left her room after that. *Cold Comfort Farm*, however, takes place circa 1955 in an alternate Earth in which Britain and Nicaragua fought a war in 1945.

"...The so-called 'Witch House' to be found on Pickman Street in Arkham, Massachusetts..."
The Witch House is from H.P. Lovecraft's short story "Dreams in the Witch House" (*Weird Tales* vol. 22 no. 1, July 1933). "Dreams in the Witch House" is about a modern scholar's discovery of the link between colonial-era witchcraft and modern metaphysical speculations.

"...The castle known as Yspaddaden Penkawr..."
Yspaddaden Penkawr is from *The Mabinogion*, a collection of Welsh legends and myths assembled at some point in the middle of the eleventh century. The two surviving complete versions of *The Mabinogion* are found in *The White Book of Rhydderch* (ca. 1325) and *The Red Book of Hergest* (ca. 1400). Yspaddaden Penkawr appears in "How Culhwch Won Olwen."

> They journeyed until they came to a vast open plain,
> wherein they saw a great castle, which was the fairest
> of the castles of the world. And they journeyed that day

until the evening, and when they thought they were nigh
to the castle, they were no nearer to it than they had
been in the morning. And the second and the third day
they journeyed, and even then scarcely could they reach
so far.

"...The gloomy but imposing sight of Exham Priory, with its dismal history
of ineffectual pest-control..."
Exham Priory is from H.P. Lovecraft's short story "The Rats in the Walls"
(*Weird Tales* v3n3, March 1924). The Priory has a rat problem which
eventually overwhelms the inheritor of the Priory.

"...The small but friendly railway station found in Llaregyb..."
Llaregyb is from Dylan Thomas' *Under Milk Wood, a Play for Voices*
(1954). Llaregyb is a small, sleepy Welsh village. In *Under Milk Wood*
the village is "Llaregub," as in "bugger all" spelled backwards. "Bugger
all" is British vernacular for "nothing."

"...The great national embarrassment, since its discovery in 1673 by
Captain Robert Owemuch, of the floating island Scoti Moria, alternatively
known as Summer Island..."
Captain Robert Owemuch and the Floating Island (a.k.a. Scoti Moria
a.k.a. Summer Island) are from "Frank Careless"' novel *The Floating
Island or a new Discovery Relating the Strange Adventure on a late
Voyage from Lambethana to Villa Franca, Alias Ramallia, to the
Eastward of Terra Del Templo: By three Ships, viz., the 'Pay-naught,'
the 'Excuse,' and the 'Least-in-Sight' under the Conduct of Captain
Robert Owe-much: Describing the Nature of the Inhabitants, their
Religion, Laws and Customs* (1673). Floating Island is a small island
located in the middle of the Thames-Isis Gulf, off the coast of England.
The island floats away in winter and hides until the summer, hence its
names. Floating Islands' inhabitants are as described.

"...The picturesque and world-famed English university town of Camford,
which most recently achieved some notoriety due to the efforts of
Professor Presbury..."
Camford and Professor Presbury are from Arthur Conan Doyle's short
story "The Adventure of the Creeping Man" (*Strand Magazine*, March
1923). In that story Professor Presbury attempts to grow younger by
injecting himself with monkey gland extract.

"...It was here, on the River Thames's banks somewhere between Godstow and Folly Bridge in 1865 that the presumed abduction of a little girl took place...the girl in question, sensitively known as 'Miss A.L.'..."

The little girl, "Miss A.L.," and the text following are references to Lewis Carroll's *Alice's Adventures in Wonderland*. "A.L." stands for Alice Liddell, the little girl for whom the Reverend Charles Lutwidge Dodgson, a.k.a. Lewis Carroll, wrote *Alice*. Miss A.L. is here drawn similarly to the Alice of John Tenniel, the classic artist of *Alice's Adventures in Wonderland*.

Page 164. "...There were two less happily-concluded sequels to her exploits, the first taking place in 1871..."

The Reverend Dodgson published *Through the Looking Glass*, the sequel to *Alice's Adventures in Wonderland*, in 1871.

"...During the occasion of a family visit to the Deanery of Christ Church College, Oxford."

The real Alice Liddell lived at the Christ Church Deanery, and her father was the Dean of Christ Church. "Miss A.L." may be a composite of the real Alice Liddell and the fictional Alice of the books, who among other things was older than the real Alice Liddell and had a much different appearance.

"The child's hair-parting was now worn on the other side, and on examination it appeared that the positions of the organs in her body had been reversed."

This is a reference to "The Hunting of the Snark." In "The Banker's Fate," the Banker is grabbed at by the Bandersnatch, and faints, with the result:

> He was black in the face, and they scarcely could trace
> The least likeness to what he had been:
> While so great was his fright that his waistcoat turned
> white—
> A wonderful thing to be seen!

"Apparently in consequence of this, Miss A.L. could no longer keep down or digest her normal food..."

Dextrocardia situs inversus totalis is a rare congenital cardiac malformation in which the normal anatomy of the heart and visceral organs are reversed. The condition is not fatal, however. What kills Miss A.L. is the reversal of her body's enzymes. Many important organic molecules, including sugars and amino acids, exist in two forms, known as stereoisomers, which are mirror images of each other. But usually in biological systems only one isomer is active and so can be broken down by the human body's enzymes and used for fuel or to create proteins. The human body's enzymes have specific spatial orientations, so that receptor sites are positioned to accept only one of the two isomers. If Miss A.L.'s reversal was complete to the molecular level, then her enzymes would be oriented so that they could no longer make use of the stereoisomers of sugar and amino acids found in normal food, and she would starve to death.

The motif of the reversal of organs also appears in H.G. Wells' short story "The Plattner Story" (*New Review*, April 1896).

"An Oxford clergyman named Dr. Eric Bellman led the group..."
Dr. Bellman appears in from "The Hunting of the Snark."

"Bellman Expedition sketch by Miss Beever, 1876."
The picture notes that the Expedition takes place in Godstow. Godstow was the location where Dodgson originally told the Wonderland story to Alice Liddell and her sisters.

Page 165. "...The mention of a form of local fauna called a 'jub-jub'..."
The "jub-jub" or "jubjub" bird is mentioned in both "The Hunting of the Snark" and in *Alice Through the Looking Glass*.

"Asked how one might find this place, Bellman grew agitated and snatched up a page out of my notebook, claiming that it was a perfect map of how the island might be reached. The page in question, I should note, was yet unused and thus entirely blank...."
From "The Hunting of the Snark:"

> He had bought a large map representing the sea,
>> Without the least vestige of land:
> And the crew were much pleased when they found it to be
>> A map they could all understand.
> "What's the good of Mercator's North Poles and Equators,
>> Tropics, Zones, and Meridian Lines?"
> So the Bellman would cry: and the crew would reply
>> "They are merely conventional signs!
>
> "Other maps are such shapes, with their islands and capes!
>> But we've got our brave Captain to thank:
> (So the crew would protest) "that he's bought us the best—
>> A perfect and absolute blank!"

"He would only say, 'The last word that he spoke was 'boo.'"
In "The Hunting of the Snark" the last words of the Baker are, "It's a Boo-" (For the Snark was a Boojum, you see).

"...And certain tunnels found beneath an island in East Anglia, at Winton Pond..."
Winton Pond is from Graham Greene's short story "Under the Garden" (*A Sense of Reality*, 1963). In the middle of Winton Pond is a small island underneath which are a web of tunnels, complete with a strange pair of inhabitants and a great trove of treasure of all the valuable rubbish people have ever lost. One of the subterranean inhabitants refers to certain characters from Wonderland.

"...Coal City..."
Coal City is from Jules Verne's novel *Les Indes Noires* (1877). Coal City, a subterranean city located beneath central Scotland, is a very productive mine and tourist attraction.

"...Vril-ya Country..."
Vril-ya Country is from Edward Bulwer-Lytton's novel *The Coming Race* (1871). The Vril-ya are a race which has constructed a utopia in a ravine deep beneath Newcastle.

"...The Roman State..."

The Roman State is from Joseph O'Neill's novel *Land Under England* (1935). The Roman State is a fascistic subterranean nation underneath England, reachable via a trapdoor at the base of Hadrian's Wall. Although the Roman State's origin is unknown, its clothes, language and ships are at the very least influenced by the Romans.

"...Harthover Place in Yorkshire..."

Harthover Place is from Charles Kingsley's *The Water-Babies.*

"...Nightmare Abbey on the edge of Lincolnshire, a place so cursed that its afflictions almost seem amusing..."

Nightmare Abbey is from Thomas Love Peacock's Gothic novel *Nightmare Abbey* (1818). Nightmare Abbey is a dilapidated family mansion haunted by a gloom of melancholy which eventually overwhelms its guests.

"...Alderly Edge, a windswept and remote location in the hills of Cheshire, is reputed to conceal the entrance to a massive cave containing scores of mediaeval knights in some state of suspended animation."

Alderley Edge is a real location in Cheshire, and local legend has it that King Arthur and his knights still sleep underneath the Edge's sandstone cliffs. Its mention here may also be a reference to Alan Garner's *The Weirdstone of Brisingamen* (1960). In the novel 140 knights in silver armor lie in enchanted sleep in the cave Fundinelve underneathAlderly Edge, waiting for the chance to fight the evil Spirit of Darkness. Garner made use of the real legend for the book.

"...The ancient ruins of Diana's Grove in Staffordshire, not far from Mercy Farm and the nearby ancestral pile of Castra Regis, home to the illustrious Caswell family until the sad events of their annus horribilus in 1911..."

Diana's Grove, Mercy Farm, the Castra Regis, and the Caswell family are all from Bram Stoker's *Lair of the White Worm* (1911). In the novel an ancient, evil white worm, which had survived since prehistoric times in the tunnels beneath England, plagued several Englishmen and women, all the while in the form of a beautiful woman, before finally being killed through the suitable application of dynamite.

The phrase "annus horribilis," or "horrible year," was used by Queen Elizabeth II to describe 1992, when she suffered from the marital problems of her children, the publication of Andrew Morton's book on Princess Diana, and a fire which badly damaged Windsor Castle.

"Annus horribilis" also works as a Latinate pun hinting at the White Worm. "Annu-" is Latin for year, but "Annelida" is the taxonomic phylum to which earthworms, and presumably the White Worm itself, belonged.

"...Thus 'Nania' is a Vril-ya word denoting sin, or evil..."
The word "Nania" does not appear in *The Coming Race*, but "Naria" does:

> Na, which with them is, like Gl, but a single letter, always, when an initial, implies something antagonistic to life or joy or comfort, resembling in this the Aryan root Nak, expressive of perishing or destruction. Nax is darkness; Narl, death; Naria, sin or evil. Nas—an uttermost condition of sin and evil—corruption.

The point of this passage may be a jab at C.S. Lewis' Narnia. The Vril-ya Country is a kind of utopia, which practices religious tolerance among other virtues. The Narnia stories are thinly veiled allegories for Christianity, with the lion Aslan a Christ metaphor. To the Vril-ya, the ethos of Narnia would be evil.

"...A hand-written note refers the reader to an apple-tree currently being grown as a government project at Kew Gardens..."
See the notes to Page 173.

"...Narnia?..."
Narnia is a reference to C.S. Lewis' Chronicles of Narnia books, *The Lion, the Witch, and the Wardrobe* (1950), *Prince Caspian* (1951), *The Voyage of the Dawn Treader* (1952), *The Silver Chair* (1953), *The Horse and his Boy* (1954), *The Magician's Nephew* (1955), and *The Last Battle* (1956). In this series children from Earth venture to the fantasy world of Narnia and have various adventures there.

"...Up in Northumberland, upon the North Sea coast, stands Bamburgh Castle...this, then, was Joyeusegarde, the fortress raised directly after the Roman withdrawal from these shores in the fifth century, where Launcelot of Camelot lived in adultery with Arthur's wife, Guinevere."
There is a real Bamburgh Castle, on the edge of the North Sea, in Northumberland. It stands on the site of an earlier fort, built in the middle of the fifth century. The original fort's name was "Din Guayrdi." This name was taken by the Arthurian romancers, including Malory, and given to Lancelot as his home. In the Arthurian myths Lancelot lives in "Joyeuse Garde" or "Joyous Gard," a castle he rescued from an evil enchanter. The castle's name had formerly been "Dolorous Gard," but after his capturing of the castle and breaking of the spell Lancelot changed its name.

"The ceiling gapes, collapsed, so that an oar of sunlight falls across this vault and stripes the carven form at rest on his sarcophagus. The elements and keepsake-hunters both have scoured its features with unkindness, so that little save a weathered granite knob remains to represent the noble countenance, and many details of his armour and effects may likewise be rendered indistinct. The dogs curled at his feet are mostly disappeared, with one a formless lump, the other nothing save a paw. Ah, ill-made knight, that thy unmaking should prove more ill yet, with all about thy funeral stones now tumbled into disrepair. The moss encroaches, and men's minds forget the eyes, the brow, his streaming beast-mane hair."
Some of Prospero's other diary entries, as below on Page 169, are in iambic pentameter or close to it. This entry is not, although the final two lines can be broken down in that way:

> Ah, ill-made knight, that thy unmaking should
> Prove more ill yet, with all about thy fun-
> -eral stones now tumbled into disrepair.
>
> The moss encroaches, and men's minds forget
> The eyes, the brow, his streaming beast-man hair.

Page 166."...Phenomena of a more whimsical, fantastic nature, such as Gort Na Cloca Mora..."
Gort Na Cloca Mora is from James Stephens' novel *The Crock of*

Gold (1912). *The Crock of Gold* is about two philosophers who argue with each other and encounter some leprechauns. Gort Na Cloca Mora is the home of the leprechauns. *The Crock of Gold* was the source for the musical *Finian's Rainbow* (1946), written by E.Y. Harburg and Burton Laine, which featured the song "How Are Things in Glocca Morra?"

"..The nearby glen, Glyn Cagny..."
Glyn Cagny is from *The Crock of Gold*. Glyn Cagny is a glen associated with the two philosophers of *The Crock of Gold*.

"...A peculiar breed of salmon said to be the most profound and learned creatures in all Ireland."
The salmon appear in a pond in Glyn Cagny in *The Crock of Gold*. The salmon originally appear in Irish folklore. In the legends there is, near the River Boyne, a fountain of water known as "Connla's Well." Near this well grow the Nine Hazels of Poetic Art. The nuts from the trees fall into the well, and the salmon in the well, known as the *Fintan*, eats the nuts and so knows all things, gaining the name the Salmon of Knowledge. In the legend of Deimne Finn, a.k.a. Fionn mac Cumhail, a.k.a. Finn McCool, Deimne is told by his master Finneces the Druid to catch and cook the *Fintan*. Deimne does this, but while cooking the *Fintan* he burns his thumb on the fish's grease. He puts his thumb on his mouth to cool it, accidentally eats the grease, and so gains the gift of wisdom.

"...The domain of The Sleepers of Erinn, where Irish god-king Angus Og and his bride Caitlin are believed to now reside..."
The Sleepers of Erinn, Angus Og, and Caitlin are all from *The Crock of Gold*. Angus Og is one of the ancient gods of Ireland; his other name is "Infinite Love and Joy." Caitlin is the daughter of one of the two philosophers of *The Crock of Gold*. The Cave of the Sleepers of Erinn is Angus Og's home.

"...The Lake of the Cauldron..."
The Lake of the Cauldron is from "Branwen, Daughter of Llyr," in *The Mabinogion*, in which it functions as described here. The legend of the Cauldron is generally considered to prefigure the story of the Holy Grail.

"...The peculiarly modern-seeming 'Giant's Garden' that surrounds an outsized tower near Camford. Unbelievably, these ruins were not discovered until 1888..."

The Giant's Garden is from the Oscar Wilde story "The Selfish Giant" (*The Happy Prince and Other Tales*, 1888). This charming story is about a giant, his garden, and the children who visit the garden.

"...Nearer to Dublin, we find Leixlip Castle..."

Leixlip Castle, Redmond Blaney, and Jane Blaney are from Charles Maturin's novel *The Castle of Leixlip* (1820). Leixlip Castle has, as the text here mentions, a dark history, with Redmond Blaney's daughters being murdered by their husbands or taken by fairies.

"...The famous spectral seafood vendor, Miss Malone..."

Miss Malone is actually sweet Molly Malone, from James Yorkston's song "Cockles and Mussels" (1884). After dying of a fever Molly Malone walks the streets of Dublin, crying, "Cockles and mussels alive, alive o!"

"...A demolished eighteenth century building in the centre of the city, once known as 'The Red House'..."

The Red House is from J. Sheridan Le Fanu's novel *The House by the Churchyard* (1863). The hand which haunted Mr. Harper's red house is the ghost of an ancestor's hand, which had been mutilated.

"Forty miles east of Galway stands a house that presently belongs to a middle-aged gentleman, one Mr. Mathers. Local legends or tall tales suggest that Mathers' house may somehow form a gateway to a strangely different Ireland..."

This is a reference to the novel *The Third Policeman* (1940) by Flann O'Brien, a.k.a. Brian O'Nolan, a.k.a. Briain ÓNuallàin. Mr. Mathers' house is the home of the quite dangerous Police Inspector Fox as well as a gateway to a hellish Ireland.

"...The unearthly ruins we discover on the windswept western coast of Ireland. These apparently once formed a house built on a wild crag jutting out above a chasm..."

This house is from W.H. Hodgson's novel *The House on the Borderland*

(1908). The House on the Borderland, inhabited by the old man and his sister mentioned in the text, is the gateway to a world of evil swine monsters.

"...The island known as that of Saint Brendan the Blessed."
This is from Charles Kingsley's *The Water-Babies*.

"...We should first comment on Coal City..."
This is from Jules Verne's *Les Indes Noires*.

"...The remarkable underground world extending from the New Aberfoyle caverns..."
The New Aberfoyle caverns appear in Jules Verne's *Les Indes Noires*.

"...The cave-world of the Roman State..."
This is from Joseph O'Neill's *Land Under England*.

Page 167. "...Equally-elusive Brigadoon..."
Brigadoon is from Alan Jay Lerner's musical *Brigadoon* (1947). Brigadoon is a Scottish village whose inhabitants awake only one day every century. Lerner based *Brigadoon* on Friedrich Gerstäcker's short story "Germelshausen" (*Secret and Eerie Stories*, 1862). Gerstäcker's original story was considerably darker than *Brigadoon* and was about a German village.

"...Airfowlness, on Scotland's western coast where what seem to be courts or parliaments of sea birds are held annually..."
Airfowlness is from Charles Kingsley's *The Water-Babies*. Airfowlness is the location where thousands of hooded crows hold their yearly parliament, to boast of what they had done the previous year and to bring one of their own to trial.

"...Or Coradine, the fascinating matriarchal settlement up to the north of Scotland..."
Coradine is from W.H. Hudson's *A Crystal Age*. Coradine is a kind of utopia set in northern Scotland.

"...The more evasive settlements, such as the place known as the Glittering Plain, which also has a second, secret name, the speaking of which is forbidden, but which is, reputedly, 'The Acre of the Undying.'"
The Glittering Plain, a.k.a. The Acre of the Undying, is from William Morris' novel *The Story of the Glittering Plain which has also been called the Land of Living Men or the Acre of the Undying* (1891). The Glittering Plain is a kingdom on the coast of northern Scotland. Those who enter the valley are granted immortality, but after this they may never leave.

"...The City of Ayesha..."
Ayesha and her city Kôr are from H. Rider Haggard's *She*. Ayesha is She-Who-Must-Be-Obeyed, the immortal goddess of the African city Kôr.

"...A remote isle to the North of Scotland, famous for its wreckers and its pirates, called the Isle of Ransom."
The Isle of Ransom is from *The Story of the Glittering Plain*.

"...The fateful expedition to The Blazing World..."
The Blazing World is from *Observations upon Experimental Philosophy. To which is added the Description of a New Blazing World*.

Page 169. "Landed in Philomela's kingdom..."
This is a reference to Samuel Gott's utopian *Novae Solymae libri sex* (*Nova Solyma, the Ideal City, or Jerusalem Regained*, 1648), in which Philomela robs and murders her guests as described here. *New Jerusalem* is, though, about a Christian utopia.

"We passed by the Capa Blanca Isles, where bullfighting occurs, a beastly sport which some animal-lover really should persuade them to abandon."
The Capa Blanca Isles appear in Hugh Lofting's novel *The Voyages of Doctor Dolittle* (1923). In that novel Dr. John Dolittle persuades the bulls to chase a matador from the slaughter ring and then perform various tricks, winning the crowd and causing the abolition of bullfighting. However, the events of *The Voyages of Doctor Dolittle* take place, according to the narrator, "many years ago," and so bullfighting must

have made a comeback between the time of Dolittle's visit and Mina's visit, which takes place in the 1930s. (See the notes to Page 159.)

"Further south was Mayda, Island of the Seven Cities..."
Mayda, Island of the Seven Cities, appears in Washington Irving's travelogue *The Alhambra* (1832). Mayda is inhabited by the descendants of Portuguese who fled Portugal in 734 to escape the Moors. Mayda's cathedrals are built of basalt and decorated with many golden ornaments.

"...Nor upon Nut Island, though we saw that island's fishermen, Nutanauts..."
Nut Island and the Nutanauts come from Lucian of Samosata's *True History* (Second century C.E.). *The True History* has accounts of places on Earth but is notable for being the earliest science fiction space travel novel.

"East lay the coast of Coromandel, a small independent country on the edge of Portugal, where was raised the castle of a locally-famed nobleman, the Yonghi-Bonghi of Bo."
There is a real Coromandel, the southeastern coastal region of India, but this Coromandel is the fictional one, with the Yonghi-Bonghi of Bo from Edward Lear's "The Courtship of Yonghy-Bonghy-Bò" (*Laughable Lyrics*, 1877), one of Lear's great nonsense rhymes.

"...An Isle called Lanternland..."
Lanternland, and the glowing Lords and Ladies, are from the anonymously written *Le Voyage de Navigation que Fist Panurge, Disciple de Pantagruel* (*The Journey of Panurge, Disciple of Pantagruel*, 1538), and then again in François Rabelais' satire *Le Cinquiesme et Dernier Livre des Faicts et Dicts du Bon Pantagruel* (*The Fifth and Final Book of the Deeds and Sayings of the Good Pantagruel*, 1564). Gargantua was a giant of medieval Celtic and Gallic legend which Rabelais adapted for his satirical works, which hold up surprisingly well as comedy.

"We found an Isle called Lanternland by some..."
Prospero's journal entries are often (and appropriately) in Shakespearean iambic pentameter, albeit slightly off the ten-beat line.

The first two sentences of Prospero's entry can therefore be broken down like so:

> We found an Isle called Lanternland by some
> Where great Demosthenes burned midnight oil
> And putting in to shore at my command
> Upon its soil saw men to glow-worms turned;
> Each Lord and Lady dressed with glass and gem
> That caught the shine of wanton candle-flame.
> Jewelled crest and diamond hem, blazing they pass
> No two the same, their radiance near divine.

"Not far away an oracle is found; a bottle in a crypt upon an isle where did sweet Bachus make a vineyard grow. The bottle speaketh with a cracking sound, and I did like its augurs not at all."
The Oracle in the Bottle is from Rabelais' *The Fifth and Final Book of the Deeds and Sayings of the Good Pantagruel.*

"...Past the Lotus-Eater's land of yellow sand and endless afternoon..."
The Island of the Lotus-Eaters appears in Homer's *Odyssey* (circa Ninth century B.C.E.), while the *lotophagi* (lotus eaters) also appear in Herodotus' *The Histories* (circa 430 B.C.E.). The "yellow sand" and "endless afternoon" is a reference to Alfred, Lord Tennyson's "The Lotus-Eaters" (1832), in which the island is described as seeming "always afternoon" and having "yellow sand." The Lotus Eaters feed on lotus blooms and so forget the cares and concerns of mortals.

"...Ogygia too we passed..."
Ogygia is from Homer's *Odyssey*. Ogygia was the island on which the nymph Calypso lived.

"...This ring-shaped island, that is called only 'Her'..."
The island of Her and its silent swan are from Alfred Jarry's *Gestes et Opinions du Docteur Faustroll, Pataphysicien* (*Gestures and Opinions of Dr. Faustroll, Pataphysician*, 1911). Jarry's absurdist work is scabrous, foul, and brilliant.

"...A Cyclops is, one of that fearsome breed whereof Odysseus spake..."
In the *Odyssey* Odysseus outwits a Cyclops.

"...Past the Imaginary Isle..."
The Imaginary Isle is from Anne Marie Louise Henriette d'Orléans, Duchesse de Montpensier's *Rélation de L'Isle Imaginaire* (*Relation of the Imaginary Island*, 1659). *L'Isle Imaginaire* is a utopia burlesquing France.

"...A pois'nous land called the Great Garabagne..."
The Great Garabagne is from Henri Michaux's novel *Voyage en Grande Garabagne* (*Voyage to Grand Garabagne*, 1936). Great Garabagne is a land where each traveller meets his own monsters and despairs.

"Next we came to Aiolio..."
Aiolio appears in the *Odyssey*. Aiolos Hippotades is the King of the Winds and keeps violent winds in ox-skin sacks.

"...The mountain Animas raised up near Soria, where once Knights Templar walked."
The mountain Animas, a.k.a. Monte de las Animas, a.k.a. Mountain of the Spirits, appears in Gustavo Becquer's short story "El Monte de las ánimas" (*Leyendas*, 1871). The Monte de las Animas, or Mountain of the Spirits, was a former stronghold of the Templars before the Castilians slaughtered the Knights.

"Beyond the straits verdant Anostus lay..."
Anostus appears in Claudius Aelianus' *Varia Historia* (second century C.E.).

"Portugal has the republic of Andorra..."
Andorra (the fictional concept, not the real country) is from Max Frisch's *Andorra* (1961), a novel about a violently pro-Christian and anti-Semitic country in the Pyrenees.

"More interestingly, in Spain's La Mancha province, is the landbound island, Barataria, where twenty years before Prospero's voyage a squire named Sancho Panza ruled, albeit only for a week. Not far from Barataria we find a grotto, Montesino's Cave, the sole account of which is that of Panza's master, Don Quixote..."
La Mancha, Barataria, Sancho Panza, Montesino's Cave, and Don Quixote are all from Miguel de Cervantes Saavedra's comedy *El*

Ingenioso Hidalgo Don Quixote de La Mancha (The Ingenious Knight, Don Quixote de la Mancha, 1605-1615).

Page 170. "...The tomb of the hero Durandarte..."
Although the tomb of Durandarte appears in *Don Quixote de La Mancha*, Durandarte is part of medieval Spanish myth and was supposedly killed at the Battle of Roncesvalles, as chronicled in *The Song of Roland.*

"...The willfully eccentric country Exopotomania..."
Exopotomania appears in Boris Vian's *L'Automne à Pékin (The Fall of Peking*, 1956), a novel about a desert utopia.

"Further east is Andrographia..."
Andrographia is from Nicolas Edme Restif de la Bretonne's *L'Andrographe (The Andrographer*, 1782). De la Bretonne was a French author who wrote a little bit of science fiction and a lot of pornography and rubbish.

"...The iron-clad castle of the 16th century sorcerer Atlante..."
Atlante's castle appears in Ludovico Ariosto's *Orlando Furioso* (1516), one of the great medieval epics.

"Next comes a Pyrenean city that apparently cannot be named for reasons of what is puzzlingly described as 'theological security.' Its southern half contains a mansion, Triste-le-Roy, reached by committing murders at the three points of a mystic triangle..."
The city which cannot be named, and the mansion Triste-le-Roy, are from Jorge Luis Borges' short story "La Muerte y la Brújula" ("Death and the Compass," *Ficciones,* 1956). The city cannot be named because to do so would involve uttering the secret name of God.

"...We pass the garrulous land of Auspasia..."
Auspasia, the noisiest and most talkative nation in the world, appears in Georges Duhamel's novels *Lettres d'Auspasie (Letters from Auspasia,* 1922) and *La Dernier Voyage de Candide (The Last Voyage of Candide,* 1938).

"...To reach Bengodi..."

Bengodi, and its Parmesan cheese, appear in Giovanni Boccaccio's *Decameron* (1353), an influential collection of Italian stories, some of which were later used by Chaucer in his *Canterbury Tales*.

"...There are also gemstones unique to Bengodi, including an invisibility-bestowing heliotrope used in the first experiments of Hawley Griffin."

In Wells' *The Invisible Man* there is no evidence of a heliotrope in Griffin's first experiments, although Griffin surely qualifies as an unreliable narrator. By Griffin's own account, he discovers invisibility in this way:

> I will tell you, Kemp, sooner or later, all the complicated processes. We need not go into that now. For the most part, saving certain gaps I chose to remember, they are written in cypher in those books that tramp has hidden. We must hunt him down. We must get those books again. But the essential phase was to place the transparent object whose refractive index was to be lowered between two radiating centres of a sort of ethereal vibration, of which I will tell you more fully later. No, not these Röntgen vibrations—I don't know that these others of mine have been described. Yet they are obvious enough. I needed two little dynamos, and these I worked with a cheap gas engine.

In the 1933 film version of *The Invisible Man* heliotrope is a major ingredient for Griffin.

"...Close to the Balearic Islands is Tryphême..."

Tryphême appears in Pierre Louÿs's novel *Les Aventures du Roi Pausole* (*The Adventures of King Pausole*, 1900). In the novel Tryphême operates much as described here.

"North, within French territory, is Papafiguiera..."

Papafiguiera, or Papefiguiera, is from Béroualde de Verville's *Le Moyen de Parvenir* (*The Way to Succeed*, 1610). *Le Moyen de Parvenir* was one of a number of late Renaissance French menippean (combining prose and verse) satires.

"These include Ptyx, Bran Isle..."
Ptyx and Bran Isle both appear in Alfred Jarry's *Gestes et Opinions du Docteur Faustroll, Pataphysicien.*

"...Clerkship..."
The island of Clerkship appears in François Rabelais' *Le Quart Livre des Faicts et Dicts du Bon Pantagruel (The Fourth Book of the Deeds and Sayings of the Good Pantagruel,* 1552).

"...Laceland..."
Laceland is from Alfred Jarry's *Gestes et Opinions du Docteur Faustroll, Pataphysicien.*

"...Leaveheavenalone..."
The island of Leaveheavenalone is from Kingsley's *The Water Babies.*

"...Breadlessday..."
Breadlessday appears in Rabelais' *The Fifth and Final Book of the Deeds and Sayings of the Good Pantagruel.*

"Amorphous Island..."
Amorphous Island appears in Jarry's *Gestes et Opinions du Docteur Faustroll, Pataphysicien.*

"Ruach, the 'Windy Island'..."
Ruach appears in Rabelais' *The Fourth Book of the Deeds and Sayings of the Good Pantagruel.*

"In between are Cyril Island (a self-propelled volcano that is currently the home of Captain Kidd)..."
Cyril Island is from Jarry's *Gestes et Opinions du Docteur Faustroll, Pataphysicien.*

"...the Fortunate Islands (which include the Isle of Butterflies..."
The Fortunate Islands and the Isle of Butterflies are from *The Journey of Panurge, Disciple of Pantagruel.*

"...Fragrant Island..."
Fragrant Island is from Jarry's *Gestes et Opinions du Docteur Faustroll, Pataphysicien.*

"...The pie-island Pastemolle..."

Pastemolle appears in *The Journey of Panurge, Disciple of Pantagruel*.

"...Thermometer Island..."

Thermometer Island appears in Denis Diderot's *Les Bijoux Indiscrets* (*The Indiscreet Jewels*, 1748). Diderot, the famous encyclopedist and philosopher, also wrote erotica, which *Les Bijoux Indiscrets* is.

"...The flower-carpeted peninsula of Flora..."

Flora appears in Ferdinand Raimund's "The Bound Imagination" (*Sämtliche Werke*, 1837), a dramatic fairytale.

"North is Lubec, a town in south Provence founded by colonists from Thermometer Island, with all the genital peculiarities so common in that place."

Lubec is from Béroualde de Verville's *Le Moyen de Parvenir*. The textual link between de Verville's work and Diderot's is Moore's invention. In Lubec, as mentioned, the genitalia of men are removed and stored in the Town Hall. On Thermometer Island the genitalia of men and women are peculiarly and geometrically shaped, but not removed.

"Trinquelage..."

The castle of Trinquelage appears in Alphonse Daudet's *Lettres de Mon Moulin* (*Letters From My Windmill*, 1866), a collection of mostly humorous stories about Daudet's native Provence.

"...To the west is Nameless Castle..."

Nameless Castle is from Denis Diderot's *Jacques le Fataliste et Son Maître* (*Jacques the Fatalist and His Master*, 1796), a comedy about a servant and his master.

"...The kingdom of Poictesme, guarded by the Fellows of the Silver Stallion."

Poictesme appears in the works of James Branch Cabell, most notably *Jurgen* (1919), in which the Fellowship of the Silver Stallion appears. *Jurgen* is a brilliant satirical comedy set in a fantasy Europe.

"A like-named group exists in modern Nimes..."

I am unaware of another Fellowship of the Silver Stallion aside from Cabell's.

"Further west, in what is now Auvergne, we have a medieval province that shared borders with Poictesme, known as Averoigne."
Averoigne is from the outstanding stories of Clark Ashton Smith, among which was "A Rendezvous in Averoigne" (*Weird Tales*, April/May 1931). Averoigne is one of the locations of Smith's fantasy stories.

"...The subterranean Grande Euscarie..."
Grande Euscarie appears in Luc Alberny's *Le Mammoth Bleu* (*The Blue Mammoth*, 1935), a novel about a subterranean world.

"...Where the buried kingdoms of the Fatipuffs and Thinnifers are found."
The kingdoms of the Fattipuffs and the Thinnifers appear in André Maurois' *Patapoufs et Filifers* (1930), part of Maurois' juvenalia.

"...We find Baron Hugh's Castle..."
Baron Hugh's Castle appears in the 1942 film *Les Visiteurs du Soir* (*The Visitors in the Evening*), a romance about two minstrels sent by the Devil to tempt the desperate and unwary.

"...The modest and agrarian republic Calejava, founded by one Dr. Ava in the 1600s upon communitarian ideals, described by Mina Murray in her journal notes as 'scrupulously fair; screamingly dull.'"
Calejava and Dr. Ava are from Claude Gilbert's *Histoire de Calejava* (*History of Calejava*, 1700). The reason that Mina finds Calejava so dull is that there are no forms at all of entertainment in Calejava, it being a communitarian, work-oriented utopia.

"...The sunken city Belesbat..."
There is a real Belesbat, a castle in Boutigny in France, but this is a reference to the murderous Belesbat, in Claire Kenin's novel *La Mer Mystérieuse* (*The Mysterious Sea*, 1923).

"...A separate sunken city (named by its discoverers as, simply, 'Disappeared')..."
The sunken city of Disappeared appears in Victor Hugo's short story "La Ville disparue" ("The Disappeared City," *La Légende des Siècles*, 1859).

"...The Atlantean colony, Atlanteja..."
Atlanteja appears in Luigi Motta's *Il Tunnel Sottomarino* (*The Undersea Tunnel*, 1927), a Vernean novel of piracy and undersea adventure.

"...Outposts of the Streaming Kingdom..."
The Streaming Kingdom, mentioned on Page 162, appears in Jules Supervielle's *L'Enfant de la Haute Mers*.

"...We passed above Le Douar..."
Le Douar appears in the novel *L'Enigme du "Redoutable"* (*The Enigma of the "Redoubtable,"* 1930) by J.H. Rosny (jeune).

Page 171. "...We saw the Isle of Boredom..."
The Island of Boredom appears in Marie Anne de Roumier Robert's *Les Ondins* (*The Water Sprites*, 1768), a *voyage imaginaire*.

"...We saw Magic Maiden's Rock..."
Magic Maiden's Rock appears in Vasco de Lobeira's *Amadis de Gaula* (*Amadis of Gaul*, 1350-1508), one of the greatest of the Iberian epics and the work responsible for Don Quixote's madness.

"...We passed Realism Island..."
Realism Island is from G.K. Chesterton's "Introductory: On Gargoyles" (*Alarms and Discursions*, 1910), Chesterton's essay criticizing Realism in art.

"We carried on past Cork (not Cork in Ireland, obviously) that Lucian described."
The island of Cork appears in Lucian of Samosata's *True History*.

"The first is Alca, where the native penguins were transformed to humans by the Angel Gabriel..."
The island of Alca appears in Daniel Defoe's *The Further Adventures of Robinson Crusoe* (1724). This was Defoe's sequel to *Robinson Crusoe*. The penguins and the Angel Gabriel appear in Anatole France's *L'Ile des Pingouins* (*Penguin Island*, 1908), which made use of Alca.

"...The former Isle of Asbefore, once part of an archipelago, with its fellow islands (Farapart, Jumptoit, Incognito) now seemingly sunken; Asbefore has known only one incident of interest, this being a successfully repelled invasion by a group of turkey hunters from the town of Bang-Bang-Turkey..."

The islands of Asbefore, Farapart, Jumptoit, and Incognito and the city of Bang-Bang-Turkey all appear in Jacques Prévert's *Lettre des Îles Baladar* (*Letter from the Baladar Islands*, 1952), one of his books for children.

"...The mouth of the Atlantic tunnel..."

The trans-Atlantic tunnel appears in Luigi Motta's *The Undersea Tunnel*.

"Further inland is Brocéliande forest..."

The forest of Brocéliande is mentioned on Page 162 above.

"Next we reach Banoic..."

In Arthurian myth Banoic, a.k.a. Benwick, was the home of King Ban and his son, Launcelot.

"...This area was subsumed in the Hurlubierean Empire..."

The empire of Hurlubiere appears in Charles Nodier's *Hurlubleu, Grand Manifafa d'Hurlubiere* (1822), a satire of philosophy.

"...Is the proposed site of the city Morphopolis..."

Morphopolis appears in Maurice Barrère's novel *La Cité du Sommeil* (*The City of Sleep*, 1909). The site is "proposed" because the events of *The City of Sleep* take place in 1950, and *The New Traveller's Almanac* was written in 1931.

"...The eight-sided Abbey of Theleme..."

The Abbey appears in François Rabelais' *La Vie Très Horrifique du Grand Gargantua* (*The Very Horrific Life of the Great Gargantua*, 1534). The scandalous magician and writer Aleister Crowley (1875-1947) took "do as thou wilt shall be the whole of the law," his famous motto, from Rabelais, and followers of Crowley sometimes use the term "thelemic" to describe themselves.

"...The giant Gargantua, who, amongst other things, provided Paris with its name during the 16th century, when he discharged the contents of his massive bladder. The luckless citizens were washed away or drowned by a great flood of urine that poured steaming from the much-relieved colossus, who, when he viewed the destruction his emission had provoked, could not contain his mirth. At this, those who'd survived the deluge angrily cried, 'Look! He's drowned us *par ris* (for a laugh),' with the unlucky city known as Paris ever after."

This event occurred in François Rabelais' *Gargantua and Pantagruel* (1532). In Chapter 17 of the First Book we read:

> And they pressed so hard upon him that he was constrained to rest himself upon the towers of Our Lady's Church. At which place, seeing so many about him, he said with a loud voice, I believe that these buzzards will have me to pay them here my welcome hither, and my Proficiat. It is but good reason. I will now give them their wine, but it shall be only in sport. Then smiling, he untied his fair braguette, and drawing out his mentul into the open air, he so bitterly all-to-bepissed them, that he drowned two hundred and sixty thousand, four hundred and eighteen, besides the women and little children. Some, nevertheless, of the company escaped this piss-flood by mere speed of foot, who, when they were at the higher end of the university, sweating, coughing, spitting, and out of breath, they began to swear and curse, some in good hot earnest, and others in jest. Carimari, carimara: golynoly, golynolo. By my sweet Sanctess, we are washed in sport, a sport truly to laugh at;—in French, Par ris, for which that city hath been ever since called.

"...Such as the Amran period, when France was Aquilonia and was ruled briefly by a Swedish warrior-king named Amra, though some suggest this was a nickname meaning 'lion' or 'lionheart.'"

Amra, Aquilonia, and the Swedish warrior-king are all from the "Conan" stories of Robert E. Howard. The "Swedish warrior-king" is Conan, who gained the name "Amra," or "the lion," while pirating with the Shemitish she-devil Bêlit.

"...The cruel Melnibonean empire, these remains including the corroded hilt of a black sword..."

The Melnibonean empire and the black sword are from the Elric of Melnibonè books of Michael Moorcock. The black sword is Stormbringer, the soul-sucking blade of Elric.

"Like most French cities, Paris has its own 'Parthenion Town,' bordello districts with permitted, regulated prostitution."
Parthenion Town is from Nicolas Edme Restif de la Bretonne's *Le Pornographe* (*The Pornographer*, 1769). Restif is commonly credited with coining the terms "pornographer" and "pornography."

"Less graspable is Neverreachhereland..."
Neverreachhereland appears in André Dhôtel's *Les Pays Où L'On N'Arrive Jamais* (*The Country One Never Reaches*, 1955), a novel about a lost teenager seeking to return to Neverreachhereland.

"Beneath the city's Opera House exist the caves where in 1881 the deranged and hideous 'Phantom' carried out his crimes."
The Opera House and the Phantom appear in Gaston Leroux's novel *The Phantom of the Opera* (1911).

"In 1913, Mina Murray and her second extraordinary league..."
The "second extraordinary League" will appear in future *League* series.

"...Their French counterparts Les Hommes Mysterieux..."
As the following list of characters indicates, French popular fiction is filled with characters who would easily qualify for a French League. The best guides in English to them are Jean-Marc and Randy Lofficier's *French Science Fiction, Fantasy, Horror and Pulp Fiction* (2000), the Lofficiers' *Shadowmen* (2003), and my *Encyclopedia of Fantastic Victoriana* (forthcoming, 2005) and *Encyclopedia of Pulp Heroes* (forthcoming, 2006). The groups may have gotten their name from the first chapter of Arnould Galopin's *Le Docteur Oméga*: "L'Homme Mystérieux."

"...Aeronaut Jean Robur..."
Robur, mentioned in passing in the first *League* series, is the aeronaut hero of Jules Verne's novel *Robur the Conqueror* (1887) and then the megalomaniacal villain of Verne's *The Master of the World* (1904).

"...The frightening night-sighted Nyctalope..."
The Nyctalope was created by "Jean de La Hire," a.k.a. Adolphe d'Espie De La Hire, and appears in a series of novels from 1908 through the mid-1950s, beginning with *L'Homme Qui Peut Vivre Dans L'Eau* (*The Man Who Could Live in the Water*, 1908). The Nyctalope was the first real super-hero of French pulp literature, having super-powers—he could see in the dark and had an artificial heart—and a group of faithful assistants.

"...Just prior to A.J. shooting him..."
The identity of "A.J." is revealed in the notes to Page 192, below.

"...Their disputed 'Jean Valjean' graffiti..."
Jean Valjean is from Victor Hugo's novel *Les Misérables* (1862).

"..The Graveyard of Unwritten Books, in chambers under the Hotel de Sens..."
The Graveyard of Unwritten Books beneath the Hôtel de Sens was created by the Turkish writer Nedim Gürsel and appears in the novel *Son Tramway* (*His Tram*, 1900). The Graveyard, also known as the "Well of Locks," is the home of all books forbidden by authorities across the world.

"...Just outside Paris lies Lofoten Cemetery, with its crows grown fat on human flesh and its reported spectres."
Lofoten Cemetery appears in the symbolist poet Oscar Venceslas de Lubicz Milosz's *Les Sept solitudes, poèmes* (*The Seven Solitudes, Poems*, 1906). The crows of Lofoten feed on the cold flesh of the recently dead and have grown quite fat on this diet. The spectres are of the dead, who are, according to some, less dead than some famous living people.

"Nearby there is Montmorency, where the scientist Martial Canterel maintains his villa, Locus Solus, with its many wonderful inventions."
Martial Canterel and Locus Solus are from Raymond Roussel's novel *Locus Solus* (1914). Canterel is an inventor and scientist who creates several remarkable inventions, including two formulae for resurrecting corpses.

"Les Hommes Mysterieux"
"The Mysterious Men." See the notes to Page 172 below.

Page 172. "Also near Paris is the city Fluorescente, built on avant-garde philosophies."
Fluorescente was created by noted Dadaist Tristan Tzara and appears in *Grains et Issues* (*Grains and Exits*, 1935).

"...Yet another subterranean site, this being the notorious Suicide City. This dismal refuge of the world's failed suicides was found during 1912 Police investigations of an underground rail line between Bastille and Vincennes, and was allegedly founded by survivors of London's notorious Suicide Club, disbanded 1882."
Suicide City appears in José Muñoz Escamez's *La Ciudad de los Suicidas* (*The City of the Suicides*, 1912). Escamez wrote the novel as an informal sequel to Robert Louis Stevenson's "The Suicide Club" (*London*, June-October 1878).

"...We come to Etretat and Hollow Needle, cave-lair of Arsene Lupin."
Etretat is a naturally formed spindle of rock off the coast of Normandy. In Maurice LeBlanc's novel *L'Aiguille Creuse* (*The Hollow Needle*, 1909), Arsène Lupin uses a cave inside the spindle, which he calls "the Hollow Needle," as his secret hideout. LeBlanc's Arsène Lupin is the foremost example in English and French literature of the gentleman thief.

"As with his rival Fantomas..."
Fantômas, the Lord of Terror, the Genius of Evil, appears in a series of stories and novels in the 1910s by Pierre Souvestre and Marcel Allain. Fantômas is a brilliant and utterly ruthless Parisian crime lord whose crimes are ingenious in their evil.
The "Les Hommes Mysterieux" illustration on Page 171 shows five members of the French version of the League. From left to right they are as follows:

- The woman is only a statue that references nothing.
- The standing man is Fantômas. He is in the same disguise he wore in the 1913 Louis Feiullade-directed film serial *Juve contre Fantômas*.
- The character seated in the boat and wearing a full-face mask is the Nyctalope.

- The standing man, wearing a tuxedo and top hat, is Arsène Lupin.
- The man holding a rifle is Jean Robur. His outfit is similar to the one worn by Vincent Price in the 1961 film *Master of the World*.
- The odd, floppy armed creature running in the right side of the panel is a Martian from Arnould Galopin's *Le Docteur Oméga*. *Le Docteur Oméga*, mentioned in the notes to Page 68, Panel 2, is about Doctor Omega, an inventor-adventurer, who goes to Mars and fights various Martians, some of whom are quite like the one seen here.

"Further north is Quiquendone, on the Escaut in Flanders, where in 1870 a deranged engineer named Dr. Ox turned townsfolk into violent beasts with side effects from gas-lighting experiments."
Quiquendone and Dr. Ox are from Jules Verne's novel *Une Fantasie du Docteur Ox* (*A Fantasy of Dr. Ox*, 1874). Quiquendone was the location Dr. Ox chose in which to install a modernized lighting system, with unfortunate results.

"Dr. Ox, believed dead, was in fact admitted to a nearby township, Expiation City, built for purposes of ethical atonement and said to have aided in the rehabilitation of various master villains."
Expiation City appears in P.S. Ballanches' *La Ville des Expiations* (*The City of Expiations*, 1907). In the novel Expiation City is a dictatorship created for the sole purpose of social re-education and the atonement of moral and spiritual weaknesses. The novel does not mention specific master villains who have sought expiation.

"North, the castle of the murderer Bluebeard stood..."
Bluebeard and his castle appear in Charles Perrault's "La Barbe Bleue" ("The Blue Beard," 1697). The traditional story of Bluebeard is that he would take a young wife and eventually murder her, with Bluebeard's last wife discovering this awful fact and seeing to Bluebeard's death.

"...Further south was the retreat of the deformed noble called 'The Beast.'"
The Beast, of the legend (also novels, films, television shows, and films) of Beauty and the Beast was created by Marie Leprince de Beaumont and appears in "La Belle et La Bête" ("The Beauty and the Beast," 1757).

"Eastwards lie two demolished fortresses, one home to an inbred Royal family cursed by cataleptic fits, with lovely Princess Rosamund as the most famous sufferer."

"Princess Rosamund" is better known as "Princess Rosamond," or the "Sleeping Beauty" of folk legend. Moore may also be bringing in the sleep-prone Princess Rosamond from George MacDonald's fairy tale *The Wise Woman, a Parable* (1875).

"The other fort, Carabas Castle, had been previously called Ogre Castle until the ogre was provoked into transforming into a mouse and promptly eaten by a talking feline dressed in striking footwear."

Carabas Castle appears in Charles Perrault's "Le Maître Chat ou Le Chat Botté" ("The Master Cat or the Boot-Wearing Cat," 1697). The ogre was taunted into this transformation by the talking feline in striking footwear, otherwise known as Puss-in-Boots.

"...Alleged to have been made by Merlin for the great knight Tristan. Called the Fountain of Love..."

This is a reference to Thomas Bulfinch's *Legends of Charlemagne, or, Romance of the Middle Ages* (1862), in which Bulfinch describes "two fountains, the one constructed by the sage Merlin, who designed it for Tristram and the fair Isoude."

"Xiros, further east, is a notoriously haunting land..."

Xiros was created by Jorge Luis Borges and appears in "El Zahir."

"Westward, Devil's Island was ruled by the giant Bandaguido, with his daughter Bandaguida and their child, until the dynasty was overthrown in the 3rd century A.D."

Devil's Island, Bandaguido, and Bandaguida are from *Amadis of Gaul*.

"Nearby is Abdera, famous for its devotion to the horse..."

Abdera is a part of traditional Greek and Roman myth, appearing in (among other places) the *Physiologus Latinus* (Fourth century B.C.E.), a bestiary of antiquity.

"Lemuel Gulliver's margin-notes conjecture that the banished intellectual horses of Abdera may have sired the Houyhnhms..."

The Houyhnhms are talking horses of human intelligence who appear in Jonathan Swift's *Gulliver's Travels*.

"...We find the ruins of the morbid city Ptolemais, bordered by the Charonian Canal..."
Ptolemais and the Charonian Canal appear in Edgar Allan Poe's "Shadow: A Parable" (*Phantasy Pieces*, v1, 1842), one of Poe's shorter and creepier works.

"...While over Phlegra are the floating remnants of the avian citadel Cloudcuckooland, founded by Pesithetaerus in 400 B.C."
Cloudcuckooland and Pesithetaerus appear in Aristophanes' play *The Birds* (414 B.C.E.). Pesithetaerus was an Athenian who founded the floating fortress Cloudcuckooland. It was intended to be a keep for birds of all species, but they ended up using it to starve the gods into submission and lay claim to rulership over the world.

"Westwards are still more islands. Aiaia, Circe's island, is amongst the most well-known, along with Scylla and Charybdis (now without their monstrous dwellers) and the Wandering Rocks, a group of now-unmoving islands that were said once to have clashed together, as remarked on by Captains Ulysses and Jason. Also popular is Siren Island..."
All of these refer to places and characters from Greek myths.

"Not far off, the volcanic isle Pyrallis..."
Pyrallis appears in Pliny the Elder's *Inventorum Natura* (*Natural History*, First century C.E.), one of the first great encyclopedic works.

"Below Mediterranean waters we find the Arabian Tunnel leading to the Red Sea, its existence proved by Nemo, Sikh submariner, who released marked fish in the Gulf of Suez, these fish later turning up near Syria."
The Arabian Tunnel, Nemo, and the experiment with marked fish are all from Jules Verne's *20,000 Leagues Under the Sea*.

"The tunnel's length comes close to intersecting with another shaft, this being the Arcadian Tunnel linking Greece with Italy, once said to be the haunt of satyrs and reserved for bitterly unhappy lovers..."
The Arcadian Tunnel first appears in Jacopo Sannazaro's *Arcadia* (1501), a pastoral idyll.

"...We're near the Straits of Otranto and the castle of the same name, empty since the 18th century, when it was plagued by apparitions, which included a giant helmet covered with black plumage."

The Castle of Otranto appears in Horace Walpole's *The Castle of Otranto* (1765), one of the earliest and greatest of the Gothic novels.

"Further north is Portiuncula..."
Portiuncula, where visitors go to recapture something lost in their past, appears in Stefan Andres' *Die Reise Nach Portiuncula* (*The Trip to Portiuncula*, 1954).

"...While under Italy we find Meloria Canal..."
Meloria Canal is from Emilio Salgari's *I Naviganti Della Meloria* (*The Seamen of Meloria*, 1903), one of Salgari's many novels of nautical adventure.

"Across Italy rotted webs of string are found, complex and covering several acres, remnants of the mobile town Ersilia..."
Ersilia is from Italo Calvino's *Le Città Invisibili* (*The Invisible Cities*, 1972), in which Marco Polo tells Kublai Khan about several fabulous cities in the Khan's empire.

Page 173. "In Torelore on Italy's west coast..."
Torelore appears in *Aucassin et Nicolette* (*Aucassin and Nicolette*, Fourteenth century C.E.), one of the greatest of all medieval romances.

"Islands nearby include the one where Prospero, his daughter and his spirits dwelled in 1600."
Prospero and his island are from Shakespeare's *The Tempest*.

"Ennasin Island, close to Sicily..."
Ennasin Island is from François Rabelais' *The Fourth Book of the Deeds and Sayings of the Good Pantagruel*.

"...While nearby lie the industrious island of the Busy Bees..."
The island of the Busy Bees is from Carlo Collodi's *The Adventures of Pinocchio* (1883).

"...The Island of the Day Before..."
The Island of the Day Before appears in Umberto Eco's novel of the same name, *The Island of the Day Before* (1994). In Eco's novel the Island of the Day Before is in the Pacific, on the other side of the International Date Line, hence the name of the island.

"Back on the mainland, in the Apennines we find the ruined Abbey of the Rose..."
The Abbey of the Rose is from Umberto Eco's *The Name of the Rose* (1980), a mystery set in the Fourteenth century.

"...And the ill-famed Castle of Udolpho..."
The Castle of Udolpho is from Mrs. Ann Radcliffe's *The Mysteries of Udolpho* (1794), one of the greatest of all Gothic novels.

"...The hill-top town of Pocapaglia..."
Pocapaglia appears in *Fiabe Italiane* (*Italian Fables*, compiled by Italo Calvino, 1956), a collection of local Italian fables.

"...Switzerland and prosperous Goldenthal..."
The fictional places of Switzerland and Goldenthal appear in Johann Heinrich Daniel Zschokke's *Das Goldmacherdorf* (*The Village of the Gold Maker*, 1817), a fairytale which was influential in the German *dorfgeschichte*, or "village stories," movement of the 1840s.

"...The snow-swept realm of King Astralgus and his alpine spirits..."
The realm of King Astralgus (or Astragalus) appears in Ferdinand Raimund's *Der Alpenkönig und Der Menschenfeind* (*The Mountain King and the Misanthrope*, 1928), a comedic fairytale play.

"While south upon the Austrian border is the Balbrigian and Bouloulabassian United Republic..."
The Balbrigian and Bouloulabassian United Republic appears in Max Jacob's *Histoire du Roi Kaboul Ier et du Marmiton Gauwain* (*The History of King Kaboul the 1st and the Marmiton Gauwain*, 1903), a symbolist fairytale.

"...Perhaps the smallest and most socially retarded country in the world, the Duchy of Grand Fenwick, founded in the 17th century by Sir Roger Fenwick, his insufferable Englishness preserved in both the Duchy's language and its customs. European commentators, while surprised by Grand Fenwick's continuing survival, feel the Duchy will hang on as long as it doesn't do anything ridiculous such as declaring war on the United States."

The Duchy of Grand Fenwick appears in Leonard Wibberley's novel *The Mouse that Roared* (1954) and its several sequels. In *The Mouse that Roared* the Duchy of Grand Fenwick, bankrupted by cheap California wine, declares war on the United States in the hope that reparation funds from the U.S. will save Grand Fenwick.

"Fenwick should not be confused with the nearby Grand Duchy..."
The Grand Duchy first appears in E.T.A. Hoffmann's *Der Goldene Topf* (*The Golden Pot*, 1814) but was featured in several of Hoffmann's works. *The Golden Pot* is about the war for the soul of a hapless young student.

"...Famous for its feline prodigy, Murr Cat (a relative of the boot-wearing cat who ruled Carabas Castle in Ardennes)."
The Murr Cat appears in E.T.A. Hoffmann's *The Life and Opinions of the Tomcat Murr* (1820). The link between Murr and Puss-in-Boots appears in the original novel.

"Zaches came from the alpine village of Weng..."
Although Zaches appears in Hoffmann's *The Golden Pot*, Weng is from Thomas Bernhard's *Frost* (1963). The textual link between the two is Moore's invention.

"...West of Munich lies delightful woodland where our coachman said a place known as 'The Wood Between the Worlds' was sometimes found..."
The Wood Between the Worlds appears in C.S. Lewis' *The Magician's Nephew* (1955), one of Lewis' *Chronicles of Narnia* novels.

"Nearby stood Runenberg..."
Runenberg is from Ludwig Tieck's "Der Runenberg" (*Taschenbuch für Kunst und Laune*, 1804), a fable about a young man who ventures too far on to a mountain and meets the fairy Woodwoman.

"...Our eventual destination, Horselberg..."
Horselberg, a.k.a. Venusberg, is from Richard Wagner's opera *Tannhäuser* (1845), although the more erotic elements were added by Aubrey Beardsley in his *Under the Hill* (1897).

"I much preferred to witness how Queen Venus makes her unicorn Adolphe sing each morning..."
Queen Venus masturbates Adolphe.

"...We find the remarkable city of holes, Cittabella..."
Cittabella was created by Lia Wainstein and appears in the novel *Viaggio in Drimonia* (1965).

"...And the nearby Nexdorea..."
Nexdorea is from Tom Hood's *Petsetilla's Posy* (1870), a fairytale much influenced by *Alice in Wonderland*.

"Northwest lies the deserted Palace of Prince Prospero, no relative to our Duke of Milan, with its seven different-coloured chambers, that was devastated by an outbreak of the Red Death in the 16th century."
The Palace of Prince Prospero is from Edgar Allan Poe's short story "The Masque of the Red Death" (*Graham's Magazine*, May 1842).

"...We pass the troubling police-state of Meccania..."
Meccania appears in Gregory Owen's novel *Meccania, the Super-State* (1918). Meccania is troubling because it is a state completely regimented and controlled by the government—the ultimate in totalitarian dystopias.

"...And come to Micromona..."
Micromona was created by Karl Immerman and appears in *Tulifäntchen, Ein Heldengedicht in drei Gesängen* (*Tulifäntchen, a Hero Poem in Three Songs*, 1830), a verse satire.

"...Percy left us at the border and went on to nearby Silling Castle (owned by some nobles saved by Percy from the guillotine)."
Silling Castle is from Donatien-Alphonse-François, Marquis de Sade's novel *120 Days of Sodom* (1785). The implication of this passage is that the noblemen Percy saved from the guillotine are the four noblemen who are the protagonists of *120 Days of Sodom*.

"...Suggested we should head on to Cockaigne, sometimes known as Cuccagna..."
Cockaigne/Cuccagna is from the *Le Dit de Cocagne* (*The Sayings of Cocagne*, Thirteenth century C.E.) and then Marc-Antoine Le Grand's

Le Roi de Cocagne (*The King of Cocagne*, 1719). Cocagne, or Cockaigne, is the French equivalent of Utopia. In the Middle Ages numerous Cocagne myths were told about "a land of fabled abundance, with food and drink for the asking."

"On our last day we visited a builders that exported houses made of food (cottages of gingerbread and such) to other parts of Germany." Although *Le Dit de Cocagne* and *Le Roi de Cocagne* certainly refer to houses made of food, the allusion to the story of Hansel and Gretel is Moore's creation, rather than being in either work.

"Also in Germany is Mummelsee, a supernatural lake providing entrance to the subterranean realm of Centrum Terrae..." Mummelsee and the Centrum Terrae appear in Johann Hans Jakob Christoffel von Grimmelshausen's *Der Abenteuerliche Simplicissimus Teutsch* (*The Adventurous Simplicissimus Teutsch*, 1668), a picaresque novel about a soldier's life.

"Or perhaps a trip to Nuremberg might be in order. Here, in Presidential antechambers, is a curious wardrobe granting access to the otherworldly 'Kingdom of the Dolls.'" The wardrobe and the Kingdom of the Dolls first appear, in very alien (to modern eyes) form, in E.T.A. Hoffmann's "The Nutcracker and the King of the Mice" (*Die Serapionsbruder*, 1818-1821), and then in a softened form in Alexandre Dumas (père)'s "The Nutcracker of Nuremberg " (*Histoire d'une Cassenoisette*, 1845). These both form the basis for the modern Nutcracker ballet. As far as I know C.S. Lewis' use of a similar wardrobe, in *The Lion, the Witch, and the Wardrobe*, was coincidental.

"It was from this strange realm, or areas adjacent, that an apple pip was taken and used to grown the privately-kept tree within Kew Gardens mentioned in our last installment." This is the answer to the reference on Page 165: "...a hand-written note refers the reader to an apple-tree currently being grown as a government project at Kew Gardens..." Kew Gardens is a real place in Surrey, and is home to the Royal Botanical Gardens, which are home to a range of conservation programs dedicated to the preservation of endangered plants.

"...we find the subterranean haunt of vagrants known as Under River, and, nearby, a ruined mansion called the Black House, both locations famous only in the psychiatric history of a violet-eyed young derelict who turned up in 1907, out of nowhere. Alienists were fascinated by the detail of the man's delusions, which concerned a sprawling castle to which he was heir, its architecture and its rituals described so vividly that many still believe his 'Castle Gormenghast' exists, although no trace was ever found."

Under River and Black House both appear in Mervyn Peake's novel *Titus Alone* (1959). The violet-eyed young man and Castle Gormenghast are from Peake's Gormenghast trilogy of novels: *Titus Groan* (1946), *Gormenghast* (1950), and *Titus Alone*. The violet-eyed young man is Titus Groan, the seventy-seventh Earl of Gormenghast, who adventures through the vast, crumbling city-castle of Gormenghast.

"Northward lies Auenthal, home of author Maria Wuz..."

Auenthal and Maria Wuz appear in Johann Paul Friedrich Richter's *Leben des vergnügten Schulmeisterlein Maria Wuz in Auenthal* (*Life of the Happy Schoolmarm Maria Wuz in Auenthal*, 1793), one of the foremost novels of the German Romantic period.

"Pierre Menard, second to chronicle the history of Don Quixote, was influenced by Wuz..."

Pierre Menard appears in Jorge Luis Borges' "Pierre Menard, Author of Don Quixote" (1939), a fictional essay about Menard, a French symbolist who wants to create his own version of *Don Quixote* and does so by copying Cervantes' *Don Quixote* word-for-word.

Page 174. "Still further north is Berlin, near the Falun Fault..."

The Falun Fault appears in E.T.A. Hoffmann's *Die Bergwerke zu Falun* (*The Mines of Falun*, 1819), a novella about a miner in the Falun Fault who discovers supernatural creatures in the mines.

"...the underground realm of the Regentrude..."

Regentrude appears in Theodor Storm's *Die Regentrude* (*The Rainmaiden*, 1868), a story about a young girl who enters a subterranean realm to awaken a sleeping "rainmaiden" and so end a drought.

"Next we reach Hamburg and the quarter called Sainte Beregonne..."
Sainte Beregonne appears in Jean Ray's horror story "La Ruelle
Ténébreuse" ("The Shadowy Alley," 1932).

"Further east is Auersperg Castle, gothic home of the notorious
19th-century black magician Axel Auersperg..."
Axël d'Auërsperg and his castle are from Philippe-Auguste Comte de
Villiers de L'Isle-Adam's *Axël* (1890). *Axël* is a symbolist play most
famous for the line, "Live? Our servants will do that for us!"

"...While off the Baltic coast are the Ear Islands, where live the Auriti..."
The Ear Islands and the Auriti appear in Pliny the Elder's *Natural History*.

"Westward in Belgium, in a valley outside Brussels, are colonies
collectively referred to as Harmonia..."
There are two Harmonias, both very similar and which together fit the
description given here: Charles Fourier's Harmonia, found in *Théorie
des Quatre Mouvements* (*Theory in Four Movements*, 1808), and
Georges Delbruck's *Au Pays de L'Harmonie* (*The Country of
Harmony*, 1906).

"On the Dutch border is the independent land of Gynographia..."
Gynographia was created by Nicolas Edme Restif de la Bretonne and
appears in his *Les Gynographes* (*The Gynographers*, 1777). Percy
finds it not as enjoyable as he had hoped because fidelity is obligatory in
Gynographia.

"Nearby in Holland is the sleepy hamlet of Vondervotteimittis..."
Vondervotteimittis, the "finest place in the world," is from Edgar Allan
Poe's short story "The Devil in the Belfry" (*Saturday Chronicle*, 18
May 1839).

"Just off the coast of Holland is the island Laiquihire, reportedly the
home of unseen deities..."
Laiquihire appears in *Voyage Curieux d'un Philadelphe Dans des
Pays Nouvellement Découverts* (*The Strange Trip of a
Philadelphian in a Newly Discovered Country*, 1755). The "unseen
deities" are the Invisible Deities, who sometimes reveal themselves when
they engage in human activities.

"...We must travel northward past the Mer-King's underwater realm near Denmark..."
The Mer-King's aquatic kingdom appears in Marie Anne de Roumier Robert's *The Water Sprites* and in Hans Christian Andersen's *The Little Mermaid* (1835).

"In northeast Greenland stand the hills known as the Devil's Teeth..."
The Devil's Teeth were created by Paul Alperine and appears in the novel *La Citadelle des Glaces* (*The Fortress of Ice*, 1946).

"...Which include Estotiland, whose folk are skilled in every science save that of navigation, and Drogio..."
Estotiland and Drogio are from Nicolò and Antonio Zeno's *Dello Scoprimento dell'Isole Frislanda, Eslandia, Engrovelanda, Estotilanda e Icaria, Fatto Sotto il Polo Artico dai Due Fratelli Zeno (Of the Discovery of the Islands Frislanda, Iceland, Greenland, Estotiland, and Icaria, near the North Pole, by the Two Brothers Zeno*, 1558), one of the most notorious of Renaissance cartographic hoaxes.

"On the Icelandic mainland we discover the extinct volcano Hekla..."
In real life Hekla is the most active volcano on Iceland. The Hekla mentioned here appears in Tommaso Porcacchi's *Le Isole Piu 'Famose del Mondo* (*The Most Famous Islands of the World*, 1572), a Renaissance atlas.

"Westward lies the extinct volcano Snaefells Jokull, which in 1863 was used by Hamburg's famed Professor Lidenbrock to enter the vast realm discovered by the 16th-century Icelandic scholar, Arne Saknussemm."
These all appear in Jules Verne's novel *Journey to the Center of the Earth* (1864).

"Some of this underground lies beneath the north of Scotland, and may be connected with Coal City, Roman State and Vril-ya country, mentioned in our previous installment."
Coal City is from Jules Verne's *Les Indes Noires*. The Roman State is from Joseph O'Neill's *Land Under England*. The Vril-ya country is from Edward Bulwer-Lytton's *The Coming Race*.

"East lies the Norwegian coast and Daland's Village, the only known port where the famous Flying Dutchman was allowed to land..."
Daland's Village appears in Richard Wagner's *The Flying Dutchman* (1843), an opera about the infamous Flying Dutchman.

"...Another tangle of sub-surface realms, such as Nazar..."
Nazar was created by Baron Ludvig Holberg and appears in *Nicolai Klimii Iter Subterraneum Novam Telluris Theoriam Ac Historiam Quintae Monarchiae Adhuc Nobis Incognitae Exhibens E Bibliotheca B. Abelini (The Journey of Niels Klim to a New Underground World, Setting Forth the Theory and History of Five Kingdoms Hitherto Unknown to Us, From the Library of B. Abelin,* 1741), a poem about Nils Klim's journey to the center of the Earth.

"Nazar has links with caves in central Norway's Dovre Fjell mountains, where trolls have been seen as recently as the late 19th century."
The trolls of the Dovre Fjell mountains appear in Henrik Ibsen's play *Peer Gynt* (1867).

"...The undersea realm Capillaria..."
Capillaria is from Frigyes Karinthy's *Capillaria* (1921), a satirical work of science fiction on the sexual contract between men and women.

"Passing on through Sweden, formerly Cimmeria..."
There were, historically, Cimmerians in the Crimea in Russia. (The name "Crimea" is derived from "Cimmeria"). The Cimmerians are also mentioned in Homer's *Odyssey* (xi, 12-19) and Herodotus' *The Histories* (iv, 11-13). But the specific reference here is to Robert E. Howard's Conan stories. In the Conan stories Cimmeria is located in southern Denmark. The Cimmerians themselves are the ancestors of modern Celts.

"...The stunning ruins of the Snow Queen's Castle..."
The castle of the Snow Queen appears in Hans-Christian Andersen's fable "Snedronningen" ("The Snow Queen," 1844).

"Southwards, at Finland's tip, are friendlier places such as Moominvalley, Daddy Jones' Kingdom and the Lonely Island, all inhabited by an unusually pacifistic breed of troll..."

Moominvalley, Daddy Jones' Kingdom, and the Lonely Island are all from Tove Jansson's delightful Moomintroll books, which begin with *The Little Trolls and the Great Flood* (1945).

Page 175. "...Visited by Wilhelmina Murray and a youthful male friend during 1912. Miss Murray and her paramour..."
The identity of Mina's paramour, the "A.J." mentioned on Page 171 above, is revealed in the notes to Page 192 below.

"We passed Klopstokia, a remarkable small country full of athletes..."
Klopstokia appears in the film *Million Dollar Legs*.

"...The tiny and yet somehow monstrous kingdom seized by the horrendous King Ubu the First in 1896."
King Ubu the First appears in Alfred Jarry's trilogy of plays, *King Ubu*, *Cuckold Ubu* and *Slave Ubu*, all written in 1896.

"...We saw the distant outline of Klepsydra Sanatorium, where Dr. Gotard's time-reversal theories recently made news."
Klepsydra Sanatorium and Dr. Gotard appear in Bruno Schulz's *Sanatorium pod Klepsydra* (*The Sanatorium Under the Obituary Notice*, 1937), an absurdist story cycle.

"...The rejuvenating fountain in Ayesha's kingdom..."
Ayesha's kingdom appears in H. Rider Haggard's She books, beginning with *She: A History of Adventure*.

"Our carriage took us through the City of the Happy Prince..."
The City of the Happy Prince was created by Oscar Wilde and appears in the short story "The Happy Prince" (*The Happy Prince and Other Stories*, 1888).

"From Strelsau, the capital of Ruritania..."
Strelsau and Ruritania appear in the Zenda novels of Anthony Hope Hawkins, beginning with *The Prisoner of Zenda*.

"...Heading south to Lutha..."
Lutha is from Edgar Rice Burroughs' novel *The Mad King* (1914), about a mentally unstable European king.

"Along the way we passed a frightening edifice known only as 'The Castle'..."
The Castle appears in Franz Kafka's novel *Das Schloss* (*The Castle*, 1926).

"...Then through a nearby valley where there's said to be a penal settlement..."
The penal settlement is from Franz Kafka's novel *In der Strafkolonie* (*In the Penal Colony*, 1919).

"...The valley led into Wolf's Glen..."
Wolf's Glen was created by Carl Maria, Freiherr von Weber, and Johann Friedrich Kind and appears in *Der Freischütz* (*The Freeshooter*, 1821), one of the great German romantic operas.

"...We drove west to Kravna on Czechoslovakia's eastern border, where I should have liked to visit the still-standing Tower of Suleiman."
This is meant to be a reference to the city of Slavna and its Tower of Suleiman, part of the country of Kravonia, from Anthony Hope's novel *Sophy of Kravonia* (1906). There is a slight chronological discrepancy here. Mina is supposed to have written this in 1912, but Czechoslovakia was not formed until 1918. In 1912 what would later become Czechoslovakia was still a part of the Hapsburg Monarchy and Austria-Hungary. But even in 1912 there was a native movement for independence and the formation of an independent "Czechoslovakia." Perhaps Mina was aware of that and was in sympathy with their desire for independence? Alternatively, the *Almanac* editors may have changed her regional reference to "Czechoslovakia" so that modern readers would recognize it.

"...The independent countries of Sylvania and Freedonia..."
Sylvania and Freedonia both appear in the Marx Brothers film *Duck Soup* (1933).

"At last we reached the castle high in the Carpathians where He lived once..."
Mina is referring to Castle Dracula.

Page 176. "He died out on the ice, that dreadful, beautiful old man."
This reference is something of a mystery. Presumably Mina is referring
to Dracula, but in *Dracula* he died in his coffin on the road in front of
Castle Dracula, cut through the throat and stabbed in the heart. The
Creature, in *Frankenstein*, is assumed to have died on an ice floe, but
there's no reason for Mina to be thinking about him. It's possible that
this is a reference to Dracula's death on a frozen river in the 1964 film
Dracula, Prince of Darkness. Or perhaps Moore is making reference
to a story which will appear in a later *League* series.

"The one disquieting thing that we discovered was a sheaf of mildewed
letters written to the former occupant by persons from a Transylvanian
city east of Belgrade. These, I hope, were writ in rust-brown ink, though
the content, with its cheerful reminiscences of awful acts performed on
earlier visits, suggests otherwise."
This is a reference to Selene, a city of vampires which was created by
Paul Féval and appears in *La Ville Vampire* (*City of Vampires*, 1875).
In the novel Mrs. Ann Radcliffe (mentioned above as the author of *The
Mysteries of Udolpho*) and a group of vampire hunters destroy the
vampire lord Goetzi, the leader of Selene.

"In Transylvania we passed the ruins of Castle Karpathenburg..."
Karpathenburg Castle is from Jules Verne's novel *Le Château des
Carpathes* (*The Castle of the Carpathians*, 1892).

"...The most astonishingly dismal town I've ever seen, this being called
the City of Dreadful Night."
The City of Dreadful Night appears in James Thomson's "The City of
Dreadful Night" (1874), a poem about a joyless, hopeless city.

"...The family name. Bathory."
Countess Elizabeth Bathory (1560-1614), a Hungarian noblewoman,
is infamous for her torture of girls and her bathing in their blood. In local
legends she was reputed to be a vampire, and it is possible that the real
Count Dracula was related to Bathory on the Hungarian side of his
family.

"Yorga."
Yorga appears in the horror films *Count Yorga, Vampire* (1970) and
The Return of Count Yorga (1971).

"I even fancied I caught sight of the name Hapsburg, though in this I surely was mistaken."

I am unaware of a fictional or historical vampire named Hapsburg, although this may be a reference to a metaphorical vampire, the Hapsburg royal family. This may be a reference to mandibular prognathism, or "Hapsburg Jaw," a condition which makes the face seem unnaturally long, similar to Stoker's description of Dracula in *Dracula*.

"...We found a pleasant inn quite near Evarchia on the Black Sea."
Evarchia appears in Brigid Brophy's *Palace Without Chairs* (1978), a modern day fairytale set in an imaginary Eastern European socialist monarchy.

"...Then hired a boat to carry us to Leuke..."
Leuke is a part of Greek myth, appearing in, among other places, the *Aethiopis* (circa 650 B.C.E.) by Arctinus of Miletus, one of the earliest poets of Greece. A later and more salacious version, undoubtedly relating to the spirit which moved Mina to conjugal activity, appears in James Branch Cabell's *Jurgen*.

Page 177. "...Beneath the waters of Drake Passage..."
Drake's Passage is a real place off the southern coast of South America.

"The science-pirate Captain Nemo, who kept a base at nearby Lincoln Island in the South Pacific..."
Lincoln Island appears in Jules Verne's *The Mysterious Island*. In the novel Lincoln Island is Nemo's volcano base.

"...First mate Ishmael..."
Ishmael, part of the crew of the *Nautilus* in *League* v1, is the narrator of Herman Melville's *Moby Dick* (1851).

"...What we have come to call the ghost submersible, an vehicle much like *The Nautilus*, which I had thought to be unique. Broad Arrow Jack has recently returned from Tierra del Fuego, where he'd been put ashore to learn whatever might be known of this elusive craft, and served us up an interesting account of his discoveries; The locals tell tales of an English naval sergeant, one James Winston Pepper, lost at sea in 1870, supposedly dragged down by undertows through emerald waters and eventually washed up upon the shores of a subsurface paradise where harmony reigned everywhere. The realm, named Pepper's Land after the sergeant, is reputedly the source of the garishly-coloured phantom submarine we've sighted. It may also be the home of a malignant species of blue dwarf or troll (perhaps related to the Nordic kobolds) that turns up occasionally in Argentina..."

All of these are references to the Beatles' charming animated film *Yellow Submarine* (1968). The "ghost submersible" is the Yellow Submarine. "James Winston Pepper" is the discoverer of Pepperland. The "emerald waters" is the Sea of Green. The "malignant species of blue dwarf" is the Blue Meanies. And their location, and the presence of the Blue Meanies in Argentina, is based on an exchange between the Chief Blue Meanie and his Second, Max: "It's no longer a blue world, Max. Where shall we go?" "Argentina?" "James Winston Pepper" is derived from Paul McCartney's first name, James, and John Lennon's middle name, Winston.

"...Until the occasion of his death in May, 1909..."
It may only be coincidence that the man most commonly associated with the cinematic version of Nemo, James Mason, was born on 15 May 1909.

"...A Miss Diver, whose connection to the Captain is unclear but who made entries in the logbook of the *Nautilus* commencing in the later months of 1910."
This is a reference to Jenny Diver, from John Gay's plays *Beggar's Opera* (1728), *Polly* (1728), and Bertolt Brecht's play *Three Penny Opera* (1928). In *Three Penny Opera* Jenny Diver sings "Pirate Jenny," about "the Black Freighter" which is coming to punish the guilty and rescue her.

"...A great cluster of small islands called the Riallaro Archipelago..."
The Riallaro Archipelago appears in John Macmillan Brown's *Riallaro, the Archipelago of Exiles* (1901) and *Limanora, the Island of Progress* (1903), both about island utopias near the Antarctic.

"Aleofane, or 'Gem of Truth'...Fanattia...Figlefia...Spectralia and neighboring Astralia...Haciocram...Kloriole, Broolyi, Swoonarie, Limanoria...Coxuria..."
All of these islands appear in *Riallaro* and *Limanora*.

"Southeast of Riallaro we find Manouham, famed for its fascinating open-sided tombs, and nearby Letalispons..."
Manouham and Letalispons are from the Abbé Pierre François Guyot Desfontaines' *Le Nouveau Gulliver, ou Voyage De Jean Gulliver, Fils Du Capitaine Gulliver* (*The New Gulliver, or the Voyage of Jean Gulliver, Son of Captain Gulliver*, 1730). *Le Nouveau Gulliver* was an unauthorized sequel to Swift's *Gulliver's Travels*, written by Swift's French translator and detailing the adventures of Gulliver's son Jean.

"Both these islands are near Juan Fernandez, not far off the coast of Chile, as is neighboring Frivola, the Frivolous Island."
The islands of Juan Fernandez and Frivola were created by the Abbé Gabriel François Coyer and appear in his *A Discovery of the Island Frivola: Or, the Frivolous Island* (1750), a *voyage imaginaire* (imaginary voyage).

"...The delightful children-governed isle of Meipe..."
Meipe appears in André Maurois' *Meïpe ou La Délivrance* (1929). Meïpe, founded by Michelle Maurois, the four-year-old daughter of André Maurois, is that wonderful land where teachers never teach and children do not need to be polite when speaking to grown-ups.

"...The Land of Parrots..."
The Land of Parrots appears in Pierre Charles Fabiot Aunillon, Abbé Du Guay de Launay's *Azor, ou Le Prince Enchanté* (*Azor, or the Enchanted Prince*, 1750), a novel about an island populated by mutes and a parrot which changes the lives of the mutes.

"...And the obscure immensity known as Mount Analogue."
Mount Analogue is from René Daumal's *Le Mont Analogue* (1952). In the novel Mount Analogue's heights reach to Heaven itself.

"Paradise Island..."
Paradise Island was created by "Ambrose Evans" and appears in *The Adventures, and Surprizing Deliverances, of James Dubourdieu, And His Wife* (1719), the supposedly true story about a shipwrecked man living a utopian life on an island of natives whose lives are devoted to love.

"...Nearby Coral Island..."
Coral Island was created by R. M. Ballantyne and appears in *The Coral Island* (1858), a Robinsonade (*Robinson Crusoe*-like novel) about three British boys who are stranded on a tropical island.

"...The pink island known as Rose..."
The completely pink island of Rose appears in Mervyn Peake's *Captain Slaughterboard Drops Anchor* (1939), a pirate novel.

"...One Captain Clegg (affiliated in some way to the adventurers assembled by ship's surgeon Lemuel Gulliver)..."
Captain Clegg is the alternate identity of the Reverend Dr. Syn.

"The Pirates' Conference, Rose Island."
See the notes to Page 178 below.

Page 178. "...On The Black Tiger, owned by Slaughterboard, who is a good man and an enemy to none of us, though I like his yellow bunkmate not a bit."
The Black Tiger and Captain Slaughterboard are from *Captain Slaughterboard Drops Anchor*. Slaughterboard's "yellow bunkmate" is an elf, the "Yellow Creature," who Slaughterboard captured on his first trip to Rose Island. In the novel the two were simply master and servant, but Moore has revealed that they were bunkmates, just as many real pirates took male lovers.

"Blood was there, strutting and twirling his moustache..."
Blood is a reference to Captain Blood, from Rafael Sabatini's *Captain Blood* (1922), one of the classic novels of adventure and piracy.

"...And also John Silver, hopping around and cackling..."
"Long" John Silver appears in Robert Louis Stevenson's novel *Treasure Island* (1883).

"Pugwash I cannot make up my mind about. He seems a rather soft and inoffensive little chap, not at all cut out for life on the high seas."
Captain Horatio Pugwash, a rather amiable sort for a pirate, appears in the first issue of the British comic *Eagle*, in 1950, and then on *Captain*

Pugwash, a BBC cartoon, beginning in 1957. The "not at all cut out for life on the high seas" may be a reference to the style of animation of the television cartoon, which involved cardboard cut-outs, similar to the animation style currently seen on *South Park*.

"Hook, on the other hand, while very capable, is an enigma..."
Captain Hook is from J.M. Barrie's novel *Peter Pan* (1904).

"Blood got in a foppish slapping-match with Pysse-Gummes..."
Pysse-Gummes is a reference to "Captain Pissgums," the S. Clay Wilson pirate character who appears in *Zap Comics* in such immortal adventures as "Captain Pissgums and his Pervert Pirates Meet Ruby the Motorcycle Dyke."

On Page 177 the "The Pirates' Conference, Rose Island" sketch shows the pirates who attended the Conference. From left to right, the probable lineup is as follows:

- the Reverend Dr. Syn as Captain Clegg. The Clegg portrayed here somewhat resembles Peter Cushing, who played Clegg in the 1962 Hammer Films production *Captain Clegg*.
- Long John Silver (with the parrot on his shoulder)
- Captain Blood (to the right of Long John Silver)
- Captain Pugwash (short, portly man in the foreground)
- Captain Slaughterboard (to the right of Captain Blood)
- Tom the Cabin Boy (Captain Pugwash's sidekick)
- Captain Hook
- Possibly Slaughterboard's "Yellow Creature," wearing a wig to cover his ears and horns?
- Captain Pissgums (whose visual resemblance to Alan Moore is surely coincidental)

"...We pass Orofena..."
Orofena appears in H. Rider Haggard's *When the World Shook* (1918), a novel about an ancient Atlantean civilization awakened from suspended animation in the present day.

"Slightly further north (although apparently maintaining strong diplomatic connections with Meipe, above) is Maïna..."
Maïna is from André Maurois' *Voyage au Pays de Articoles* (1927), a satiric Lost Race novel.

"...We sight the changing-coloured sands that bound Cook's Island..."
Cook's Island was created by E. Nesbit and appears in *The Phoenix and the Carpet* (1904), a novel about four children who buy a used carpet and discover a Phoenix egg wrapped inside.

"...We encounter the vast Mardi Archipelago, containing fascinating realms such as the island of maimed and one-legged gladiatorial enthusiasts, Diranda and witch-isle Minda or Valapee, Isle of Yams..."
The Mardi Archipelago, Diranda, Minda, and Valapee are from Herman Melville's *Mardi and a Voyage Thither* (1849), a satirical South Seas adventure story.

"...We pass by Hunchback Island..."
Hunchback Island appears in Abbé Pierre François Guyot Desfontaines' *Le Nouveau Gulliver*.

"...One of the peculiar areas of the South Pacific that local islanders believe inspires men to communicate in song, such as the beauteous Bali Hai near Japan..."
Bali Hai is from the Rodgers & Hammerstein musical *South Pacific* (1949), which was based on James Michener's *Tales of the South Pacific* (1947).

"Zara's Kingdom, ruled by British-educated Princess Zara and a sextet of exemplary Englishmen, including Captain Corcoran who'd previously served aboard Her Majesty's Ship *Pinafore*."
Zara's Kingdom, Princess Zara, and Captain Corcoran are from Gilbert & Sullivan's *Utopia Limited; or, The Flowers of Progress* (1893). The H.M.S. *Pinafore* is a reference to Gilbert & Sullivan's musical *H.M.S. Pinafore* (1878).

"One puzzling incident recorded by this Captain in his memoirs concerns Marsh's Island, close to Zara's Kingdom and named after Captain Obed Marsh of Innsmouth, Massachusetts, who dropped anchor there in 1830."
Captain Obed Marsh and Innsmouth, Massachusetts are from H.P. Lovecraft's horror story "The Shadow Over Innsmouth" (*The Shadow Over Innsmouth*, 1936).

"Islanders from Zara's land believe that Marsh's Island is the haunt of hideous fish-like humanoids called 'Deep Ones'..."

In "The Shadow Over Innsmouth" Obed Marsh, traveling through the South Seas, discovered an island on which lived a "woman" who he took as his bride and who returned with him to Innsmouth. The "woman" was actually a Deep One, a member of the aquatic fish-humanoids who worship the evil alien god Dagon.

"When I was a boy an eldritch book informed me I'd inherited the Innsmouth Look.

I'd gills and wide-spaced eyes, you see, and I frolicked at the bottom of the deep blue sea

(He frolicked at the bottom of the deep blue sea).

I went to the ocean depths most willingly, and now I am a tentacled monstrosity

(He went into the ocean depths most willingly, and now he is a tentacled monstrosity)."

The "Innsmouth Look" is from "The Shadow over Innsmouth." The "Innsmouth Look" is a facial deformity that the descendants of Obed Marsh and his Deep One bride develop as they grow older, a deformity which presages their change into a Deep One.

The joke behind these lyrics is that they describe what happens to the narrator of "The Shadow Over Innsmouth" in the style of Gilbert & Sullivan, specifically to the tune of Sir Joseph Porter's solo from Act One of *H.M.S. Pinafore*. For comparison, here is the first verse:

Sir Joseph:
    When I was a lad I served a term
    As office boy to an Attorney's firm.
    I cleaned the windows and I swept the floor,
    And I polished up the handle of the big front door.
Chorus:
    He polished up the handle of the big front door!
Sir Joseph:
    I polished up that handle so carefullee
    That now I am the Ruler of the Queen's Navee!
Chorus:
    He polished up that handle so carefullee
    That now he is the Ruler of the Queen's Navee!

"This is Noble's island, close to Ecuador, where an English biologist (apparently employed by British Military Intelligence) performed experiments of a most confidential nature that we nonetheless believe to have involved hybridisation, during the late 19th century. This belief, we should add, is supported only by the testimony of the clearly half-demented hermit Edward Prendick, who Miss Wilhelmina Murray and her colleague Allan Quatermain encountered on their trip to the South Downs during the terrible Martian incursion in the latter half of 1898."

Noble's Island and Edward Prendick appear in of H.G. Wells' *The Island of Dr. Moreau*, in which Dr. Moreau retreats to Noble's Isle in disgrace after the barbarous cruelty of his experiments is revealed. In the novel there is no stated link between Moreau and British Military Intelligence.

"...Such as Hoste, an island republic..."

Hoste appears in *Les Naufragés du "Jonathan"* (*Survivors of the Jonathan*, 1909), a novel about a shipwreck. *Les Naufragés* was written by Jules Verne and later heavily rewritten by his son Michael.

"...Or Geometer's island..."

Geometer's Island appears in Abbé Desfontaines' *Le Nouveau Gulliver*.

"Not far away are Greedy Island...adjacent Doctor's Island...Foolyk...Philosopher's Island..."

These are all from Abbé Desfontaines' *Le Nouveau Gulliver*.

"...We next come to Rampole Island..."

Rampole Island was created by H.G. Wells and appears in *Mr. Blettsworthy on Rampole Island* (1935), a novel about an Englishman who is shipwrecked on an island of "savages" who end up adopting him as a "sacred fool."

"...Just south of Villings, an attractive island purchased recently..."

Villings appears in Adolfo Bioy Casares' *La Invención de Morel* (*The Invention of Morel*, 1941), a novel about romance and metaphysics.

"A little west of Villings we find Brisevent, in an archipelago known as the Marvellous Islands..."

Brisevent and the Marvellous Islands are from Charles Sorel's *La Maison des Jeux* (*The House of Games*, 1642), a novel of social analysis.

"Bordering this group of curiously-populated islands to the east is Houyhnhnms Land..."
Houyhnhnms Land appears in Jonathan Swift's *Gulliver's Travels.*

"...we pass the fair, enlightened pagan island of Eugea..."
Eugea was created by Népoumucène Lemercier and appears in *L'Atlantiade, ou La Théogonie Newtonienne* (*The Atlantiade, or the Newtonian Theogony*, 1812), a long poem about Atlantis.

"...Inhospitable Nimatan with its exquisite lunatic asylums..."
Nimatan, or Nimpatan, appears in John Holmesby's *The Voyages, Travels, and Wonderful Discoveries of Captain John Holmesby* (1757), a Gulliver's Travels-like imaginary voyage.

"...The former Roman colony of Oceana..."
The island utopia Oceana appears in James Harrington's *The Commonwealth of Oceana* (1656), a utopia controversial at the time of its publication for its republican politics.

"...The idealistic republic known as Spensonia..."
The utopian country of Spensonia appears in Thomas Spence's *A Description of Spensonia* (1795) and *The Constitution of Spensonia* (1798).

"...The acclaimed 'perfect society' known as Utopia..."
Utopia is from Sir Thomas More's *Utopia* (1516), the most famous of all utopian works and from which the word "utopia" came to mean an idealized society.

"During the early sixteenth century, Utopia was ruled by the extraordinary giant Gargantua, and was indeed the birthplace of his son, the similarly-sized Pantagruel."
Gargantua and Pantagruel's stint on Utopia appears in François Rabelais' *Pantagruel Roi des Dipsodes* (1532).

Page 179. "Traveling on past Spidermonkey Island..."
Spidermonkey Island is from Hugh Lofting's *The Voyages of Doctor Dolittle.*

"Here we find Vendchurch's Island..."
Vendchurch's Island was created by "Ambrose Evans" and appears in
*The Adventures, and Surprizing Deliverances, of James Dubourdieu,
And His Wife*.

"...And Fonesca..."
Fonesca, or Fonseca, is from the anonymously-written imaginary voyage
A Voyage to the New Island, Fonseca, Near Barbadoes (1708).

"Here too is Oroonoko Island..."
Oroonoko Island may be a reference to Aphra Behn's *Oroonoko, or
the Royal Slave* (1678), a novel about a slave uprising in the British
colony of Surinam and Oroonoko, the royal slave who leads the revolt.

"...And the quarrel-free Ferdinand's Island..."
Ferdinand's Island is from Johann Michael Fleischer's *Der Nordische
Robinson* (1741), a German Robinsonade.

"One is the island of Speranza, sometimes called the Island of Despair,
where one Rob Crusoe, late of York, spent many years of loneliness
and hardship following his shipwreck there during the last days of
September, 1659."
Speranza, a.k.a. the Island of Despair, a.k.a. Crusoe's Island, and Rob
Crusoe are from Daniel Defoe's *The Life and Strange Adventures of
Robinson Crusoe, of York, Mariner* (1719).

"Ironically, well within swimming distance of Speranza is an island known
as Herland..."
Herland appears in Charlotte Perkins Gilman's *Herland* (1916), a feminist
utopia.

"...Such as Tacarigua..."
Tacarigua is from Ronald Firbank's *Prancing Nigger* (1924), about a
family of West Indians who attempt, unsuccessfully, to gain entrance
into high society.

"Cannibal Island, nearby..."
Cannibal Island is from Francois Guillaume Ducray-Duminil's *Lolotte
et Fanfan* (1788), a children's story about a pirate island.

"...While Chita is an island famous for its trees like giant lettuce..."
Chita is from Pierre-Mac Orlan's *Le Chant de l'Équipage* (1949), a novel of adventure metaphorically about Orlan's experiences in WWI

"The Isle of Birds, much more hospitable..."
The Isle of Birds is from Eléazar de Mauvillon's *Le Soldat Parvenu* (*The Upstart Soldier,* 1753).

"We also have the pirate island San Verrado..."
San Verrado appears in Francois Guillaume Ducray-Duminil's *Lolotte et Fanfan.*

"...And the feared Zaroff's Island, owned by an expatriate Russian Count whose pass-times include hunting human beings."
Zaroff's Island, and the expatriate Russian Count Zaroff, are from Richard Connell's short story "The Most Dangerous Game" (*Colliers,* 19 January 1924)

"Cacklogallinia is ruled by chickens..."
Cacklogallinia appears in "Captain Samuel Brunt"'s *A Voyage to Cacklogallinia* (1727), a novel about a voyage to the moon in a balloon drawn by birds.

"...The isle belonging to the Milanese Duke and occultist Prospero..."
Prospero is from Shakespeare's *The Tempest*, which puts Prospero's Island in the Mediterranean, but Robert Browning's "Caliban Upon Setebos" (1864) places the island in the Caribbean.

"Within the Patagonian region of south Argentina we find Leonard's Land..."
Leonard's Land appears in Jean-Gaspard Dubois-Fontanelle's *Aventures Philosophiques* (1766).

"Further north, not far from Buenos Aires, we find Babel..."
Babel is from Jorge Luis Borges' "La Biblioteca de Babel" ("The Library of Babel," *El Jardin de Senderos que se Bifurcan,* 1941), a story about a library which contains all books ever written or which will ever be written.

"...The first being the Palace of Justice..."

The Palace of Justice is from Marco Denevi's "El primer cuento de Kafka?" ("Kafka's First Story?" *Falsificaciones*, 1966), a story written in the Kafka style about a Kafka-esque "Palace of Justice."

"The other major edifice of note in Babel is the city's spectacular library..." The library of Babel is from Jorge Luis Borges' "The Library of Babel."

"...We find Madragal, with its history of skirmishes with Parapagel..." Madragal, or Maradagal, and Parapagel, appear in Carlo Emilio Gadda's "Acquainted With Grief," (*Letteratura*, 1941), a fictional autobiography set in an imaginary South American country.

"Meanwhile, on the eastern border between Argentina and its neighbor Chile exists Cesares Republic..." Cesares (or Cessares) Republic appears in James Burgh's *An Account of the First Settlement, Laws, Form of Government and Police of the Cessares* (1764), a novel about a utopian religious community.

"...Within the upper reaches of Chile itself, is Agzceaziguls..." Agzceaziguls is from Charles Derennes' "Les Conquérants D'Idoles" ("The Conqueror of Idols," *J'ai Vu*, 9 May-20 June 1919), a story about Native Americans in a fictional country near Chile.

"...Stands a solitary Pink Palace..." The Pink Palace is from Marco Denevi's short story "La Niña Rosa" (*Falsificaciones*, 1966).

"Bolivia, as we continue north, is home to the immense lake (or small inland sea) known as Lost Time..." Lost Time appears in Gabriel Garcia Marquez's short story "El Mar Del Tiempo Perdido" ("The Sea of Lost Time," *La Increible y Triste Historia de la Cándida Erendira y de su Abuela Desalmada*, 1972).

"...Between Paraguay, Brazil and Argentina is Roncador..." Roncador was created by Herbert Read and appears in his novel *The Green Child* (1935), a kind of sequel to Plato's *Republic*.

"Speranza" The shape of the clouds above Crusoe's head, and the way he musingly fondles the mouth of the goat, are likely not coincidental.

Page 180. "...The fabled Incan kingdom known as El Dorado..."
The legend of El Dorado first appears in print in Sir Walter Raleigh's
The Discoverie of the Lovlie, Rich and Beautiful Empyre of Guiana
(1596).

"...By a young Swiss-German millionaire named Aurie Goldfinger..."
Aurie (or Auric) Goldfinger appears in Ian Fleming's novel *Goldfinger*
(1959), in which Goldfinger bedevils James Bond.

"In the Andean hills of Ecuador, as an example, there exists a valley in
the shadow of Mount Parascotopetl where all of the populace are blind
from birth..."
This is a reference to H.G. Wells' short story "The Country of the Blind"
(*The Strand*, April 1904).

"...While high in the Colombian Andes we find Golden Lake..."
Golden Lake appears in Daniel Defoe's *A New Voyage Round the
World* (1724), one of Defoe's travel books.

"...The delightful almond-scented village of Macondo..."
Macondo appears in Gabriel Garcia Marquez's novel *Cien Años de
Soledad* (*100 Years of Solitude*, 1967).

"Passing on into Venezuela we find (or, in fact, don't find) Ewaipanoma..."
Ewaipanoma appears in Sir Walter Raleigh's *The Discoverie of the
Lovlie, Rich and Beautiful Empyre of Guiana*.

"...Just past ill-starred Nolandia we reach Happiland..."
Nolandia and Happiland appears in Sir Thomas More's *Utopia*.

"Aglaura, north of Happiland..."
Aglaura is from Italo Calvino's *Invisible Cities*.

"Further north, upon the coast, we come to Watkinsland..."
Watkinsland appears in Doris Lessing's *Briefing for a Descent into
Hell* (1971), a novel of "inner space fiction" about a man who begins on
a tropical shore and ends in a trip across the universe.

"Not far from Watkinsland to the northwest is Quivera..."

Quivera was created by Vaughan Wilkins and appears in *The City of Frozen Fire* (1950), a novel about a Welsh colony discovered in South America.

"Deep within the forests of the Amazon, for instance, is reputed to exist the ancient jungle kingdom known as Mu..."
One of the classics of crackpot crypto-archaeology is James Churchward's *The Lost Continent of Mu* (1926) which posited a pre-historic and now sunken continent in the Pacific Ocean called "Mu." This Mu, however, appears in Hugo Pratt's Corto Maltese comics, specifically *The Secret of Tristan Bantam* (1981) and *Mu* (1988). Maltese is an adventurer who searches for the land of Mu in the forests of the Amazon.

"...Quite possible the same kingdom described by the great 19th century traveller Candide and his instructor Dr. Pangloss as 'the Fabulous Land'..."
Candide and Dr. Pangloss are from Voltaire's *Candide* (1759). Presumably the "Fabulous Land" mentioned here is the same as the El Dorado which the pair encountered.

"In other sources Mu is sometimes known as 'Yu,' or 'Yu Atlanchi'..."
Yu-Atlanchi is from A. E. Merritt's novel *The Face in the Abyss* (1931). Yu-Atlanchi is an Incan Lost City.

"...It is near here that the world-famous 'bird girl' Riolama or Rima was discovered..."
Riolama/Rima appears in W.H. Hudson's novel *Green Mansions* (1904). Rima is a notable predecessor to Tarzan. In *Green Mansions* she lives in British Guiana, along the Orinoco river.

"Jacob Epstein's statue of Riolama still stands next to the same artist's rendering of Edward Hyde in London's former Serpentine Park..."
There was a real Jacob Epstein, a sculptor who carved a relief of Rima as a tribute to W.H. Hudson shortly after Hudson's death in 1922. The relief is in Hyde Park.

"The most astonishing of Brazil's mystery sites, which we have saved for last, is Maple White Land..."
Maple White Land appears in Arthur Conan Doyle's *The Lost World*.

"Goldfinger Expedition, 1928"
In this picture the young Auric Goldfinger is gesturing. To his right is a young-looking Odd Job, who in *Goldfinger* is Goldfinger's Korean assassin.

Page 181. "Some few miles down the Amazon from the volcanic plateau, for example, is a secluded lake known as the Black Lagoon by local Indian tribes..."
The Black Lagoon appears in the Jack Arnold directed films *The Creature from the Black Lagoon* (1954) and *Revenge of the Creature* (1955). In the films the male Creature is fixated on Kay Lawrence (played by Julie Adams). If the Scientific Expedition to the Black Lagoon (seen in the illustration on this page) killed the female Creature, it might explain why the male Creature was obsessed with a female human.

"These may be some hitherto unknown Silurian throwbacks..."
This is a reference to an episode from the British science fiction television series *Dr. Who*: "Dr. Who and the Silurians" (1970), written by Malcolm Hulke. In that episode the Silurians are race of intelligent reptilian humanoids who ruled Earth during the dinosaur age.

"...There is the miserable Island of Birds..."
The sad Island of Birds appears in Michel Tremblay's *Contes Pour Buveurs Attardés* (1966), a collection of fantasy stories.

"...Not to be confused with the Isle of Birds found in the Caribbean..."
The Isle of Birds in the Caribbean appears in Eléazar de Mauvillon's *Le Soldat Parvenu*.

"...We have Waferdanos..."
Waferdanos appears in the anonymously written *Voyage Curieux d'un Philadelphe Dans des Pays Nouvellement Découverts* (1755), a utopian novel.

"...The submarine country Capillaria..."
Capillaria is from Frigyes Karinthy's *Capillaria*.

"The ruins of another previously mentioned underwater passage, namely the Atlantic Tunnel..."
The Atlantic Tunnel appears in Luigi Motta's *The Undersea Tunnel*.

"...A number of the islands (once known as 'The Wicked Archipelago')..."
The Wicked Archipelago appears in Lucian of Samosata's *True History*.

"These include the notoriously rain-swept Buyan Island..."
Buyan Island appears in Karl Ralston's "Buyanka" (*The Songs of the Russian People*, 1932), an investigation into the roots of Russian legend and folklore.

"...Cheese-like Caseosa and the startling island Cabbalussa...neighboring Dream Island..."
Caseosa, Cabbalussa, and Dream Island appear in Lucian of Samosata's *True History*.

"Yspaddaden Penkawr castle in Wales..."
Yspaddaden Penkawr appears in *The Mabinogion*. Yspaddaden Penkawr is mentioned on Page 163.

"Idol Island and Winkfield's Island..."
Idol Island and Winkfield's Island are from "Unca Eliza Winkfield"'s *The Female American* (1767), a Robinsonade with a female protagonist.

"Further south, however, on the island of Militia, we find mention of a man-mimicking variety of shrub known as a Simlax..."
Militia, or Melita, and the Simlax shrub appear in Pliny the Elder's *Natural History*. There is a real Simlax plant, *Simlax officinalis L.*, otherwise known as sarsparilla, but the Simlax of Pliny was a maiden who was transformed into a plant by the gods for loving another woman's husband.

"...The mobile vegetation on the nearby Island of Moving Trees..."
The Island of Moving Trees is from Miguel de Cervantes Saavedra's *Los Trabajos de Persiles y Sigismunda* (*The Trials of Persiles and Sigismunda*, 1617), a Byzantine romance which Cervantes considered his greatest work.

"Prospero's occasional companion Captain Robert Owe-much... Ursina... Vulpina..."
Captain Owe-much, Ursina, and Vulpina are from "Frank Careless"' *The Floating Island*.

"...The Island of Fortune...the Island of Chance...Philosophy Isle..."
The Island of Fortune, the Island of Chance, and Philosophy Isle appear in Abbé Balthazard's *L'Isle Des Philosophes Et Plusieurs Autres* (*The Island of the Philosophers and Several Others,* 1790), a look at possible utopias.

"...An isle that is but recently risen from the sea, a mere outcrop of rock that as yet goes unnamed but which to me appears as though shaped like a fine York ham..."
This is a reference to Ham Island, which appears in Jules Verne's *Le "Chancellor"* (1875).

"The Island of the Palace of Joy..."
The Island of the Palace of Joy appears in Matteo Maria Boiardo's *Orlando Innamorato* (1487), an epic about the adventures of the knight Orlando.

"...A very pretty gentleman that I once met, by name Orlando..."
Orlando is from Matteo Maria Boiardo's *Orlando Innamorato*, Ludovico Ariosto's *Orlando Furioso*, and Virginia Woolf's *Orlando* (1928). The comment that he is "very pretty" is a reference to Orlando's sex change, from male to female, in Woolf's *Orlando*.

"...But illusions of the sorcerer Malagigi."
The sorcerer Malagigi is from Matteo Maria Boiardo's *Orlando Innamorato*.

"This mention of a person named Orlando is far from unique in the League's annals, though as we shall see the gender of this person seems to vary..."
In Virginia Woolf's *Orlando* the titular character changes sex, literally overnight.

"...Rossum's Island..."
Rossum's Island appears in Karel Capek's *R.U.R.: Rossum's Universal Robots* (1920), the play which gave the world the word "robot."

"...Commencing with Quarll Island..."
Quarll Island appears in Peter Longueville's *The Hermit* (1727), one of the most popular of the *Robinson Crusoe* imitations.

Page 182. "...nearby Treasure Island, where the pirate captain Flint..."
Treasure Island and Captain Flint are from Robert Louis Stevenson's
Treasure Island.

"...Glubbdubdrib, Balnibari and Laputa..."
Glubbdubdrib, Balnibari and Laputa are from Jonathan Swift's *Gulliver's
Travels*.

"...Captain Sparrow's Island..."
Captain Sparrow's Island appears in S. Fowler Wright's *The Island of
Captain Sparrow* (1928), a Lost Race novel in which the heroine is
threatened by the descendants of pirates on a tropical island.

"...Brobdingnag..."
Brobdingnag is from Jonathan Swift's *Gulliver's Travels*.

"...Great Mother's Island..."
Great Mother's Island is from Gerhart Hauptmann's *Die Insel der
Grossen Mutter* (1924), a utopian novel.

"...And Orphan Island."
Orphan Island, a feminist utopia, appears in Rose Macaulay's *Orphan
Island* (1924).

"Up in the great northwest expanses of the Klondike region, for example,
stands Thieves City..."
Thieves City was created by Maurice Level and appears in the novel
La Cité des Voleurs (*The City of Thieves*, 1930).

"...A tropical oasis known as Dead Man's Valley..."
Dead Man's Valley, a.k.a. Tropical Valley, appears in Pierre Berton's
The Mysterious North (1956), a fantasy about the northern frontier of
Canada.

"...The Valley of the Beasts..."
The Valley of the Beasts appears in Algernon Blackwood's "The Valley
of the Beasts" (*Romance Magazine*, March 1921), a horror story about
a valley in which all animals live in harmony, until a human hunter invades
it.

"...Haunted Island..."
Haunted Island appears in Algernon Blackwood's "A Haunted Island" (*Pall Mall Magazine*, April 1899), a novel about a haunted island in the Canadian woods.

"...Nearby Canadian Floating Isles..."
Canadian Floating Isles appear in Charles M. Skinner's *Myths and Legends of Our Own Land* (1896), a collection of bizarre "true" Canadian and New England stories.

"...The frankly absurd area called Rootabaga Country..."
Rootabaga Country was created by Carl Sandburg and appears in *Rootabaga Stories* (1922), a collection of children's stories set in the American Midwest.

"Elsewhere in Washington State we discover Chisholm Prison, thought to be escape-proof until the ingenious professor Van Dusen did just that during the first years of the twentieth century..."
This is a reference to "The Problem of Cell 13" (*Boston American*, 30 Oct-5 Nov 1905), perhaps the most famous of Jacques Futrelle's Thinking Machine stories. Professor Van Dusen is the "Thinking Machine," a very clever crime solver. The Thinking Machine stories are set in and around Boston, Massachusetts, and Chisholm Prison is likely Charlestown Prison rather than a prison somewhere in Washington.

"...The logging town of Twin Peaks..."
This is a reference to David Lynch's horror television show *Twin Peaks* (1990).

"...we find areas of dense forest sometimes called 'The Deep, Deep Woods' by locals. Doll-like creatures have been seen here..."
This is a reference to Johnny Gruelle's children's story *Raggedy Ann in the Deep Woods* (1930).

"...A supposedly-haunted dell within the Deep, Deep Woods called Glastonbury Grove..."
Glastonbury Grove appears in *Twin Peaks*. In *Twin Peaks* Glastonbury Grove, a circle of twelve sycamore trees, is the doorway to the Black Lodge, the home of the evil plaguing the woods and the town of Twin Peaks.

"Moving through Oregon we pass by Cricket Creek (one of the places where there have been various reports of living dinosaurs..."
Cricket Creek is from Evelyn Sibley Lampman's *The Shy Stegosaurus of Cricket Creek* (1955). In *The Shy Stegosaurus* Cricket Creek is in the desert of the American southwest.

"...Upon the nearby coast the city of Mahagonny..."
Mahagonny was created by Bertolt Brecht and appears in *Aufstieg und Fall der Stadt Mahagonny* (*The Rise and Fall of the City of Mahoganny*, 1929), a satire of American life.

"...Near Mendocino, we find France-Ville..."
France-Ville is from Jules Verne's novel *Les 500 Millions de la Begum* (*The Begum's 500 Millions*, 1879), about France-Ville, a utopian community built by a Frenchman, and Steeltown, a city dedicated to the building of weapons and the destruction of France-Ville.

"Some distance further down, now Monterey, at a number 5 Thallo Street in Pacific Grove, lives the intriguing although somewhat musty-smelling scientist Tyco M. Bass..."
Tyco M. Bass appears in Eleanor Cameron's *The Wonderful Flight to the Mushroom Planet* (1954), a science fiction novel about two boys and their spaceship.

"...While San Francisco is home to the Western American Explorer's Club, whose Professor William Waterman Sherman was involved in the mysterious '21 Balloons' incident of 1883."
The Western American Explorer's Club, Professor William Waterman Sherman, and the 21 Balloons Incident of 1883 are from William Pène Du Bois' *The Twenty-One Balloons* (1947), a novel which tells the story about Professor's Sherman hot-air balloon trip and his crash-landing on a remote volcanic island.

"Out in rural California, not far from Merced, is the long-established settlement called iDEATH, famed for its watermelons. Hardened sugar from there is used to make trout-hatcheries, cabins, sculptures or indeed almost anything one might require. Continuing south, past a vast spread of rusted, obsolete machinery from the 19th century known locally as The Forgotten Works..."

iDEATH and the Forgotten Works are from Richard Brautigan's *In Watermelon Sugar* (1964), a surrealistic novel set in a post-apocalyptic world.

"...Just past Mexico's border, to the charming villa of Don Diego de la Vega where the masked adventurer known as The Fox was sighted during the nineteenth and even early twentieth centuries."
Don Diego de la Vega was the Zorro, the Fox, in Johnston McCulley's Zorro stories, beginning with "The Curse of Capistrano" (*All-Story Weekly*, 9 August 1919). The first Zorro stories took place in the early part of the Nineteenth century, but as McCulley and then other authors created sequels to McCulley's first Zorro stories, successors to Zorro appeared throughout the century and into the start of the Twentieth century.

"...Thought to be the birthplace of the fabled lumberjack Paul Bunyan and his celebrated blue ox, Babe..."
Paul Bunyan and Babe are American legends, and any number of myths were told about them starting in the 1870s.

"The crewman, a fellow named Lebowsky, had been formerly a member of the Naiad race of Scoti Moria, but it is not known if he continued the traditional Naiad habits of smoking and nine-pins once established in America, or indeed if he produced any subsequent offspring of any note." This is another piece of Moorean back-engineering, referring to an ancestor of The Dude and Mr. Lebowski from Ethan and Joel Cohen's film *The Big Lebowski* (1998). The Dude is a chain-smoking bowler.

"...The ruined city of Tcha, a supposedly Atlantean colony on the Yucatan peninsula."
Tcha was created by L. Frank Baum and appears in *The Boy Fortune Hunters in Yucatan* (1910), one in the "Boy Fortune Hunter" series of novels about a group of youthful treasure hunters who traveled around the world, finding profit and glory wherever they went.

"While giving mention to Louisiana's marvelously atmospheric Yoknapatawpha County..."
Yoknapatawpha County is from William Faulkner's Yoknapatawpha stories and novels, including *The Sound and the Fury* (1929) and

Absalom, Absalom (1936). However, in the Faulkner novels Yoknapatawpha County is in Mississippi, not Louisiana. In addition, if Yoknapatawpha were in Louisiana it would be Yoknapatawpha Parish, not County.

"...The New Mexico ranch home of the early 20th century gunfighter and balladeer Gene Autry. While the famous singing cowboy's home is not itself remarkable, beneath it sprawls the subterranean empire of Murania..."
Gene Autry (1907-1998) was a real person, but this passage is a reference to the fictional Gene Autry, who appears, along with the underground kingdom of Murania, in the 1935 film serial *The Phantom Empire*.

"...The massive underground land Atvatabar..."
Atvatabar was created by William R. Bradshaw and appears in *The Goddess of Atvatabar* (1892), one of the classic Hollow Earth novels.

"...The similarly subterranean Etidorhpa's Country..."
Etidorhpa's Country appears in John Uri Lloyd's *Etidorhpa or the End of the Earth* (1895), one of the lesser-known Hollow Earth novels.

"...Cave systems in Kentucky..."
This is a reference to the Mammoth Cave system of central Kentucky. The Mammoth Cave system is the largest such in the world, with over 200 miles of surveyed passages and a possible hundred more connected to it.

"...The Inca Tunnel running from the same Kentucky caves towards Peru..."
The Inca Tunnel is from Emilio Salgari's *Duemila Leghe Sotto l'America* (1888), a novel about a long underground passage beneath the United States, ending in Peru amongst the treasures of the Incas.

"Orlando."
Orlando's pocket watch has a question mark on it, which is the symbol of the League of Extraordinary Gentlemen.

Page 183. "...To the east beyond the wildernesses of Drexara..."

Drexara was created by Abbé Antoine Francois Prevost and appears in *Le Philosophe Anglais* (1731), one of Prevost's adventure novels.

"...Are the Appalachian hills where Silver John (a balladeer and possibly a colleague of Gene Autry)..."
Silver John, a.k.a. John the Balladeer, was the memorable creation of Manly Wade Wellman and appears in a number of short stories and collections, beginning with "O Ugly Bird!" (*The Magazine of Fantasy and Science Fiction*, December 1951).

"...The hillbilly settlement called Dogpatch, with its famously attractive females, and the nearby Valley of the Shmoon, where little edible food is grown, but where nobody goes hungry."
Dogpatch and the Valley of the Shmoon both appear in Al Capp's comic strip *Li'l Abner* (1934-1977). The Shmoon (plural of Shmoo) are the most edible beasts in creation.

"Westwards, meanwhile, lies Oklahoma, another location that seems to inspire men to song and dance, at least to judge by the Nature Theatre of Oklahoma..."
This is a reference to Rodgers & Hammerstein's musical *Oklahoma!* (1955) and to the Nature Theatre of Oklahoma, which appears in Franz Kafka's *Amerika* (1927).

"Northwards, over Kansas, there would seem to be some massive flaw in space, as mentioned earlier, permitting access to extensive extra-worldly territories..."
This is a reference to the Oz books by L. Frank Baum, the first of which was *The Wonderful Wizard of Oz* (1900). In the Oz books Dorothy Gale and others made use of several portals to get to Oz, including the one in Kansas seen in *The Wonderful Wizard of Oz*.

"Further north still, in Wyoming, we discover Lake LaMetrie and its legendary talking monster..."
This is a reference to Wardon Curtis' short story "The Monster of Lake LaMetrie" (*Pearson's Magazine*, August 1899). The "talking monster" was an "elasmosaurus" into which Edward Framingham had his brain transplanted.

"...Eastwards in Montana is Red Gap, where displaced English butler Marmaduke Ruggles..."

Red Gap and Marmaduke Ruggles are from Harry Leon Wilson's novel *Ruggles of Red Gap* (1915), about an English butler whose services are won in a poker game by a wealthy family of the American West. In *Ruggles* Red Gap is located in eastern Washington.

"...The famous former Texas Ranger and masked vigilante John Reid, shortly prior to Reid's retirement to the coast to raise a family."

John Reid is better known as the Lone Ranger, from *The Lone Ranger* radio show, which began in 1933. Reid's retirement to "the coast" is a reference to the Green Hornet, who first appears in 1936 on *The Green Hornet* radio show. The Green Hornet's secret identity is Britt Reid, and it is established in *The Green Hornet* that Britt Reid is a descendant of John Reid.

"Iowa has Rampart Junction..."

Rampart Junction is from Ray Bradbury's short story "The Town Where No One Got Off" (*Ellery Queen*, October 1958), a town no outsider has visited for twenty years, and for good reason.

"...In the forgotten county of Apodidraskiana is the haunt of fugitives called Dotandcarryone Town..."

Apodidraskiana and Dotandcarryone Town are from Thomas Love Peacock's *Crotchet Castle*.

"Great Cypress Swamp is of more interest to us as the site of certain grim events, at a neighbouring graveyard, which involved a Mr. Randolph Carter of Massachusetts."

This is a reference to H.P. Lovecraft's short story "The Statement of Randolph Carter" (*The Vagrant* n13, May 1920).

"Great Cypress Swamp also runs into Okeefenokee Swamp, upon the Georgia/Florida border, where yet more talking animals have been reported..."

Although the Okeefenokee Swamp is a real place, the talking animals of Okeefenokee Swamp appear in Walt Kelly's classic comic strip *Pogo* (1941-1973).

"Higher up the coast, in Carolina, it appears that youthful ingenuity is prized with both South Carolina's Readestown..."
This is a reference to the dime novel character Frank Reade, his son, Frank Reade, Jr., and his grandson, Frank Reade III. Frank Reade was created by Harold Cohen and first appears in *Boys of New York* #28 (28 February 1876). Frank Reade and his kin were brilliant boy inventors who used their steam- and later electric-powered inventions and vehicles to enrich themselves and kill vast numbers of non-WASPs.

"...And North Carolina's Wrightstown named for rival boy inventors..."
Wrightstown is a reference to dime novel character Jack Wright, who was created by Luis Senarens and first appears in *Boys' Star Library* #216 (18 July 1891). Like Frank Reade, Jr., who Wright was friendly rivals with, Jack Wright was an ingenious boy inventor who used his electricity-powered vehicles to enrich himself, adventure around the world, and kill people who didn't look like he. In the original stories Wrightstown was only an hour's train ride north of New York City. Moore might have moved Wrightstown to North Carolina as a reference to the Wright Brothers' first airplane flight at Kitty Hawk, North Carolina.

"...While neighbouring Bayport has found fame within the last few years as home to many mysteries requiring intervention by teen-aged youths for their solution."
Bayport is the home of teenaged sleuths Frank and Joe Hardy, a.k.a. the Hardy Boys, created by Edward Stratemeyer and Leslie McFarlane and debuting in *The Tower Treasure* (1926). In the Hardy Boys novels the location of Bayport is left ambiguous, but it is relatively close to New York City.

"In Virginia, various local authors (such as Musgrave, Kennaston and Townsend, all of Fairview, close to Lichfield)..."
These individuals appear in James Branch Cabell's novel *The Cream of the Jest* (1917).

"...Have referred to local legends that concern a hunting party of three men that set out from the Jamestown colony during January, 1610, of whom no trace was ever found, save for a journal which tells how the hunters stumbled on 'a terrible Place' and concludes with the disturbing entry 'Staires! We have found staires!'"

This frightening event appears in Mark Z. Danielewski's haunted house novel *House of Leaves* (2000).

"A little north, in Maryland, stands the spectacular estate of Arnheim..." Arnheim was created by Edgar Allan Poe and appears in the novel *The Domain of Arnheim* (1847).

"...The dismal ruins of the Usher property..." This is a reference to Edgar Allan Poe's short story "The Fall of the House of Usher" (*Burton's Gentleman's Magazine*, September 1839).

"...Near Philadelphia...are the remains of Mettingen..." Mettingen appears in Charles Brockden Brown's *Wieland or the Transformation* (1798), a significant early American Gothic novel.

"...The eerily dilapidated summer-houses in the swamp called Gone-Away Lake, close to Creston..." Gone-Away Lake is from Elizabeth Enright's *Gone-Away Lake* (1957), a novel about a small, decaying summer community.

"...The reported talking pigs and other animals of upstate Centerboro..." This is a reference to Walter R. Brooks' "Freddy the Pig" books, the first of which was *To and Again* (1927).

"...To the river Island of the Fay..." The Island of the Fay was created by Edgar Allan Poe and appears in the short story "The Island of the Fay" (*Graham's Lady's and Gentleman's Magazine*, June 1841).

"...The allegedly-haunted town of Sleepy Hollow..." Sleepy Hollow is from Washington Irving's short story "The Legend of Sleepy Hollow" (*The Sketch Book*, 1820).

Page 184. "...The small Dutch settlement famed for its well-known case of genuine suspended animation, one Van Winkle..." This is a reference to Rip Van Winkle, who was created by Washington Irving and appears in the short story "Rip Van Winkle" (*The Sketch Book*, 1820).

"...The nearby town of Hadleyburg, formerly famous for its decency, has only known shame since its much-deserved humiliation by a passing stranger during 1899 "

This is a reference to Mark Twain's novel *The Man Who Corrupted Hadleyburg* (1899).

"Close to New York City is Roadtown..."
Roadtown is from Edgar Chambless' *Roadtown* (1910), a technological utopia.

"...While in New York itself a basement of unknown location is believed to be the resting place of Flatland, an entirely flat environment in which live two-dimensional beings..."
Flatland is a two-dimensional world created by Edwin A. Abbott and appearing in the novel *Flatland* (1884). In Rudy Rucker's short story "Message Found in a Copy of Flatland" (*The 57th Franz Kafka*, 1983), Flatland is in the basement of a Pakistani restaurant in London.

"Neighbouring Connecticut is unremarkable save for the proverbially pretty and agreeable womenfolk to be found in the small town of Stepford..."
Stepford and the very pretty women, who are actually robots, appear in Ira Levin's novel *The Stepford Wives* (1972) and the 1975 and 2004 films of the same name.

"...The matriarchal settlement of Coradine in Scotland..."
Coradine is from W.H. Hudson's *A Crystal Age*.

"...The old colonial city of Arkham..."
Arkham is from the various Cthulhu Mythos stories of H.P. Lovecraft.

"...The feared property in nearby Maine owned by a terrible munitions dealer named (I think) Belasco..."
Belasco and the feared property in Maine are from Richard Matheson's novel *Hell House* (1971).

"...The area surrounding the town of Jerusalem's Lot that has developed an evil reputation..."
Jerusalem's Lot is from Stephen King's novel *Salem's Lot* (1975).

"...And even made a pretty-sounding village called Eastwick sound alarming..."
This is a reference to John Updike's novel *The Witches of Eastwick* (1984).

"...A Massachusetts lunatic, Whateley by name..."
This is a reference "Old Wizard Whateley," who appears in H.P. Lovecraft's short story "The Dunwich Horror" (*Weird Tales* vol. 13 no. 4, April 1929).

"...Lucifer himself would one day 'set his cleft hoof' on the town."
This is a reference to the events of John Updike's *The Witches of Eastwick*.

"...Magical tokens to be found at a Victorian house on Walden Street in Concord..."
This is a reference to the Hall family house in Jane Langton's *The Diamond in the Window* (1962) and its several sequels. The plot of each novel centers on seemingly-ordinary magical objects—a stained-glass window and a sinister jack-in-the-box, a swing, a stereoscope, a tattered American flag, a bike—that lead the Hall children Eleanor and Eddy, and later their stepcousin Francesca (Frankie), to magical adventures.

"...'Sartin talking toad-things, like,' that might be found at Whiton House on the South Shore."
This is a reference to Edward Eager's novel *The Time Garden* (1958). The "talking toad-thing" is a reference to the Natterjack, the friend of the novel's protagonists.

"As we passed a lofty and forbidding residence in rural Massachusetts that our driver called Hill House..."
This is a reference to Shirley Jackson's wonderful haunted house novel *The Haunting of Hill House* (1959).

"...He told us of an awful-sounding lottery held in a nearby town, invariably resulting in the winner's murder..."
This is a reference to the events of Shirley Jackson's short story "The Lottery" (*The New Yorker*, 26 June 1948).

"...When we passed Beaulieu, a walled town on the Miskatonic River leading into Arkham..."
The walled town of Beaulieu appears in Ralph Adams Cram's *Walled Towns* (1919), an urban utopia.

"...A peculiar dream-territory accessible from certain (or perhaps I should say 'sartin') places in or around Arkham..."
This is a reference to the Dreamlands, mentioned in several stories by H.P. Lovecraft: "The Silver Key" (*Weird Tales* vol. 13 no. 1, January 1929), "Through the Gates of the Silver Key" (with E. Hoffmann Price, *Weird Tales* v24 n1, July 1934), and *The Dream-Quest of Unknown Kadath* (1943).

"...The architecturally peculiar 'Witch House'..."
The Witch House is a reference to H.P. Lovecraft's "Dreams in the Witch-House."

"...Arkham's Miskatonic University..."
Miskatonic University is a fictional university which appears in or is referred to in many of Lovecraft's "Cthulhu Mythos" stories.

"...A scholar, a young man said to have some knowledge of this world of dreams, named Randolph Carter."
Randolph Carter appears in five H.P. Lovecraft stories: "The Statement of Randolph Carter" (*The Vagrant*, May 1920), "The Unnamable" (*Weird Tales* v6 n1, July 1925), "The Dream-Quest of Unknown Kadath" (*Beyond the Wall of Sleep*, 1943), "The Silver Key" (*Weird Tales* v13 n1, January 1929), and "Through the Gates of the Silver Key" (with E. Hoffmann Price, *Weird Tales* v24 n1, July 1934).

"Allan seemed perplexed, saying he recognized the name from somewhere..."
Allan recognizes Randolph Carter because of the events of the text story "Allan and the Sundered Veil" from the *League of Extraordinary Gentlemen* v1.

"...Citing a talking cat that had been seen on Mulberry Street in nearby Springfield..."
The talking cat is seen in Dr. Seuss' *The Cat in the Hat* (1955), while

Mulberry Street is a reference to his *To Think I Saw It On Mulberry Street* (1937). Springfield, Massachusetts is the birthplace of Theodore Geisel, a.k.a. Dr. Seuss.

"...The dream-world town of Ulthar."
Ulthar appears in H.P. Lovecraft's short story "The Cats of Ulthar" (*The Tryout*, vo. 6 no. 11, November 1920) and "The Dream-Quest of Unknown Kadath." The cat may be from Ulthar because the citizens of Ulthar are themselves cats.

"...I stood almost naked in a derelict and filthy room..."
This event is described in "Allan and the Sundered Veil."

Page 185. "...In Government investigations into the United Avondale Phalanstery..."
The Phalanstery is mentioned on Page 162.

"...The ambiguous figure Orlando..."
Orlando is mentioned on Page 181.

"...Seemingly affiliated to the Prospero, Gulliver and later Murray groups..."
In the internal chronology of the two *League of Extraordinary Gentlemen* series Moore and O'Neill have shown and hinted at several Leagues. (Future *League* series will delve into the history of these Leagues). These Leagues include

- Prospero's Men: Prospero, the Duke of Milan, Caliban, and Ariel, from William Shakespeare's *The Tempest*; Christian, from John Bunyan's *The Pilgrim's Progress*; and Captain Robert Owe-Much, from "Frank Careless"' *The Floating Island*.
- Baron Münchhausen, from Rudolf Raspe's *Baron Münchhausen's Narrative of His Marvellous Travels and Campaigns in Russia*. Although the Baron is not associated with any individual Leagues that we know of, his silhouette appears in the British Museum among portraits of other Leagues, and we may suppose that the Baron was an agent of those who run the Leagues, if not a member of one.
- The eighteenth-century League: Lemuel Gulliver, from Jonathan Swift's *Gulliver's Travels*; Sir Percy Blakeney and Lady Marguerite Blakeney, from Baroness Emmuska Orczy's *The*

Scarlet Pimpernel; The Reverend Dr. Syn, from Russell Thorndike's *Doctor Syn*; Mistress Hill from John Cleland's *Fanny Hill*; and Natty Bumpo, from James Fennimore Cooper's five "Leatherstocking" novels.

- The nineteenth-century League: Mina Murray, Allan Quatermain, Captain Nemo, Dr. Jekyll/Mr. Hyde, and the Invisible Man.
- The Pre-War League: Mina Murray, Allan Quatermain (see the notes to Page 192 below), and Professor Challenger, from Arthur Conan Doyle's *The Lost World*. This group is hinted at on Page 189.

Leagues from later in the Twentieth century and the Twenty-First century will appear in future *League* series.

The 2003 film *The League of Extraordinary Gentlemen* hinted at other Leagues:

- A twelfth-century League whose members included Robin Hood, from English folk myth; the Black Arrow, from Sir Walter Scott's *The Black Arrow* (1883); and Ivanhoe, from Sir Walter Scott's *Ivanhoe* (1819). This League is chronologically inapt, as *The Black Arrow* is set during the War of the Roses, more than two hundred years after the events of *Ivanhoe*.
- A seventeenth-century League whose members included the Four Musketeers, from Alexandre Dumas' "Musketeers" novels, beginning with *The Three Musketeers* (1844); Captain Blood, from Rafael Sabatini's *Captain Blood* (1922); and the Sea-Hawk, from Rafale Sabatini's *The Sea-Hawk* (1915). This League is chronologically inapt; *The Sea-Hawk* is set at the time of the Spanish Armada's defeat, in 1588, while *Captain Blood* takes place in the 1680s and the Musketeers novels takes place in the first half of the Seventeenth century.

These Leagues, however, are not canonical, as they were not mentioned in the pages of *League* itself.

"...The base that he maintained at Lincoln Island..."
Lincoln Island appears in Jules Verne's *The Mysterious Island*. In the novel Lincoln Island was Nemo's volcano base.

"...Also made use of an underground port known as Nautilus Island..."
Nautilus Island appears in Jules Verne's *20,000 Leagues Under the Sea*. Nautilus Island is an underground port inside of an extinct volcano.

"Upon the seabed east of his volcanic grotto, his log notes a great proliferation of stone ruins that Nemo thought to be the submerged townships of Atlantis..."

This is a reference to *20,000 Leagues Under the Sea*, in which Nemo shows Arronax the underwater ruins of "Atlantis."

"...The much feared and fabled Nameless City..."

This may be a reference to the Nameless City of H.P. Lovecraft's short story "The Nameless City" (*Wolverine*, November 1921). "The Nameless City" introduces Abdul Alhazred, who in Lovecraft's fiction is the "Mad Arab" who wrote the blasphemous book *The Necronomicon*. "The Nameless City" is about a nameless city "remote in the desert of Araby" which is home to a portal to a luminous, other-dimensional abyss. The Nameless City is loosely based on the real city of Irem or Iram, which is mentioned in the Qur'an in Sura 89:6-8:

> Seest thou not how thy Lord dealt with the 'Ad (people),-
> Of the (city of) Iram, with lofty pillars,
> The like of which were not produced in (all) the land?

Irem is located in Arabia, however, rather than the Sahara. In Lovecraft's story "Medusa's Coil" (*Weird Tales*, 1939) Atlantean ruins in the Sahara are mentioned.

This may also be a reference to Pierre Benoit's *L'Atlantide* (1919), a novel in which two French Army officers discover a lost Atlantean colony in the Sahara desert ruled over by an Ayesha-like queen.

"We sailed past bleak Mongaza Island, where with good eyes you can see the horrid idol raised beside the so-called Boiling Lake. A giant called Famongomadan apparently sacrificed young virgins to the idol in the early sixteenth century..."

Mongaza Island and the details of the virgin sacrifice can be found in *Amadis of Gaul*.

"...by which time I thought science had assured us the giant race of Earth's prehistory was long extinct."

This is a reference to the *Almanac* text on Pages 166 and following, which established that giants from various stories had existed on Earth but that the race had died out centuries ago.

"Traveling on we passed Mogador..."
Mogador appears in the works of Alberto Ruy-Sanchez, beginning with
Los Nombres Del Aire (1987), a novel about a woman's life inside the
walled, North African-style city of Mogador.

"...I barely noticed the Fixed Isle..."
The Fixed Isle appears in *Amadis of Gaul*.

"...The isle of Lixus whereupon gold hornet-bees drone busily about the
island's sole surviving gold-leafed tree..."
Lixus and its gold insects appear in Pliny the Elder's *Natural History*.

"...We put to shore near Nouakchott upon the western coast of
Mauritania."
Nouakchott is the capital of Mauritania. In 1900 and 1901 it was a
small village.

"We avoid the islands known as the Harmattan Rocks..."
The Harmattan Rocks appear in Hugh Lofting's *Doctor Dolittle's Post
Office*.

"...Soon pass the isle called No-Man's-Land..."
No-Man's-Land appears in *Doctor Dolittle's Post Office*.

"...Coming at last in sight of Nacumera..."
Nacumera and its dog-headed inhabitants appear in Sir John Mandeville's
Voiage and Travayle of Sir John Maundevile (1357). The Nacumerans
are modern versions of the Cynocephali, which were first mentioned in
Pliny the Elder's *Natural History*.

"...A place that I have previously heard of, called the Island of the
Blessed..."
The Island of the Blessed appears in Lucian of Samosata's *True History*.

"We travel onward, passing by Wild Island..."
Wild Island appears in Ruth Stiles Gannet's *My Father's Dragon* (1957),
a novel about the narrator's father, who runs away as a child to rescue
an exploited baby dragon.

"It may be that the dragon has its origins on Silha, further south..."
Silha appears in Sir John Mandeville's *Voiage and Travayle of Sir John Maundevile*.

"Silha is the most northerly island of the Dondum Archipelago..."
The Dondum Archipelago appears in the *Voiage and Travayle of Sir John Maundevile*.

"...the minor continent Genotia, some miles off the coast of German Southwest Africa."
Genotia appears in Louis Adrien Duperron de Castera's novel *Le Theatre des Passions* (1731). In 1890 "German Southwest Africa" is what is now Namibia.

Page 186. "...the Mithras-worshippers found in Ximeque, Genotia's largest region. Gynopyrea, on Genotia's southern coast, is infamous for its effeminate behavior..."
Ximeque and Gynopyrea appear in *Le Theatre des Passions*.

"...past Neopie Island..."
Neopie Island appears in *Le Theatre des Passions*.

"Pandoclia, nearby, is similar..."
Pandoclia appears in *Le Theatre des Passions*.

"Nimpatan, a large island of silk-garbed and gold-worshipping scoundrels..."
Nimpatan appears in John Holmesby's *The Voyages, Travels, and Wonderful Discoveries of Capt. John Holmesby*.

"...after his death by one Miss Diver..."
Miss Diver is mentioned on Page 177.

"...the famed seagoing Iraqi adventurer Sindbad."
Sindbad appears in *The Arabian Nights* (14th-16th century C.E.).

"The most southerly of these islands is Canthahar..."
Canthahar, or Cantahar, appears in de Varennes de Mondasse's *La Découverte de L'Empire de Cantahar* (1730), a novel about the discovery of Cantahar by a ship blown far off course.

"...While nearby Cucumber Island..."
Cucumber Island appears in Rudolph Erich Raspe's *Baron Münchhausen's Narrative of His Marvellous Travels and Campaigns in Russia.*

"Three unnamed islands mentioned in the manuscript are probably those settled by the now-obligatory shipwrecked Englishman, a sometime-associate of Lemuel Gulliver named Sir Charles Smith who was cast up there during 1740, and called by him New Britain."
Sir Charles Smith and New Britain appear in Pierre Chevalier Duplessis' *Mémoires de Sir George Wollap* (1787-1788), a Robinsonade.

"Further north, just south of Madagascar, is the isle of Taprobane with its fabulous City of the Sun..."
Taprobane and the City of the Sun appear in Pliny the Elder's *Natural History.*

"...While on nearby Bustrol he reports that the inhabitants have formed themselves into perfect square provinces."
Bustrol appears in Simon Tyssot de Patot's *Voyage et Avantures de Jaques Massé* (1710), a utopian novel.

"...The northern swamp-isle of Aepyornis..."
Aepyornis appears in H.G. Wells' "Aepyornis Island" (*Pall Mall Budget*, 27 Dec 1894). The Aepyornis were real, however; they were a genus of flightless birds native to Madagascar. It's thought that Aepyornis eggs were the source of the legends of the Rocs.

"...The giant avian Rocs that he had once encountered further north."
Sindbad encountered the Rocs on the Island of the Roc in *The Arabian Nights.*

"He also notes that some way east of Madagascar is an island where the cliffs, viewed from the sea, resemble nothing so much as a massive human skull, where monstrously proportioned primates had allegedly been seen, along with dragons, Rocs, and other creatures of that nature."
Skull Island, a.k.a. the Island of the Mists, appears in *King Kong* (1933), from the Edgar Wallace's "King Kong" (*Boys' Magazine*, 1933).

"...Just north-east of Madagascar off the coast of Mozambique, although not mentioned by the legendary Iraqi sailor, there exists a mountainous island where in 1782 a stranded Englishwoman, Mrs. Hannah Hewit, built not only her own house of clay bricks but also a mechanical man as a companion (and possibly, as certain sailors' stories have indecently suggested, as a paramour)."
This island, "Hewit's Island," appears in Charles Dibdin's *Hannah Hewit* (1796), a Robinsonade with a female protagonist.

"...Meillcourt, further north still, was in Sindbad's time the province of the peaceful Troglocites and Quacacites..."
Meillcourt, the Troglocites and Quacacites all appear in Jean Baptiste de Boyer, the Marquis d'Argens' *Le Législateur Moderne, ou, Les Mémoires du Chevalier de Meillcourt* (1739), a utopian novel.

"...While on nearby 'Island of Iron' Marbotikin Dulda..."
Marbotikin Dulda appears in Pierre Chevalier Duplessis' *Mémoires de Sir George Wollap*.

"Rondule, the island furthest south, ruled by a hundred chieftains..."
Rondule, or Rondisle, appears in *Mémoires de Sir George Wollap*.

"...While on Lamary the naked locals hold women in common..."
Lamary appears in Sir John Mandeville's *Voiage and Travayle of Sir John Maundevile*.

"A sub-group of islands nearby, the Waq archipelago, are said by Sindbad to be ruled by women..."
The Waq archipelago appears in *The Arabian Nights*.

"...Sindbad makes the mystifying observation that it would make a bad place for a small group of schoolboys to be marooned."
This is a reference to William Golding's novel *Lord of the Flies* (1954).

"Feather Island, not far off..."
Feather Island appears in Fanny de Beauharnais' *Rélation très véritable d'une Isle Nouvellement Découverte* (1786), a utopian novel.

"To the north, the isle where stands the Mihragian Kingdom..."
The Mihragian Kingdom appears in *The Arabian Nights.*

"...While King's Kingdom, on an adjacent island, is believed to be the burial site of Solomon, son of David."
King's Kingdom appears in *The Arabian Nights.*

"The island empire Pentixore is close at hand..."
Pentixore appears in Sir John Mandeville's *Voiage and Travayle of Sir John Maundevile.*

Page 187. "...And off Somalia's coast exists the rival Azanian Empire..."
The Azanian Empire appears in Evelyn Waugh's *Black Mischief* (1932), a satire about an attempt by an African ruler to modernize his country.

"Double Island, which seems to both rise and submerge at will, lies to the east..."
Double Island appears in George Maspero's *Les Contes Populaires de l'Egypte Ancienne* (*Popular Stories of Ancient Egypt*, 1899), a collection of ancient Egyptian folk tales.

"...While Camphor Island, known for its generous camphor trees..."
Camphor Island appears in *The Arabian Nights.*

"...And giant horned animal, the karkadann..."
The karkadann is mentioned in *The Arabian Nights* as a Persian unicorn which is snatched up by a Roc while an elephant is speared on its horn. The karkadann was based on the rhinoceros.

"...As does the island of the Diamond Mountains..."
The Diamond Mountains appear in *The Arabian Nights.*

"Continuing north we pass Old Man of the Sea Island, with its terrible ancient inhabitant reputedly killed by Sindbad, though we only have the mariner's own word for this, and the island of the Mountain of Clouds..."
Old Man of the Sea Island and the Mountain of Clouds both appear in *The Arabian Nights.*

"The nearby Island of Grey Amber, meanwhile..."
The Island of Grey Amber appears in *The Arabian Nights*.

"...Whereas Bragman, the Land of Faith, was so devout and dull that Alexander couldn't be bothered to conquer it."
Bragman appears in Sir John Mandeville's *Voiage and Travayle of Sir John Maundevile*.

"The people of the Island of Connubial Sacrifice, at least as they're described by Sindbad..."
The Island of Connubial Sacrifice appears in *The Arabian Nights*.

"Manghalour, off the coastline of Saudi Arabia..."
Manghalour appears in Louis Rustaing de Saint-Jory's *Les Femmes Militaires* (1735), a utopian novel.

"...The linguistically extraordinary island known as Polyglot..."
Polyglot appears in the *Liber Monstrorum de Diversis Generibus* (Ninth century C.E.), a medieval bestiary.

"...And also Taerg Natib..."
Taerg Natib, or Taerg Natrib, appears in William Bullein's *A Dialogue Both Pleasant and Pitiful, Wherein is a Goodly Regimente Against the Fever Pestilence, with a Consolation and Comfort against Death* (1564), a work of political philosophy.

"In the Arabian Sea near the mouth of the Persian Gulf we have Calonack..."
Calonack appears in Sir John Mandeville's *Voiage and Travayle of Sir John Maundevile*.

"...Further west, Parthalia is inhabited by giants of great longevity..."
Parthalia is from William Bullein's *A Dialogue Both Pleasant and Pitiful*.

"...We have the mountainous country Ardistan..."
Ardistan appears in Karl May's *Ardistan and Djinnistan* (1909), a symbolical fairy tale about sin and redemption.

"...By League associates William Samson Senior and his son, also called William Samson, the feared (and currently famed) 'The Wolf of Kabul.'" William Samson, Sr. appears in *League* v2 as the League's carriage driver, beginning on Page 61. William Samson, "the Wolf of Kabul," is a character in the British comics *Wizard* and *Hotspur* beginning in 1922. He is Bill Sampson (or "Samson"), an agent for the British Intelligence Corps operating on the Northwest frontier of India. The Wolf's father is not mentioned in the original comics. William Samson, Sr. is Moore's creation, an example of what Moore calls "back-engineering."

"A triple-headed volcano called Djebbel Allah on the northern borders makes a hazard of the route to neighboring El Hadd, home of the much-admired white lancers, while nearby lands such as Djinnistan, Djunubistan, Ussulistan, Tshobanistan, and the giant-built isthmus known as the Chatar Defile..."
Djebbel Allah, El Hadd, Djinnistan, Djunubistan, Ussulistan, Tshobanistan, and the Chatar Defile are all from Karl May's *Ardistan and Djinnistan*.

"...I have a good mind to let Chung take his Clicky-Ba to the whole bloody lot of them..."
Chung was the native servant of the Wolf of Kabul. "Clicky-Ba" was the iron-edged cricket bat which Chung used to kill his enemies.

"...The adjacent warring lands of Farghestan and the old Christian kingdom of Orsenna..."
Farghestan and Orsenna appear in Julien Gracq's *Le Rivage des Syrtes* (*The Shore of Syrtes*, 1951), an allegorical novel about cultural suicide.

"The Garamanti tribe inhabiting the Rifei mountains in Afghanistan..."
The Garamanti tribe and the Rifei mountains appear in Antonio de Guevara's *Libro Llamado Relox de los Principes, en el Cual va Encorporado el Muy Famoso Libro de Marco Aurelio* (*The Dial of Princes*, 1527), a pseudo-historical apocrypha.

"...Where we find the mountain-ringed land of Tallstoria..."
Tallstoria appears in Sir Thomas More's *Utopia*.

"...a visit to Samarah and its splendid palace Alkoremi is advised..."
Samarah and Alkoremi appear in William Beckford's *Vathek* (1787), one of the great Arabesque gothics.

"...The fabulously jewelled and mosaic-decorated City of Sand..."
The City of Sand appears in Jean d'Agraives' *La Cité des Sables* (1926),
a novel of aerial adventure.

"...At the end of beautiful Fakreddin Valley is the ruined palace
Ishtakar..."
Fakreddin Valley and the palace of Ishtakar appear in William Beckford's
Vathek.

"...As mentioned by both the notorious Lord Byron and his fellow poet
William Ashbless..."
William Ashbless is the invention of Tim Powers and James Blaylock.
The pair had used the name as a pseudonym to publish their cowritten
poetry. Later, when they needed a name for a poet in their books, they
independently used Ashbless' name.

"...The almost unreachable city of Jannati Shah..."
Jannati Shah is from George Allan England's *The Flying Legion* (1920),
a Lost Race novel about a golden city found in the depths of the Arabian
desert.

Page 188. "...The gemmed remains of Irem Zat El-Emad, or Irem
with the Lofty Buildings..."
Irem Zat El-Emad appears in *The Arabian Nights*.

"Northwest we pass Golden Mountain, where a sultan's treasure horde
was once concealed..."
Golden Mountain appears in Emilio Salgari's novel *Il Treno Volante*
(*The Flying Train*, 1904).

"...And skirt the Christian city Nova Solyma in Israel..."
Nova Solyma appears in Samuel Gott's *Novae Solymae Libri Sex*.

"...We find the ruined palace-principality called Here or Ici..."
"Ici," a.k.a. "Here," appears in Philippe Jullian's novel *La Fuite en
Egypte* (*Flight into Egypt*, 1968).

"..a barge-trip down the curious Brissonte River..."
The Brissonte appears in *Liber Monstrorum de Diversis Generibus*.

"Not far from the Brissonte, upon the beaches close to Alexandria, is Monsters' Park."

Monsters' Park appears in Maria Savi-Lopez's *Leggende del Mare* (1920), a collection of myths and legends about the sea.

"Further south is Heliopolis..."

The fictional Heliopolis appears in *Die Zauberflöte* (1791) by Wolfgang Amadeus Mozart and Emanuel Schikaneder. Fittingly for the world of *League*, *Die Zauberflöte* is full of Masonic symbolism and imagery.

"...While upon the border with Sudan exists the subterranean Sunless City..."

The Sunless City appears in Albert Bonneau's novel *La Cité Sans Soleil* (1927).

"...The ever-young and slender gallant named Orlando, who adventured in North Africa during the sixteenth century, apparently a male during this part of his or her career."

The titular character in Virginia Woolf's *Orlando* changes sex overnight. The Orlando of Woolf's novel did not begin adventuring before the 1630s. Moore, however, has linked this Orlando to Matteo Maria Boiardo's *Orlando Innamorato* and Ludovico Ariosto's *Orlando Furioso*, thus making the character much longer lived than Woolf's character.

"...And therein sought the Kingdom of the Amphicleocles..."

The Kingdom of the Amphicleocles appears in Charles Fieux de Mouhy's *Lamekis* (1735), a novel about an ancient Egyptian's subterranean adventures and his discovery of a utopian civilization.

"We passed the ruined citadel of Bou Chougga..."

Bou Chougga appears in A. Certeux's *D'Algérie Traditionelle* (*Traditional Algeria*, 1884), a collection of traditional Algerian folklore.

"Beyond Bou Chougga is a dreadful place, beside the yellow waters of the sluggish Zaire, where acre after acre of the ground is choked with sickly lilies and the clouds hang fixed within the dismal sky. The region is called Silence..."

The land of Silence appears in Edgar Allan Poe's short story "Silence: A Fable" (*The Baltimore Book*, 1839).

"At last we reached Abdalles, neighbor to the Kingdom of the Amphicleocles..."
Abdalles appears in Charles Fieux de Mouhy's *Lamekis*.

"Heading into Chad we had the Mountains of the Moon behind us to the north..."
The Mountains of the Moon are mentioned in Ptolemy's *Geography* (circa Second century C.E.) and in Ludovico Ariosto's *Orlando Furioso*. There are real Mountains of the Moon, in East Africa along the western border of Uganda.

"...Umbopa fairly put the wind up Curtis, Good and I by telling us that we were now in Arimaspian Country..."
Sir Henry Curtis and Captain Good are Quatermain's companions in *Allan Quatermain*. Arimaspian Country appears in a number of accounts, including Herodotus' *History* and Pliny the Elder's *Natural History*.

Page 189. "...Then, a mile south, Curtis tripped upon a skeleton half buried in the undergrowth that looked like that of some enormous lion, yet had a beak, and now we don't know what to think."
This may be a reference to the reaction to pre-twentieth-century finds of *Protoceratops andrewsi* in the deserts of Mongolia. It was thought that these fossils might have created the legends of lion-sized, bird-headed animals.

"...We made camp in Albino Land, a region sparsely populated by albino Negroes..."
Albino Land appears in Voltaire's *Essai sur L'Histoire Générale et Sur les Moeurs et L'Esprit des Nations Eepuis Charlemagne Jusqu'a Nos Jours* (*Essay on the General History and on the Morals and Spirit of Nations From the Days of Charlemagne to Our Own*, 1756), a history of the world.

"Whatever idle thoughts I had of these grew dim, however, when we moved south into Makalolo..."
Makalolo appears in Albert Robida's *Voyages tres extraordinaires de Saturnin Farandoul dans les 5 ou 6 parties du monde* (1879), a gentle parody of Jules Verne's work in which Saturnin Farandoul encounters Captain Nemo and Phileas Fogg, among others.

"...The many local tribes such as the ferocious Bulanga and the utterly dreadful wife-trading cannibals of the M'tezo, who eat all their spare relatives."
The Bulanga and M'tezo appear in Norman Douglas' *South Wind* (1917), a fictional exploration of the pleasures of the hedonistic life.

"We skirted round a hamlet called Ben Khatour's Village..."
Ben Khatour's Village appears in Edgar Rice Burroughs' novel *The Son of Tarzan* (1915).

"...We came into the kingdom Pal-Ul-Don."
Pal-Ul-Don appears in Edgar Rice Burroughs' novel *Tarzan the Terrible* (1921).

"...Not wholly unlike the supposed gryphon skeleton we'd found in Arimaspian Country, but bigger, with a ruff of bone behind the head and two rhino-like horns grown from the beak..."
This is a reference to the Gryfs of Pal-Ul-Don in *Tarzan the Terrible*. The Gryfs are a species of small Triceratops.

"...The miles-high peaks called by the local people Saba's Breasts, which mark the plateau Kukuanaland..."
Saba's Breasts and Kukuanaland appear in H. Rider Haggard's *King Solomon's Mines*.

"...Abyssinia and the neighboring Kingdom of Ishmaelia..."
Ishmaelia appears in Evelyn Waugh's *Scoop, a Novel about Jerusalem* (1938), about a naive British journalist sent to Africa to cover an impending revolution.

"Before Ishmaelia came to prominence, however, Abyssinia itself was commented upon at length by League associate Orlando, visiting the area in the early sixteenth century. 'How many years, I wonder, has it been, or centuries, since last I knew the pleasure of these sands between my toes? Travelling without company I soon came to those dear, familiar ruins in the north, set on their stone plateau; those tumbled relics of a city that I still walk in my dreams of childhood, where my girlish fingertips still know each dent in each worn stone as though it were a long lost cousin. Tethering my horse I found my way through the familiar labyrinths and chambers, mounting finally the old iron ladder to our city's central courtyard, or at least its remnants. Some of my old fellows left their hole-like dwellings at the city's outskirts to come to greet me, though the Troglodyte condition is much worse in them, and this has advanced since last we met. I hardly could make out a word they spoke, though our discourse was amiable, and they seemed most amazed to find me now a man, insisting that I drop my britches and provide them evidence of this. I asked after my much-beloved old Greek friend, Mr. Cartaphilus, but from what I could make out of their reply they have not seen him for some time, and think that he still roams the world disconsolately, seeking some eventual cure for what he views as our abiding curse."

This is a reference to the City of the Immortals, which appears in Jorge Luis Borges' "El Inmortal" (*El Aleph*, 1949). In the story "Mr. Cartaphilus" is the poet Homer under a pseudonym. "Cartaphilus" is one of the older names of Ahasuerus, or the Wandering Jew, who in Christian legend is forced to wander eternally as atonement for his failure to recognize Jesus as the Messiah. "Cartaphilus" was first used in 1228 in Roger of Wendover's *Flores Historiarum* (*Flowers of History*) in reference to "a porter of the hall in Pilate's service."

"...And continued on to Nubia where perfumed Senapho is ruler..."
Nubia and Senapho appear in Ludovico Ariosto's *Orlando Furioso*.

"It is at Saba here in Abyssinia, though, that Solomon and Sheba's tomb is found..."
Saba appears in Sir John Mandeville's *Voiage and Travayle of Sir John Maundevile*.

"I journeyed on, and rode a while beside the Marvellous River..."
The Marvellous River appears in Jean, Sire de Joinville's *Histoire de Saint Louis* (1309), a biography of Louis IX.

"I heard the music of sun-worshipers with gongs and cymbals, carried on a dusk breeze from the Temple of the Sun in Mezzorania..."
Mezzorania appears in Simon Berington's *The Memoirs of Sigy Gaudentio di Lucca* (1737), about an isolated African utopia.

"Elsewhere in the same document Orlando makes mention of the City of the Apes..."
The City of the Apes appears in *The Arabian Nights*.

"The Island of the Palace of Joy..."
The Island of the Palace of Joy appears in Matteo Maria Boiardo's *Orlando Innamorato*.

"...Part of the larger country known as Freeland..."
Freeland appears in Dr. Theodor Hertzka's *Freiland*.

"Close by, on Tanganyika's coastline we find Jolliginki, where the Land of Monkeys is located."
Jolliginki and the Land of Monkeys appear in Hugh Lofting's novel *The Story of Doctor Dolittle* (1922).

"...A school-friend of George Edward Challenger..."
Professor Challenger appears in three of Arthur Conan Doyle's novels and two short stories, beginning with *The Lost World*.

"...Discovered the purportedly two-headed animal that caused such an intense curiosity amongst zoologists and scientists..."
This is a reference to the pushmi-pullyu, from Hugh Lofting's *The Story of Doctor Dolittle*.

"...Until the discovery of the Piltdown Man in 1912."
The Piltdown Man was a hoax perpetrated in 1912 by Charles Dawson, an amateur paleontologist, who claimed to have found the remains of a new species of man in a gravel pit near Piltdown, England near Sussex.

"...There is Bong Tree Land..."
Bong Tree Land appears in a number of Edward Lear poems, beginning with "The Owl and the Pussy Cat" (*Nonsense Songs, Stories, Botany and Alphabets*, 1871).

"...passing swiftly through Basilisk Country..."
Basilisk Country appears in Pliny the Elder's *Natural History*.

"...we reach Butua in Bechuanaland."
Butua appears in the Marquis de Sade's *Aline et Valcour* (1795), a "philosophical novel." Bechuanaland was a section of what is now Botswana. The British annexed it in 1885.

"…An occasional resort for the depraved aristocrats of Silling castle…"
Silling castle, referred to on Page 173, appears in the Marquis de Sade's
120 Days of Sodom.

"North of here, in German Southwest Africa, there stands the city of
Beersheba…"
Beersheba appears in Italo Calvino's *Invisible Cities*.

"On our first day, out walking in the hot, damp forests near the coast,
we stumbled on a most peculiar site, being a long abandoned hut
apparently untouched by either local folk or wildlife. You will think me
mad, but there seemed something strangely English about this abode,
with its clay cladding and its window grids of woven branches; its roof
thatched after a style I am sure I've seen in Devon. Inside was a quaint
stone fireplace and rudimentary furnishings, and I had quite a nasty turn
when I happened upon a baby's crib containing a small skeleton, though
Allan reassured me that the bones appeared to him to be those of an
infant monkey, possibly some unfamiliar species of gorilla."
This is a reference to Edgar Rice Burroughs' novel *Tarzan of the Apes*
(1912). The hut is the location where Tarzan's father and mother died,
while the bones belong to the dead child of Kala, Tarzan's ape mother.

Page 190. "…Into eastern Mauritania where, we were told, exist
two isolated outposts of the Roman Empire, Castra Sanguinarius and
Castrum Mare…"
Castra Sanguinarius and Castrum Mare appear in Edgar Rice Burroughs'
novel *Tarzan and the Lost Empire* (1929).

"…The marvellous oasis of Giphantia…"
Giphantia appears in Charles Francois Tiphaigne de la Roche's
Giphantia (1760), a proto-science fictional *voyage imaginaire*.

"…And past the walled and dead City of Brass…"
The City of Brass appears in *The Arabian Nights*.

"Here, in a quarter of the city that tourists have named 'the Interwoven
Zone,' Allan made his by-now furtive enquiries of a seedy-looking chap
who had the sweet, medicinal aroma on his dusty clothing that I now
associate with opium, and we were led through narrow streets to a

stone house with cool, dark rooms where we were introduced to one of the most utterly repellent and unsettling individuals that it has been my misfortune to encounter. Squatting in a corner swathed in shapeless robes, with only one deformed hand visible, clutching the fuming mouthpiece of a hookah pipe, I would not even swear our host was human. A pretty but subdued young Arab boy lay curled up like a dog upon the rush mat where the creature sat, but had a frightened air to him and did not meet our eyes. Our host's voice, issuing from the darkened cave-mouth of his cowl, was guttural yet sounded somehow slippery. We were informed that we were in the presence of a...I believe the word was 'Mudwunk' or 'Mugwump' or something like that...and that this creature could provide us with whatever drugs or sexual activities we might desire."
This is a reference to William S. Burroughs' "Interzone" (a.k.a. the "Interwoven Zone") and the Mugwump, which appears in a few of Burroughs' works, including *Naked Lunch* (1959). The Mugwump is a nasty quasi-human thing, in Burroughs' words "obscene beyond any possible vile act or practice." The similarity between Moore's description of the Mugwump and Carroll's description of the Caterpillar in *Alice in Wonderland* may not be coincidental.

"...The French intended to transform this area, with interlinked canals, to a 'Saharan Sea.'"
The proposed Saharan Sea appears in Jules Verne's *L'Invasion de la mer* (1905). The Sea was also suggested as a possible project in the real world, though never attempted.

"...A reputed cannibal-and-sorcerer infested region called Crotalophoboi Land..."
Crotalophoboi Land appears in Norman Douglas' *South Wind.*

"...The prosperous kingdom of Macaria..."
Macaria appears in Samuel Hartlib's *A Description of the Famous Kingdom of Macaria* (1641), one of the lesser known utopias.

"...And soon passed into Brodie's Land..."
Brodie's Land appears in Jorge Luis Borges' "El Informe de Brodie" (*Doctor Brodie's Report*, 1970), about a land where humans evolved into beasts.

"Headed for Niamey..."
Niamey is Niger's largest city.

"...The outskirts of the city known as Blackland..."
Blackland appears in Jules Verne's *L'Etonnante aventure de la Mission Barsac* (1919), a novel about a French mission in West Africa which ends up in Blackland, a mysterious desert city.

"...We rode on into Uziri Country, where we similarly tried our hardest to avoid the fierce Waziri tribe."
Uziri Country and the Waziri Tribe appear in Edgar Rice Burroughs' novels *The Beasts of Tarzan* (1914), *Tarzan and the Jewels of Opar* (1916), and *Tarzan the Untamed* (1919).

"The valley country Midian, where the people were converted to fanatically devoted Christians..."
Midian appears in Edgar Rice Burroughs' novel *Tarzan Triumphant* (1919).

"...The legendary minarets of Opar glinting high above that citadel's impregnable and massive walls..."
Opar appears in Edgar Rice Burroughs' *The Return of Tarzan*, *Tarzan and the Jewels of Opar*, and *Tarzan the Invincible*.

Page 191. "In French Sudan we managed to pass through the Valley of the Sepulchre without becoming caught up in a theological dispute between the separate 12th century Crusader colonies of Nimmr, and its sister city at the valley's other end."
Nimmr and the Valley of the Sepulchre appear in Edgar Rice Burroughs' novel *Tarzan, Lord of the Jungle* (1928).

"...A secret and forbidden city ruled by a fierce warrior queen, we next camped by the great volcano Tuen-Baka, in which we believed this Kingdom (called Ashair by local tribesmen)..."
Ashair and Tuen-Baka appear in Edgar Rice Burroughs' novel *Tarzan and the Forbidden City* (1938).

"The deep, enormous footprint, possibly from some variety of dinosaur.."
If this is a reference to something in particular I am unaware of it.

"We passed on through the outer reaches of the Great Thorn Forest where we had a startling encounter with the towering tribeswomen of Alali..."
The Great Thorn Forest and Alali appear in Edgar Rice Burroughs' novel *Tarzan and the Ant Men* (1924).

"...The tribesmen of nearby Minuni..."
Minuni appears in Edgar Rice Burroughs' *Tarzan and the Ant Men*.

"Riding into Fantippo..."
Fantippo appears in Hugh Lofting's *Doctor Dolittle's Post Office* and *Doctor Dolittle and the Secret Lake*.

"District EC7, corresponding roughly with the British Protectorate of Uganda, had Ayesha's city, Kor, listed amongst its prominent addresses."
Kor appears in H. Rider Haggard's *She*. "EC" is British postal code for "East Central," which in the real world covers the eastern end of central London. The London EC district is subdivided into EC1 to EC4; there is no EC7.

"...Through the jungle region known as the Ape Kingdom by its natives..."
The Ape Kingdom appears in Edgar Rice Burroughs' *Tarzan of the Apes*.

"...Where the drumming of the simian hominids' famed 'Dum-Dum' ceremony echoed on the wind above the forest canopy..."
The "Dum-Dum" ceremony appears in *Tarzan of the Apes*. This may also be a reference to the "Dum-Dum" ceremony which appears in the *Tarzan* parody, "Melvin of the Apes," written and drawn by John Severin and appearing in *Mad Magazine* #6 (August/September 1953).

"...They passed the Kingdom of the One-Eyed..."
The Kingdom of the One-Eyed appears in Jean Gaspard Dubois-Fontanelle's *Aventures philosophiques*.

"...The droppings-fouled great wall bounding the city of Xujan..."
Xujan appears in *Tarzan the Untamed*.

"...Passing through the Empire known as Ponukele-Drelchkaff..."

Ponukele-Drelchkaff appears in Raymond Roussel's *Impressions d'Afrique* (1910), a poem about a fantastical Africa.

"...the famed Viceroyalty of Ouidah..."
Ouidah appears in Bruce Chatwin's *The Viceroy of Ouidah* (1980), a novel about a Brazilian slave trader in Dahomey.

"In the north, they say, is Sleepless City..."
Sleepless City is a legend of the Hausa people of west Africa.

"...Carry your remains to Fixit City on Nigeria's Bauchi Plateau..."
Fixit City is a Hausa legend.

"Dead's Town, deep in the Nigerian bush..."
Deads' Town appears in Amos Tutuola's *The Palm-Wine Drinkard and His Dead Palm-Wine Tapster in the Deads' Town* (1952), a collection of hallucinatory African fairytales.

"...The cruel and insanely capricious more northerly town, Unreturnable-Heaven."
Unreturnable-Heaven appears in Amos Tutuola's *The Palm-Wine Drinkard and His Dead Palm-Wine Tapster in the Deads' Town*.

"We saw swamp-bound Wraith-Island.."
Wraith-Island appears in Amos Tutuola's *The Palm-Wine Drinkard and His Dead Palm-Wine Tapster in the Deads' Town*.

Page 192. "On our way we had the most delightful treat of falling in amongst a herd of the most civilised and gentle elephants that I have ever seen, one of whom I thought I saw wearing a small golden crown atop his head..."
This is a reference to the Babar books of Cecile, Jean and Laurent de Brunhoff, which began in 1934 with *The Story of Babar*.

"...The horrid little hut, deep in the Congo and still ringed by decomposing heads on poles, where ivory-trader's agent Kurtz met his deserved demise..."
This is a reference to Joseph Conrad's novel *The Heart of Darkness* (1901).

"...Members of the Amahagger tribe..."
The Amahagger tribe appears in H. Rider Haggard's *She*.

"...Ruled by a native Amahagger woman posing as Ayesha (whom, they learned, was now believed to have been reincarnated somewhere off in Asia)."
This is a reference to H. Rider Haggard's novel *Ayesha: The Return of She* (1905), a sequel to *She*.

"We saw the name 'Orlando' and word that I thought might have been the ancient Greek for 'Homer.'"
This is a reference to Jorge Luis Borges' "El Inmortal." In the story one of the Immortals in the City of the Immortals is Homer.

"We traveled north through Blemmyae Country..."
Blemmyae Country appears in Pliny the Elder's *Natural History*.

"...Until we reached his much-beloved lost land of Zuvendis..."
Zuvendis appears in H. Rider Haggard's *Allan Quatermain*.

"...Just prior to Allan's death we found out that a son of his he'd thought long dead (also called Allan)..."
Quatermain's son is mentioned in several of Haggard's books, beginning with *King Solomon's Mines*. His death is described in *Allan Quatermain*. Quatermain's son, in the books, is named "Harry." The reason that he is here called "Allan" is—and this is spoiling the surprise, I admit—that Quatermain and Mina are faking Quatermain's death and lying to British Intelligence, who she knows will read her diaries, about the efficacy of the Fire of Life. In proper pulp fashion Quatermain fakes his own death and returns as his son, "Allan, Junior," or the "A.J." mentioned on Page 171 and following.

Page 193. "...By 1901 the dreadful airship wars afflicting early twentieth century Europe were already underway."
This is a reference to H.G. Wells' *War in the Air* (1908), a novel in which a world war is fought using armadas of airships.

"...The delayed and yet surprisingly successful British lunar expedition by Professor Selwyn Cavor..."

Professor Cavor, who appears in *League* v1, and his lunar expedition appear in H.G. Wells' novel *The First Men in the Moon* (1901). The expedition was delayed due to the events of *League* v1.

"...Such as several unsubstantiated sightings of reputedly deceased detective Sherlock Holmes, which would not be confirmed until the following year."
Sherlock Holmes "dies" in the Arthur Conan Doyle short story "The Adventure of the Final Problem," which was published in 1893. The next Holmes story was *The Hound of the Baskervilles*, which was published in 1901-1902. *The Hound of the Baskervilles*, however, was set in the years before Holmes "died." Holmes returned to action in "The Adventure of The Empty House," which was published in 1903. In the world of *League*, the events of the Sherlock Holmes stories occur during the year in which they were published, rather than the years which the stories state they occur. So, for example, "The Empty House" is dated in the spring of 1894, but in the world of *League* it takes place in 1903.

"...The sole survivor of an expedition into these alarming territories during the 1870s, this being the Reverend Dr. Eric Bellman, was confined."
Dr. Bellman is mentioned on Page 161. The Bellman Expedition is from Lewis Carroll's *The Hunting of the Snark*.

"...Possibly as part of a two-year investigation into 'borderland' or 'gateway' sites such as the Mathers house discussed in our first chapter, although journals from this period are either missing or suppressed. During 1904 they were investigating rural English locations such as Winton Pond near Ipswich or Smalldene in Sussex..."
These sites are mentioned on Page 161.

"...Until 1906 that they came to travel overseas again. At this time England was preparing to embark upon an Anglo-Russian Convention covering Afghanistan, Tibet and Persia that would extend Britain's influence within the European power blocs."
The Anglo-Russian Convention took place in our world from October 1905 to August 1907, at which time an entente was reached essentially ending the Great Game of espionage, addressing Afghanistan and Tibet, and dividing Persia, the cause of much Russian-British antagonism, into three spheres of influence.

"Here, to Australia's southwest there is the island kingdom of Antangil, largely Catholic by inclination, where the seasons seem to happen all at once and where a strange amphibious lion-faced creature thrived until the breed was hunted to extinction in the 18th century."

Antangil appears in *Histoire du grand et admirable Royaume d'Antangil inconnu jusques à présent à tous historiens et cosmographes* (1616), the first French utopia, possibly written by Joachim du Moulin.

"Some distance east of Antangil we find a longer list of since-exterminated species (unicorns, winged horses, concave dromedaries with a hollow where the hump should be) upon the minor continent Terre Australe..."

Terre Australe appears in Gabriel Foigny's *Les Aventures de Jacques Sadeur dans la découverte et le voyage de la Terre Australe* (1676), a South Seas utopia.

"Travelling further, to the southeast of New Zealand lie the weed and coral-crusted ruins of Standard Island..."

Standard Island appears in Jules Verne's *L'Ile à hélice* (*The Floating Island*, 1895).

"Not far north from this looming hulk are the Jumelles..."

The Jumelles appear in de Catalde's *Le Paysan gentilhomme, ou Avantures de M. Ransay: avec son voyage aux Isles Jumelles. Par Monsieur de Catalde* (*The Peasant Gentleman, or the Adventures of M. Ransay, with His Voyace to the Jumelles Islands, by Mr. Catalde,* 1737), a French utopia.

"...While further east lie prehistoric Caspak and the nearby Oo-Oh..."

Caspak and Oo-Oh were created by Edgar Rice Burroughs and appear in the novel *The Land That Time Forgot* (1918).

"...Cousins of the Vril-ya found beneath Newcastle in the north of England."

The Vril-ya are mentioned on Page 165.

"Meanwhile, in the southern reaches of Australia itself we come to what remains of Farandoulie, close to the largely-rebuilt city of Melbourne..."

Farandoulie and the destruction of Melbourne appear in Albert Robida's *Voyages très extraordinaires de Saturnin Farandoul dans les 5 ou 6 parties du monde.*

"Moving further north, it is still possible to see small tribes of Erewhonians..."

Erewhon appears in Samuel Butler's *Erewhon* (1872) and its sequel *Erewhon Revisited* (1901). *Erewhon* is one of the most famous of utopias.

"North of Australia exists a massive spread of islands, ranging from the somewhat puritanical but brightly-dressed folk of Altruria..."

Altruria was created by William Dean Howells and appears in *A Traveller from Altruria* (1894), a genial utopia.

"...On to savage Flotsam..."

Flotsam appears in Edgar Rice Burroughs' novels *The Cave Girl* (1913) and *The Cave Man* (1917).

"...And the Mayan colony of Uxmal in the east."

Uxmal appears in Edgar Rice Burroughs' *Tarzan and the Castaways* (1964).

"Westward, just east of Altruria there is the island of New Gynia, where women rule."

New Gynia appears in Joseph Hall's *Mundus Alter et Idem, Sive Terra Australis Ante Hac Semper Incognita* (1605) and *Utopiae, Pars II* (1613), a satirical description of London which may have partially inspired *Gulliver's Travels*.

"...We raised our anchor and went east, so coming presently to Lilliput..."

Lilliput appears in Jonathan Swift's *Gulliver's Travels*.

Page 194. "This largest island of the Indonesian chain was misidentified as recently as 1753, called Bingfield's Island by one William Bingfield, late of England...here we put in and visited the kingdom of Melinde, being fortunate to journey there during a lull in its incessant slave-trading war with neighboring Ganze, and going on from here came to Kronomo..."

Bingfield's Island, Melinde, Ganze, and Kronomo appear in *The Travels and Adventures of William Bingfield, Esq.: Containing, as Surprising a Fluctuation of Circumstances, both by Sea and Land, as ever befell one Man, by "William Bingfield"* (1753).

"Southeast of Java we came by the massive island of Australia and were much perplexed...the island was divided as two separate countries, the most easterly known as Sporoumbia...neighboring Sevarambia, to the west, was much more civilised and pleasing..."

The island of Australia and its countries of Sporoumbia and Sevarambia appear in Denis Veiras' *Historie des Sevarambes, peuples qui habitent une partie du troisième continent, communement appelé la Terre Australe* (1677-1679), the first libertine (hedonistic and anti-religious) utopia.

"...We passed first by Pathan, where trees grow honey, meal and wine..."
Pathan appears in Sir John Mandeville's *Voiage and Travayle de Sir John Maundevile.*

"...While off to port we saw both Pala, where the potent moksha fungus may be found, and oil-rich neighboring Rendang."
Pala and Rendang appear in Aldous Huxley's *Island* (1962), a South Seas utopia.

"North of New Guinea we passed through the Luquebaralideaux Islands..."
The Luquebaralideaux Islands appear in *The Journey of Panurge, Disciple of Pantagruel.*

"Heading east we moored quite near Cuffycoat's Island..."
Cuffycoat's Island appears in André Lichtenberger's *Pickles ou Récits à la mode anglaise* (1923).

"...The towering volcanic island of Manoba to the south..."
Manoba appears in Paul Scott's *The Birds of Paradise* (1962), the fictional autobiography of an Anglo-Indian.

"...And also sighted off New Guinea's eastern coast the great island Bensalem, that once traded with Atlantis..."
Bensalem was created by Francis Bacon and appears in *New Atlantis* (1627), a utopia.

"...And a place that local seafarers have told us has been lately settled by the shipwrecked family of a Swiss pastor, named by them New Switzerland."

New Switzerland appears in Johann David Wyss' *The Swiss Family Robinson* (1812-1827).

"Some way off Bensalem we could also see the lonely isle of Uffa..."
Uffa is mentioned, in Arthur Conan Doyle's short story "The Adventure of the Five Orange Pips" (*Strand Magazine*, November 1891), as one of the locations of Sherlock Holmes' untold tales: "of the singular adventures of the Grice Patersons in the island of Uffa."

"...Since it is my intent to take our fellowship as far as wondrous Balnibarbi and Laputa."
Balnibarbi and Laputa appear in Jonathan Swift's *Gulliver's Travels*.

"On our way we skirted Yoka Island, with its shaven-headed samurai..."
Yoka Island appears in Edgar Rice Burroughs' *The Mucker* (1914), a romance about a low-born brute winning the hand of an upper class lady.

"...And the extensive island commonwealth of Oceana..."
The fictional Oceana appears in James Harrington's *The Commonwealth of Oceana*.

"Further on, we came at last to the familiar waters of Glubbdubdrib, Island of Sorcerers..."
Glubbdubdrib appears in Jonathan Swift's *Gulliver's Travels*.

"Though I entreated my companions to refuse this generous offer, Mr. Blakeney was most adamant, insisting on the company of a revered and ancient ancestor from his own lineage. When conjured, this shade proved to be not wholly the aristocratic personage of Blakeney family legend, but instead the spirit of a one-eyed horse thief with a desperate mania for public self-pollution. Disheartened with the vision of his heritage provided by this squinting, pizzle-waving apparition, Mr. Blakeney fast succumbed to melancholia, insisting that we sail without delay on the next morning's tide."
I don't know who the "pizzle-waving apparition" might be a reference to. It's possible that this is a reference to the first Sir Percy Blakeney, who appears in Baroness Orczy's *The Laughing Cavalier* (1914) and *The First Sir Percy* (1920). The first Sir Percy was a vagabond, but

there's nothing in the text themselves that refers to him either squinting, stealing horses, or engaging in public self-pollution.

"Thus we came to the larger isle of Luggnagg, further north..."
Luggnagg appears in Jonathan Swift's *Gulliver's Travels*.

"...He thought his immortality and brow-mark traits he and his kind had inherited from some long-distant forebear, said in legend to have been a visitor to Luggnagg, come from distant Abyssinia, where our informant thought there might exist a city of undying folk like he."
This city is the City of the Immortals from Jorge Luis Borges' "El Inmortal."

Page 195. "...Passing Tracoda to the east..."
Tracoda appears in Sir John Mandeville's *Voiage and Travayle of Sir John Maundevile*.

"East of Tracoda, I have heard, exist three islands named for their distinctly coloured sands, green, red, and black..."
Green Sand Island, Black Sand Island, and Red Sand Island appear in Tancrede Vallerey's *L'Ile au sable vert* (1930).

"...There hung the dark mass of Laputa, flying island homestead of the science-and-learning preoccupied Tomtoddies..."
Laputa appears in Jonathan Swift's *Gulliver's Travels*.

"...When I suggested we sail on and try to spot the language-obsessed island called Locuta that a son of mine once told me he had found..."
Locuta and Gulliver's son Lemuel Gulliver Junior appear in Mrs. E.S. Graham's *Voyage to Locuta; A Fragment by Lemuel Gulliver Junior* (1817), one of several unofficial sequels to *Gulliver's Travels*.

"We passed east of Zipang, or of Japan as it is these days called..."
"Zipangu" was what Marco Polo called Japan in *The Travels of Marco Polo*.

"...And went south by way of Formosa, which possesses off its coast another smaller island of the same name..."
The smaller island of Formosa appears in George Psalmanaazaar's *Description de l'isle Formosa* (1704), a fictional account of Formosa.

"...Northwest of Borneo, we saw the mountain Tushuo rising from the sea..."

Mount Tushuo appears in the anonymously written *The Compendium of Deities of the Three Religions* (Third century B.C.E.), an early Chinese collection of myth and legend.

"...And heading on passed by the Island of the Roc..."

The Island of the Roc appears in *The Arabian Nights*.

"Nearby we saw another, smaller island, situated opposite a river mouth in nearby Borneo. Protected by a reef it seemed fecund and full of life, yet to my knowledge it has never been explored or named."

This may be a reference to R.M. Ballantyne's *The Coral Island*.

"We sailed on past the Isle of Salmasse, where some trees grow meal while others drip a fearful venom..."

In some translations of Sir John Mandeville's *Voiage and Travayle of Sir John Maundevile* the isle of "Pathen" is said to have

> trees that bear meal, whereof men make good bread and white and of good savour; and it seemeth as it were of wheat, but it is not allinges of such savour. And there be other trees that bear honey good and sweet, and other trees that bear venom, against the which there is no medicine but one....

Moore may be using as his source a translation of Mandeville in which this section is credited to the island of "Salmasse."

"...And came likewise by the islands Raso (where men will be hung if they fall ill)..."

In some translations of Sir John Mandeville's *Voiage and Travayle of Sir John Maundevile* "Raso" is translated as "Caffolos."

"...And strange Macumeran, where the hound-headed populace adore their ox-god with unfathomable rituals and barking, howling incantations."

Macumeran, or Nacumera, appears in Sir John Mandeville's *Voiage and Travayle of Sir John Maundevile*.

"Finally we reached the gulf of Siam, mooring near the isle of Tilibet, a place that I myself had never visited yet which was recommended to me by my eldest son, John, who himself is something of a traveller, as with my various other children and descendants."

Tilibet and Gulliver's son John appear in the Abbé Pierre François Desfontaines' *Le Nouveau Gulliver*.

Page 196. "Whilst the company of the immortal Struldbruggs can ofttimes become dispiriting and lead the mind to a consideration of one's own mortality, the Tilibetans, who can talk when scarcely a day old..."

The Struldbruggs and the Tilibetans appear in the Abbé Pierre François Desfontaines' *Le Nouveau Gulliver*.

"...We discovered an enormous isle called India that clearly was not the more famed sub-continent known by that name..."

The island of India was created by Warren Lewis and his brother C.S. Lewis when both were children.

"...With nearby a strange island where the trees seemed merely balls of cottonwool glued onto posts, inhabited by animals in human dress, of which I must confess Mr. Bumppo bagged a couple."

Boxen, the island with the trees of cottonwool, was created by C.S. Lewis and his brother Warren Lewis when both were children.

"It transpired our island was in fact a Phoenix-governed Animal Republic..."

The Animal Republic appears in Jean Jacobé de Frémont d'Ablancourt's *Supplément de l'Histoire Véritable de Lucien* (1654), a *voyage imaginaire* which is a kind of sequel to Lucian of Samosata's *True History*, mentioned on Page 169 and following.

"Thus did we pass Mask Island..."

Mask Island appears in Charles Fieux de Mouhy's *Le Masque de Fer* (1746), an early version of the story of the Man in the Iron Mask which Alexandre Dumas later retold. See the notes below to Box #16 of the Game of Extraordinary Gentlemen.

"Here, I'm told, exists the kingdom of Agartha, veiled divinely from the memory of man, the throne of which is decorated with the figures of two million gods, with its existence central to the very continuity of mankind and...but I confess that I have quite forgot the point I sought to make, or why I ever thought this place important."

Agartha appears in Saint-Yves d'Alveydre's *Mission de l'Inde en Europe* (1885), the book which introduced the concept of Agartha, or "Shambhala," to the West. The memories of Agartha are removed from humans by the gods.

"...Finally we put ashore on Feather Island..."

Feather Island appears in Fanny de Beauharnais' *Rélation très véritable d'une Isle Nouvellement Découverte*.

"Nemo speaks of being taken by his father as a boy to visit Lomb, a city on the western coast of India near Mangalore..."

Lomb appears in Sir John Mandeville's *Voiage and Travayle of Sir John Maundevile*.

"He comments witheringly on this beast-worship practiced by his countrymen, with reference to Goatland, just northwest of Lomb..."

Goatland appears in Charles Fieux de Mouhy's *Le Masque de Fer*.

"...But he reserves his deepest scorn for the religious manias of Mabaron, a ten-day journey north of Lomb..."

Mabaron appears in Sir John Mandeville's *Voiage and Travayle of Sir John Maundevile*.

"Much more to the Captain's taste is Mancy, almost opposite to Mabaron on India's eastern coast..."

Mancy appears in *Voiage and Travayle of Sir John Maundevile*.

"Nemo also comments favorably upon the Pygmy Kingdom on the Dalay River just northeast of Mancy..."

The Pygmy Kingdom appears in *Voiage and Travayle of Sir John Maundevile*.

"Likewise meeting his approval we find Jundapur, in the northwest..."

Jundapur appears in Paul Scott's *The Birds of Paradise*.

·"The Sikh submariner, however, speaks less fondly of the feared Black

Jungle, on its island in the Ganges delta..."
The Black Jungle appears in Emilio Salgari's *I Misteri della Jungla Nera* (*The Mystery of the Black Jungle*, 1895), the first of Salgari's "Sandokan" novels.

"...Passing by Calcutta, came upon the east shore of the Ganges to the more alluring and yet no less fearsome kingdom known as Gangaridia..."
Gangaridia appears in Voltaire's *La Princesse de Babylone* (*The Princess of Babylon*, 1768), Voltaire's version of *The Arabian Nights*.

Page 197. "...Into the Sacred Valley, beyond the Great Rungit Valley..."
The Sacred Valley appears in Maurice Champagne's novel *La Vallée Mystérieuse* (1915).

"Here, in the morning, looking north, we saw the River Physon in its devil-haunted valley that is said to be a way to Hell, and heard the distant yet incessant sound of fiendish drums and trumpets with which that dire valley ever rings."
The River Physon appears in Sir John Mandeville's *Voiage and Travayle of Sir John Maundevile*. It had formerly appeared in a letter supposedly written by Prester John and sent to the Roman Emperor.

"Beyond it, father told me, was a nameless isle whereon lived giants, each as tall as five like him, while further northward yet were women who had precious stones for eyes, that they might slay men as the basilisk doth."
Both of these islands appear in Sir John Mandeville's *Voiage and Travayle of Sir John Maundevile*.

"...Wherein was found the island kingdom of Pentexoire, governed once by the immortal Prester John."
Pentexoire, or Pentixore, appears in Sir John Mandeville's *Voiage and Travayle of Sir John Maundevile*.

"Also, he spoke of the Dream Kingdom, near to Bactria..."
The Dream Kingdom appears in Alfred Kubin's *Die andere Seite: Ein phantastischer Roman* (*The Other Side: A Fantastic Novel*, 1908), a novel about a utopian dreamland.

"On our way here from Formosa across the East China Sea we passed Alcina's Island, near to Japan's coast, where I once travelled some five hundred years ago..."
Alcina's Island appears in Ludovico Ariosto's *Orlando Furioso*.

"...Including the sad tale of a young local beauty, Cho-Cho-san, with family still living in the nearby streets, who'd killed herself some few years after her desertion by the handsome U.S. Naval officer she'd married in the early 1890s."
Cho-Cho-San appears in John Luther Long's novel *Madame Butterfly* (1903), the source of the modern musical.

"She laughed delightfully and said that I was flirting with her, warning me that I should take care not to visit Titipu, a nearby town where the Mikado had decreed that such flirtation was a crime that merited beheading."
Titipu appears in Gilbert & Sullivan's musical *The Mikado* (1885).

"On our way we passed by the minor continent Hsuan, where in 90 BC the Emperor Wu Ti revived the lately-dead by burning incense..."
Hsuan appears in Tung-fang Shuo's *Accounts of the Ten Continents* (First century B.C.E.), a fictional Chinese travelogue.

"...And sailed on by those two enticing isles, Babilary, whereon women rule..."
Babilary appears in the Abbé Pierre François Desfontaines' *Le Nouveau Gulliver*.

"...And Women's Island, where there are no men at all."
Women's Island appears in the anonymously written *Le Livre de merveilles de l'Inde* (1883-1886), a fictional travelogue of India.

"The first place that I went to was Albraca..."
Albraca appears in Matteo Maria Boiardo's *Orlando Innamorato*.

"...It appears to be a man-like monkey or perhaps an ape-like man...a signboard placed within the cabinet identified this strangely noble beast, in Chinese characters, as 'Great Sage, Equal to Heaven,' though even after I'd painstakingly translated this, I was left none the wiser."

The "Great Sage, Equal to Heaven" is the Monkey King, Sun Wu'Kung, who appears in *Hsi-yu chi* (*Journey to the West*), which was written by Wu Ch'eng-en (1500?-1582).

Page 198. "...Described to their immediate forebears by a famous wandering storyteller called Kai Lung during the nineteenth century."
This is a reference to Ernest Bramah's Kai Lung, whose charming stories first appear in *The Wallet of Kai Lung* (1900).

"...I passed through a dreadful city called Perinthia..."
Perinthia appears in Italo Calvino's *Invisible Cities*.

"...Where walking in the desert by the falling light of day I reached a place called Watcher's Corner..."
Watcher's Corner appears in Pinhas Kahanovitch's *Gedakht* (1922), a collection of Jewish fantasy and occult stories.

"Some distance further west I saw the mountain Waiting Wife..."
Waiting Wife Mountain appears in the anonymously written *Tal-Ping Geographical Record* (921 C.E.), a fictional Vietnamese atlas.

"...Passing the towering scaffold-city of Isaura..."
Isaura appears in Italo Calvino's *Invisible Cities*.

"I continued south, and after some great while reached Gala, an agreeably appointed kingdom..."
Gala appears in André-François de Brancas-Villeneuve's *Histoire ou Police du royaume de Gala* (1754), a utopian novel.

"...Amongst the jungles of Cambodia, I saw the tunnel-riddled but majestic city of Pnom Dhek, its neatly-tended gardens rising from the shrieking, growling greenery, and not far off saw also great Lodidhapura..."
Pnom Dhek and Lodidhapura appear in Edgar Rice Burroughs' novel *The Jungle Girl* (1931).

"...Near Mandalay I ventured in Gramblamble Land and visited the famous city Tosh, beside Lake Pipple-popple."
Gramblamble Land, Tosh, and Lake Pipple-popple appear in Edward Lear's *The History of the Seven Families of the Lake Pipple-popple* (1865).

"From Gramblamble Land I ventured north across the Southwest Wilderness..."
The Southwest Wilderness appears in Tung-Fang Shuo's *The Book of Deities and Marvels* (First century B.C.E.).

"I had a dreadful time kept as a hostage at a monastery of sinister Bon sorcerers, a place called So Sa Ling..."
This is a reference to *A Tibetan Tale of Love and Magic* (1938) by Alexandra David-Neel. In the book, a travelogue, a Tibetan bandit tells Neel the story of the monastery of the Bon sorcerers.

"After some days further travel I beheld Mount Tsintsin-Dagh, the lamasery of the Silent Brothers there atop its pinnacle."
Mount Tsintsin-Dagh appears in Paul Alperine's *Ombres sur le Thibet* (1945), an adventure novel set in Tibet.

"By this means I came firstly to True Lhassa..."
True Lhassa appears in Maurice Champagne's *Les Sondeurs d'Abîmes* (1911), a novel about a subterranean city underneath the Himalayas.

"...I also avoided the mysterious cloudy valley just north of True Lhassa, where two rival cults of sorcerers (or perhaps more-than-human supernatural forces) called the White Lodge and the Black Lodge are believed to be at war..."
The White Lodge and the Black Lodge as warring magical forces are a part of basic theosophical teaching as well as a feature of several novels involving "Eastern" magic, most notably Talbot Mundy's, as in his *Ramsden* (1926). David Lynch, who used the concept of the Lodges in his television show *Twin Peaks* (1990), has acknowledged that he got the concept from the theosophists.

"...At last I came to the lovely valley in the shade of the blue mountain called Mount Karakal, where is the beautiful bronze-dragon-decorated lamasery of Shangri-La."
Mount Karakal and Shangri-La appear in James Hilton's novel *Lost Horizon* (1933).

Page 199. "...We rattle first through Dodon's kingdom..."
Dodon's Kingdom appears in Alexander Pushkin's "The Golden

Cockerel" (1835), a story based on Washington Irving's poem "The Legend of the Arabian Astrologer."

"When I said I thought that this was tosh, Allan replied that Tosh was actually a city in the heart of Burma. Much as I adore him he can be intensely irritating when he thinks he's being humorous."
As mentioned on Page 198, Tosh is a city in Burma.

"Heading on to Moscow we gave a wide berth to Pauk...
Pauk appears in Fyodor Dostoyevsky's *Besy* (*The Possessed*, 1871-1872), a political tract about the appearance of five radicals in a small provincial town.

"...A long, deep sleep, during which I endured a dreadful, muddled dream where I appeared to be in Moscow, although not the Moscow of our present day, but rather as it might be in, say, twenty years or so. There was some nonsense that concerned a large black talking cat, and a well-dressed man that according to the logic of the dream I knew to be the Devil. I awoke quite unrefreshed..."
Mina has dreamed about Mikhail Bulgakov's excellent novel *Master i Margarita* (*The Master and Margarita*, 1966).

"...Passing by the wretched remnants of the town of Gloupov..."
Gloupov appears in Mikhail Saltykov-Shchedrin's *Istoriya Odnogo Goroda* (*The History of a Town*, 1869-1870), a satire of Russian bureaucracy.

"...We travelled through the large, apparently borderless town of Ibansk..."
Ibansk appears in Aleksandr Zinoviev's *Ziyayushchie Vysoty* (*The Yawning Heights*, 1976), a novel criticizing the Soviet Union.

"Take Paflagonia, for example...or nearby Blackstaff...or else Crim Tartary..."
Paflagonia, Blackstaff, and Crim Tartary appear in William Makepeace Thackeray's fairytale, "The Rose and the Ring" (1857).

"...I must say our ride through the city of Phyllis seemed to offer fascinating views at every turn..."
The city of Phyllis appears in Italo Calvino's *Invisible Cities*.

"Just as intriguing was the city of Despina on the Black Sea's northern coast."
The city of Despina appears in Italo Calvino's *Invisible Cities*.

"Just east of Despina, in the Tartary Desert, we saw from far off the fortress Bastiani..."
The Tartary Desert and the fortress Bastiani appear in Dino Buzzati's *Il Deserto dei Tartari* (*The Tartar Steppe*, 1940), a classic of Italian absurdist fantasy.

"It stands upon the edge of Abcan, a wide territory in constant darkness due to Abcan's emperor persecuting Christians."
Abcan is a reference to Sir John Mandeville's *Voiage and Travayle of Sir John Maundevile*.

"...A little further south we found the sprawl of caverns, rocks and whirlpools wherein the poetic dreamer Alastor maintained his cave-retreat..."
Alastor's cavern appears in Percy Shelley's poem "Alastor or the Spirit of Solitude" (*Alastor*, 1816).

"More southerly still we passed through the land of Gondour..."
Gondour appears in Mark Twain's *The Curious Republic of Gondour* (1875), one of Twain's satires.

"...We spent some time travelling in Amazonia, or Feminy, a land of women which extends from here into the west of China..."
Amazonia, a.k.a. Feminy, appears in Sir John Mandeville's *Voiage and Travayle of Sir John Maundevile*.

"North of Feminy we passed through Ivanikha, where the peasantry are all named Ivan..."
Ivanikha appears in Yevgeniy Zamyatin's "Ivany" (*Dva Rasska Dlja Vzroslych Detej*, 1922).

"...Crossing the boundless, junk-filled country known as 'X'..."
X appears in Tibor Déry's *G.A. úr X.-ben* (*Mr. A.G. in the City of X*, 1963).

"...Came finally into the province called the Land of Wonder..."
The Land of Wonder appears in Isaac Leib Peretz's *Ale Verk* (*Comlete Works*, 1912), a work of Jewish fantasy.

Page 200. "...Passing the half-constructed city Thekla..."
Thekla appears in Italo Calvino's *Invisible Cities*.

"Similarly half-done was the nearby city Moriana..."
Moriana appears in Italo Calvino's *Invisible Cities*.

"Eudoxia, a little further east..."
Eudoxia appears in Italo Calvino's *Invisible Cities*.

"Nearby Zemrude was more ambiguous..."
Zemrude appears in Italo Calvino's *Invisible Cities*.

"Octavia, in the northeast, is a fragile cobweb-city of rope walkways strung across a chasm..."
Octavia appears in Italo Calvino's *Invisible Cities*.

"...While further on Valdrada, built above a lake, seemed no more real than its perfect reflection..."
Valdrada appears in Italo Calvino's *Invisible Cities*.

"From here we headed south to Vladivostok, passing through the Land of the Goat Worshippers..."
The Land of the Goat Worshippers appears in the Abbé H.L. Du Laurens' *Le compère Mathieu ou les Bigarrures de l'esprit humain* (*Mathieu the Accomplice, or the Multicolored Pattern of the Human Spirit*, 1771), a work of philosophy often seen as licentious and anti-clerical.

"...And saw fabled Xanadu, wild vegetation bursting upwards through the holes in its long-ruined pleasure dome..."
Xanadu appears in Samuel Taylor Coleridge's poem "Kubla Khan" (*Christabel: Kubla Khan, A Vision; The Pains of Sleep*, 1816).

"...Past the high-piled platform city of Zenobia..."
Zenobia appears in Italo Calvino's *Invisible Cities*.

"...Through daily replaced Leonia with massive waste-heaps on its outskirts..."
Leonia appears in Italo Calvino's *Invisible Cities*.

"...And amongst the ringed canals of Anastasia, city of unlimited desire."
Anastasia appears in Italo Calvino's *Invisible Cities*.

"We went through Urnland, famed for horsemanship..."
Urnland appears in Jorge Luis Borges' short story "Undr" (*New Yorker*, 1975).

"We saw Mount Poyang, with its dog-flesh eating deity..."
Poyang Mountain appears in Liu Ching-Shu's *Garden of Marvels* (Fifth century C.E.).

"We went southwards through Eusapia, which has a subterranean double of itself built underneath it..."
Eusapia appears in Italo Calvino's *Invisible Cities*.

"...And also Queen Ayesha, believed by Orlando to be at present incarnated in the land of Kaloon, also to the west."
Queen Ayesha first appears in H. Rider Haggard's *She*. After her seeming death in *She* Ayesha reappears in the Asian country of Kaloon in *Ayesha: The Return of She*.

"...And were shown the way to Mount K'un Lun, sometimes called Hes or Fire Mountain, further west."
Mount K'un Lun is a part of Chinese mythology, perhaps appearing first in the anonymously written *The Book of Mountains and Seas* (Fourth century B.C.E.), a collection of Chinese geography and folklore. Hes, a.k.a. Fire Mountain, appears in *Ayesha: The Return of She*.

"...Hsi Wang Mu, the Royal Mother of the West..."
Hsi Wang Mu is the queen of immortals in Taoist mythology.

"Orlando spoke quite wistfully about a gathering of immortals said to happen every three thousand years or so atop the mountain's peak..."
In Taoist/Chinese mythology Hsi Wang Mu's peach tree bears its sole fruit every three thousand years.

"We travelled on instead west from Kaloon through Chitor. Here we saw the Victory Tower..."
Chitor and the Victory Tower are mentioned by Sir Richard Francis Burton in a note to his translation of *The Arabian Nights Entertainment* (1885-1888).

"...Where an insubstantial creature known as the A Bao A Qu will follow the ascendants..."
This is a reference to Jorge Luis Borges' *The Book of Imaginary Beings* (1969), a bestiary of fantastic creatures.

"We went with her through the lovely Kingdoms of Radiant Array and Joyous Groves, north of the Himalayas, thus avoiding the ill-favoured Kingdom of Myriad Lights..."
I don't know what these refer to.

"She showed us, in the poignant ruins of his kingdom, Trees of Sun and Moon that spoke with Alexander once, foretelling his demise..."
The Trees of the Sun and the Moon are a part of Persian legend, as is their foretelling of the fate of Alexander the Great.

"...And we three lounged delightfully beneath them, gorging on their fruit, said to provide five hundred years of life."
I am unaware of the Persian legend of the Trees of the Sun and the Moon also including anything about long-life-bestowing fruit. Possibly Moore and O'Neill are hinting that the grove of the Trees of the Sun and Moon is also the Garden of Hesperides from Greek mythology, in which golden apples of immortality grow?

Page 201. "Logbooks loaned to the current editors by a Miss Diver..."
"Miss Diver" is mentioned on Page 177 above.

"...A daughter that she has named Janni, for her mother..."
This could mean that Jenny Diver is Nemo's daughter or wife, one of the people Nemo mentions returning to on Page 150.

"...The islands of the archipelago called Megapatagonia..."
Megapatagonia was the creation of Nicolas Edme Restif de la Bretonne

and appears in *La Découverte australe par un homme-volant* (1781). Megapatagonia is an archipelago which is exactly opposite France and so its culture is an inverse of the French, down to its capital "Sirap."

"...An almost identical archipelago that ran not from Tierra del Fuego to Earth's southern pole, as was the case with Megapatagonia, but instead stretched from the Orkney Islands in the north of Britain to the planet's arctic reaches, called the Blazing World."
The Blazing World is mentioned on Page 161. It was created by Margaret Cavendish and appears in *Observations upon Experimental Philosophy*.

"...Circling the shining island of fire-elementals called Pyrandia..."
Pyrandia was created by Jean Jacobé de Frémont d'Ablancourt and appears in his *Supplément de l'Histoire véritable de Lucien* (1654). Pyrandia is the country of the Firemen, whose skin is made of flame and who live as long as they have something to feed their fires.

"...In an area called by some the Academic Sea, we discovered...three-sided Caphar Salama."
The Academic Sea and three-sided Caphar Salama were created by Johann Valentin Andreae and appear in his *Reipublicae Christianapolitinae Descriptio* (1619). Caphar Salama and its capital Christianopolis are a kind of utopia.

"...We discovered the Leap Islands..."
The Leap Islands were created by James Fennimore Cooper and appear in *The Monikins* (1835), a rare work of fantasy by Cooper.

Page 202. "...Putting into Aggregation Harbour on the Isle of Leaphigh we found a society that was less eerie and unnerving than the backwards-speaking half-world we had lately quit. The folk of the Leap Islands are not mere degraded humans but are rather monkey-men called Monikins..."
Aggregation Harbour, the Island of Leaphigh, and the Monikins appear in Cooper's *The Monikins*.

"...The wealthy, pious city Christianopolis that I would have gladly sacked were it not fortified in so impregnable a fashion..."

Christianopolis appears in Johann Valentin Andreae's *Reipublicae Christianapolitinae descriptio*. The city is overtly Christian, hence Nemo's distaste for it. It is quite impressively fortified with several towers, walls, and a single impregnable citadel.

"...The capital of a place I've heard tell of that is called Antarctic France. Although there are intriguing rumours of immortals that survive the centuries encased in ice..."
Antarctic France and the ice-enclosed immortals were created by Robert-Martin Lesuire and appear in his *L'Aventurier Français* (1782).

"The island is called Tsalal..."
Tsalal was created by Edgar Allan Poe and appears in the novella *The Narrative of Arthur Gordon Pym of Nantucket* (1838).

"...Where the schooner *Jane Guy*, come from Liverpool, was wrecked in 1828, its crew and passengers reportedly all massacred by the fierce, sturdy blackamoors that are this curious isle's inhabitants."
This is an accurate representation of the events of *The Narrative of Arthur Gordon Pym*.

"Then there is the great aversion of the natives to the colour white, which seems to be connected with some awful figure from the island's ancient folklore, their great dread for which is conveyed by a stream of frantic, chattered syllables that sound like 'Te-ke-li-li.'"
This is from *The Narrative of Arthur Gordon Pym*, but also incorporates some material from H.P. Lovecraft. In *Pym* it is "gigantic and pallidly white birds" which scream "tekeli-li." Lovecraft, however, wrote a kind of sequel to *Pym*, *At the Mountains of Madness* (1931), in which the monstrous Shoggoth utters the phrase.

"Knowing Tsalal to have connections with a place called Present Land..."
Present Land is from *The Narrative of Arthur Gordon Pym*.

"...The chasm that provided entrance to the underground Empire of the Alsondons."
The Empire of the Alsondons was created by Robert-Martin Lesuire and appears in *L'Aventurier François*.

"...We drew close to the ring of icy peaks, the so-called Iron Mountains that surround the plateau..."
The Iron Mountains appear in the anonymously written *Voyage au centre de la terre* (*Voyage to the Center of the Earth*, 1821).

"...The arrival at this spot of the survivors from the shipwrecked whaler *Mercury* during November in 1906."
This is likely a transcription error; the *Mercury*'s shipwreck appears in *Voyage au centre de la terre*, but in that story it is said to have shipwrecked in 1806, not 1906.

"...A vast hole, apparently quite bottomless, that only later did I think might be the mythic aperture which leads to the vast subterranean world called Pluto..."
The polar passage to Pluto appears in *Voyage au centre de la terre*.

"...We continued into Present Land, at which point I discovered that my timepiece had quite simply stopped, all moments here being subsumed within the present."
Hence the name "Present Land," which appears in *The Narrative of Arthur Gordon Pym*.

"I have disturbing intimations of a tall white shape, much larger than a man, that coincide with memories of one of my crew screaming, and half-glimpses of a kind of sphinx..."
The white shape is from *The Narrative of Arthur Gordon Pym*. The sphinx appears in Jules Verne's sequel to *Pym*, the novel *The Ice Sphinx* (1897).

"All I may know with certainty is that when we at last arrived on the far side of that ringed range, close to a group of peaks that I've since named the Mounts of Madness..."
The "Mounts of Madness" are a reference to the "Mountains of Madness," which appear in H.P. Lovecraft's *At the Mountains of Madness*. In Lovecraft's novel the mountains are only informally given that name by the narrator.

"It seemed the long-abandoned and half-buried relic of some citadel..."
This and the following sentences are references to the City of the Old Ones in Lovecraft's *At the Mountains of Madness*.

"I do not wish to pain myself with the detailed recounting of what happened in those hellish tunnels, save to say that we encountered something that might best be characterized as intellectually precocious slime or froth."

The slime is a Shoggoth, which appears in H.P. Lovecraft's *At the Mountains of Madness*.

"I had crossed above the subterranean land known as Kosekin Country..."

Kosekin Country appears in James De Mille's *A Strange Manuscript Found in a Copper Cylinder* (1888), a combination of satire and utopia.

Page 203. "...Or by some accounts Plutonia..."

Plutonia is from Vladimir Obruchev's *Plutonia* (1924), the story of a trip in time back to the Stone Age.

"...The services of an old Czechoslovakian ex-naval man named Rudolf Svejk..."

Rudolf Svejk is from Jaroslav Hašek's *The Good Soldier Švejk* (1912).

"...The briefly-famed Elisee Reclus Island...Cristallopolis, a geyser-heated colony of France...Maurel City, a near-simultaneously established colony, this time American..."

Elisee Reclus Island, Cristallopolis, and Maurel City all appear in Alphonse Brown's *Une Ville de Verre* (1891).

"Mounts of Madness"

The Mounts of Madness have a visual similarity to the helmet of Torquemada, a character from Kevin O'Neill's earlier series "Nemesis the Warlock," which appears in the British comic *2000AD*.

Page 204. "...Headed on past Vichebolk Land..."

Vichebolk Land appears in André Lichtenberger's *Pickles ou récits à la mode anglaise*.

"...That odd ensemble's senior member Lemuel Gulliver claimed he'd discovered Vichebolk Land in 1721..."

This is also from *Pickles ou récits à la mode anglaise*.

"...We saw, wading along the icecap's coastline, two gigantic and bipedal reptiles...the North Pole Kingdom..."
The North Pole Kingdom and its population of civilized dinosaurs were created by Charles Derennes and appear in *Le Peuple du Pôle* (1907), a Lost Race novel about a race of peaceful reptilian humanoids discovered at the North Pole by French aviators.

"...The claw-carved ice caves that comprise the region called Polar Bear Kingdom..."
Polar Bear Kingdom and its polar bear citizens appear in Mór Jókai's *20,000 Lieues Sous Les Glaces* (*20,000 Leagues Under the Ice*, 1876), a Lost Race novel.

"...Had been lately visited by representatives of an American who manufactured phosphate drinks and was most anxious in securing the pictorial rights to any suitably appealing bear activity, for purposes of advertising."
This is a reference to the 1993 "Polar Bears" ad campaign created by the Creative Artists Agency for Coca-Cola.

"...The representatives had next struck further north in hope of finding an elusive polar witch-doctor with whom they sought to make a similar agreement."
This is a reference to the famous 1930s Coca-Cola ad campaign which featured Santa holding a Coke.

"...The mountain-door of nearby subterranean Mandai Country..."
Mandai Country appears in Hirmiz bar Anhar's *Iran* (1905), a collection of Persian legends.

"...Gaster's Island, sometimes called the island of the Belly-Worshippers, and even saw one of the isle's processions as it wound along the shore, holding a hideous idol-figure of the island's ravenous god Manduce aloft."
Gaster's Island and Manduce appear in François Rabelais' *The Fourth Book of the Deeds and Sayings of the Good Pantagruel*.

"It appeared to be a veritable sea of frozen words..."
The Sea of Frozen Words appears in Rabelais' *The Fourth Book of the Deeds and Sayings of the Good Pantagruel*.

"…The German word 'Volk'…"
Volk, in German, means "folk."

"…The word 'optative' (which we believe may be connected with Greek grammar)…"
The *Oxford English Dictionary*'s definition of "optative" is "1. Grammar. Having the function of expressing wish or desire. 2. Characterized by desire or choice."

"…The delicious-looking word 'Vulpecula'…"
Vulpecula is a small northern constellation between Hercules and Pegasus.

"…The stark volcanic rock known as Queen Island, as discovered by the most unfortunate Captain John Hatteras in 1861."
Queen Island and Captain Hatteras appear in Jules Verne's *Voyages et aventures du Capitaine Hatteras* (1866).

Page 205. "…Giant Thule…"
The island of Thule, ten times as large as Great Britain, appears in Diodorus Siculus' *The Library of History* (First century B.C.E.), Strabo's *Geography* (First century B.C.E.), and Procopius' *The Gothic War* (Fourth century C.E.).

"…Fabulous Hyperborea."
Hyperborea is first mentioned in Pliny the Elder's *Natural History*.

"Thule, with its demon-worshipping and hide-clad savages the Scritifines…"
Thule and the Scritifines appear in Procopius' *The Gothic War*.

"…In the freakishly warm territory called The Back of the North Wind…"
The Back of the North Wind appears in George MacDonald's *At the Back of the North Wind* (1870), a novel about a poor stable boy in Victorian London who becomes involved in fantastic journeys.

"We have already met one of the somewhat wistful-looking folk that live here, who explained that this land was the realm of the North Wind himself, an elemental and titanic figure, seldom wholly visible save when in belting rain or snow, who sat at some kind of portal near the ice-bridge that we'd seen, joining Hyperborea with the polar icecap. We bade *adieu* to this rather forlorn and sorry chap (in old and faded naval uniform, if I recall correctly)..."

The "elemental and titanic figure" is from MacDonald's *At the Back of the North Wind*, but I don't know who the man in the naval uniform is.

"The picnic I had started to describe above was interrupted when we were surrounded by a group of most insistent...well, I dare say one would have to call them toys, since they were none of them a living being in the strict sense of that phrase, though they possessed both animation and intelligence. Bursting from out the undergrowth to ring us round came hordes of what appeared to be diminutive stuffed bears, their glass eyes glinting with an eerie, keen intelligence. Commanding them from his bright yellow vehicle was what looked for all the world to be a small boy made from painted wood, his conical blue hat tipped with the tiny bell of silver that had first alerted me."

The "small boy made from painted wood" is Noddy, who appears in Enid Blyton's *Noddy Goes to Toyland* (1949) and its sequels. Noddy is a wooden doll who drives a taxi cab in Toy Town.

"Their realm, the quaintest little town, with houses that seem made from building-blocks, is Toyland."

Toyland was created by Enid Blyton and appears in *Noddy Goes to Toyland*. Toyland is a country populated by toys and nursery rhyme characters. There is a Toyland in Victor Herbert's play *Babes in Toyland* (1903), but the two are not the same.

"Apparently, sometime around 1815, an inventor by the name of Spalanzani had enlisted the assistance of a manufacturer of spectacles, a doctor named Coppelius, to help with the construction of a mechanism so ingenious in its working that it might be said almost to think and live...the beautiful doll-woman that resulted from this partnership was named Olympia..."

Spalanzani, Coppelius, and Olympia (or "Olimpia") appear in E.T.A. Hoffman's "The Sand-Man" (*The Night-Pieces*, 1817), a frightening early story of horror.

"...Her consort, who, although he might be honestly described as artificial or constructed life, was not by any means a toy. For one thing, it appeared that he was fashioned out of human flesh, his musculature rather frighteningly pronounced, as with an anatomical exhibit. We learned that this at once horrific and yet somehow noble individual was the creation of a young, ambitious European doctor who had known Doctor Coppelius and, two years after the creation of Olympia, had sought to emulate the elder man's achievement by constructing his own artificial being, this time from the fragments of dead men and galvanised by an electric current."

This is the Creature, from Mary Shelley's *Frankenstein; or, The Modern Prometheus* (1818).

Page 206. "...An underground realm of vast size called Pluto or Pellucidar by some..."
The underground land of Pellucidar appears in a number of Edgar Rice Burroughs' novels, beginning with *At the Earth's Core* (1922).

"...Atvatabar..."
Atvatabar was created by William R. Bradshaw and appears in *The Goddess of Atvatabar*.

"...Or else Ruffal by others..."
Ruffal appears in Simon Tyssot de Patot's *La vie, les avanture, and le voyage de Groenland du Révérend Père Cordelier Pierre de Mesange* (1715), an early French utopia.

"We were told to steer clear of Evileye Land..."
Evileye Land appears in Apollonius of Rhodes' *Argonautica* (Second century B.C.E.) and Pliny the Elder's *Natural History*.

"...The territory of a powerful and ferocious arctic 'sha-man' or witch-doctor who dwelled slightly further to the north..."
This person is explained below.

"...Toyland was occasionally visited by someone she described as a 'bold, fearless black balloonist,' an explorer that she thought we might well be advised to meet."
The identity of the "bold, fearless black balloonist" will be revealed in a future *League* series.

"...a strange and mournful figure crouched before a deer-hide wigwam howling penitently...he wore, as his magician's robe, a fresh-flayed reindeer hide reversed so that the skin was outermost, its bloody red by now turned almost black, lined by the fur inside that stuck out in a trim around the garment's edge...he told us between moans of anguish that he was the 'sha-man' of the North Pole, charged at the mid-winter solstice with delivering the gift of cheer to all the homes on Earth...this breach of the magician's most important yearly ritual was met by the witch-doctor's fierce invisible familiars, or 'little helpers' as he called them..."

The idea of Santa Claus as a psychedelic-mushroom-imbibing shaman is not original to Moore. In 1980 the British journalist Rogan Taylor theorized that the traditional image of the red-and-white-robe-wearing Santa Claus evolved out of centuries of Siberian tradition, with the reindeer being a stock animal for the Siberian Lapps, flights through the air being a part of shamanic tradition, the red and white of Santa's robe being the color of the hallucinogenic fly agaric mushroom, and Santa's trips up and down chimneys being similar to the way that shamans' spirits enter and leave a shaman's yurt.

"...past the meteoric aggregate some call 'The Real North Pole'..."
The Real North Pole appears in M.P. Shiel's *The Purple Cloud* (1901), an early after-the-Apocalypse novel.

"...the Sea of Giants..."
The Sea of Giants appears in Tommaso Porcacchi's *Le isole piu 'famose del mondo* (1572), an early world atlas.

"...coming into Peacepool by Jan Mayen's Land. Peacepool itself, where there is said to live an enigmatic and benign old woman known as Mother Carey..."
Peacepool and Mother Carey appear in Charles Kingsley's *The Water-Babies*.

Page 209. The Game of Extraordinary Gentlemen. The Game originally appeared in *America's Best Comics 64 Page Giant* (2000), an anthology of stories from various ABC comics. In the *Giant* was a *League* feature, the "Game of Extraordinary Gentlemen."

Some squares have not been annotated. Those omitted repeat previous squares, as with the Spring-Heeled Jack references (see Box #1 below), or have no literary references.

Kevin O'Neill has admitted that the game is designed so that it cannot be completed or won.

Box #1. "Jump 5 spaces with Spring-Heeled Jack." This is a reference to Spring-Heeled Jack, the subject of British folklore and penny dreadfuls. Urban and rural legends about Spring-Heeled Jack, a devil-faced creature who spat blue and white flames and attacked women, circulated in Britain beginning in the mid-1830s. A play about Spring-Heeled Jack appeared in 1863, and the first penny dreadful with Spring-Heeled Jack as the central character appeared in 1867. Several penny dreadfuls with Spring-Heeled Jack followed, the best-known being Charlton Lea's in 1890, which featured a nobleman wearing a special suit which allowed him to jump great distances and to fight crime.

Box #2. "Blackballed from the Diogenes Club." The Diogenes Club was created by Arthur Conan Doyle and appears in two of his Sherlock Holmes stories: "The Greek Interpreter" (*Strand Magazine*, September 1893) and "The Adventure of the Bruce Partington Plans" (*Strand Magazine*, December 1908). The Diogenes Club is "the queerest club in London," and "now contains the most unsociable and unclubbable men in town," including Holmes' brother Mycroft.

Box #3. "Refreshments with Ally Sloper." Ally Sloper, seen on Page 149, Panel 1, was a British comic strip character and a sort of heroic, roguish everyman.

Box #4. "Help Detective S. Blake solve Mystery of Edwin Drood." "Detective S. Blake" is a reference to Sexton Blake, "the schoolboy's Sherlock Holmes." Blake was created by Harry Blyth and first appears in *The Halfpenny Marvel* #6, 20 December 1893. Blake is a gentleman detective who appears in nearly 4000 stories through 1968 and is one of the most-published characters in the English language.

The "Mystery of Edwin Drood" is a reference to Charles Dickens' novel *The Mystery of Edwin Drood* (1870). *Drood*, left unfinished at the time of Dickens' death, has remained a mystery because of the unclear state in which it was left; though there is an obvious suspect, the murderer's identity will never be known for sure, and because Edwin Drood's body is never found, there is the possibility that no murder was committed.

Box #5. "Fleet Street: Get tragic haircut," is a reference to Sweeney Todd, the Demon Barber of Fleet Street. Sweeney Todd is the lead character in a London urban legend which began around 1820. In these stories Todd was a barber on London's Fleet Street who killed his clients and turned them into meat pies, which Todd and his partner Mrs. Lovett then sold. The story of Sweeney Todd first appears in a penny dreadful in 1840 and as a play in 1842, with numerous prose and stage retellings of the story following through the Nineteenth and Twentieth centuries.

Box #6. "Dr. Nikola has you in thrall." "Dr. Nikola," whose name is seen on Page 31, Panel 4, is a reference to Guy Boothby's Dr. Nikola, one of the first major arch-villains of fiction.
The phrase "has you in thrall" is likely a reference to John Keats' poem "La Belle Dame Sans Merci" (1819), in which the lead character, enchanted by La Belle Dame, is warned by her former victims, "La Belle Dame Sans Merci/Hath thee in thrall!"

Box #7. "Time Traveller: Throw again, but move backwards." The Time Traveler is the hero from H.G. Wells' *The Time Machine*.

Box #8. "Professor Gibberne slips you his New Accelerator." "Professor Gibberne" and his "New Accelerator" are references to H.G. Wells' "A New Accelerator" (*Strand Magazine*, December 1901). In the story Professor Gibberne invents "accelerator," a drug which gives the human body the ability to move three times as quickly as normal.

Box #9. "Fan-Chu Fang, Prince Wu-Ling and Wu Fang need a fourth for Mah Jong," accompanied by an illustration of three old, evil-looking Chinese men. These characters were all Yellow Peril opponents (see the "Yellow Peril" essay in *Heroes and Monsters* for more information on this character type) who plagued heroes in magazines, books, and films in the first few decades of the Twentieth century.

Fan-Chu Fang was the Chinese arch-enemy of Dixon Brett. Brett was a gentleman detective in the mold of Sherlock Holmes and Sexton Blake and appears in story papers and novels in the 1910s and 1920s. Fan-Chu Fang, the "Wizard Mandarin," was a "veritable archangel of evil"; he was an agent of the Chinese government who worked toward the downfall of British Empire, going so far as to raid Buckingham Palace itself.

Prince Wu-Ling was the Chinese arch-enemy of Sexton Blake. The Prince, the "descendant of a dynasty which could trace its philosophy back to the time when the Anglo-Saxon race was unheard of," longed "from the innermost depths of his princely nature to feel the heel of the East on the West, to carve a path of saffron through a field of white, to raise on high Confucius, Buddha, and Taoism across all the world."

There were five characters named Wu Fang during the years before World War II. The first appears in the 1914 movie serial *The Exploits of Elaine*. He was a standard Yellow Peril character who was the enemy of Arthur Reeve's "science detective" character Craig Kennedy, the "American Sherlock Holmes." The second Wu Fang, also a standard Yellow Peril character, appears in the 1918 movie serial *The Midnight Patrol*. The third Wu Fang appears in the 1928 serial *Ransom*, written and directed by George B. Seitz, who had also written and directed *The Exploits of Elaine*. The Wu Fang in *Ransom* was a simple Yellow Peril anti-American terrorist and not the same character from *The Exploits of Elaine*. The fourth Wu Fang was the arch-enemy of Norman Marsh's Detective Dan, a.k.a. Dan Dunn, Secret Operative No. 48, who appears in an eponymous comic strip in 1932 and eight Big, Little books beginning in 1933. Dunn's Wu Fang was the "King of the Dope Smugglers, with diabolical, fiendish cunning, aided by a horde of depraved gangsters, and an endless stream of money squeezed from human blood, corruption and degradation." The fifth Wu Fang was the protagonist of the 1935-1936 pulp *The Mysterious Wu Fang*. Created by Robert Hogan, the pulp Wu Fang was headquartered in Limehouse. He was a mad scientist who bred monstrous new species of poisonous insects and snakes and who planned to conquer the entire world.

Box #10. "Even Gunga Din's ghost is a better man than you." Gunga Din appears in Rudyard Kipling's poem, "Gunga Din" (1890). Gunga

Din is the *bhisti*, or water-carrier, for the narrator's regiment. Din dies saving the narrator, inspiring the line, "You're a better man than I am, Gunga Din!"

Box #11. "Steal Moonstone for Dr. Nikola, or return to start." The "Moonstone" is a reference to Wilkie Collins' *The Moonstone* (1868), one of the most significant mystery novels of the Nineteenth century. The stone in question is a fabulous gem, a yellow diamond with a curse on it.

Dr. Nikola appears in Box #6.

Box #12. "Mowgli mistakes you for Dr. John Doolittle." Rudyard Kipling's feral child Mowgli is introduced in the short story "In the Rukh" (*Many Inventions*, 1893) and went on to appear in several stories, books, and films. Mowgli is raised by wolves in the forests of India and is able to speak with the animals.

Dr. John Doolittle first appears in Hugh Lofting's *The Story of Doctor Dolittle*. Dr. Dolittle has the ability to speak with the animals and eventually devotes himself full-time to dealing with them.

Box #13. "The Black Cat attempts to neuter you." This a reference to Edgar A. Poe's short story "The Black Cat" (*Philadelphia United States Saturday Post*, 19 August 1843), seen in the group portrait on the back cover of the first *League* collection. In "The Black Cat" the narrator hangs his good, black cat Pluto, only to find that the act was worse than a sin; it was a mistake.

Box #14. "Find Pip's fortune. Estelle seems restless." In Charles Dickens' *Great Expectations* (1860), Pip is the youthful hero of the novel. He has various misadventures as he tries to earn his way in life, and he falls in love with Estella, the adopted daughter of the wealthy Miss Havisham.

Box #15. "Oh, rotten luck! Suffer premature burial and retire from the game!" This is probably a reference to Edgar Allan Poe's short story "The Premature Burial" (*Dollar Newspaper*, 31 July 1844), the account of several examples of being buried alive.

Box #16. "Prison. Don iron mask." This is a reference to Alexandre Dumas' *The Man in the Iron Mask,* which is one third of Dumas' novel *Le Vicomte de Bragelonne* (1848-1850). The novel, the last of Dumas' trilogy about the life of d'Artagnan of the Musketeers, is about, among other things, the famous historical mystery of the Man in the Iron Mask, the true king of France who is held in prison with an iron mask on his face to conceal his identity.

Box #18. "Catch Moby Dick. Return to port at square 6 and see a Doctor." In Herman Melville's *Moby Dick* (1851), Moby Dick is the great white whale which Captain Ahab and the crew of the whaler *Pequod* pursue. The "see a Doctor" comment is a reference to the mayhem caused in *Moby Dick* when the great white whale is finally caught.

Box #19. "McTeague the dentist seems distracted." This is a reference to Frank Norris' *McTeague* (1899), a novel about a dentist, McTeague, who has no license to practice dentistry and is subject to greed. These twin flaws lead to McTeague's gruesome downfall.

Box #20. "Spurt forward 4 spaces aboard Good Ship Venus." "The Good Ship Venus" is a traditional naval and rugby song with lyrics like "The captain had a daughter/Was swimming in the water/Delighted squeals came as the eels/Entered her sexual quarter." (That is one of the more printable quatrains). The song was also recorded by the punk group the Sex Pistols in their 1980 album/documentary *The Great Rock'n'Roll Swindle*.

Box #21. "Robur shows you his Great Eyrie." Robur was created by Jules Verne and appears in *Robur the Conqueror* and *The Master of the World*. Robur, mentioned as one of Les Hommes Mysterieux on Page 171, is a rogue engineer who designs a new and powerful aircraft and uses it to threaten the world. Robur's "Great Eyrie" is his mountain hideaway in North Carolina.

Box #22. "Lake LaMetrie Monster stops for a chat." The "Lake LaMetrie Monster" is a reference to Wardon Curtis' "The Monster of Lake LaMetrie." The Monster, mentioned on Page 183, is an elasmosaurus into whose body is put the brain of a human. Initially the human controls the elasmosaurus' body and can talk, but eventually the human succumbs to the body's animal nature.

Box #23. "Become obsessed with Numerology." In numerology and Illuminati conspiracy theory the prime number 23 has significance, with Kabbalists defining it as "union with the Godhead" and Aleister Crowley defining 23 as "parting, removal, separation, joy, a thread, and life."

Box #24. "Fail to recognize Nick Carter." Nick Carter is the detective/ adventurer created by Ormond G. Smith and John Russell Coryell. Carter debuted in the short story "The Old Detective's Pupil" (*New York Weekly* v41 n46, September 18, 1886). Carter appears in over 2000 stories and novels and went through several incarnations from dime novel detective hero to Sherlock Holmes copy to hard-boiled private eye to ruthless spy in his century-long career. Nick Carter was a master of disguise, which is why he is not recognized in his disguise as a little girl. Moore noted that on the covers of *The Nick Carter Library* Carter is shown in various disguises, from a Chinese boy to an African-American, and so it amused Moore to show Carter in his disguise as a little girl.

Box #25. "Great Cthulhu wants you." Great Cthulhu is the "god of elder days" from H.P. Lovecraft's Cthulhu Mythos stories.

Box #27. "Old Mr. Fogg offers you a lift." Mr. Fogg is Phileas Fogg, the world traveler from Jules Verne's novel *Around the World in Eighty Days*.

Box #28. "Thrashed by Rosa Coote. Crawl like a worm to square 33." Rosa Coote, created by William Dugdale, first appears in the pornographic novel *The Convent School, or Early Experiences of A Young Flagellant* (1876). Rosa Coote, who appears in the first *League* series, thrashes the player because of her penchant for flagellation.

Box #29. "Mr. Wm. Bunter Senior sends you for pies." Mr. Wm. Bunter Senior is William George "Billy" Bunter, who was created by Charles Hamilton and appears in over 1500 stories and novels, beginning in 1908 in the British story paper *The Magnet*. Bunter was a greedy, cowardly, cunning, foolish, and gluttonous schoolboy.

Box #30. "If you stole Moonstone, Raffles coshes you for it." The Moonstone is mentioned in Box 11, above. Raffles is A.J. Raffles, the creation of E. W. Hornung. Raffles, who first appears in *Cassell's*

Magazine in 1898, is one of the best known of the gentleman thieves. To "cosh" is to strike with a blackjack.

Box #31. "Meet chap with dreadful appendectomy scars, on ice floe." This is a reference to Mary Shelley's *Frankenstein,* in which Victor Frankenstein's final confrontation with his patchwork man occurs on an Arctic ice floe.

Box #32. "Jim Hawkins produces his wrinkled parchment." Jim Hawkins is the boy hero of Robert L. Stevenson's *Treasure Island.* He and a group of pirates follow a parchment to find buried treasure.

Box #33. "At her castle in Styria, Camilla drinks your health." In J. Sheridan Le Fanu's horror story "Carmilla" (*The Dark Blue*, December 1871), Carmilla is a female vampire who preys on the innocent in Styria, a rural Austrian province along the Hungarian border.

Box #34. "In Ruritania Black Michael sends you to square 36." Black Michael and Ruritania appear in Anthony Hope Hawkins' *The Prisoner of Zenda*. Ruritania is a fictional central European kingdom in which Rudolf Rassendyll duels with the evil Rupert of Hentzau. Black Michael is the wicked Duke of Strelsau in the novel.

Box #35. "Sir Francis Varney bites you. Deuced bad show!" Sir Francis Varney, a vampire, first appears in J. M. Rymer's novel *Varney the Vampyre, or The Feast of Blood* (1845). Varney is seen in the group portrait on the back cover of the first *League* collection, while the illustration of Varney accompanying the text here is a visual quotation from the cover of Rymer's novel.

Box #37. "King Solomon's Mines: You can afford an extra turn." This is a reference to H. Rider Haggard's *King Solomon's Mines*, the first novel to star Allan Quatermain. The mines themselves hold the fabled lost treasure of King Solomon.

Box #38. "Hank Morgan from Connecticut seems disoriented." In Mark Twain's *A Connecticut Yankee in King Arthur's Court* (1889), Hank Morgan is a Connecticut engineer and the embodiment of hardheaded Yankee can-do pragmatism. Through a knock on the head he is sent back in time to the court of King Arthur.

Box #39. "Meet Dr. Van Helsing. If bitten by Varney, Retire from Game." In Bram Stoker's *Dracula*, Dr. Van Helsing is the aging vampire hunter who helps Mina and Jonathan Harker kill Dracula.

Box #41. "Lilliput. Big yourself up." Lilliput, in Jonathan Swift's *Gulliver's Travels*, is an island of six-inch-tall natives.

Box #43. "Join Mr. Kurtz for a drink." "Mr. Kurtz" is a reference to Joseph Conrad's *Heart of Darkness*. Kurtz, an agent for a company of ivory traders, becomes corrupted by the power he gains over the natives of the Belgian Congo.

Box #44. "Curipuri: Man-apes and giant reptiles." "Curipuri" is a reference to Arthur Conan Doyle's *The Lost World*, in whichl the curupuri is a spirit dreaded by the natives of the Amazon.

Box #45. "Brobdingnag: Suffer penile dementia. Return to 41 and regain self-esteem" Brobdingnag. in Jonathan Swift's *Gulliver's Travels*, is an island of giants whose stature might well inspire penile dementia.

Box #46. "Readestown: Frank Reade Jnr. builds you a pair of steam-boots." "Readestown" and "Frank Reade Jr." are references to the Frank Reade, Jr. series of dime novels. Readestown is mentioned on Page 183 above. Created by Luis Senarens, Frank Reade, Jr. is a boy inventor and adventurer who is as successful in coming up with wonderful new inventions, like "steam-boots," as he is in exploring the world and wiping out non-white natives.

Box #47. "Sleepy Hollow. Rest your head for 1 turn." "Sleepy Hollow" is a reference to Washington Irving's "The Legend of Sleepy Hollow," mentioned on Page 183 above, about a small town in upstate New York purportedly haunted by a headless horseman.

Box #48. "Receive white feather." This is a reference to A.E.W. Mason's novel *The Four Feathers* (1902), in which a young British pacifist refuses to fight in the Sudan, and is given four white features by his friends and fiancée as a sign of contempt for his "cowardice." The phrase "to show the white feather," to display cowardice, predates Mason's novel, but *The Four Feathers* is likely the source Moore is referring to here.

Box #49. "Baltimore Gun Club sends you aloft." The Baltimore Gun Club, which appears in Jules Verne's novels *From the Earth to the Moon* and its sequel *Autour de la Lune* (*Around the Moon*, 1870), is a group of Baltimore gun fanciers who decide to travel to the moon by shooting a manned shell at it.

Box #50. "Take Trans Atlantic Pneumatic Tube." The "Trans Atlantic Pneumatic Tube" is a reference to Michel Verne's "An Express of the Future" (*Strand Magazine*, December 1895), in which a pneumatically-driven train carries passengers under the Atlantic.

Box #51. "The Harkaway boys don't like your tan. Thrashed and sent back 6 spaces." "The Harkaway Boys" are a reference to Bracebridge Hemyng's stories about Jack Harkaway and his family, who first appear in *Jack Harkaway's Schooldays* in 1871. The Harkaway boys, whose father, Jack, appears in a portrait on the back cover of the first *League* collection, were adventurous schoolboys who traveled around the world. The Harkaway boys would not like someone's tan and would thrash them for it is because they were biased against the non-English, especially those who had darker skin than they, and often used malicious pranks and physical violence against them.

Box #52. "John Melmoth recounts an anecdote. Miss five turns." "John Melmoth" is a reference to Charles Maturin's *Melmoth the Wanderer* (1820), the greatest of all Gothic novels. In the novel John Melmoth sells his soul to the devil in exchange for lengthened life. He then spends most of the novel bewailing his fate and looking for someone to take his place. The novel is lengthy, and Melmoth is long-winded, which is why the player misses five turns while Melmoth tells a story.

Box #53. "Join sight-seers at cylinder in crater. Retire from game." "The cylinder in crater" is a reference to H.G. Wells' *The War of the Worlds*. Why the player is forced to retire from the game can be seen on Pages 37-40.

Box #55. "Willie and Tim have a question. Sadly, their speech is unfathomable." Willie and Tim, seen on Page 112, Panel 2, are the friendly tramps Weary Willy and Tired Tim, two of the earliest recurring characters in British comics. They were created by Tom Browne and first appear in the comic *Illustrated Chips* in 1896.

Box #56. "Stuck in Grimpen Mire for 1 turn." In Arthur Conan Doyle's *The Hound of the Baskervilles*, Grimpen Mire is the dangerous section of Dartmoor just north of Baskerville Hall where the notorious Hound is said to prowl.

Box #57. "Moulin Rouge. Lose virginity." The Moulin Rouge was a combination theater, concert hall, and dance hall, full of artists (like Henri de Toulouse-Lautrec), dancers, and prostitutes. It opened in Paris in 1889 and quickly became famous as the symbol and embodiment of Parisian *joie de vivre* and *fin de siecle* dissipation.

Box #58. "Robbed by Arsène Lupin." Arsène Lupin, the most famous of the gentlemen thieves, was created by Maurice LeBlanc and first appears in the magazine *Je Sais Tout* in 1905. Lupin was a mysterious master thief, similar to Raffles (see Box #30 above), who stole from society but also fought for good.

Box #59. "Rue Morgue: Assist C. August Dupin and miss a turn, or go to square 61." The "Rue Morgue" and "C. August Dupin" are references to E. Allan Poe's detective, C. Auguste Dupin, and his first case, "The Murders in the Rue Morgue" (*Graham's Magazine*, April 1841). Dupin appears on pages 23-36 of the first *League* collection.

Box #62. "Absinthe break. Go to the dogs." Absinthe, a.k.a. The Green Fairy, is a strong herbal liqueur, usually around 120 proof, which was popular during the Nineteenth century with aesthetes and intellectuals. Its ingredients vary, and although its primary ingredients are alcohol and wormwood, the formula is often augmented with other herbs such as anise, licorice, hyssop, veronica, fennel, lemon balm and angelica. Absinthe gained a deserved reputation for being toxic if taken in large quantities, and its use was banned across the United States and Europe from 1912-1915.

Box #63. "Broad Arrow Jack shows you the Golden Rivet, but worse things happen at sea." Broad Arrow Jack, seen in *League* as a member of the crew of the *Nautilus*, is the hero of E. Harcourt Burrage's "Broad-Arrow Jack" serial (*The Boys' Standard*, 1866). Broad-Arrow Jack is John Ashleigh, an Englishman who runs afoul of thieves while emigrating to Australia. He is branded with the broad arrow but recovers and continues with his adventures.

The Golden Rivet is a reference to naval folklore. Crewmen new to a ship were told that one of the rivets in the lower part of a ship's hull was made of gold and that they should find it. No such rivet existed, of course. On some ships the search for the golden rivet was also used as an excuse to sexually initiate the new crewman.

Box #65. "Sargasso Sea. Miss a turn." The Sargasso Sea is an area of the Atlantic Ocean where the winds, mixed by the Gulf Stream and the North Equatorial Current, move in a circle, thus causing ships powered only by sail to be trapped in it. It is known for the distinctive blue quality of its waters and its vast islands of seaweed. The Sargasso Sea appears in the first Captain Nemo novel, *20,000 Leagues Under the Sea*.

Box #66. "Oh, no, it's Fungal Disease." This may be a reference to the William Hope Hodgson story, "The Voice in the Night" (*Blue Book*, November 1907), about two castaways on a North Pacific island who become infected with a fungus which transforms their entire bodies. H.P. Lovecraft's *The Shunned House* (1928) also features a fungus, this one haunting an old house in Providence, Rhode Island.

Box #67. "Doctor Moreau will see you now. Spend rest of game on all fours." In H.G. Wells' *The Island of Dr. Moreau*, the cruel Doctor Moreau attempts (unsuccessfully) to turn animals into men.

Box #68. "Treasure Island welcomes offshore investors." This is a reference to Robert Louis Stevenson's *Treasure Island*.

Box #69. "Lulu breaks your heart." "Lulu" is a reference to Frank Wedekind's plays *Earth-Spirit* (1895) and *Pandora's Box* (1902). In the plays Lulu is a German femme fatale who leaves a trail of broken hearts and fortunes behind her. She ultimately ends up destitute and plying her trade on the streets of London and is finally murdered by Jack the Ripper. The two Wedekind novels were used as the source for the silent film *Pandora's Box* (1928) in which Lulu was played by Louise Brooks.

Box #71. "Henry Hobson says go back 1 or forward 4." This is a dual reference, to Henry Hobson, of Harold Brighouse's novel *Hobson's Choice* (1915) and to the phrase "Hobson's choice." In the novel

Hobson's Choice Henry Hobson is a Lancashire bootmaker who must deal with several rebellious daughters. The phrase "Hobson's choice" is a reference to Thomas Hobson (1549-1631), a hostler in Cambridge, England, who always offered his customers only that horse which was closest to the door. The phrase "Hobson's choice" has come to mean no choice, to take what is offered or nothing.

Box #73. "Buy Crystal Egg from Mr. Cave." "The Crystal Egg" and "Mr. Cave" are references to H.G Wells' "The Crystal Egg," seen above on Page 25, Panel 3.

Box #74. "Lidenbrock Sea crossing rougher than usual." The Lidenbrock Sea is a reference to Jules Verne's *Journey to the Center of the Earth*. The Lidenbrock is an underground sea, filled with various prehistoric creatures, that subterranean explorers are forced to cross.

Box #75. "Severin's been a bad boy." Severin appears in Leopold von Sacher-Masoch's novel *Venus in Furs* (1870). Sacher-Masoch, whose name was the source for the term "masochism," wrote *Venus in Furs* to detail his masochist fantasies. The novel is about Severin, a dissipated dilettante who falls in love first with a statue of Venus and then later with his neighbor, Wanda, who resembles the statue and who indulges Severin's taste for the lash.

Box #76. "Kapitan Mors will fly you to square 82." "Kapitan Mors" is a reference to Captain Mors, the heroic protagonist of the German dime novel series *Der Luftpirat und Sein Lenkbares Luftschiff* (*The Pirate of the Air and His Navigable Airship*), which ran from 1908 to 1911. Captain Mors was a Captain Nemo-like character who fought for good and for Earth against villains both human and alien. Mors is shown to be one of Robur's correspondents in the first *League* collection and is mentioned in the Game on Page 224.

Box #77. "Pére Ubu screams abuse. Ignore him. He's Polish." "Pere Ubu" is a reference to Alfred Jarry's trilogy of absurdist plays, *King Ubu*, *Cuckold Ubu*, and *Slave Ubu*. Ubu is an unpleasant authoritarian monster given to vulgarities, including "merdre," a nonsense word close to "merde," the French word for "shit." "Ignore him, he's Polish" is a reference to Alfred Jarry's speech on *King Ubu*'s opening night: "The action, which is about to start, takes place in Poland, that is to say,

Nowhere." The reason Poland is Nowhere is that in the 1890s there was no independent country of Poland. Poland had been occupied and partitioned in the 18th and 19th century, and in the 1890s was occupied by the Russians, Prussians, and Austrians.

Mina and Allan pass by Ubu's kingdom on Page 175.

Box #78. "Dishonored by Harry Flashman. Sting with shame for 2 missed turns." The character Harry Flashman, who first appears in Thomas Hughes' novel *Tom Brown's Schooldays* (1857) as a bullying schoolboy who torments Tom Brown, became popular in the modern era through George Macdonald Fraser's "Flashman" novels, beginning with *Flashman; From the Flashman Papers 1839-1842* (1969). As an adult Flashman is no improvement over his childhood self; he remains an unlikeable cad and scoundrel.

Box #79. "Bed down with exotic beauty, wake up with The Beetle. Lie back and think of England." In Richard Marsh's *The Beetle*, the Beetle is a giant, deformed beetle which is inhabited by the soul of an Egyptian princess. She can transform herself into the beetle, into a beautiful Egyptian woman, and into an ugly old man, which explains the change alluded to here.

Box #80. "Flatland. Perhaps a private education might help." This is a reference to Edwin A. Abbott's *Flatland*, mentioned on Page 184.

Box #82. "The Purple Terror is starting to grow on you." This a reference to Fred M. White's short story "The Purple Terror" (*Strand Magazine*, September 1899), a tale about a carnivorous plant.

Box #83. "A humbling experience with Mr. Heep. Feel soiled, even if you win." "Mr. Heep" is a reference to Uriah Heep, a character in Charles Dickens' *David Copperfield* (1850), who is a vile blackmailer and one of Dickens' most despicable villains.

Box #86. "Maiden Voyage of the *Titan*. Ghastly Business." The "voyage of the *Titan*" is a reference to Morgan Robertson's novel *Futility* (1898), in which he wrote about a *Titanic*-like ship which is struck by an iceberg. The *Titan* is referred to on Page 115, Panel 4 of the first *League* collection.

Box #87. "Professor Cavor coats you with his special paste. The moon seems awfully big tonight." "Professor Cavor" is a reference to H.G. Wells' *The First Men in the Moon*. Cavor, seen on Page 52 of the first *League* collection, is the short, fat scientist who invents a paste, "cavorite," which cancels gravity. Cavor and the narrator of the novel use it to travel to the moon.

Box #88. "Wonderland. Throw 6 to stay where you are. Otherwise, move counter in reverse." Wonderland is the magic land that Alice visits in Lewis Carroll's *Alice's Adventures in Wonderland* and *Through the Looking Glass*. "Throw 6 to stay where you are. Otherwise, move counter in reverse" is a reference to Chapter 2 of *Through the Looking Glass*, when the Red Queen tells Alice that "Now, HERE, you see, it takes all the running YOU can do, to keep in the same place. If you want to get somewhere else, you must run at least twice as fast as that!"

Box #100. "Well, call me Kallikrates! It's the Fountain and Heart of Eternal Life! Hurrah! Jolly well done! Now join Mr. Melmoth for a long lunch." "Kallikrates" is a reference to H. Rider Haggard's *She*. Kallikrates was an Egyptian who Ayesha, the immortal goddess and She Who Must Be Obeyed, loves yet slays. The "Fountain and Heart of Eternal Life" are references to the source of Ayesha's immortality.

Page 211. The poster that is part of the "Exhibition Extraordinary" is the cover to *League of Extraordinary Gentlemen* v2 n1. The entire illustration can be seen on Pages 4-5 above.

Page 212. This image is the cover to *League* v2 n2.

Page 213. This image is the cover to *League* v2 n3. This scene is set in the British Museum, the headquarters for the League.

Moving counterclockwise, beginning with Mina, the references are as follows:

The book Mina is holding has "Apergy" and "1880" on it. This is a reference to Percy Greg's novel *Across the Zodiac* (1880), in which apergy, a "repellant force" that works very much like anti-gravity, is discovered and used to transport the protagonist to Mars. Apergy later appears in John Jacob Astor's novel *A Journey in Other Worlds* (1894) and in Jack London's short story "A Thousand Deaths" (*The Black Cat*, May 1899).

The map of Mars behind Mina is dated 1880. Presumably it was compiled by the hero of *Across the Zodiac*. The map resembles real maps made by the astronomer Percival Lowell (1855-1916), who theorized that life might exist on Mars.

The top picture on the left bears the caption "timore Gunclub 1865." This is a reference to the Baltimore Gun Club, of Jules Verne's *From the Earth to the Moon* and its sequel, *Round the Moon*. In *From the Earth to the Moon* the Gun Club uses a giant artillery piece to fire a manned projectile to the moon.

The bottom picture on the left bears the caption "Augustus Bedloe." This is a reference to the protagonist of Edgar Allan Poe's short story "A Tale of the Ragged Mountains" (*Godey's Lady's Book*, April 1844). In that story Bedloe walks into the Ragged Mountains outside of Charlottesville, encounters a strange city, and has an out-of-body experience.

The submarine-like model below the portrait of Augustus Bedloe bears a placard with the words "Astronef," "proposed by," "ofessor Hart," and "eaton York." This is a reference to George Griffith's "A Visit to the Moon" (*Pearson's Magazine*, January 1900), a short story in which Rollo Lenox Smeaton Aubrey and Lilla Rennick visit Mars in the *Astronef*, a spaceship designed by Lilla's father.

The black cat is a statue of the Egyptian goddess Bast/Bastet. The placard on the pedestal reads "C. Cave, Naturalist and Dealer," is a reference to H.G Wells' "The Crystal Egg."

The upside down scabbard has the word "Phra" inscribed on it. This is a reference to Edwin L. Arnold's novel *The Wonderful Adventures of Phra the Phoenician* (1891). Phra is a Phoenician trader from the first century B.C.E. who is reincarnated through the centuries.

The rabbit inside the glass jar, wearing a jacket and holding a watch, is the White Rabbit from Lewis Carroll's *Alice's Adventures in Wonderland.*

The skull with the Roman centurion helmet has a tag reading "Lepidu." This is a reference to Edwin L. Arnold's novel *Lepidus the Centurion* (1901), a novel in which an Englishman in the modern era finds the living body of a Roman centurion, Lepidus, trapped in a tomb which has recently been uncovered.

What looks like a wooden mallet is actually the head of Pinocchio, from Carlo Lorenzini's *The Adventures of Pinocchio* (1881). Pinocchio must have lied very badly just before he died, because his nose is quite long. His nose points towards the lower lefthand corner of the cover. The two oval spots on his head are his eyes, his mouth is just visible below his nose, and on the side of his head is his ear. His body is not visible; obviously he was decapitated.

Inside the glass case are three stuffed animals:

* The first, a toad, is likely the Frog Footman from Lewis Carroll's novel *Through the Looking-Glass* (1872), based on the John Tenniel illustrations.
* The second, a rat, is likely Mr. Rat from *The Wind in the Willows*.
* I have been unable to place the reference to the third creature, a penguin in a military or marching band uniform.

The axe and the cape and bonnet are likely references to Little Red Riding Hood. Her basket is at the foot of the red hood.

The hookah is probably the water pipe of the caterpillar in Lewis Carroll's *Alice's Adventures in Wonderland,* as is the playing card figure. The hookah appears to be attached to the pump at the top of the jar containing the two of spades.

The cat is a reference to Edward Lear's *Nonsense Alphabet*, in which he writes, "C was a lovely Pussy Cat; its eyes were large and pale; And on its back it had some stripes, and several on his tail." Lear's drawing of the Pussy Cat is nearly identical to the cat seen here.

Hanging to the left of Little Red Riding Hood's hood is a dressing gown. It may be the gown in which Sherlock Holmes customarily lounged, or it may be Griffin's gown, which Mina discovers on Page 69.

In the upper right corner of the page is a shadowed bust of Pallas Athena. Presumably this is the "pallid bust of Pallas" on which sat the raven in Edgar Allan Poe's poem "The Raven" (*The New York Mirror*, January 1845).

The bat-winged figure in the case to the left of the Pussy Cat may be the suit of Spring-Heeled Jack, seen in Box #1 of the Game of Extraordinary Gentlemen.

The burning lamp is often how Aladdin's Lamp is pictured.

The picture with the caption "1889" may be a reference to Mark Twain's novel *A Connecticut Yankee in King Arthur's Court*, which was published in 1889. The larger figure is holding a helmet from a medieval suit of armor.

The picture below that, with what looks like a Roman centurion holding a badminton racket, may be a picture of the main characters from *Lepidus the Centurion*.

The black globe with the placard "The Steel Globe" is a reference to Robert Cromie's novel *A Plunge into Space* (1890), about a scientist who builds a fifty-foot sphere of black metal and travels to Mars with a group of friends.

Kevin O'Neill notes:
> Inside the glass case are the following:
> - The frog from illustrator Randolph Caldecott's "A Frog He Would A-wooing Go" (1883).
> - The rat is from Beatrix Potter.
> - The figure in military costume is from "Les Animaux" (1842) by Jean Ignace—Isidore Grandville.
> - The batwing cat in upper right background is also from "Les Animaux."
> - The dressing gown is Griffin's.

Page 214. This image is the cover to *League* v2 n4.

Page 215. This image is the cover to *League* v2 n5.

Page 216. This image is the cover to *League* v2 n6.

Page 217. This image is the cover to the "Bumper Compendium" which reprinted *League* v2 n1 and n2.

Page 218. This image is the cover to the "Bumper Compendium" which reprinted *League* vol. 2 n3 and n4.

Page 219. The "Colour and Save Page" is similar to ones which appear in British comics like the *Rupert the Bear* Annuals.

This image may have been an alternative cover to *League* v2 n5.

Kevin O'Neill notes:
> This colour and save page was reproduced from a photocopy of the original cover for #5. The courier company lost the original art en route to Wildstorm, and in the meantime Alan thought it gave away too much of the story so we replaced it with an alternate version.

Page 220. The "Cautionary Fable" may be a play on Ogden Nash's *The Boy Who Laughed at Santa Claus* (1957), which begins

> In Baltimore there lived a boy.
> He wasn't anybody's joy.
> Although his name was Jabez Dawes,
> His character was full of flaws.
>
> In school he never led his classes,
> He hid old ladies' reading glasses,
> His mouth was open when he chewed,
> And elbows to the table glued.
> He stole the milk of hungry kittens,
> And walked through doors marked NO ADMITTANCE.
> He said he acted thus because
> There wasn't any Santa Claus.

and ends quite badly for Jabez Dawes.

The poster in the first illustration which reads, "Extra, The League of Extraordinary Gentlemen #6 Delayed. Ink on the Track. Now Due January" is a reference to "leaves on the tracks," the traditional response given by British Rail for delays in train service. Moore and O'Neill are no doubt also having some fun with those fans who complained about the delays in the release dates of the later issues of the second *League* series.

Page 221. "How to Make Nemo's *Nautilus*" is an homage to similar diagrams in British story papers like the *Rupert the Bear* Annuals.

"Simon and Sally" may be a reference to the two children characters in the British comic strip "Simon and Sally," which was drawn by Mike Noble and appears in the comic *Robin* beginning in 1953.

The names for the forms of the paper are allusions to the sexual positions described in the *Kama Sutra*, the Indian guide to love and marriage written by the Indian sage Vatsyayana sometime between the Second and Fourth century C.E.

Vishnu is one of the three most important gods in the Hindu pantheon. Vishnu makes up the divine triad with Brahma and Shiva. Vishnu is the sustainer and maintainer of the universe.

"Rhanipur," or Ranipur, is a town in Uttar Pradesh in north central India.

The Thuggee, or Thugs, were a group of religious assassins in India who strangled travelers for the glory of the goddess Kali.

Bhang is an Indian drink made from the leaves and flowers of the *Cannibis sativa* plant, which also produces marijuana.

Kevin O'Neill notes:
> The two smiling kids are more like the generic happy kids from numerous 1920s-1930s British comics—I think Alan has a soft spot for Roy Wilson's art on *Happy Days*—but then, so do I.

Page 222. I've been unable to decipher any of the Martian writing on this page. It's possible that it is not decipherable, and that Kevin O'Neill is simply teasing the reader.

Kevin O'Neill notes:
> Give up on the Martian writing Jess. Believe me, nothing to
> see here.

"That same year, Giovanni Virginio Schiaparelli first saw 'canals' on Mars..."
In 1877 Giovanni Schiaparelli (1835-1910), the well-respected astronomer and director of the Milan Observatory, examined Mars through his telescope. The surface of Mars cannot usually be seen with any clarity, but Schiaparelli was looking at Mars when the distance between Mars and the Earth was at its minimum. Schiaparelli saw straight lines crisscrossing Mars' surface, and used the word *canali* to describe them. *Canali*, in Italian, means naturally-occurring grooves or channels. Schiaparelli was not the first to see these grooves or to describe them as *canali*. Father Pietro Secchi (1818-1878), one of the earliest astrophysicists, had examined Mars and mapped it in 1876, using the word *canali* to describe the grooves. Schiaparelli drew on Secchi's observations and expanded them, creating a new map of Mars. The English-speaking public misinterpreted the word *canali* to mean "canals" and took this to mean that the grooves were artifically constructed and so were evidence of the existence of Martians.

"...it was not until 1894 that Percival Lowell realised these were irrigation systems and that Mars was inhabited, founding the Lowell Observatory at Flagstaff, Arizona, to study 'Mars as the Abode of Life' in its many startling varieties."
In 1895 the American astronomer Percival Lowell (1855-1916) published four essays in *The Atlantic Monthly* on the atmosphere, water situation, canals and oases of Mars. These essays were collected and published later that year as *Mars*. In *Mars* Lowell argued for the existence of intelligent life on Mars.

The Lowell Observatory is a real place, and it was established in Flagstaff, Arizona by Lowell in 1894, but its purpose was and remains scientific. *Mars as the Abode of Life* is the title of a book written by Lowell and published in 1910.

"...such as those reported in 1895 by both the visionary Mrs. Smead..."
In 1895 the American medium Mrs. Smead claimed to have communicated with her dead daughter and brother-in-law, both living on Mars. Smead described canals and Martians, who greatly resembled humans.

"...and the seeress 'Mirielle'..."
I have been unable to place this reference.

"During the 'Mauve Nineties'..."
The 1890s were described as the "Mauve Decade," due to the perception that mauve pervaded the Decadent literary movement of those years.

"...Carl Jung's 15-year-old case study 'Miss S.W.' in 1899..."
In 1899 one of Carl Jung's patients, "Miss S.W.," then only fifteen years old, described while in trances her travels to Mars. "Miss S.W." described canals and Martians making use of flying machines.

"...the medium Helene Smith..."
From 1894-6 "Helene Smith," a Swiss medium whose real name was Catherine Muller, had visions of Mars while hypnotized. Smith described meeting Martians and speaking with them, and described the Martian language as similar to French.

"...the prehistoric 'Green City' of Varnal."
Varnal is mentioned on Page 13, Panel 1 above.

"..subject of Théodore Flournoy's 1899 biography 'From India to the Planet Mars'..."
Theodore Flournoy was a psychology professor at the University of Geneva who published *From India to the Planet Mars, a Study of a Case of Somnambulism with Glossolalia* in 1899. The book was a psychological and unsympathetic treatment of Muller, who Flournoy thought was faking her visions in order to get attention.

"...a reference to the planet's abundant Princess population."
This is a reference to Dejah Thoris, the titular princess of Edgar Rice Burroughs' first John Carter of Mars series, *A Princess of Mars*.

Page 223. This is an homage to similar puzzles in British comics like the *Rupert the Bear* annuals.

Kevin O'Neill notes:
> Hidden in the tree above Dr. Moreau's head are Pip, Squeak and Wilfred, among others.

Page 224. The game at the top of the page is an homage to similar illustrations in British comics.

"Campion Bond's Moral Maze" is an homage to similar mazes in British Comics.

The comment that "one path leads to wealth and status, the others to being found dead in the woods" is a reference to Dr. David Kelly. Dr. Kelly, a British scientist, told the BBC that the British government's dossier on Iraq was "sexed up" by the Blair administration. Dr. Kelly later said that if the U.K. assisted in the invasion of Iraq he would be "found dead in the woods." Five months later Dr. Kelly's body was found in Oxfordshire woodlands.

"Mors" refers to Captain Mors, the lead character from the German dime novel *Der Luftpirat und Sein Lenkbares Luftschiff.* Captain Mors is mentioned in Box 76 of the Game of Extraordinary Gentlemen.

Robur is the lead character in Jules Verne's *Robur the Conqueror* and *Master of the World.*

"The Doctor" refers to the Devil Doctor of Limehouse, who may or may not be Fu Manchu. The Doctor was the one of the villains of the first *League* series.

"M" refers to both the head of MI5 and to Professor Moriarty, who was one of the villains of the first *League* series.

Page 225. It's unclear whether this image is intended to have actually taken place in the world of *League.*

Kevin O'Neill notes:
> No, this image falls outside *League* continuity as I drew it
> as a promotional Christmas card for a friend, Justin Ebbs,
> and his Just Comics company.

The "Millennium Kestrel" may be a reference to the *Millennium Falcon* in the *Star Wars* trilogy of movies. A kestrel is a kind of falcon.

"My Big Donkey," "Proper Little Madam Career Pack," and "Sweet Cigarettes" are not actual games. "Leaf on the Track, A Game of Patience" is a reference to British Rail's excuse of "leaves on the tracks" as an explanation for slow and late trains.

I am unaware of Poe the Cat as a reference to anything.

Page 226. This is the full image of Gullivar's carpet. I have been unable to decipher any of the writing. It is possible it is not meant to be deciphered.

Kevin O'Neill notes:
> Stop reading the carpet, Jess, it's bad for you—I won't tell
> you again!

KEVIN O'NEILL INTERVIEW

Jess Nevins: How did you first get involved in *League*? Did Alan Moore just ring you up one day and say, "I've got this idea for a Victorian comic?"

Kevin O'Neill: Not quite. It was funny, I was in Comic Showcase, a comics store in London, and Paul Hudson, the owner, had heard a rumor on the Internet that I was working on a project with Alan Moore. I said I didn't know that, that was news to me, I hadn't spoken to Alan in a while, but by coincidence that week I was having to ring Alan because of some letter that Fleetway Publishing was sending out asking people to sign away rights and stuff like that, so there was a number of us ringing each other and making sure that everyone understood what it meant and no one was going to sign it anyway. So I rang Alan and we were chatting about this, and right at the end of the conversation he asked me if I'd be interested in this project he was thinking of. And he described, briefly, the *League of Extraordinary Gentlemen*, and I was just amazed. It was the greatest idea I'd ever heard. Any artist would give his eyeteeth to draw that combination of characters and work with Alan. And so I said I was definitely interested. I guess this would have been 1996, late 1996, somewhere around then. He sent me the synopsis he'd done of the story, a kind of outline, which possibly Jim Lee had seen by then, and we really worked from there. We were just talking over things from very early sketches, which were mostly off the mark if I recall. We talked about maybe giving Allan Quatermain tribal scars on his face, but that got dropped along the way, because he could hardly be undercover if he had a face covered in tribal scars. So that's really pretty much how it started. And then I got the first gigantic script, and Alan is always very courteous and always says that if there's a better way of drawing it, go ahead, but Alan's way is always spot-on, so to deviate from it is like deviating from the blueprints of a house, really.

JN: That actually ties into a couple of other questions. How does working with Moore differ from working with other authors?

KO: Well, principally I've worked with Pat Mills, and Pat, way back, at the beginning of *2000AD*, had the reputation that Alan now has, for producing big fat scripts with a lot of detail. Not as much detail as Alan, and the storytelling is different—Alan is the greatest architect of sequential graphic storytelling in the world, while Pat's certainly got a more bombastic style. I'd worked briefly with Alan before, on a "Green Lantern Corps" story, and some other bits and pieces, so I kind of knew his approach was different from Pat's. Pat encouraged my input on the stories themselves. The kind of work we were doing suited that approach. With Alan, it's very precise, and there's also that slight fear in the back of your head of letting him down, that some of these great scenes he's conjured up, these fantastic moments are not going to be quite as good once they're laid down on paper. But it made me reconsider my career at that point as well because I had been in a bit of a doldrums before I got *League*. Pat and I had been involved with people who were developing a *Marshal Law* movie, and that distracted me from the comics business for a while, so when I got back into it I was doing fill-in jobs and bits and pieces. I'd probably drawn way too many guns and people blowing up and heads blowing off, and so doing something which couldn't have been more different was when I started the series finding the right tone, the right approach for the artwork took a little while, took a few pages to find itself. It must have been ten pages or so into the first episode before I really thought I was getting to grips with it. Alan's very encouraging as indeed was Pat—I'm a self-taught artist, and so my grounding is sort of shaky, so I was learning on the hoof with both those gentlemen, and I think *League* in particular has prompted some really different work from me than I might have expected from myself a few years ago.

JN: You'd said, in 1999, in an interview for *Submedia Magazine*, that "The *League of Extraordinary Gentlemen* was a real change. It had a female protagonist and some of the hardest stuff I've ever had to draw— people doing nothing. It's much easier to blow someone's head off than to do long scenes with smoking-jackets." Do you still find the more static, less dynamic scenes difficult to draw?

KO: I'm more used to them now, and I really enjoy them. Because Alan puts in little touches of body language and glances and looks, and is perhaps part of the reason for the success of the book, and we seem to have many more female readers than certainly I've experienced with books I've previously worked on—I think people are genuinely attracted by the smaller moments because they build to the bigger moments. They have very human touches, which the new story we're doing develops, and it's a huge amount of fun. Alan's feedback, when they work well, is so positive, it makes me enjoy them even more. The big drama scenes, the huge operatic scenes, I should expect to come easy, because I've drawn a lot of that kind of material over the years, those scenes actually have more power because of the quiet moments that lead up to them.

JN: What were some of the other challenges involved in envisioning the universe of the *League*?

KO: When I first started on *League* I guess the temptation for me, and this was from habit, was to have a lot of jokey Victorian signs and—not quite graffiti, but things written on walls and painted on advertisements and such, kind of like a Victorian *Marshal Law* landscape or something.

JN: Sort of like a *Mad Magazine* sort of—

KO: Yeah, too much wordplay and such, but that was really invading Alan's territory. It was inappropriate. And once we'd become entranced by the idea of using more than just the fictional characters who are the principles, using as much from a fictional background as possible, including, in what I'm doing at the moment, including fictional ads on the sides of buildings and so on referring to fictional commercial companies, it became richer—it's more challenging. I'm reading a lot more and chasing stuff down, that's a huge amount of fun. Actually, I think people perhaps have the impression that there's a great deal of research involved, in our view of London in particular, and to a degree that's true, but even before working on the book I'd lots and lots of books on Victorian and Edwardian London. It interests me. I grew up in the 1950s, and there were still acres and acres of bomb sites, lots of Victorian streets, the docks around Woolwich and so on. It was black and grimy and sooty and bomb damaged and sort of interesting and exciting. So I've always been interested in that, but London in our book is different. It's just kind of skewed slightly. It is a fantasy London, it's based on real London architecture but in some scenes it's taller or squat, or in others it's squatter and uglier. That was really the challenge, it was just hitting the right mood. And also, what people's expectations are when you have, say, the Limehouse sequence. We wouldn't be in Limehouse much, but I wanted it to be as visually interesting as I could possibly make it and Alan's writing in that sequence is very powerful and very dark and I kind of had a lot to live up to.

JN: In the scripts, how much direction is there for the actual art? How much direction is there for the look of the characters, and the look of the universe? How much of that comes from Moore, how much from the original novels and stories, and how much from you?

KO: Let me think. As I said, we talked over the characters, roughly what ages they would be, originally, and I started looking up the books, and I remember mentioning to Alan that in *Mysterious Island* Captain Nemo is revealed as Prince Dakkar, an Indian prince, and Alan got quite excited by that, and we talked about Nemo wearing an Indian costume, and that motif carrying through to the *Nautilus* and the interior of the *Nautilus*. That was in discussion, and—I found that as far as possible I was looking at the earliest visual references for any of the characters. Mostly they were, I won't say disappointing, but take *20,000 Leagues Under The Sea*. You have a kind of bearded, European looking Nemo, and in *Mysterious Island* I think he has a white beard. The poor artist, the revelation that Nemo was Indian was changed from him being revealed to be Polish, I believe. So that wasn't particularly useful, and I did say to Alan that it'd be nice if he had an Indian style *Nautilus*, but that doesn't fit the description in the books, so this is a new *Nautilus*; the earlier one had been lost and this one has replaced it. So a lot of it is discussion. In the scripts Alan is very precise on where people are standing, where they are relative to one another, the continuity in tracking people around the room, tracking from shot to shot, he's extraordinarily detailed, I've never worked with as much detail, which took me a while to get used to. But once I did I found it enormously helpful. And Alan does give descriptions of important details that need to be included. I guess I have a fair amount of freedom on buildings and docks and stuff like that. The *Nautilus*—oddly enough I think my *Nautilus* veers from Alan's description, because it was going to be originally festooned in

Indian statues and things, but I found that I couldn't make it work in continuity, shifting the angles of something absolutely covered in that amount of detail would have been difficult. And then I was kind of scribbling around on that kind of squid-encircling-a-whale image, which seemed right to me, and a few Indian details on the design to make it work. So it's kind of give and take, and I don't think I've done anything that Alan hasn't liked, there've been some odd things that have happened, like Mr. Hyde's size developed from a very early ad, which became the back cover for the first six issues, of the big Hyde hand with the other hands on top. Alan had suggested, when we were talking about a teaser ad, doing something like the end of the first issue of *Fantastic Four*, where they put their hands on top of one another, and it's a kind of Three Musketeers thing as well, isn't it? We thought that might be interesting, and so when he said that Hyde's hand would be a bit bigger, I drew this enormous hand, and actually I think it looked pretty good, but scaling the hand up to the rest of the body, obviously Hyde by then was this enormous figure. The other curious thing about Hyde is his dark coloration in the comic was an accident of design, really. I did the color notes for Ben Dimagmaliw and at the first appearance of Hyde I'd put a note saying that Hyde's dark because he's in the shadows, but Hyde became dark permanently. A dark figure, he didn't keep the skin tone of Jekyll. But we liked it, we liked—Ben's wonderful dark coloring there was a perfect complement to the rest of what we were doing on the book. I think we all have degrees of freedom, but we're trying to— I guess it's a vision we all agree on, how the book should be.

JN: Were there any particular moments or characters or scenes that were favorites or that you're particularly proud of?

KO: From the first series, I think the climax of issue six, I think— Moriarty's airship coming under attack, I think that whole issue in the first series is my absolute favorite. I think it all kind of comes together. In the second series, there's a really nice scene where Mina's walking around the pub, and she has a conversation with Hyde in his room—I just think that's—I like that, because it's a quiet moment, but it was very scary. Maybe another scene later in the second series where Mina is crying, looking out of the frame crying, because some of these things are very subtle, and my style, before I started the series, was very bombastic. That kind of thing is difficult. I think in issue six of the first series, the big scenes with the balloon approaching the airship were images which I was comfortable with. And I think we wanted, because the series was running so late as well, but we definitely wanted to go out with a bang and make the wait worthwhile.

JN: One of the things that I've found with *League* is that people tend to put every panel under a magnifying glass and trace all sorts of possible references. I've had a lot of people say that individual panels are references to some of the work you've done with *2000AD*, panel homages to *Nemesis* or even *Metalzoic*. Do you see a continuity between your earlier work and your work on *League*?

KO: I suppose there might be something subliminal in that, there's no deliberate references to earlier series. I think principally because it would throw the balance of a series to refer to stuff which has no real connection to it--

JN: Well, maybe not a direct reference, but—I think it was in the *Almanac* you drew Lovecraft's "Mountains of Madness," and a couple of people said, "Oh, this is similar to a panel in *Nemesis*." Is there a desire on your part to draw these things in a similar way?

KO: I guess. The Lovecraft thing and the *Nemesis* thing, the deeply gabled roofs, dark buildings with round windows or skewed expressionist windows, is just the way I like to draw anyway, whether I'm drawing it for *Nemesis* or for stuff for *League* for the *Almanac*. I think that's just a consequence of that kind of architecture appealing to me, the expressionist style appealing to me. It's fun to draw. But it wasn't very consciously a reference I was aware of anyway, before you mentioned it.

JN: Where do you see *League* fitting in with the rest of your body of work?

KO: Interesting question. I guess if you'd asked me in 1995 I wouldn't have seen something like *League* coming, even though *Nemesis*, the very first serial which would have been published but we delayed it, was a Victorian world, it was called "The Gothic Empire." I only drew a couple of episodes and then we abandoned it and drew a different serial,

Nemesis. Pat went back to the Gothic serial later and by then I had sort of quit *2000AD* and it was continued by other hands. But I was always interested in Victorian material, but I never thought—I never saw myself drawing Captain Nemo and the other characters even though I've always had an interest in earlier proto-pulp fiction. I've collected books on penny dreadfuls and so on, it's always fascinated me, but I never really knew that anyone else was interested. I don't know. It's been a very lucky change of direction, because like I said I was growing a little tired of just drawing things blowing up, and I had mentioned to people in recent years, certainly before *League*, that maybe one day I'd quite like to draw a romance comic or something with a female character, and most people laughed. They didn't see that at all. And Alan works with artists—I guess he doesn't always pick people who perhaps an editor would pick, for instance, or a publisher. He sees something different coming out of the working relationship to something that an editor might predict to be the consequence of teaming two people together. I always wanted to do something that was very English, but really *Nemesis* and *Marshal Law* and *Ro-Busters* and things like that are very fanciful, they're either American or alien or just plain bizarre. This is a very English book.

JN: Have you found yourself getting, maybe not burned out, but a little tired of all the Victoriana? I imagine that, after having spent seven years drawing these characters and then reading the books you might be looking forward to moving on to more recent time periods.

KO: I did enjoy it. I've always enjoyed it. What I found is that we are now shifting gears into various new time periods, it's starting all over again, and that's got its own delights and its own problems, of course, a new set of things to look up and get involved with. I think we've had a great deal of fun with the Victorian period, but we never really saw the book as the *Justice League*. Characters have been killed off, and things are moving along, and it's shifting. So its period setting and its line-up are obviously going to change from series to series. And that's as it should be. I think it makes it much more exciting for the readers. I'm sure that it would be easy to just maintain the thing as it is, just to keep its core members and keep having new adventures, but it's more exciting that it's shifted the way it has. Characters have died in memorable ways, Nemo has left, Allan and Mina's relationship has disintegrated at the end of this book, but it shifts again in the next one. That's all good, that makes it very exciting to work on.

JN: How long does doing the research for an average issue take you?

KO: It really does vary. On the Martian book, issue four, when we had the episode with Barnes Bridge blowing up, I did go down to Barnes, the old railway bridge, to do some sketches and take some pictures, because even though it doesn't appear on much more than a couple of pages, three or four pages, it was important to get it right. There was just something about being on the scene, I couldn't find any good photographic refs in books, so it wasn't too great a distance for me to travel and to go and look at it. There was a day of doing that. The other stuff—when I get a script from Alan I immediately sort out what I've got a reference for or what I need to get a reference for whatever we're doing. But I honestly couldn't tell you, Jess. (Laughs) I honestly don't know. If I actually came up with a figure it would probably shock Scott Dunbier, so I probably won't even think about it. (Laughs)

JN: Well, for the purposes of the interview I'll just say that it takes you about thirty minutes a day. Do you use any people as character models?

KO: No, there's—I've never used, never had people modeling for any of these—most of the characters I've drawn have been so bizarre that no one looks like them anyway, but—

JN: No one looks like Torquemada?

KO: No, no one looks like Torquemada, thank God. When we started the book, funnily enough, we were talking about what they would look like, and I vaguely remember us talking about Quatermain, because obviously there's the Stewart Granger film. And we did talk about Sean Connery, and I remember mentioning Connery in *Robin and Marian*, where he was obviously much older, and *The Rock*, where he's kind of grizzled—these kinds of films. It's sort of ironic the way that turned out. But Quatermain in the comic series doesn't actually look like that, doesn't look like Connery. When I was thinking about it and reading the books I thought, really, John Hurt, the actor, looks like Rider Haggard's description, but clearly Quatermain, in some ways, is a wish dream fantasy of Rider Haggard. I was looking at pictures of Rider Haggard as an old man, and Quatermain is vaguely, vaguely like him but not terribly close. And then the others, I just kind of winged it.

JN: Okay—a few specific questions. You've said in the past that sometimes in *League* you include pieces of architecture which were theorized but never realized, like the Monument in Pudding Lane in volume two and St. Paul's Cathedral in volume one. Were there any others that the rest of us missed?

KO: I'd have to go through it, but off the top of my head I'd say no, because they may yet still appear. It was fun to have the opportunity to fit the more outrageous proposals into a landscape without completely distracting from everything else that was happening. Also, we had a lot of our action take place along the Thames, and some of the things that we wanted to get in or that would have been nice to have got in just wouldn't have appeared there. They just wouldn't have been appropriate. But they will appear in the future. It's never too late.

JN: What were some of the other Easter eggs you snuck into the book? Some people caught the figures from the Quality Street Chocolates in the street scene in volume two. Were there any others?

KO: That one doesn't exist. I think people are seeing Quality Street figures where there aren't any. Me and Alan laughed about that, because it's actually not a bad idea, but they're slightly the wrong time period. I think they're Regency characters on Quality Street. I think perhaps people are seeing shadows where they are not, and possibly missing stuff—in the scene where the Invisible Man brutalizes Mina, he knocks her over a table. And one of the items on the table is the Portland Vase, a Roman vase which was smashed by a mad Irishman back in 1845. They've clearly taken it off display, repaired it, and put it safely in this office, where it ends up of course smashed again by Mina knocking it over. That's on the page where she is punched by the Invisible Man. A lot of stuff I'd put in as I go along or Alan had deliberately mentioned something, and I thought, "Oh, this might be amusing, let's drop it in and see if people notice it, and if they don't it doesn't matter."

JN: One of the items in the second volume that drew the most interest from the fans was everything in Martian in the first issue. A lot of people seemed to fixate on that. How much of what was in Martian, from the dialogue to what's on Gullivar Jones' carpet, is—first of all, was the script in Martian your idea or was that Alan Moore's?

KO: That was Alan's. It was very terse dialogue between Gullivar and the green Martians for the most part. And Alan wanted it written in an alien script, and there's an instruction to letterer Bill Oakley to that effect. But we were talking about it, and I said, well, I'll give it some thought, and, in a bit of synchronicity, there was something in *Fortean Times*, the English magazine—I don't know if you've ever seen it, but *Fortean Times* had a page which was material allegedly channeled from Mars. It was from a book called *From India to the Planet Mars*, by I think Theodore Flournoy. On this page there were these sort of charmless drawings and a strange drawing of what I think was purported to be a Martian woman which some medium had channeled down to the page. And a page of writing, allegedly Martian handwriting. And I looked at that, and my first thought was, "Maybe we could use that," because that's a nice fictional reference or, depending on your belief, a nice real reference. But when I looked at it more closely I realized that it wasn't a terribly good fake of what an alien language might look like or an invented or lost language might look like—just someone's doodling, maybe she had got an idea from looking at some Islamic symbols or something. It wasn't terribly good. So I gave it a bit more thought and thought I'll have a go at lettering those sequences, the Martian sequences, and if Alan doesn't like them we'll have Bill redo them. It would save me the step of sending the artwork to America for Bill to letter, and there wasn't a great deal of Martian in it so it wouldn't have taken me much longer to do. I came up with two little fonts, one which was bold lettering of about 30 characters, and a less bold group which was about 150 Martian characters. And those were randomly sort of scrambled around the carpet, which I drew originally as a black and white line drawing just to test the lettering effect and carpet details before starting the opening page's closeups of the carpet. The carpet doesn't actually say anything that I can recall. I should hold it up to a mirror to make sure I didn't. And now you're going to tell me that there's something reversed there.

JN: No, I've given myself several headaches by holding it up to mirrors and trying to figure out what an individual symbol might mean, and I've come up with nothing.

KO: (Laughs) Good. I shall double check, but I'm pretty certain you're right. I think the carpet, I'm on pretty safe grounds that it's just pure design. When I came to do the Martian word balloon lettering, there were two things about it. One was, I wanted it to fit in balloon shapes. In theory, if it was Martian lettering, if it was truly alien, it could be scripted in straight lines or vertical lines down the page, but that's all very cumbersome and overstated. The other thing, when I was looking at it, was that if someone was saying a short sentence, it should be a short burst of Martian writing, and if someone was saying something slightly longer, it should be slightly longer. So what I did was write it out on a bit of tracing paper and then flop the tracing paper over, and some of the words, I realized I could turn into these character designs I had and then just drop random Martian character designs in there as well, so it had a sort of rhythm to it, but there's no logic, there's no great plan to it. There are a few real words which you can possibly just about still make out. Some of the word balloons I shall double-check, some of them might be completely reversed English but so transformed by the Martian character form that you just couldn't read them. There is something underlying it all, it made it look a little bit more credible as a script, as a language.

JN: In the *Traveller's Almanac* there were some watermark illustrations. Were those anything in particular?

KO: Yeah, let me look for it to remind myself. In the first episode, the illustration that's on the cover of the *New Traveller's Almanac*, with Her Majesty's Stationery Office printed on it, which was in red in the book, that fake cover, that image, of a kind of Mayan compass calendar image, was a watermark in the first chapter of the *Almanac*—in fact it's still there in the collection, but you just couldn't really see it or make it out. The next one, that ended up as a watermark because it was a mistake on my part. I'd drawn a unicorn. It was meant to be an illustration for the Marvellous Islands, which showed a centaur. So it should have been a centaur skeleton, which would have made sense, but for some reason I drew a unicorn skull, and then Alan pointed that out, so I drew a different illustration for the Marvellous Islands, a very simple thing, and we used the unicorn image as a watermark.

JN: Your depiction of the Martian Tripods is quite striking and memorable, and yet it's fairly different from a lot of the other Tripods that have come before. Was there a particular inspiration for your depiction of the Tripods, or was it just you having fun with them?

KO: Well, the Tripods—I've always loved *War of the Worlds* since I was a kid, I absolutely adored the book, and I probably have seen all the earliest illustrated *War of the Worlds*—there's some wonderful Belgian illustrations, there are some great Tripod pictures, but they tend to sort of roll around a little bit and perhaps look a little bit foolish. I'm sure that in real life, looking like that, they'd scare the life out of you, but they just seem like boilers on wobbly legs. And you often couldn't see the basket on the back of the Tripods in those early illustrations, sometimes you could, sometimes you couldn't, the scale was sometimes bigger than Wells described, sometimes it was smaller, and the cowl on top was never quite like he described it, I'm sure I've not got it exactly as he described it either, because I think Wells in particular is often a bit mean with detail. Certainly anyone trying to draw the Time Machine has got a huge problem, because there's virtually nothing useful for an artist to work on. Tripods are a little bit better, because you have many descriptions. What I did with the Tripod legs was give them a kind of insect configuration. They look like they can walk. I think they improved as I went along. I did about four or five different ones and they all had different merits. Some of them looked scarier than the finished one, but didn't work from any other angles but one angle, from the front or from the sides. The one I ended up using is the one that was most useful in the round. I tried to be pretty faithful to Wells even though some of it doesn't make sense. Like, in the book you can see the occupants of the Tripods operating the controls, which suggests that perhaps somewhere a marksman with a rifle could have picked them off. So I tried to make the cockpit of the thing look a bit more protected. I think he was writing very fast. I know that—the *War of the Worlds* I've got is a heavily annotated version from a few years ago with lots of variant versions and chapters and things that he changed for the American version and later editions, so it's quite interesting. In fact, when I started the book I went through *War of the Worlds* and plotted it out, day by day, and got it down on paper, so we could work out exactly how many Tripods there were per cylinder, and when they landed, and where they were every day, and what the state of the Thames was, and then I sent that all off to Alan. I think we were reasonably faithful. The Primrose Hill thing we dealt with as swiftly as we could. There's lots of nice details in *War of the Worlds* which would have been interesting to fit in if there'd been room, like the Martians brought along creatures which they were clearly feeding from, like vampires, which I thought was a nice touch. I think we had talked about doing something with that, but in the end there simply wasn't room, because it is always as much about the League as it is about *War of the Worlds*—we're not doing a *Classics Illustrated War of the Worlds*. There's lots of great stuff in the book, it's wonderful, and there are moments in the second chapter—I'm sure you spotted it—where there's conversations from the book taking place in the background, which just gives it, which just brings the sweep of Wells into our world.

ALAN MOORE INTERVIEW

Jess Nevins: Was there a specific idea or moment which inspired the storyline for the second *League* story, or did it just grow naturally from the first *League* series?

Alan Moore: It grew from the fact that—as you know, we had been originally keeping this rough dating scheme that things happened in the years that they were published in. We noticed that *War of the Worlds* was published in August 1898. This was during the writing of the first series, which we had set for other reasons in the early part of 1898. So we figured that if we were going to get the Martian invasion in, that more or less had to be the second book, if we were going to keep to that rough chronological scheme, that the Martian invasion of Earth took place in August of 1898. So that was the main incentive, because that seemed like too big a fictional event to ignore, and it also seemed to offer lots of interesting possibilities, like, for example, it enabled us to present a view of the fictional Mars, and—well, there were lots of dramatic possibilities for the story, although as we progressed with it I found that, actually, the Martian invasion, it's a very big event that's happening in the background of the second volume. But actually that's kind of like the way that Wells handles it. Wells is much more concerned with the foreground lives of tiny little human beings who don't really see or understand all of the conflict, but just have it suddenly descend upon them. And that is probably because a whole book focusing upon the unfathomable menace of the Martians would have been very boring, and that's presumably why Wells decided to foreground the human reaction, and that's probably the only way you could really successfully— it's one of the better ways to successfully tell that kind of story, that kind of invasion story, whether you're talking about an alien invasion or whether you're talking about a military invasion. It's more likely that you're going to focus upon the people on the ground rather than the invading military forces. That was pretty much why we decided to go for the Mars invasion as the second book.

JN: As you were saying that I was reminded about our first interview, where you talked about the great British tradition of apocalyptic fiction, and you mentioned *Day of the Triffids*.

AM: Yeah, Wyndham and tons of books. *Day of the Triffids* and *War of the Worlds* are kind of scientific apocalypses, but there were, oh, tons of books written in the early twentieth century that were predicting the invasion of England. There were lots of imaginary war or future war stories that were essentially apocalyptic fiction.

JN: When you were saying that it reminded me that I'd read, a couple of months ago, *The Battle of Dorking*, the first British future war novel, and it's very similar to *War of the Worlds*, in that it really does focus on the little people, the experiences of one soldier.

AM: On the invaded rather than the invaders. Yeah, I think that that is, it just seems to be the natural way to do it. You can—for one thing, if you're focused on the Martian invaders or the foreign soldiers, then they're going to lose their shock value. You're going to find out too much about them, they're going to become familiar, which goes against the grain of the whole thrust of the invasion story, which is of some sort of aliens, whether from other worlds or other countries, flooding into your home world, your home country, and changing everything. And the fact that the shock of their Otherness is one of the most appealing things about that kind of fiction. So probably it's just the most sensible and convenient way of telling that sort of story, because by keeping focused upon the human figures in the foreground, some of the sense of threat, the sense of shock, and the sense of Otherness can be retained in the background monsters. I'm not surprised that the fiction does most generally tend to take that kind of slant. It's the easiest way to do a story like that, to tell the truth.

JN: Did anything about the second series change while you were writing it, or had you planned it out very precisely before you wrote it?

AM: No, I hadn't planned it out precisely. Most of the stuff in it occurred to me while I was writing it. I knew that there would be an invasion of England, that we would follow as closely as possible the sequence of events in Wells' book. I kind of realized fairly early on, probably while I was writing that first issue, it probably occurred to me that Griffin would almost certainly side with the Martians, just because they were both written by the same person. It seemed to me that Griffin would probably think, "Oh, those Martians, they're written by H.G. Wells as well, so I'd better bond with them." And, also, given the fact that Griffin is a kind of megalomaniac lunatic, who sincerely wants to rule the world, it struck me that he might strike some sort of bargain with the Martians and that he'd probably get killed. Griffin is too unstable a character—like Hyde, in a different way, it occurred to me that both Griffin and Hyde are essentially too unstable, psychologically, to survive for very long, realistically. Both of them are psychopathic, in different ways, and Hyde seems especially to have some deep theme of self-hatred, perhaps connected with his dual nature. Hyde hates Jekyll, certainly, and Jekyll hates Hyde. That sort of self-hatred, it generally leads to self-destructiveness. And it occurred to me that, really, in any sort of real psychological situation, although we are used to having a chaotic monster as a member of our super teams these days, if they were really that chaotic they wouldn't last that long. This is why the Hulk has never made a successful member of the Avengers, I guess. It just seemed that those two characters would probably be dead by the end of the book, which is why by the time I was writing the *Almanac* for issue number one I was sufficiently confident to state that by the end of the book there were only two members of the original League left following the Martian invasion, because it seemed to me that, yeah, Griffin and Hyde would get themselves killed, and Nemo, I can't see him working for the British Empire for longer than about six months without becoming outraged, having a temper tantrum, storming off. And that seemed to work well in that it would pare the League down to a two-man core membership ready for their new adventures in the Twentieth century. And I'd also got the idea, from the book, from *War of the Worlds*—I was more or less tied to what happened in there, so I knew that at the end of the book it would at least have to seem as if the Martians had died of the common cold. This is what gave me the idea for some sort of germ warfare, some sort of biological disease weapon. That got me thinking about Dr. Moreau, and after checking the dates I found that *The Island of Dr. Moreau* actually preceded all of those anthropomorphic, humanized animals that teemed all over British children's fiction during the early twentieth century. So it struck me as a potentially interesting and amusing conceit if we were to make Dr. Moreau's horrific animal experiments the root of the genesis of all of these much-loved children's characters that seemed to be half-human, half-animal, like Mr. Toad or Ratty and Mole, or Rupert Bear, or Tiger Tim or any of these other figures. So the story kind of grew. I'd got a rough idea. By the time I'd got that first issue finished I had got a rough idea. There were events that I thought might make it into the final story which eventually had to be left out. There were events that I'd not really imagined which suddenly found their way in. It's an odd process, because you're trying not to contradict what has been established in the works of other writers, at least not too badly, and trying to come up with original ideas, original takes upon the subject matter, within the confines of that. That's pretty much how it happened. It grew organically. Once I'd realized that Griffin was going to die I remembered we'd done that thing in the first series where we'd made it apparent that Hyde can actually see Griffin, which seemed too good to waste.

JN: So that wasn't a deliberate foreshadowing, back then, it was just—

AM: No, it was just that I was, when I was thinking about Hyde, it just suddenly occurred to me that his senses, being more bestial than human perceptions, might actually be wider than ordinary human perceptions, and that he might be able to see Griffin. And I also thought that, well, if he did, if he was able to see Griffin, he wouldn't tell him, because, being Hyde, this would give him a secret advantage that he could perhaps exploit at some later date. So, having thought of that, I thought, "Okay, so Hyde kills Griffin. Why does Hyde kill Griffin?" And since I'd already shown a kind of dawning respect between Hyde and Mina during the first volume, where in the scene on the airship, where Mina has been slapping Jekyll's face to effect the change, and all of a sudden he changes to Hyde and grabs Mina's hand, and is quite likely to tear her arm off or something, and she just tells him that he's hurting her and she would be very grateful if he'd let her go, and he does, and I thought that that seemed to imply something about the way that Hyde perceives Mina, that she can control him, or reason with him, or reach him in some way when other people can't. And that was what led to that quite oddly touching little scene in issue two, when the two of them are talking in Hyde's room, which just wrote itself. And it established this connection between Mina and Hyde. Not a romantic connection, but—Hyde's feelings for Mina are a bit more complicated than his feelings for the rest of the world. It wouldn't be love, exactly, but an absence of hate, which is probably the best that Hyde could manage. So with that all set up, the order of events tended to dictate itself, and it all led up to that rather horrible sequence in issue five, which I still find myself alternately shuddering at and chuckling over. That was pretty much how the story came together. Fairly organically. Once we knew that we were going to be handling the Martians, then the events in the story tended to suggest themselves.

JN: Some people have wondered, do you usually outline in detail before you begin writing or do you just write and then revise in a second draft? Something like *Watchmen*, for example—

AM: Oh, I never do second drafts, no. No, it's all first draft. Everything that anyone's ever read of mine, with the possible exception of the last chapter of *Voice of the Fire*, where that is a second draft. But everything else, generally, the first episode is in print by the time that you're writing episode three, so you can't, you haven't got the luxury that book authors have, of going back and changing a character, making something more convenient for yourself. You've more or less got to train yourself to get it right the first time. That's how it happens. You have to anticipate stuff that, even if you don't know what it is you're doing, you have to at least leave room for it. It's an instinctive thing. With that first issue, it was something that I wanted to do, to show what the geopolitical situation on Mars might be, if you were to incorporate a lot of the various different Martian fictions that have been written over the years. So I knew I wanted to do that, and I knew I wanted some big, spectacular battle scene, where you didn't have to have much in the way of commentary or language, where you could just show this huge, spectacular alien battle. And at the end, yeah, you see the crashed spacecraft and the League members going to inspect it. That was a lot of fun, and it gave me time to think, and I didn't set up anything there that contradicted later things. And while I was writing it I was getting a better idea of what the shape of the rest of the story might be, or at least key events. But, that said, even when you've got that, you get to something like issue four, and when I was thinking, "How do I start this issue?" Then I came up with that whole scene with the dozens of people all fleeing upon the railway train that stalls upon the bridge near Mortlake, and you have the Tripod waiting along the river and smashing down the entire bridge. It's quite a dramatic little scene, the small boy being rescued by the *Nautilus*. I'd got no idea until I actually sat down to write those pages that that scene was going to be there. It was just something that suggested itself at that point. So you get a kind of rough grasp of the main plot points that you're going to need to fit in, and you just proceed carefully from there and hope that you haven't forgotten something or left something out that you're going to need in issue five. It seems to work out pretty well, most of the time.

JN: Was there anything that appeared in the second series that you'd originally planned to appear in the first series?

AM: Don't think so, no. There was nothing that was—no, I don't think so. There was nothing that was left out for lack of room, say, in the first series that we had to put in the second series. The way that the characters behaved, it's obvious that some of it has to go in the second series. No, there was nothing that, we got to issue six of Book One and thought, "Oh, it's a pity we didn't get this scene in or that scene," because that was a whole different story. The kind of scenes in that first book would have involved Fu Manchu and Moriarty, and we thought we'd got pretty well all the great scenes that we wanted to show with those characters. So, no, it was all new stuff for the second volume.

JN: Was there anything that you wanted to work into the second series that you didn't get the chance to use? You'd previously mentioned a possible tie between Gullivar Jones' carpet and the *Beano* series "Jimmy's Magic Patch."

AM: Yeah, well, that was one of those things, an idle thought that in the *Beano* series "Jimmy's Magic Patch" you've got a British schoolboy who buys a pair of trousers, somehow he comes by a pair of trousers that have been mended with a square from a magic carpet. There is a patch made out of carpet material which has been used to mend this boy's trousers. Now, actually, that doesn't make much sense right from the word go, people don't generally use squares of carpet material to mend their trousers with, but this was British comics and it was the forties. Kevin had suggested that maybe Gullivar Jones' carpet could have been the source of this square of carpet material that Jimmy's magic patch was made from, and I had originally got some vague idea for a scene in which an anxious Gullivar Jones, worried about what the Martians might be doing upon Earth, uses his carpet to fly back to Earth, which is how he got to Mars in the first place, so I presume that interplanetary travel wouldn't have been a big problem for him. So he gets back to Earth, but he probably gets back the week after the invasion has ended, and he happens to land somewhere near London where he's unfortunate enough to run into a group of gypsies, probably those from Arthur Morrison's *Child of the Jago*, who murder him and steal all of his possessions, including the magic carpet. That would have explained how the original gypsies who provided Jimmy with the magic patch for his trousers, where they got it from. But that doesn't fit in at all with the chronology of Gullivar Jones, who returned to Earth and lived a happy life and lived to a ripe old age, presumably. So to make this connection with a minor character from British comics would have meant violating the continuity of a more important character. There wouldn't have been very much point to it. It would have just been a cute little tie-up for continuity obsessives that would have actually probably done more damage to the continuity than it would have reinforced it. So, bad ideas, stupid ideas, they perhaps look appealing to start with, but it soon becomes apparent that, no, a scene like that would add nothing to the story. Even if it did seem cute to you at the time, it's better to let it go.

JN: Some fans had the expectation that John Carter and Gullivar Jones would make a reappearance later in the series, charging to the rescue or something like that. Was that ever a consideration?

AM: No. Like I say, I was trying to follow Wells' book, and Wells' book makes no mention of the League of Extraordinary Gentlemen saving the day, much less John Carter and Gullivar Jones turning up from space and defeating the Martians. In Wells' book it's obvious that the Martians have died of a disease, so all I was able to do was to change the details of how they died of the disease. No, that first issue, I got pretty much all of my Martian riffs out of my system with that one. That'snot to say that we might not revisit Mars at some point in the future. I think me and Kevin have decided that some time between 1900 and 1950 the Martians wipe themselves out in some way, so that by the time Ray Bradbury's *The Silver Locusts* [*The Silver Locusts* was the British title of *The Martian Chronicles*—Jess] reached Mars, then it was a dead planet, with only the ghosts of former civilizations drifting around. That was our rough thinking. But, again, whether we'll ever get the chance to actually detail that or not, I don't know.

JN: The first League series was almost lighthearted while the second took a, well, darker turn. You'd said that William Samson, the father of the Wolf of Kabul, was created at the time of the American invasion of Afghanistan. Was the tone of the second *League* series at all influenced by current events?

AM: Yeah. There's always been, even in the first *League* series, yes, it was lighthearted, but I began writing that in 1998. It was set in 1898. And so there was a kind of connection, even from the first book, at least in my head, between this kind of unstable period approaching the turn of the Twentieth century and this unstable period approaching the turn of the Twenty-first century. And there was always that sort of parallel feeling. But, yeah, certainly in the second book when I realized that there's quite a few little things in *War of the Worlds* that did chime with what was happening in Afghanistan. The very fact that it's a war, for one thing. That there is a war going on. I suppose there's bound to be some parallels. And the idea, say, for example, over here, while I was writing the second volume, where our horrifically right-wing but luckily blind and therefore beyond criticism home secretary, David Blunkett, he was talking about how in the wake of September the eleventh—one of these kind of ridiculous right-wing ideas that the politicians over here put forward to try and mirror the even more ridiculous right-wing ideas that politicians over there have been putting forward—was that every immigrant, every Muslim citizen, should be made to have to accept loyalty tests, proofs of good citizenship. There were various suggestions about what this might be. Some sort of questionnaire where they'd be asked to name all the members of the England football team, or swear allegiance to Tony Blair or the Queen or something. Most of the things would have meant that I and most of my family and friends would have been thrown out of the country straight away. It was ridiculous. It was just this kind of xenophobic fear of people turning up from overseas who had a different way of life to us. So that was probably what fed in to the title of Chapter Two, "People of Other Lands," and the impassioned plea, I think it was at the end of issue three, where it was saying, "Let this magazine be your proof of loyal citizenship! God save the Home Secretary!" There were moments where it seemed that I could at least make some little comment.

Again, the atmospherics of this story set roughly a century ago do coincide quite nicely with the political atmosphere of our present day. When Mina Murray is talking, I think in issue two, about how the sky had previously seemed something that sheltered humanity, but now that these alien cylinders had turned up, it's suddenly an object of fear, and that seemed to me to have a resonance, post-9/11, with the sheltering skies of America, which up until September the eleventh, 2001, had done a pretty good job of keeping America free of the kind of bombardment and aerial warfare that the rest of the world has been putting up with since Guernica. But after 9/11 I bet there's a lot of people walking around squinting occasionally at the sky if they hear an airplane passing. Again, it strikes a chord of resonance with the death-from-the-sky that Wells was proposing in *War of the Worlds*. There are connections between this century and previous centuries, and I always find that it suits the atmospherics if you can, kind of subtly, connect the time in which your story is set and the time in which your readers are living. It never does any harm, and it can sometimes give an extra level of resonance to the story.

JN: Do you think future League stories—I mean, the ones that are going to be set in different time periods—will share those atmospherics?

AM: Well, possibly. We'll have to see what happens when I'm actually writing them. The thing is, if I was to, say, do a series set in America in the fifties, which I've talked about, then I'm sure that whatever the elements were in that story, that I would probably find that there were parallels and connections with whatever was happening in whatever year it was that I got around to writing that story. If you've got the right sort of eye, it's not difficult to see possible points of connection in these different worlds and different times. So I should imagine League stories set in the future or even League stories set further in the past will—the times in which I'm writing those stories will probably color the way that the story turns out, it will probably color the way in which I choose which facts or which characters to include. So, yeah, there'll probably always be some fairly arch references to present day situations somewhere within the text of the *League*. I wouldn't rule that out by any means.

JN: One interpretation of the two *League* series has the first one as essentially showing Sherlock Holmes' England, the hansom cabs, Moriarty, Mycroft, the sort of Holmesian London, while the second series shows Wells' England, the forests, the rural areas, Moreau, the Crystal Egg, and so on. Was that deliberate or did that just—

AM: No, I don't think so. That's not really the way that we thought of it. It's just that Moriarty was the obvious villain for the first book, so, yeah, there are a lot more Sherlockian references in that first volume. The second volume, the Martians are the main enemy, so I suppose that, yeah, they're going to color the landscape if they are the predominant forces in it, but, no, it's meant to be the same world, it's not meant to be, "This is the Conan Doyle England, this is a Wells England," because there are Wellsian elements in the first book and there are Conan Doyle elements in the second book. It's not as neat as that, and it's nothing that was really intended. The first book actually deals with stuff happening in other countries, at least in the first couple of episodes. It's not all London. In this one the action is split between Mars, London, and the River Bank, with this rustic jaunt to the South Downs. So, no, it wasn't an attempt to evoke a Wellsian England, it was just the way that the story tended to come out.

JN: With something like *League*, that's really dense with references, people often wonder—there's a certain level of looking at it with a magnifying glass, so that people begin to think that everything is planned ahead of time.

AM: Yeah, well, no, they can put that idea completely out of their head. If they knew—it would frankly be impossible to plan all those details ahead of time. I'm not that bright, and they're being far too generous if they think I am. Nobody's that bright. It's a lot of luck and serendipity that makes things work out just so. Some very involved thinking. I surprise myself as often as not, just when I'm looking at the original material and something will hit me, and, "Oh, I see, we could have this connected with this, and that could be connected with that, or explained by that," and it will tickle me, there will be something about it that is an appealing idea. But that'll be where the inspiration comes from, and as I'm writing the scenes perhaps further details will occur to me. But it's certainly, it's not all meticulously planned out in detail right from the word go. When I sat down to write *League of Extraordinary*

Gentlemen number one, I'd got no idea what it was going to develop into. It was still in a very rudimentary stage as a kind of "Justice League of Victorian Britain," and all the rest kind of grew out of it naturally. With the second volume, particularly with the *Almanac* section of it, that kind of expanded my vision of what the League is really all about, and made it a much more sweeping and all-encompassing vision. But, again, that was something which I hadn't really planned. We were just looking for something to put in the backup pages because we didn't want to just do another pastiche, and we hit upon the idea of the *Almanac*, and after thinking about it for a little while I suddenly realized what marvelous potential there was in it. But this is nothing that I'd got planned from the outset. These are things that occur to me as I'm going along, and that's probably why the League still feels pretty fresh. These ideas haven't been stewing for years. They have often occurred to me that morning. So there is something about—you can tell when ideas are fresh, or when they have been brewing for years, and there can be a kind of staleness to them, when it's obvious that the author has gone over this idea so many times in his or her head, that it no longer really holds any kind of fresh appeal for them, so they're unlikely to be able to communicate any kind of fresh appeal to their readers. So I have vague ideas of how things are going to be going, but I always leave loose ends and vague patchy areas that will leave room for inspiration and serendipity. It seems to be a better way of working.

JN: Do you feel that the second series is as satirical as the first?

AM: Yeah. I wasn't even sure that the first series was that satirical, quite frankly. There's elements of humor and satire in both of them. If it seems less satirical I'm not going to say that it's not less satirical, but that wasn't the intention. There's perhaps even more rather pointed satire in the second volume than there is in the first. I don't know, I think that we were—perhaps some of the satirical references in the second volume, they're a little more pointed. I don't know—oh, just little things like, in the second volume, the hardback collection, where we've got "Campion Bond's Moral Maze" at the end, in the activities pages, where it talks about various moral choices, that some lead to success and some lead to being found dead in the woods. Which is perhaps a reference to Dr. David Kelly, who also revealed things that MI5 didn't really want him to reveal and who said that, "If things get much worse I might end up being found dead in the woods," just before he ended up being found dead in the woods. So there were a few little satirical pokes like that, probably more than in the first volume. As to whether it was generally more or less satirical, I don't know. That wasn't really what I was thinking about. I don't really think of either of them as being massively satirical works. They've got elements of satire in them, but they're more works that are having fun purely by pulling down the barriers between High Literature and pulp literature and pornography and low literary forms like that. It's pulling down these snobbish barrier fancies between different genres, different levels of literature, supposed high and low literature—that has always been the most subversive thing about *The League of Extraordinary Gentlemen*. I wouldn't think of it as a work of political satire. There'll be elements of that creeping in, or social satire, but they're going to be largely incidental to the main thrust of the story, which is just the fun to be had. I'm choreographing a huge car crash of different people's worlds and characters. The satire, I don't think is a huge element in either of the *League* volumes, anyway, but probably there's more incidental satire in the second volume than there is in the first. I don't know whether that's true or not, I'm just saying that off the top of my head. Certainly it seems to me that there's probably more direct satirical digs and swipes in the second volume than there were in the first.

JN: Your plots—the Yellow Peril, the alien invasion—have been fairly archetypal. Where do you think the appeal of these iconic plots lies for the modern audience?

AM: "Archetypes" is a very generous way of describing it. "Cliches" would be another way of describing it. And the thing with cliches is that they tend to stay around for a long time because there is some element of, not truth there, but there is some element of application there. Obviously, say, that excellent Yellow Peril article that you wrote—

JN: Thank you.

AM: —in the first *League* companion, that kind of pointed out the ambivalence of our relationship with the Orient and the way that we've travestied and caricatured elements of the Oriental appearance, mind set, behavior, that we were particularly frightened of. And although things have obviously changed since Victorian times, you'll still find that at least a couple of members of, say, George Bush's "Axis of Evil" have kind of got a bit of a Yellow Peril slant to them. These are perpetual hobgoblins of the human mind that always stay fresh. Invasion, we're always terrified of invasion. Fifty, sixty years ago we were frightened of being invaded by the Germans, because that was quite likely to happen. At the moment, we're frightened of being invaded by al-Qaeda terrorists, plane bombers, suicide bombers, leading to ridiculous scenes of tanks around Heathrow Airport, as if that's going to do anything. We have the same fears, we have the same prejudices. These don't change from century to century. And so consequently I think that both of the examples you cite, the Yellow Peril, Fu Manchu, death from the air of the first series, the Martian invasion of the second series, and probably anything I do in the future—if we stick to these fairly archetypal or cliched themes, then you will probably find that they will still continue to have an appeal, because they're always, they're saying something about us, no matter which century they're set in. We're gonna read them to some degree as comments upon our own century, upon our own literature, on our own lives, and, yeah, I should think that that is probably a lot of the appeal, that the reader has had these cliches presented to them throughout their entire lives, and to suddenly re-examine them in a more knowing light can be quite revealing, and can restore perhaps some of their original charge, some of the original potency of these ideas. Let's face it, there have been lots and lots and lots of stories about alien invasions, right up to the ridiculous overkill of something like *Independence Day*, where you've got to have a flying saucer that is bigger than a city, and it's got to destroy the White House or other big, important landmarks, otherwise it's just not going to look as threatening. We've upped the ante so much with these ridiculously overstated alien invasions that it struck me that perhaps the best way to actually get an effect was to take it right back to the basics: Tripods, big metal cylinders dropping on to Horsell Common, heat rays, and this all happening in 1898, because, I suppose, the most famous or widely seen examples of the *War of the Worlds* story would be Orson Welles' radio broadcast and the George Pal film, from which examples most readers might have generally supposed the Martian invasion took place in America in the 1950s or 1930s. And I think that actually putting it back in its original setting, London, 1898—and, yes, all right, I think Wells, somewhere in *War of the Worlds*, suggests that this is happening in an unspecified point in the future, but then the whole world that he describes is so exactly like 1898 that you might just as well have set it then. And I thought that seeing these big striding Martian Tripods up against—it's not Will Smith in a high-tech fighter jet, it's mounted cavalry, Gatling guns—small potatoes. There's an obvious techno-gap between Earth and its invaders. I thought that stripping it right back to the basics, the invasion story, suddenly gave that archetypal cliche new legs. It's like the scene that the first time that the *Nautilus* surfaces, back in issue one of the first volume. Now, we in the early Twenty-first century, we're not that excited by the idea of a submarine. We've seen lots of submarines. This is no longer anywhere near as thrilling as it would have been back when Jules Verne was kicking the idea around. However, I think that that scene, in the first volume of the *League* where the *Nautilus* surfaces, has a genuine sense of wonder about it, that, yes, it is a submarine, but there's something about the way that the story is set up that means that you're almost viewing its appearance through late nineteenth-century eyes, and there's something about the way that the *War of the Worlds* is treated that gives the same impression. The fact that the Martians are invading late-nineteenth-century England means that you're forced to see the invasion through late-nineteenth-century eyes, and so it suddenly becomes that much more shocking and alien and startling. It kind of reinvests those ideas with some of the power that they originally had, which has been worn down through a lot of our successive reinterpretations of them over the intervening century.

JN: You'd said in an interview with *Third Alternative Press* that a Neo-Platonist approach to characterizing previously existing characters yielded the best results, that "a character who seems flat and boring has strayed from the ideal form of the character." So were you doing this not just with *War of the Worlds* but also with Quatermain and Mina?

AM: Yeah, to a degree. You tease the characters out, you assume that they exist somewhere in some Platonic space, that there is an ideal form of the character, and all that is important is that you be as faithful as possible to that idealized form. It's probably nonsense, but it's a nonsense that I have heard other writers subscribe to. I remember that the writer Alvin Schwartz, who was an early writer on *Superman*, he wrote a number of Superman newspaper strips, some of the comics, and he wrote a book called *A Very Unlikely Prophet*—

JN: And the atomic bomb story that got him visited by the F.B.I.

AM: Sorry, the what story?

JN: He wrote an atomic bomb story in early 1945, and that got the F.B.I. dropping by to see where he got the ideas from.

AM: Was it published by John Campbell?

JN: No, I think it was in *Superman*. Or...wait....

AM: John Campbell got visited by the Feds, didn't he, about an atomic bomb story, about three months before Hiroshima.

JN: I'll have to check where and when it appeared. But Schwartz went through the same thing, and if he's experienced the same thing as John Campbell he's in pretty good company.

AM: Well, yeah, absolutely. But one of the things that struck me in his autobiography, this *An Unlikely Prophet*, there's bits in it which I'm certain happened exactly as he said they did, and there's bits in it which I'm certain that he's made up. But one of the things that he said was, that's kind of central to his whole thesis, was when he was writing *Superman*, often he'd be in script conferences with three or four different *Superman* writers, or they'd all be sitting around talking about ideas that they'd had, and he said that it was surprising how often somebody would float an idea for a *Superman* story, and somebody else would say, "No, Superman wouldn't do that," and the other writers would think about it and would agree, "No, no, you're right, Superman wouldn't do that." And he said it came to him that, how do we know what Superman would or wouldn't do if there's no Superman? He came to the same conclusion that I put forward as a possibility, that in some ways there is some ideal form, some ideal Platonic form of these characters, existing somewhere in the reaches of the human mind, and that it's the writer's job to try and not so much invent the characters as it is to intuit them, let them speak. And I think that very much with Allan and Mina, you read the originals and you think about the characters and you extrapolate, you think, "All right, this is how the characters were then, what would they be like if these things had happened?" And you start to get an idea, you start to get an impression. So, yeah, that is pretty much how I arrive at most of my characters, really. It's working from the belief that there is a perfect realization of that character, somewhere there, and that if you are just patient enough or dig deeply enough you will be able to unearth it and present it to your readers intact. That's the theory.

JN: A lot of fans were disconcerted that the League were, in their eyes, too passive in reacting to the Martian invasion. I know that you wanted to remain faithful to the timeline and events of *War of the Worlds*. Were you also in some way trying to subvert the cliche, which these fans expected, of the heroes sort of single-handedly fighting off the invasion with guns blazing?

AM: Yeah. That probably plays well in Hollywood, but if people want that, then they've got the film that they can go and see. That's not what the books are about. The books are a much more literary experience. I know that in most Hollywood films, this is what happens at the end, that the heroes will drive off the invaders—there'll be a big shoot-out, there'll be a High Noon, there'll be a big physical conflict that will solve everything, because this is how Hollywood does its movies, which is why I don't watch many of them. Everyone's entitled to their own tastes. I think that that is kind of moronic. That's not being snooty or elitist, that's just my feelings. Other people are quite entitled to feel that that big, obvious, physical climax is required by every story, because it is required by every Hollywood story. But the world of literature is a richer and deeper place than that, and I don't really see why I needed to have the League or John Carter or Gullivar Jones suddenly turning up in a big spaceship and blasting all the aliens. What would that have done? I might as well have had Will Smith suddenly turn up through a time warp and sort the problem out. That might have been the most satisfying dramatic solution for some of my audience, but I would like to think, I would like to hope, that the majority of my audience would probably have preferred me to do something a bit more unexpected, like the stuff that I actually did do. It's so unsatisfying, it's what everybody does, it's these big, stupid clashes between good and evil, our guys and the other guys. I haven't been to see the *Lord of the Rings* films, I didn't think it was that good a book. It's kind of obvious, and I'm sure that will probably terribly offend lots of Tolkien readers or fans of the films, but it's not to my taste. And there's plenty of other stuff that will do that everywhere. It's not that I was deliberately trying to subvert the expectations of those fans, I just wasn't thinking about them very much. It just seemed to me that the best way to tell this story was the way that we told it, where you've got this use of biological weapons that is kind of shocking, given the time period that it's happening in. And you end the story on this downbeat note, with Allan just sitting there in the park, with all of those beautiful Kevin O'Neill and Ben Dimagmaliw autumn colors all around him. I think that we give our readers plenty of conflict and adventure, and, I mean—for God's sake, we actually have got Mr. Hyde physically fighting one of the Tripods at the end! I would have thought that that was satisfying enough for any of the readers. I mean, what, did they want to have Mr. Hyde fighting one of the Tripods while Mina's fighting one of the other Tripods with her vampire powers?

JN: Well, I think a lot of the readers, the ones who e-mail me about this, are preconditioned by other superhero comics, and so they expect a climax in the *League* that's similar to a climax in the average story of *Justice League* or *Avengers* or *Legion of Superheroes*, where everybody pitches in. It was disconcerting to them.

AM: The idea of disconcerting comic readers is obviously a horrific one to me. If any future *League* stuff comes out I'd hate to be going into it under false pretenses. It probably would be as well to tell everybody now that if they really do like those conventional *Avengers/Justice League/Legion of Superheroes* superteam books, then they're probably best sticking with them, because that's not really what the League is about, the League is this complex literary joke that is probably about a lot of books that they haven't read and would never be interested in reading, and I certainly wouldn't want to be leading the readership on under false pretenses or expectations that we're suddenly going to be doing stuff that's like a conventional superteam book.

JN: In fairness to them, they love the series, they just have minor cavils.

AM: Well, everyone's entitled to their own opinions, it's just that—there are similarities. It's a group of unusual, extraordinary people, which in the comic market that is a generally pretty strong selling idea. But that is where it parts company with the superhero comic. It's not even my intention to tell a good adventure story every time, necessarily. There's nothing to stop me from suddenly deciding that I might want to tell a love story using this world of fictional characters. I'm not saying that I have got any ideas for that. There'll probably always be an element of rip-roaring pulp adventure in the *League*. Probably. But I wouldn't rule out that at some point I might want to use the characters to tell a completely different sort of story. The fun that I'm having with the *League* is not in doing a new sort of superhero group. The fun that I'm having with the *League* is being allowed to run amok through the entirety of fiction, in the past, the present and the future. Copyright laws cannot stop us. We can play an elaborate, complicated literary game, which I know is not everybody's cup of tea, but it is mine. I love it. It's such fun. And I don't want to play it to the point where we're ignoring the fact that we have to tell an interesting story. The interesting story has always got to be the most important thing. But that won't necessarily be an interesting story in the terms that superhero team books kind of—the fairly limited options for an interesting story that are presented by conventional superhero team books. It probably won't be that kind of interesting story. And probably the *League*, whatever happens to it in the future, it's going to get more extreme. If there's stuff that people don't like about it now, they're going to hate it by a couple of volumes down the road, because we feel incredibly liberated by this, me and Kevin. We're having the time of our lives. We hadn't even realized that it was possible to do stuff like this before. And we're going to take it as far as we possibly can. We're almost certainly going to take it too far, because that is really the only destination worth heading for, too far. You wouldn't want to think that you'd held back, would you? That would be cheating the readers. I'd like to think that my readers expect me to occasionally gather them all in my arms and jump over a cliff. I think that that's part of the excitement. (Laughs) Of course, I might be completely wrong and they might be horrified and hate that part of my writing, but, nah, I think that most of the people who like the *League*, they're probably sniggering at the same parts that me and Kevin are, and they're probably getting excited by the same parts. One of the things that I like best about the *League*, and this is something that no superhero comic book team book could ever do, is the fact that within the space of a few pages, because the *League* is not restricted to the same fairly narrow channels that most team superhero books are restricted to, we can do anything. One of the things I was most pleased with in the second volume was the scene that starts off with Allan and Mina on the morning after they've had sex for the first time, and Allan is desperately trying to explain to

Mina his reaction to her inadvertently glimpsed scars. It starts off with this very fraught emotional atmosphere. They're very angry with each other. Then, when Allan explains that his first wife had had scars around her neck—which incidently, how cool was that?

JN: I'm sure that when you read that in the Haggard book you were pleased no end.

AM: Kevin told me about it, and I thought, "This is supernaturally perfect, this is one of those things that"—well, you were saying earlier about readers wondering whether I'd had everything planned out in minute detail from the beginning. Well, when you read something like that I can see how they'd get that impression, because it looks so incredibly clever! But, no, it just happened by accident. I'd got no idea that his first wife had got a scarred throat when I originally decided to give Mina one. Anyway, back to that scene in the forest, where he's explaining about his first wife, and talking about how that was the reason he reacted the way that he did, not revulsion. And then it becomes incredibly tender between them, it's quite emotional, and from there it moves quietly to the bit where she's showing her scars to him, where he's taking her scarf off and then he's kissing her scars, it moves very easily to the erotic. And then, when they're having sex against the tree, and you suddenly see her catching sight of something over her shoulder, and you turn over the page and there's that awful bear creature shambling towards them, then it is both ridiculous, to my mind at least very funny, and also completely horrifying. In the space of that one scene I was very pleased with the way that we moved from emotional difficulty to deep emotional compassion to eroticism to a mingling of comical absurdity and horror. You shouldn't really be able to put all those flavors next to each other. But something about the way the *League* is set up means that it's possible for us to be simultaneously deadly serious, horrifying, ridiculous—the death of Mr. Griffin is probably a scene that in the audience would have elicited mixed reactions, I would have thought. They would probably have been laughing and shuddering in about the same measure, because— partly it's really funny that the only character you could have that happen to in a comic is an invisible man. It was so perfect. When I thought of it I was laughing. When I explained it to Scott Dunbier I was laughing, because Scott was very worried about the scene, and me and Kevin were saying, "No, no, Scott, don't worry, you won't be able to see anything!" That, to me, is the beauty of the *League*, the fact that there aren't really any expectations. It could be very sexual, it could be very funny, it could be very thrilling, or it could be completely horrific, or perhaps intellectually stimulating, all in the same couple of pages. I can't think of many books that have that same easy versatility.

JN: One of the things that people have been most struck by is the portrayal of Hyde. Some people have said that he's really the central character in the story. Was that your intention all along, or did he sort of seize control?

AM: I guess that you could fairly say that Mr. Hyde is a very central character in that second book. Yeah, to some degree it surprised me as much as anybody. That first meeting between him and Mina, just the conversation in the room. When that dialogue was writing itself I found it very surprising the way it was coming out. It certainly wasn't anything that you could call tenderness upon Hyde's part. He's talking about beheading her, raping her, breaking her jaw, and you don't doubt him for a minute, that he could quite easily do these things if he was in the right mood. And he's talking about his own conflicted behavior when it comes to her, and her reaction to him, that, yeah, she's terrified of him, but on the other hand this is a side of Hyde that nobody's ever seen before. It's fascinating and quite touching in a lot of ways. Hyde is never going to turn up and bring you a bunch of flowers or a box of chocolates. He's never going to ask you for an evening at the cinema. But to have him actually tell you that he doesn't actually hate you—that's probably as close to an admission of, not love, but as close as Hyde could ever get to it, and I found him an increasingly fascinating character, because when I started thinking about Stevenson's original concept, that Hyde was all of the evil, all of the dark side of Jekyll, isolated into a different person, and I started thinking about what a stupid idea that had been, and how it would obviously lead to disaster, and that led up to one of the sequences I'm proudest of, which is Hyde sitting there at the dinner table, explaining the difference between him and Jekyll and the relationship between them, the reason why Jekyll is such a feeble wretch, and the reason why Hyde is about nine or ten feet tall and has got this huge body mass. It's because Jekyll had no drives without Hyde and Hyde had no restraints without Jekyll. Which says something, I think, about the relationship between what we would conventionally call good and evil in the human being. Our demons and our angels, they are meant to work together. Separating them is ridiculous, and can only lead to the desperate extremes that are represented by Hyde. I found myself interested in him as a character and as a sort of symbol of the conflicted nature of human beings: terrified of their dark side and hating their dark side, wanting to be rid of it, and needing it so much. It's very often that right brain, that dark, unexplored territory, that most of our essential drives are contained in. That's where they come from: Hyde's territory rather than Jekyll's. Both halves of the personality, they have to work together in unison if you're going to have any sort of integrated and whole human being as a result. And I think that I saw something tragic in Jekyll and Hyde. Hyde's only urge can be to death. He would have to be—the pain of being Hyde, unmediated by any, I don't know, more contemplative or reflective or spiritual parts of the human personality. The idea of being a creature that had, by definition, no higher attributes, where the solace of those higher attributes was forever denied to it. Hyde's life would just be rage and hatred. There wouldn't be any other options available, except for perhaps enraged hatred. It's a kind of damned soul. The only thing that you could do if you were Hyde would be to get yourself killed. You would hate the universe that you were in, you would hate yourself, you'd hate everything. That lent a kind of tragedy and heroism—I really liked the scene with Hyde, like Horatio, defending the bridge. I thought that was great, because he never stops being Hyde for a minute. He's still as hateful and violent and psychotic. And yet I bet there weren't many dry eyes in the place. I bet everybody felt kind of moved by Hyde's sacrifice, even if, as he himself points out, he's not doing it to be noble, he's doing it because he really wants to kill something. Actually, the thing that he probably wants to kill is himself. But in either instance it's not nobility that's behind it. But Hyde almost achieves a nobility in spite of himself in that scene, which I thought was kind of touching. All of the characters go through some changes in the course of the series, but if the second volume of the *League* was centered upon anybody, then it was centered upon Hyde. He was just a character that suddenly, he'd been growing in importance throughout the first book, and he kind of blossomed during the second book, which I suppose must make it all that much more unfathomable to a lot of the readers as to why we've killed or removed the three most visually interesting characters in the *League*, in this highly successful series, before the end of the twelfth issue. But, hell, that was just the way that it was going.

JN: It's interesting, the reaction I get between the traditional comics fans and the fans who are more familiar with literature than with comics. The fans who are coming at this from a literary base, they're not disconcerted or nonplused by Hyde's death or Griffin's death or the end of the 1898 League, whereas the comic book fans sort of expect that the status quo is always going to be maintained, that there's always going to be the same League, and so they're wondering—

AM: Yeah, that obviously Hyde didn't really die, so, what, did the Time Traveler take him away at the point of death, or—no, no, he's dead. The only status quo in the *League* is—if people have been bothering to read the Almanac, they might notice that we've taken the precaution of making Allan and Mina immortals.

JN: The comics fans, they take the deaths as written, but they seem to be wondering why you're doing it. They're coming at it with a very different set of preconceptions.

AM: Why we're doing it is because, realistically, those characters, we couldn't just keep them all hanging around together for the next thirty, fifty, sixty, seventy, eighty years. For one thing, it's such an unstable group, made up of such unstable characters, that that's not likely to be how it develops. Also, as we take the characters out of their Victorian milieu, then characters like Hyde and Griffin will become less appropriate. And there are other characters, on the other hand, who become available. I see the League as having a very very long history that stretches for hundreds of years and that there has been a constantly changing membership. Hell, even the Justice League of America, over their relatively short history—what, about forty years?—they've done all sorts of things! There was that weird period when they had Gypsy and Vibe. (Laughs) This is just in 40 years. I see the League of Extraordinary Gentlemen as extending over hundreds of years. So, surely, even to the mainstream comics fans—the original gold suited Iron Man is no longer in the Avengers. Things change, and in the world of literature, they change a bit more naturally than in the world of comic books. It's to be expected that some of these characters are not going to be around.

JN: It's more reflective of real life.

AM: It's more reflective of real life and it's more reflective of literature.

These characters—yes, all right, Conan Doyle brought Sherlock Holmes back when the demand was great enough. Yes, death is reversible in literature as well. But by and large people in literature are much more used to their heroes eventually dying, even if it's a series, or dying at the end of a book if it's a novel. It's a completely different set up, with different ground rules to comics. Publishing a book, yes, you can have all your characters die at the end of the book, if you want. Or, *Hamlet*, or something like that. If *Hamlet* had been a comic book series (laughs), then nobody would have died in it, because the writers would have been keeping the characters around in case somebody needed them.

JN: I don't suppose you ever saw the Arnold Schwarzenegger film, *The Last—*

AM: Actually, I know exactly what you're going to say. It's the only Arnold Schwarzenegger film that I've got the slightest shred of sympathy for. For a moment, there was the illusion that he actually had a sense of humor and was making fun of himself. Yeah, "Something is rotten in the state of Denmark, and Hamlet's taking out the trash." That was funny. "To be or not to be, that is the question." (Imitates Schwarzenegger) "Not to be." That shows the difference. Comics and Hollywood, you have to keep the hero alive, because it's a franchise. In literature, the characters are not regarded as franchises, so you are a lot more free. And actually I'd have thought the readers would have liked that, because genuinely, in the *League of Extraordinary Gentlemen*, they can't take anything for granted, we could kill anybody.

JN: Well, as I said, some of the readers are coming at this from a comic book background. They want their status quo. They want, basically, intellectual comfort food. And the ones who are coming at this from a literary background, they're more used to different fare, and so I think by and large most of the fans of *League* who—as far as I can tell, there are plenty of fans of *League* who are fans of comic books, but there are many more fans of *League* who are—

AM: We seem to be gathering—from the bookshop sales, I imagine— but we seem to be gathering a lot of people who don't usually read comic books, but who are interested in nineteenth-century literature or Rider Haggard or Conan Doyle or people like that. Which is very gratifying. This is not to despise the comic readership at all, and there are an awful lot of comic readers who also have a very solid and good literary grounding at the same time. I'm very happy to think that we're drawing readers of literature, people who are really familiar with these characters in their original literary form. To me, the test is, do they like what we're doing with it? The comic readers, yes, their point of view is important as well, but they've got no idea who Allan Quatermain is or whether we're handling him right, or anything, whereas, people who have read *King Solomon's Mines* or things like that, they're going to be much more critical, presumably, in that they are going to actually know the works of literature that we're referring to, and they're going to be able to see if we've travestied them. So far, I haven't had very many complaints. I think most people feel that we've been at least as faithful as anybody else has been, and more faithful than some, to the original sources of these characters. I think that even for the more traditional comic readers, I would think that *League* is quite refreshing because, for one thing it takes place in what has got to be the best comic book or fiction universe of all time. The Marvel Universe, the DC Universe, how could they possibly be a patch upon the Fiction Universe? That is a universe which is crammed with fascinating characters, where you can afford to have a couple killed. You can afford to have hundreds killed, and there'll still be plenty to play around with. And it does restore some of that thrill that you can't usually get in comics. I remember what an incredible sense of specialness there was back in the early sixties if I was reading a comic and a character actually died! I was incredibly shocked and moved and I thought it was a great story. Say, DC, it was obvious that their readers really liked stories in which, say, Superman died or got married or had some other continuity shattering experience. That was why they invented the "Imaginary Story," so they could allow for that without damaging their continuity. Actually, that whole thing of "this book is going to be coming out every month until the end of time or until it's cancelled," that is something which damages a lot of comics. It's like when I took over on *Swamp Thing*. I identified one of the main problems with the character that it was based on a false premise. Officially, Alec, the Swamp Thing, was trying to find a way to regain his lost humanity and become Alec Holland again. But even the dimmest reader, the most uncritical, cliche-fed reader must have realized that that was never going to happen, because that would end the series. It's like *The Fugitive* or things like that: if the series ever fulfills its premise, the series ends. Which is so limiting. That's why I had to remodel *Swamp Thing*, to get past that, so that, no, that wasn't the premise anymore. The premise was something which allowed for all sorts of possibilities, so that the reader wouldn't know what to expect. I suppose that underlines the difference between the kinds of comics I like to write and the kinds of comics I don't like to read. I'm not into reassuring my readership. I'm not into providing them with the same product every time. That might pass for consistency if you're a hamburger chain, that maybe your customers do have the right to expect exactly the same meal every time they go in, in exactly the same setting. But that's not how I operate, and I don't want to give my readers the cozy reassurance of another set of pre-packaged concepts where they already know the structure, they already know that in the last few pages it's going to look like the villain's dead but then all of a sudden he's not really dead at all and there's going to be a couple of shocking last minute blows traded before the villain's really dead, although they'll leave open the option that the villain's not really dead because there's a sequel to think about. That is how every adventure story is structured these days, and that's not something you go to for thrills, that's something you go to for reassurance. That's something that's become cozy and familiar to you. That's a thousand miles away, a million miles away, from anything that Art is supposed to be about. Art, and I do regard comics as Art, you might as well, they've got as much claim to be Art as anything else has, Art is not about reassuring people. We don't read Art to be reassured, we read Art to be challenged and to challenge our assumptions and to maybe extend our ideas in certain areas, which you can't really do without challenging them. So that's probably my agenda with *League*. And anything we do in the future, it's probably going to be only more of the same. That agenda will probably get more militant as the series goes on.

JN: What do you think was going through Hyde's mind in his final scene with Mina, before he went out and marched to his death? Did he have some sort of epiphany, or was it the culmination—

AM: A cruel epiphany. He realized—he was torturing himself as much as anything with that. He just wanted to have it once and know what it was like, even though he'd already got a pretty good idea that what it would be like would be unbearable. There's no way you could consummate it. No future in it. It's never going to work. (Laughs) Even with the most optimistic, love struck eyes in the world—and that's not a description of Hyde by any means—but even with the most optimistic and love struck eyes in the world, it's never going to work for Hyde and Mina. So, yes, let's just kiss her once, to see what that's like, and touch her breast once. If I can manage to do that without suddenly going berserk and breaking her neck, just to see what that's like, and then suffer the incredible pain of knowing that that is the only time in your entire life that you will ever have a moment of tenderness, and then do what you gotta do. Take your jacket off, walk over the bridge, and settle these Martians. And sing a song as you do it. That seemed to be Hyde's style—immense pain, immense pain held in check by immense manic strength. I should imagine that's what was going through Hyde's mind. Almost torturing himself, almost cruelty. It would have been kinder just to walk across the bridge without even saying goodbye to Mina. It would have been kinder to him and to her. But he wanted to know it just once, even if it was painful. It confirms for himself that Heaven is a cruel place, because you can't stay there. It doesn't last. It's something else to be taken from you. In fact, that was probably one of the very few things in Hyde's life which actually caused him real pain. Physically getting hurt is not a big deal for Hyde. Emotionally, there's no way he can be hurt. He doesn't have normal emotions. So to inflict that pain on himself, by choice, yeah, it seemed appropriate for Hyde, who I was starting to see as a much bigger and wiser and more complex figure than I had originally. I'd never seen Hyde as stupid. But in that second book I began to see Hyde as wise, wise where Jekyll was foolish. Not stupid where Jekyll was intelligent, wise where Jekyll was foolish. Hyde's got a much better and clearer understanding of human nature than Jekyll ever had. It's perhaps a more brutal and stark and unflinching grasp of human nature, but it's wiser because it's truer, because it's more realistic than this hopeless, doomed idealism that prompts Jekyll to separate the two of them in the first place. I really did like that scene, and I'm sure that you would have noticed "You Should See Me Dance the Polka." You got the reference?

JN: Spencer Tracy.

AM: Yeah, my favorite film. That was the one with the nude girls harnessed to the coach. Was that the Frederic March version? No, I'm sure that was the Spencer Tracy version.

JN: I missed that completely.

AM: Isn't there a dream sequence where Hyde is setting on the box of a coach with a whip—

JN: Well, this is Texas, they probably don't show that sort of thing down here.

AM: Oh, it's really, it's the scene I remember. There are these sort of semi-naked—you probably can't see a nipple, but it was pretty racy for the time—these semi-naked girls harnessed to a coach with Mr. Hyde whipping them on, while "You Should See Me Dance the Polka" plays deliriously in the background. One of my favorite film sequences.

JN: Have you noticed a difference in reaction to the series from British and American fans?

AM: I don't really notice much reaction at all because I'm completely out of the loop. I don't go to conventions, I don't read the fan press, and I don't really have anything to do with the Internet. Have you noticed any difference in reaction between the Yanks and the Brits?

JN: What I've seen and what people have said to me is—it basically splits down the middle in terms of nationality. The American fans are a lot more squeamish and appalled by the violence and sex, and the British fans aren't.

AM: That probably sounds pretty reasonable. How did the sex go down? I thought that that sex scene at the end of number four, I thought that was lovely.

JN: I did, too, and a lot of the fans whose opinions I respect did, too, but there's always the Bible Belt wing of comic book fans in America who call it "pornography."

AM: Oh, well. (Laughs) Oh, well. As long as it's the people in the Bible Belt that I'm offending. No offense, people in the Bible Belt, but they're going to be offended by almost anything. It was in the Bible Belt that the cops seized that Wonder Woman poster because that was pornography, wasn't it, a few years ago.

JN: Yeah, it was actually in the Bible Belt that they arrested a woman for selling a vibrator to a married couple, that was about 50 miles from where I live.

AM: Yeah, it was down South where I read about a couple going to prison because their little boy had mentioned to one of his friends that he'd seen daddy performing an act of oral love upon mommy, which was considered sodomy in that particular—the thing is, I can't make allowances for people like that. They're entitled to think that it's pornography and they're entitled to think that it portrays abnormal sexuality. By the same token I must be free to think that they are abnormal sexually. I think that that entire culture is, I'm afraid it's laughable. We don't have to deal with it over here so I can say this. There's no other country in the world but America where you'd put up with people like that or ideas like that. They're laughable. They're childish. That would be an embarrassment in any other country, those kind of ideas. That scene, I'm very proud of it. The quite honest, unabashed sexuality, and then that awful bit where her scarf comes unraveled, which is what it was all building up to. It wasn't about the sex, it wasn't about the nakedness of her body, it was about the nakedness of her throat. All of a sudden we see a part of Mina we've not seen before. I don't mean her naked body, we see a part of Mina's psychology that we haven't seen before, which for me overshadowed the quite ordinary sexual activity.

JN: She's suddenly vulnerable.

AM: You suddenly realize a whole lot about what she's been keeping to herself and how scarred her personality is. Not just her neck, but these are the sort of scars that go down a long way. To me that was much more important than the fact that they happened to have just had sex. Sex—we all got here because of sex. We all do it, if we're lucky. We've been doing it for millions of years. It's perhaps time we got over it and moved on. A couple of million years, that should be time for us to have gotten over our understandable panic at the idea of sexual reproduction.

JN: Did you have any trouble with ABC/Wildstorm about the sex and the violence?

AM: Nah. These are people who hired me, and they are familiar with my previous work. There's been plenty of sex and violence in my stuff right from the eighties. I'd like to think that it was handled in the best possible taste, but people pretty much know what they're getting with me by now. There was sex all the way through *Swamp Thing*, *Marvelman*, *V for Vendetta*. There was violence—all of these things. So, no, I think DC and Wildstorm understood. *League* is one of the best selling comics, at least in book form. I think in bookshops it is probably the best selling graphic novel.

JN: In pamphlet form it outsells, I think, all the Superman books, all but one of the Batman books, and everything but JLA.

AM: In the book collections it does even better. Obviously somebody likes it. Obviously there are a number of people out there who aren't offended by it, or who could swallow their revulsion if they were really pushed. I've been completely open about the fact that there'll probably be more sex in the future stuff—if that's appropriate. We're not just going to shovel it in for no reason at all, just for the sake of it. I quite like sex, myself. Call me crazy. But I think it's just as interesting to depict sex as it is to depict a couple of people trying to rip each other's windpipes out. It's part of human life, and it's an important part, and I should expect to find it turning up a lot more in *League of Extraordinary Gentleman*. Because I want to normalize it, I want to get to a point where people don't think, "Ooh, it's a sex scene!" I'd like it to get to a point where people could just think, yeah, this is just another part of the story, what are they telling us here, and not be distracted by all the boobs and buttocks.

JN: I think part of the fan reaction was that when you have Mina tell Allan to bite her neck, that gave fans a glimpse into a more—I don't want to say "kinkier," but a more complex form of sexuality.

AM: Also, it's Mina's sexuality. Why would Mina tell Allan to bite her neck, to bite her shoulder? Doesn't that tell us something about what Mina's real take upon the events in Stoker's novel was? It's not so much that I'm hinting, "Oh, Mina's a bit kinky!" for any sort of titillation reasons, it's that I'm saying she's asking him to *bite her*. She obviously finds that sexually exciting. Why would Mina find that sexually exciting? Doesn't that suggest possibly a different take upon her feelings about

Dracula? This is what I mean. We're getting over very important character information in a line of dialogue like that. It's not for titillation. It's not the kind of stuff you see in certain modern comics, Marvel Knights or Vertigo or whatever, where a reference to some sexual peccadillo is seen as spicy, as spicing the story up. That's not what it was used for. It was trying to imply that there might be a certain degree of ambivalence to Mina's reaction to what happened to her in 1896 or 1897 or whenever it was. She might not have been entirely repulsed by the king of the vampires. It might have been quite an experience. It might have left her, sexually, with a bad case of Stockholm Syndrome. These are speculations, but this is what I mean. A sex scene is a way of getting over very important character information, just as much as a fight scene is, and the reader really shouldn't be looking at it as, "Oh, this is purely thrown in for titillation." I don't really throw in anything in any of my stories just for this or just for that. There's generally some sort of story information being imparted as well, or character information. I love those scenes, but as a warning to the faint hearted there probably will be more of them in the future, so stop buying now.

JN: Why did Mina divorce Jonathan?

AM: I'm not sure who did divorce who. But…he's actually a profoundly dull little man. He's a state agent. He's not really a very interesting or fascinating or passionate man, and I figured that it would get very complicated between them after *Dracula*, because Mina's nearly fatal relationship with Dracula probably would have been the most passionate that she had ever had. It would certainly probably leave her relationship with Jonathan looking a bit pallid. At the same time, I would imagine that Jonathan, like many men of the era, would feel that Mina was tainted, that—this is not just particularly limited to the Victorian era, I believe that it's a common response among the boyfriends and husbands of rape victims, to completely turn against the victim right when she's most in need of support, because they blame her for it. "You could have resisted more. You could have resisted more, you could have done something to fight him off." This is I think what goes through the heads of a lot of men who've got no concept of what being raped is about. So, yes, she was probably getting very dissatisfied with him, he was probably suddenly afraid and revolted when he responded to Mina. She'd been dirtied in some way, and she was perhaps, perhaps she wanted it?

Perhaps there was some kind of lust in her that he hadn't seen before, something frightening. I should imagine a combination of these factors is what led to the divorce. Partly it was her, partly it was him I'm not sure which one divorced the other one, or on what grounds. Maybe we'll at some point in the future return to that, if it ever seems fruitful.

JN: Was Griffin's death a response to the rape scenes in the first *League* series, a sort of balance—

AM: No, not really. I wasn't trying to appease, "Oh, we've had a woman being nearly raped"—

JN: Well, we first see him as a rapist, and—

AM: Oh, yeah, well...I hadn't really thought of that. Yeah, if you want. It sort of provides a sort of symmetry for people who need that. But that wasn't what I thought. When I was thinking the scene through, I thought, "What would Hyde do if he got hold of Griffin?" And the answer was, "The worst possible thing. And then when he'd done that he'd think of the next worst possible thing." And he would do all of them. And rape was obviously somewhere along the line of the spectrums of the very bad things to do to the Invisible Man. And it was something that would occur to Hyde. Hyde's a monster. And terrifying, brutalizing, murdering people, that's something which is kind of cozy to him, and so, yeah. And also, it struck me as kind of funny. I have to admit it, this probably says an awful lot about me which I shouldn't be admitting in public, but I thought it was just audacious and funny, to have Mr. Hyde raping the Invisible Man, because—one of the funny things about the Invisible Man in the girls' school—I thought it was funny having the Invisible Man having sex with the girls. I know technically it was rape. I still thought it was funny, just because—it's a funny idea, people floating in space with their legs wrapped around nothing, gasping in rapture. That was funny, and so it was funny to have the Invisible Man on the receiving end, as it were, for the same reason. It's a good visual joke.

JN: Some of the fans also pointed out that Hyde's last words to Griffin in the first series were, "Bugger you, Griffin."

AM: I hadn't thought of it, but, again, they're probably attributing—the phrase, "Bugger you," in British, isn't really literal. So, there wasn't really any connection, but I suppose I could see why—it's an accidental connection. I hadn't really thought of it.

JN: Have you gotten any complaints, joking or serious, from readers about your treatment of children's characters, like Rupert the Bear and Raggedy Andy and the Cat in the Hat? Has anyone said, "I can't believe you did that to my Raggedy Andy!"

AM: What, the reference in the *Almanac*?

JN: Right.

AM: No. I'm relying upon the fact that the Almanac is sort of dense prose and I'm expecting that the readers aren't gonna get through it, to tell the truth. We don't get much response from readers anyway. But the only response I've had on, say, Rupert Bear is howling laughter, at least over here. I think that kind of tying Raggedy Ann and Raggedy Andy and their Deep Dark Woods with the Deep Dark Woods outside of Twin Peaks, and—also, it's funny you should mention that, Jess, because after I had cast Raggedy Ann and Raggedy Andy as these sinister, frightening, David Lynch twilight beings in the Almanac, I was reading an issue of *Fortean Times*, which is a journal of—I think it's available in America. It has newspaper clippings, reports of strange phenomena from around the world, articles, all sorts of things. And in its letters page it also has a regular column for people to write in their own strange experiences. And there was one from a reader that certainly made the hackles rise on the back of my neck. This guy was talking about how he'd come home one day, let himself into his house, and walked past, on his way to the kitchen or to the living room he'd walked past the bedroom and looked in, and there, amongst his wife's collection of toys, there was a life-size, four or five foot high, Raggedy Ann doll, just sitting there with the button eyes and the stitched grin, looking at him. And he thought, fair enough, his wife collected dolls and toys and teddy bears, she must have just got a new one. And he went into the kitchen and said hello to his wife and was getting himself a drink from the fridge and he said, "When did you get the new doll, then?" And she said, "What?" And he repeated himself until it became completely obvious that she had got no idea what he was talking about. And so he took her back to the bedroom, opened the door, looked in, and there was no Raggedy Ann doll. And he was at a loss for any explanation for it. Very creepy little story. So, no, I've not had any sort of complaints from Raggedy Ann or Raggedy Andy fans, but then, that's probably because in their hearts they know that it's true, that these are creepy, malefic beings from another dimension. I think that people, they can see a certain amount of love and reverence even in our awful portrayal of a character looking not too dissimilar to Rupert the Bear. We love those Rupert annuals. That's why a lot of the activity pages in the second book, like there's that origami page, which is just like the old Rupert annuals. Or the end papers, at the back, that Kevin did, with all the characters waving goodbye, almost—I think people, they understand that there is a reverence. Like when we put Babar's animal kingdom next to Mr. Kurtz's hut, there in the Almanac. We're not sort of dissing Joseph Conrad or Babar the elephant. It's just an amusing juxtaposition, because we like both of them, in our different ways, and thought that there might be something amusing in putting them next to each other.

JN: When Gullivar Jones told John Carter that he was "sorry to hear about the Princess," was that a reference to anything in particular?

AM: Not specifically. I just got a feeling that something could have happened. Not that she'd died, maybe she'd left him, or was having an affair with somebody. I don't know. It was just something that had occurred to me. I'm not even sure what I was talking about. I wanted him to just refer to Dejah Thoris. Nothing very specific. She might have died, she might have left him for another man, something unrelated in the Edgar Rice Burroughs books. I was figuring that if John Carter actually went to Mars somewhere in the aftermath of the Civil War, then the Burroughs Martian books couldn't have been published at the same time that they were set, so I figured that they all must be set in the late Nineteenth century, the Burroughs Martian books, so with that in mind, yeah, maybe Dejah Thoris had died by this point. Maybe this is some point after whatever Burroughs chronicles.

JN: Was the winged Sorn, the one that was the victim of the "flesh mechanics," was that a reference to anything in particular?

AM: Yeah, that's a reference to "The Crystal Egg." In the Crystal Egg story, the glimpse of Mars seen through the Egg shows a very spindly winged being that is glimpsed through the Crystal Egg that turns up in Mr. Cave's shop. If it's the same Mars, then what is this spindly winged being doing there? So since I did want to make it the same Mars, because it is the same author, and the two stories were written...within ten years of each other, anyway...it just struck me there might be some connection. So we decided to have a Sorn that had been given wings, as a way of explaining the glimpse of a spindly winged Martian form in "The Crystal Egg."

JN: One last reference question. At one point in the Almanac you mention that Percy Blakeney was trying to conjure up one of his ancestors but instead got a one-eyed horse thief with a "desperate mania for public self-pollution." I—

AM: That's not a reference to anything. In that particular, I forget where they are, which land they're in.

JN: Um...Glubdub...Glubdubdribb.

AM: Glubdubdribb, yeah, that's one of Gulliver's lands, isn't it, yes, where they will summon the ghosts of your ancestors, and I just thought it would be funny if the aristocratic Percy Blakeney wanted to summon a specific ancestor who turned out to be a tremendous disappointment. So it wasn't a reference to anybody special, it was just a little invention.

JN: I have to ask: have you seen the movie?

AM: No. Not only that, but I have kind of completely severed my connection with movies. I have kind of told them that actually I don't want a sequel to be made. If they do make one, fine, I believe that they can, by our contract, if they do make one, fine, but I want my name taken off of it, and I want them to give all my money to Kevin. And also, they're making some John Constantine movie, apparently, so I told them to make sure that my name wasn't on that anywhere, and that again all the money went to Rick Veitch and the various artists involved. I just don't want any connection with the—I think films are dumb. Perhaps that's a little dismissive, but hell, I'm in the mood. I think that the majority of the—I think the film medium is flawed from its inception. That's not to say that there haven't been some wonderful films made, but they are very very much the exceptions that prove the rule, and I think that the big flaw from the inception is that film has always been technologically intensive as a medium, which means that it has also been cash intensive. You need a lot of kit to make a film, as opposed to, say, writing a book or drawing a picture. You need a lot of kit, and that means a lot of money, and that kind of inevitably means that the medium is going to end up in the hands of accountants rather than creators. And I think it's difficult to argue that in most practical applications, in the greater majority of its practical applications, the film industry seems to be largely produced by and for people who have reading difficulties, and who have trouble taking on board complex ideas. This is not to say that it's not possible, as I say, to do brilliant, moving, transporting films. But you don't see many of them. I'm sure that people who love films, they can go and watch them. It's very rare that I bother to watch a movie, and even when I do, it's even rarer that it satisfies me. And, yes, there's plenty of bad comics and there's plenty of bad books and there's plenty of bad record albums, but the reason I think I hate the movie industry is that if I make a bad comic, it does not cost a hundred million dollars, which is the budget of an emergent small third world African nation. And this is money that could have gone to alleviating some of the immense suffering in this world but has instead gone to giving bored, apathetic, lazy, indifferent Western teenage boys, largely, another way of killing 90 minutes of their interminable and seemingly pointless lives. Yeah, perhaps that seems a bit harsh, but on reflection I think you'll see that I'm absolutely right. (Laughs) Sorry for this sudden surge of vitriol, but you asked.

JN: Oh, it spices up the interview.

AM: Well, good. I wouldn't want people to think that I'm getting less cranky as I get older. Yeah, not only have I not been to see the film, I've gone completely apeshit about the idea of films in general.

JN: So that's a no.

AM: No, yeah.

JN: Moving on to a happier topic…you still sound enthusiastic about doing more *League* stories. A lot of people are wondering: third *League* series? Fourth *League* series?

AM: Hopefully, yeah. Yeah, third *League* series, fourth *League* series, yeah. Dunno when, and I'm so exhausted at the moment, Jess, I am so wiped out—I know that it doesn't show in the work, at least I hope it doesn't show in the work. Part of the reason that I'm so exhausted is that I am having to work harder and harder to let it not show in the work. Before we actually do *League* volume 3 I'm going to have to take a very, very long break. But tell people not to despair. It's always possible that there might be something, I don't know what, but there's the possibility of something before *League* volume 3. There are all sorts of things we could do with the *League*. People should just keep their eyes peeled and watch this space for further announcements. The *League* as a concept, because I can have hot sex, because I can kill all the characters whenever I want, because I can jump about through the time stream like a demented fourth-dimensional grasshopper, because I can set it anywhere in the entire world of fiction, past, present, or future— it's inexhaustible. I cannot see myself *ever* losing my enthusiasm for the *League*. Of course, this could all be changed in five years or something. I could be completely fed up with it. But at the moment I can still see so much boundless potential, and I can see a book in which you could tell any kind of story using any characters that you want set in any world that you care to set it. So there will certainly be a *League* volume 3. And four, five, six, who knows? After that, as many as I have the time and inclination to write, and that Kevin's got the enthusiasm to draw. But like I say, *League* volume 3 might be quite a way in the future. We might be talking about a couple of years.

JN: Certainly the fans know this is not the generic comic that's going to be cranked out regularly, and they're willing to wait.

AM: Well, that's good. We appreciate our fans, and tell them to just have faith. We might not be leaving them to dangle until book 3. There might be other things to occupy and while away a couple of happy hours sometime between now and then. But I'm as excited and enthusiastic about the *League* as I was when I started it. In fact, more so. With the Almanac, particularly with the Almanac, I suddenly realized that I've got the whole of the geographic cosmos of fiction as our stamping ground, and since then I've worked out a timeline of the *League*'s world, in some detail, which makes it kind of fourth-dimensional, gives it a chronological axis. It's a very complete universe, and I can imagine no end of stories. When volume 3 does come out, I'm still not sure exactly what it's going to be like. At least a significant chunk of it is going to be set in 1910 and will be set in London in 1910, during the coronation of King George, when Halley's Comet was passing overhead. There'll be some interesting new characters, some interesting old characters. You'll be seeing Captain Nemo in the 1910 adventures, although I don't want to say much more than that. There are all these things that we might very well pick up on. Les Hommes Mysterieux—I've still not quite worked out how to do that one yet. It's a bit too obvious. It's an obvious idea, so a clash between the League of Extraordinary Gentlemen and their opposite numbers, it's a bit too comic-booky. There's an obvious way of doing it, so until I can think of a non-obvious way of doing it I shall perhaps be leaving that one alone. Although, who knows, I'm talking about a couple of years until book three shall be a possibility, so by then I might have the entire Les Hommes Mysterieux storyline completely hatched. These things happen.

JN: For future *League* stories are you thinking of doing more European-style stories?

AM: You mean, European as opposed to set in England?

JN: No—longer format, less episodic—

AM: Well...yes. I don't know. We hadn't really thought about it much. We might do a bit of both. It's conceivable that we might suddenly release something in a non-episodic form, purely as an album, and then the next thing after that might be episodic building to an album in the way that the first two series have. Remaining flexible is probably the main item on our agenda, so don't rule anything out. We will almost certainly be doing some kind of European-style one-off releases, hopefully when people least expect it, but volume 3 of the *League* will probably be released in comic book form and then collected. But like I say, there might be, oh, unexpected treats or surprises between now and then.

JN: Why do you think *League* resonates with the readers?

AM: Because I think that in our hearts and in our dreams and in our secret imaginations we all somehow believe that all these characters exist in the same world anyway. Like you pointed out in the essays in *Heroes & Monsters*, this has been an impulse, this intertextuality has been an impulse right since "Jason and the Argonauts," that there is this ancient urge to have our fictional characters or our gods in their fictional worlds run into each other, in the same ways that we run into each other in our material worlds. We want to see these great archetypes interact without the restrictions of authorial copyright, publisher's ownership. We want to see Sherlock Holmes meet Dracula, or Jack the Ripper, or any of these previous crossbreedings of different stories. I think that there's always been this strong impulse to link up the worlds of our imagination. There is a kind of a thrill when a character from one story suddenly shows up in another. I can remember—one of the earliest examples of it I can remember is a series of kind of lame American Western TV shows that for some reason was shown on British television back in the late fifties, very early sixties. There was one called *Bronco*, with Ty Harden as Bronco Layne, the lead cowboy hero. There was another one called *Sugarfoot* or *Tenderfoot*. And I think there was *Cheyenne* as well, a third one. And there was a kind of itinerant cowpoke named Toothy Thompson who was very much a background character, but he would show up in all three shows as the same character. These characters, although they never met, obviously all lived in the same part of the West, and they would all encounter this sort of toothless trail bum. And as a kid I found that fascinating. That was probably the first time that I actually got a taste of how strange and wonderful it was when somebody from one fiction wandered into another, that there seemed to be a really playful and exciting release of energy. And I suppose that all we've done with the *League* is to take that to an ultimate extreme. I thought that—you very generously said that the *League* was the ultimate crossover. And I think that's probably true. I'd like to think so. It's difficult to think of a bigger one. Potentially, every work of fiction that's ever been created is already crossed over somewhere in the universe of the *League*. I think that is probably the ultimate appeal. Of course, the fact that me and Kevin write and draw like angels perhaps has something to do with it. But I think that there is this big charge at seeing the whole world of fiction joined up. And, also, because I think it is probably evident on one level how much fun me and Kevin are having with it. I think that that communicates. I think that communicates with any work, how much of a buzz the artist and writer have generated for themselves while working on it. That's going to communicate to the reader. Perhaps not to all the readers, but to the majority of them. The fact that me and Kevin are having such a good time, an indecently good time—a lot of this really should be illegal—we shouldn't be allowed to get away with this. It is such gleeful fun, and I think that sense of glee probably communicates to the readers. I think that's maybe why the readers like it.

JN: Do you think *League*'s success indicates a desire on the part of the comics buying audience for more non-superhero comics?

AM: Maybe, although the *League* has got at least superficial similarities with standard superhero comics. Whether they want non-superhero comics or their superhero comics dressed differently, I couldn't really say. I'd like to think that they were going to be more eclectic and a bit more open in their taste. There's nothing more I'd like to see than a return to the incredibly healthy variety of, say, the 1950s, where there was a comic for every conceivable genre. And not only would you have a romance comic genre, you'd probably have five or six subgenres of the romance genre.

JN: Cowboy romance, sports romance—

AM: I think, *Negro Romance*, was that one of them?

JN: Yep.

AM: Right, a bit unpalatable by today's terms, but at the same time— what a good idea! There were comics about nurses, there were comics about funny animals, there were comics about cowboys, war comics, there were horror comics, ghost stories, historical adventures, cavemen comics. You want to look at a healthy comics industry, look at Japan, with all of their incomprehensible comics about mahjong. They sell, immensely. The thing is that if you want to look at anything healthy, in evolutionary terms, then a sign of life and health, in evolutionary terms, is diversity. In evolutionary terms, we generally—if you see pictures of evolutionary descent, it's either humans descending from apes or horses descending from Eohippus. The reason that these two are chosen is because us and the horses are two of the crappiest evolutionary forms in terms of diversity. There's only one species of human beings, and there's pretty much only one or two basic species of horses. If you want to look at evolutionary success you want to look at bats. There are thousands of species of bats. They have got diversity. They are healthy in evolutionary terms.

JN: I'm sure you've read the quote from J.B.S. Haldane. He was asked what he could tell about God from studying nature. Haldane said, "An inordinate fondness for beetles."

AM: Exactly! Exactly. You've only got to look at how many different sorts there are. That represents evolutionary success. They've done very well. They've diversified. There are thousands of different species. And I would say that us and the horses, we look like a very bare twig on the evolutionary tree. That's not healthy. And the same goes for comics. If comics have specialized down to the superhero comic, this one sickly strain of show dog, then comics could die out. If the superhero suddenly goes out of favor, incomprehensible and unbelievable as that might be, but there have been swings in the past of people's tastes, and things have vanished overnight. And if the comic book superhero were to suddenly fall out of favor, that could take down the entire medium with it. If there's nothing but superhero comics, then this industry ends when people's fondness for superhero comics ends, which will probably be sometime in the next twenty years? Next twenty or thirty years. That would mean that the superhero had lasted for a hundred years, which would be pretty good. It would be quite surprising.

JN: Longer than radio drama lasted.

AM: Yeah. That's probably going to happen in the next twenty years. And if superheroes are all comic books are about, then comic books and the comic medium will probably vanish along with the superhero. So obviously it makes much more sense to diversify. And I'd like to think that—it just opens up so many possibilities, a book like the *League*. You can do stories set in any kind of milieu that almost defy genre because they're playing around in so many different genres. In that second volume of the *League* you've got children's stories, science fiction, horror, all of these things are alluded to, with elements of romance and sex and everything thrown in. And there are references to cowboys in the Almanac. I'd like the *League* to be beyond genre. I'd like it to not recognize any boundaries between different artists' and writers' work, different genres, so that it was all-inclusive. This is about stories—not superhero stories, not comic book stories, not literary stories. Just purely stories, the things that we've entertained ourselves with since we were in the caves. If the *League* is about anything it is an attempt to write, an absurd attempt to write some sort of ultimate story. And that's probably all it is, ultimately.

JN: In your introduction to the Richard Corben graphic novel of W.H. Hodgson's *House on the Borderlands,* you spoke of the lack of regard with which older horror and fantasy writers like Hodgson are held. Was the Almanac an attempt by you to try and redress the problem?

AM: Well, yeah. I'm always all for spreading the word about deserving books and things like that. So the *Almanac* gave me a chance to do lots of things at once. It enabled me to actually pin down the geography and to a certain degree the history of the *League*'s world, which has opened up no end of possibilities for future stories. It also enabled me to connect up some of these fictional places and people into a whole continuous world—which country's on the border of which other country, and so on. But it also enables me to tell the readers about, oh, the Moomintroll books, or Flann O'Brien, or any of these wonderful things. Like, as we've said before, it's almost painful to contemplate someone getting through life without reading *The Third Policeman.* I can't be that cruel to my readers. They deserve to know.

JN: Or a childhood without the Moomintroll books.

AM: Yeah. That's too bleak to contemplate. People, they should know about these things. In a film- and TV-dominated culture, there is a very real danger that they won't find out about these things, or at best all they'll see is when somebody decides to make a bad movie out of them in ten years' time, they'll see a diluted Hollywood version, and will perhaps imagine that they've got the whole experience. Whereas, no, get out there, read the books, they're interesting, they're fantastic! They won't all be to your taste, but there is that whole enticing, rich world of the human imagination, which is what I suppose we're ultimately trying to map in the *Almanac*. It's providing a map for the reader. I know that we say at the end of that introduction to the Almanac that we hope that it provides lots of material for future excursions, but in a way we do, because, yeah, we know that they can't actually travel to these lands. But if they know that these lands exist in fiction, then they can go out and buy a copy of the second volume of your *League* companion and find out where they actually came from, and if they want they can read the books, and they might discover that they're embarking upon life-long love affairs with some of these books. That would be great. Like I say, I'm contemptuous of much modern culture after disco, so I'd be delighted—

JN: Even punk?

AM: Actually, I'm probably just trying to say things for effect. I loved punk. It wasn't as great as some people said it was because it had got problems. The main problem being that they hadn't thought of anywhere to go after nihilism. No, basically, much modern culture, in terms of, say, movies, television, the Internet—I am loftily contemptuous of it. I think that to overlook the traditional culture that there is in books and print media, to assume that you can get it all better on screen—I think that's cultural suicide. I think it's an incredible mistake. It's a mistake that could only be made by people who've never experienced the richness of a good book. There's no way that any kind of technology is going to ever compete with the richness that is possible with this most basic of technologies, where you've just got 26 symbols rearranged in a number of interesting ways. The word itself, print media itself, text, language, books, this is the basic technology. This is the technology on which all technologies are based. That's why the word "technology" has that "logy" part in it: writings *about* a subject. Writing. It is the original technology, and I don't think we've bettered it. It's so elegant to be able to create entire universes out of the manipulation of 26 symbols. And there is also the fact that a book—if a book is software, then the technology that that software plays upon is the most sophisticated in the universe. Human imagination has got a much higher res. than anything that X-Box and Playstation are going to be coming out with in the foreseeable future. No, a lot of this fad—and I think it is a fad, I don't think it's the future— this fad for immediate sensory overload, bells and whistles and flashing lights, this fad for peak experience all the time, no matter what the content is, no matter if the content is so incredibly shallow that it offers no kind of substance at all, as long as it's in a flashy package, then that is probably what a lot of people want. Constant flashy sensational stimulation. And that's not culture. That's fireworks display. And the critical acumen that people seem to bring to most, say, contemporary films is exactly the same critical acumen that the average five-year-old brings to a fireworks display. You're not interested in the characters or the emotional resonances or the themes or motifs—this is a fireworks display, you're just interested in the pretty lights and the bangs. And that is most modern culture. And I think that it would be a tragedy if these half-witted cultural lemmings were allowed to lead literature over the cliff in their mad dash for annihilation. I'd like to think that—yeah, all right, the *League of Extraordinary Gentlemen* is not going to solve the problem—but I'd like to think that at least it offered a possible guide to some of the riches of this incredibly rich world.

JN: Even now I'm getting e-mails from people who are turned on to authors and books, from *League* and from the Almanac.

AM: That is brilliant. I'm so pleased. Any unusual or unexpected ones?

JN: I got a rapturous e-mail from someone who'd never read Borges' "El Aleph" before.

AM: Fantastic! He was one of the people that I really wanted people to read. Borges is one of the best writers in the English language. He's in a kind of stratosphere with James Joyce and a couple of others. He is one of the very best things to ever happen to the English language. Oh, I'm so glad about that. That is lovely.

JN: *League* is baby steps for these people. It gets them started.

AM: That is so great. I am so happy. And if we're going to be keeping *League* in print forever, then it will always be available as a kind of entry point to a completely different and much bigger world that exists beyond the confines of comic books, which are fairly limited. Yeah, the world of comic books is great, and it's got a kind of nice 60 year history, and we will love it, that goes without saying, but there's a bigger world beyond it, that has been here for longer, that has produced more marvelous things, and that has much greater breadth. I think all of us owe it to ourselves to poke our head outside of this little beloved enclosure that we take so much fun in wandering around in. We really owe it to ourselves to have a peek over the wall and see what's out there. I think we might find it a very stunning experience.

INDEX